Criminals I have k  **e to.**

According to my [...] museum, someone had disabled the Brock's security system and taken the Chagall in the confusion surrounding the Stendhal faintings. To stroll out of a museum in broad daylight with a painting tucked inside one's bomber jacket took a cool head and an abundance of self-confidence.

The very qualities possessed by a certain art thief I knew only too well. An art thief who once told me that a criminal's cardinal rule was to keep things simple. An art thief who habitually wore a brown leather bomber jacket.

Along with half the men in San Francisco, I chided myself. Besides, the missing Chagall was small potatoes. Michael X. Johnson hunted bigger game.

Not that he needed the money after the Caravaggio heist last spring. Most likely Michael was lounging by the sea in Saint-Tropez, tanning himself in an indecent swimsuit. Or gambling his ill-gotten gains at the craps table in Monte Carlo. Or ensconced in a Prague penthouse, rolling around naked on satin sheets with a Czech chorus girl.

Not that I cared.

Praise for the Art Lover's Mysteries

"Delightfully different."—New Mystery Reader Magazine

SHOOTING GALLERY

AN ART LOVER'S MYSTERY

Hailey Lind

A SIGNET BOOK

SIGNET
Published by New American Library, a division of
Penguin Group (USA) Inc., 375 Hudson Street,
New York, New York 10014, USA
Penguin Group (Canada), 90 Eglinton Avenue East, Suite 700, Toronto,
Ontario M4P 2Y3, Canada (a division of Pearson Penguin Canada Inc.)
Penguin Books Ltd., 80 Strand, London WC2R 0RL, England
Penguin Ireland, 25 St. Stephen's Green, Dublin 2,
Ireland (a division of Penguin Books Ltd.)
Penguin Group (Australia), 250 Camberwell Road, Camberwell, Victoria 3124,
Australia (a division of Pearson Australia Group Pty. Ltd.)
Penguin Books India Pvt. Ltd., 11 Community Centre, Panchsheel Park,
New Delhi - 110 017, India
Penguin Group (NZ), cnr Airborne and Rosedale Roads, Albany,
Auckland 1310, New Zealand (a division of Pearson New Zealand Ltd.)
Penguin Books (South Africa) (Pty.) Ltd., 24 Sturdee Avenue,
Rosebank, Johannesburg 2196, South Africa

Penguin Books Ltd., Registered Offices:
80 Strand, London WC2R 0RL, England

First published by Signet, an imprint of New American Library,
a division of Penguin Group (USA) Inc.

First Printing, October 2006
10 9 8 7 6 5 4 3 2 1

PUBLISHER'S NOTE
This is a work of fiction. Names, characters, places, and incidents either are the product of
the author's imagination or are used fictitiously, and any resemblance to actual persons,
living or dead, business establishments, events, or locales is entirely coincidental.
    The publisher does not have any control over and does not assume any responsibility for
author or third-party Web sites or their content.

*For Sergio
and
Malcolm
What's life without laughter?*

Acknowledgments

Many thanks are due, as always, to the wonderful agent Kristin Lindstrom and our editors, Martha Bushko and Kerry Donovan.

Muchísimas gracias a Irma Herrera y Mark Levine for throwing such a fabulous release party! Merci beaucoup à Marie et François—pour le français, l'amitié, et la camaraderie. Thanks also to Bee Enos, whose voice and music inspire; and to Pamela, Jan, Charlotte, and all Cuba-loving, wine-drinking, salsa-dancing fools. Thanks to Beth Bruggeman and Kim Sullivan for the running commentary and fan mail; to Mrs. Chan for the insights of a native San Franciscan and for keeping tabs on the aliens; and to the other Mrs. Chan for her insights, pep talks, and steadfastness. To Steve Lofgren, Scott Casper, Anita Fellman, and Karen Smyers for going above and beyond the call of friendship. Thank you as well to our aunts Mem and Suzy, wonderful examples of perseverance and love. Finally, to Susan, Bob, and Jane Lawes, for their completely unbiased support and encouragement . . . and as always, a deep-felt thanks to Jace. How would any of it get done without her?

Prologue

May 10

Georges LeFleur
Hôtel Royal du Prague
Prague, Czechoslovakia

Très cher grand-père,
Why haven't you returned my calls? I've tried
Paris, Amsterdam, Rome, Jakarta. . . . *Please* call me,
if only to say you're all right. Has the Spanish Minister of the Interior dropped the felony charges yet?

I imagine you've heard that Interpol obtained the
first three chapters of your book and the proverbial
merde has hit the fan. I don't suppose you had anything to do with sending them an advance copy, did
you? I *hope* you don't think this is a joke, old man.
You'll be lucky if you don't end up dead on the
streets of Barcelona, or suspended by your fingers
from the Arc de Triomphe like your old fence, Her-
zog. Remember him? Keep that image in mind the
next time you're tempted, will you, please?

I know you are enjoying your new project, Grandfather, but surely you can see that writing a book about
your career in art forgery is one thing—the worst that
can happen is that you'll spend your declining years in

a prison cell—but publishing trade secrets for how to commit fraud, offering advice on how to sell art forgeries, and listing all of the fakes in the world's top art museums . . . was that really such a great idea? You're making some dangerous enemies. Even my father—your son-in-law, remember?—is concerned, and we both know how he feels about you.

And this book hasn't exactly made my life easier. San Francisco isn't that far from Europe, you know. I have a legitimate faux-finishing business now, and even though you think I'm wasting my life, believe me when I say that I like what I do and I don't appreciate the incessant questions about my past. Remember, you promised not to write about me! If you break that promise, *Grandpapa*, I'll come after you myself. I swear I will.

Anyway, I love you and—so help me—I miss you like crazy. *Please* keep yourself out of legal trouble long enough to visit me soon, will you? You promised.

Je t'embrasse,
Annie

June 15

Mademoiselle Annie Kincaid
True/Faux Studios
The DeBenton Building
San Francisco, California, USA

Ma très chère Annie,
So wonderful to receive from you this letter! There are few who appreciate your rare humor so much as I.

Rest assured, *ma petite*, the tome is coming along famously and shall be released October 1st to rave reviews, I have no doubt. Just the other day I was writing a few words on the economic ramifications of the traffic in *truquage* and forgeries. I adore the economists. So pragmatic.

Those old fellows at Interpol are so droll. Thank you for reminding me. I shall send them a fruit basket.

I was touched, my darling girl, by your invitation to visit sunny San Francisco. I shall see what I can do, but alas! My arthritis troubles me much in my dotage. Often do I wish for the companionship of my beloved granddaughter to ease my pains. But do not worry. I understand that your work takes priority in your heart.

Remember, *chérie*, stay strong against the naysayers!

Je t'aime beaucoup,
Grandpapa Georges

Chapter 1

With some regularity, the janitorial staff of major museums mistakes a work of modern art for trash and disposes of it in the Dumpster. Perhaps the average custodian is a keener judge of art than the average curator!

—*Georges LeFleur, in an interview with* Mother Jones *magazine*

"Anthony, that body is *not* part of the exhibit," I said for the third time, my voice rising in desperation. "*Look* at it: there's a *dead man* hanging from your *oak tree*!"

At just that moment, the San Francisco Conservatory of Music's string quartet reached the end of a lilting Mozart air, and my words rang out across Anthony Brazil's bucolic walled sculpture garden. Lighthearted conversation skidded to a halt and the well-coiffed crowd of art lovers, snooty socialites, and local celebrities gaped at me for a second before shifting their gazes to the majestic oak tree in the northeast corner. There, nestled amongst the angelhair ferns and silvery blue hydrangeas, as though it were one of artist Seamus McGraw's more macabre sculptural installations, dangled the body of a man.

For one long, surreal moment quiet blanketed the posh scene.

Then a scream split the silence.

"Call the police!" someone yelled. "Call 411!"

"It's *911*, you fool!" another shouted in reply. "It's *911*!"

Shrieks and cries and the sound of shattering wine-glasses filled the air as the overflow crowd of Anthony Brazil's A-list clients forgot their finishing-school manners and surged toward the garden's narrow gated exit, where they formed a noisy, upper-crust traffic jam.

Anthony Brazil gave me a withering glance. The verti-cally challenged proprietor of San Francisco's premier art gallery was an old friend of my father's, but he and I were not on the best of terms. Anthony had invited me to the grand opening of his swanky new gallery only in grudging recognition of my having held my tongue about his role in an art forgery scandal last spring, while I was attending the event only in the hope of landing a wealthy client or ten for my faux-finishing business. As my grandfather had taught me, a little blackmail, judiciously applied, just made good business sense.

My spotting a corpse in Brazil's oak tree was more than either of us had bargained for.

"Don't look at me like that," I said, downing the last swallow of a rich Russian River Pinot Noir, smoothing my unruly dark curls and brushing imaginary crumbs from my one and only little black dress. "*I* didn't put a body in your tree."

"My dear child, such a thought never crossed my mind," Brazil hissed in his high tenor. Although outwardly calm, his signature red bow tie trembled. "But you *do* seem to at-tract the more, shall we say, *unseemly* element of the art world, do you not?"

"You give me entirely too much credit, Anthony," I sniffed.

It was true that I had become embroiled in a scandal involving forged sketches and the theft of a priceless Caravaggio masterpiece last spring. It was also true that I had spent my seventeenth birthday in a Parisian jail cell accused—quite rightly, I must confess—of flooding the European art market with forgeries of Old Master drawings. But those charges had been dropped when no French art expert had been willing to testify that *une jeune fille américaine* was capable of such high-quality work.

After graduating from college, I reveled in an art restoration internship at San Francisco's Brock Museum until a spiteful 'expert' spilled the beans about my prior close working relationship with my grandfather Georges LeFleur, who happened to be one of the world's foremost art forgers. Banished from the fine-art world, I had spent the last several years slowly building up a legitimate faux-finishing business, True/Faux Studios. I worked long hours painting decorative finishes in homes and businesses, paid exorbitant self-employment taxes, and belonged to the Better Business Bureau. It wasn't as exciting as being a Parisian artist, but neither was it as scary as being a Parisian prisoner.

Still, although these days my life was lived on the up-and-up—mostly, anyway—a residual distrust of the police lingered. The sound of approaching sirens put my nerves on edge and seemed to rev up the crowd as well. I watched the distinguished guest director of the San Francisco Opera throw an elbow into the gut of a local radio-talk-show host as they jockeyed for position at the packed garden exit. Newly elected Mayor Joseph Green showed considerably more class by stopping to help Gloria Cabrera to her feet. Gloria was the manager of Marble World, a major stone importer in the San Francisco Bay Area, and I had seen her stare down not one but three angry contractors, their clients, and their work crews. If Gloria was vulnerable to this pack of tuxedoed hyenas I figured I didn't stand a chance and decided to try my luck exiting through the gallery.

"Don't even *think* about leaving before speaking to the police," Anthony snapped, as if reading my mind.

"What *must* you think of me?" I said, feigning shock.

Ol' Tony gave me the fish eye, and I reluctantly trailed him inside, where about a dozen less-panicky guests grazed on hors d'oeuvres and chattered excitedly about the gruesome discovery. As Brazil started working the room, reassuring anyone who would listen that this was all a dreadful misunderstanding, I grabbed a tumbler of single-malt scotch from the bar. Taking a fortifying gulp, I glanced out at the garden through the plate-glass window at the rear of the gallery. The limp body was clearly visible, thanks to the exhibit lighting. Covered in layers of fine beige dust, the corpse had a monochromatic, stonelike appearance, the face partially obscured by a drape of lank, powdery hair, and one hand wrapped mummylike in a dirty cloth.

Forcing my eyes from the ghoulish sight, I spied a Biedermier side table stacked with glossy show catalogues. Entitled "The New Anthony Brazil Gallery Presents 'Tortured Bodies, Tortured Souls: 30 Years of the Sculptural Work of Seamus McGraw,'" the introductory essay explained in impenetrable postmodern prose that McGraw's metal and leather sculptures depicting murder, torture, and mutilation offered a uniquely scathing commentary on the alienation inherent in contemporary America's death-dealing society.

Or a uniquely repulsive insight into the mind of a self-indulgent artist, I thought as I flipped through the catalogue. I paused at the black-and-white photographs of the show's largest installation, *The Postman Should Never Ring Twice*, which depicted bound and twisted figures in their death agonies, cowering at the feet of a demented letter carrier armed with hemp rope, steel thumbscrews, and something that looked suspiciously like a bronze dildo. I studied the grotesque images dispassionately. McGraw's ugly sculptures struck me as less alienated than sad—and lonely. Call me a boring traditionalist, but when it came to art my tastes were stuck in the Renaissance, an era when artists expressed humanity's noblest hopes, ambitions, and dreams. If I wanted a scathing commentary on social alienation I could read the newspaper.

I was about to toss the catalogue aside when the color photograph on the back cover, autographed in a loopy, flamboyant hand, caught my eye. Seamus McGraw posed in his studio, barefoot and dressed in baggy khaki drawstring pants and a white cotton shirt, smiling warmly at the camera. He was handsome in an aging hippy kind of way, the sharp planes of his tanned face softened by middle age, and I felt a frisson of recognition. Looking out the rear window again, I realized the corpse in the tree bore a striking resemblance to the one person who had been conspicuously absent from tonight's opening: the guest of honor, sculptor Seamus McGraw.

I had heard of artists denouncing the philanthropic hands that fed them. I had heard of artists staging dayslong performance art wherein nothing ever seemed to happen. But I had never heard of an artist building a show around his own death. *Give the man points for originality*, I thought. Perhaps McGraw had decided to become a grisly contribution to his sculptural menagerie in an attempt to achieve the ultimate synergy with his work. It seemed a lit-

tle extreme to me, but extremism in modern art was not un-
common.

Turning away from the morbid view, I nearly collided
with a fortyish brunette wearing a chic black dress that was
in imminent danger of falling off her undernourished
shoulders.

"Are stuffed mushrooms low-carb?" the woman demanded, waving the hors d'oeuvres in question under my
nose.

"You bet," I replied, though I had no idea. She looked as
though she could use the calories. Her large, horsy teeth bit
into a greasy, sausage-stuffed mushroom cap and chewed
vigorously. My stomach lurched. "I'm Annie Kincaid."

"Janice, Janice Hewett," she mumbled around a mouthful of mushroom. "My husband, Norman, and I buy from
Anthony Brazil all the time. We've never seen *anything*
like this before. Can you *imagine*? What a *gloriously* dev-
astating way to kill oneself! Not that it's not *tragic*." Janice nabbed a hot crab puff from a tray offered by a slightly
green-faced waiter and shoved it, whole, into her mouth. A
bit of the creamy filling escaped, oozing over her bottom
lip. "What *is* it with sculptors these days?"

"What do you mean?" I asked, mesmerized by the sight
of the creamy white glob slowly sliding down her pointy
chin.

"They're just *too* much trouble." She wiped her face
with a cocktail napkin and I relaxed. "Give me a nice
painter any day. You can usually deal with them, unless
they eat their paints. You know, like van Gogh?"

"Van Gogh was pretty unstable already," I objected.
Poor Vincent, I thought. A good dose of Prozac might have
eased his suffering but could also have dulled his artistic
vision, depriving the world of his astonishing genius. It

made me wonder whether Seamus McGraw had been similarly tortured by creative demons.

"Anyway," Janice said, lunging for the last bacon-wrapped water chestnut. A portly man across the steam table glared at her before slurping up a raw oyster with a loud smack of his rubbery lips. A wave of nausea rolled over me, and I tried to concentrate on what Janice Hewett was saying. "We've recently had a run-in with a sculptor, another in dear Anthony's stable of artists. Brilliant but quite *mad*, you have *no* idea. He's a contemporary of McGraw's, but not as well known these days. Robert Pascal. Have you heard of him?"

"Why yes, he's an old acquaintance of my father's," I said, surprised. I hadn't seen Robert Pascal since I was ten years old. I remembered begging him for one of his horrid little maquettes—small-scale models of sculptures that artists make to work out problems of scale and composition before taking a chisel to a block of stone or putting flame to metal—because it was perfect for my dollhouse installation, *Tattooed Barbie and Biker Ken*. My father had taken one look at that dollhouse and sent me into therapy.

My opinion of Pascal's work had not improved over the years. He was very much in Seamus McGraw's *Life Is a Suppurating Cesspool* school of art, which was not surprising since the two had studied together in Berkeley in the 1960s. To my eyes, though, Pascal's sculptures were colder than McGraw's, more disaffected than gruesome. Still, I remembered Pascal as a nice old man and had wondered if he would be here tonight.

"You know Robert Pascal? *Personally*? What luck!" Janice gushed, hitching up her dress. I braced myself. In my experience, people who gushed inevitably caused trouble. "Pascal *stole* our sculpture!"

"What sculpture?"

"*Head and Torso*," she replied, trying and failing to sound modest. *Head and Torso* was Robert Pascal's most famous piece, and by far his most haunting. Completed when he was a young man, it had generated considerable buzz and established him as a major new talent. Sadly, Pascal had never lived up to that early promise, a fact the more uncharitable art critics regularly pointed out with glee.

"Why would an artist steal his own sculpture?" I asked, but her reply was interrupted by the shrill blare of an alarm. My heart sank when I realized the sound was emanating from the Brock Museum next door. I had noticed the museum's elderly, autocratic director, Agnes Brock, chatting with Mayor Green earlier this evening, but she and I had assiduously avoided each other in a manner befitting old adversaries.

"Suicide here! Art theft there!" Janice burbled dramatically, her watery blue eyes gleaming with excitement. "And my *own* kidnapped sculpture! What could *possibly* happen *next*?"

I eyed her with distaste. I had been around plenty of art theft in my time, and more death than I cared to think about, and had found nothing thrilling about any of it. Janice placed a limp hand on my shoulder, leaned toward me, and whispered like the vapid sorority girl she must once have been, "Andy, will you do it?"

"Do what? And the name's Annie."

"Oh. Sorry. Anyway, will you talk to Pascal for us? We need *Head and Torso* returned before the Thanksgiving symphony fundraiser next week! He was only supposed to repair some minor damage; I don't know *what* is taking him so long. It has left *such* a hole in our collection, you have *no* idea!"

"Why don't you talk to him yourself?" I said, my attention drawn to the commotion unfolding outside in the sculpture garden. Uniformed officers swarmed into the flower-filled yard and started cordoning off the oak tree with yellow police tape. A sour-faced man in a rumpled brown suit was speaking with Anthony Brazil, who kept pointing toward the gallery. *Uh-oh,* I thought. *I really should get out of here.*

"Pascal won't answer his phone. Have you ever *heard* of such a thing? My Norman got so angry that he sent our man over to the studio, but Pascal wouldn't come to the door, either! There's nothing for it now but to initiate legal proceedings," she concluded with a theatrical sigh, leaning against the silk-draped bar and languidly spearing a boiled shrimp and watercress canapé.

"You mean a lawsuit? Against a little old sculptor?" I finally gave Janice my full attention. "Surely that's premature. Maybe he wasn't home when your, uh, 'man' called. Maybe he was working and didn't want to be disturbed. Maybe he'd fallen and couldn't get up."

"So you'll help us, then?" A broad smile displayed her huge teeth, decorated with bits of greenery. "That is *such* a relief, you have *no* idea."

"Really, Janice, I don't . . ."

"I'll pay you for your time, of course," she said, shrewdly targeting my Achilles' heel.

"I charge one hundred fifty an hour," I blurted, doubling my usual rate because Janice and Norman Hewett could obviously afford it.

Plus, I didn't like her.

"Done," she said.

Rats. I should have gone for triple.

Janice reached into a spangly evening bag and handed me an engraved card with her phone number on it.

"I'm willing to talk to Pascal, but I can't promise he'll return *Head and Torso . . .*" I said, the rest of my sentence

trailing off as I spotted a young cop pushing his way towards me through the milling crowd.

"You the one discovered the body?" he asked when he
reached me. His lovely features were almost feminine, his
angular face and long limbs reminiscent of the beatific
young men in Sandro Botticelli's *Madonna and Child with
Angels*. But he spoke like a cop.

I nodded. "It had been there for a while, but everyone
thought it was just another sculpture. It's a rather gruesome
exhibit."

"No shi— I mean, you ain't kiddin'," he replied. The
cop's beautiful eyes looked me up and down, and I was
torn between feeling flattered and annoyed. He was too
young and too pretty for me, anyway. "The caterer said the
body's been there at least since last night. Weird, huh?"

"Shocking," I said, ignoring Janice, who was watching
us avidly.

"Stick around, the inspector's gonna wanna talk with
you. Name and address?" He jotted down my information
and turned to Janice, who was eager to share her lack of
knowledge with a new audience.

Now that the authorities knew where to find me, it was
time to vamoose. It could be hours before the inspector got
around to interviewing me, and I saw no reason to wait. I
didn't know anything more than I had already told the an-
gelic cop. I had worked all day at my studio, and I had no
earthly idea why nobody else had noticed the figure in the
oak tree was a corpse.

To hell with Brazil's entreaties, I was breaking out of
this joint.

Since the front entrance was probably teeming with
cops, I scanned the room for an alternate exit, finally spying a door on the far side of the gallery. Biding my time
until I was hidden by the ebb and flow of the crowd, I

edged around the room, and slipped through the door which was marked *private*.

A narrow hallway led past a maze of administrative cubicles and Brazil's private office, beyond a tiny employee lunchroom and a grungy restroom, to a rear storage area jammed with wooden crates, packing materials, and surplus artwork. I threaded my way through the mess to the fire exit, which was partially blocked by a sofa-sized painting whose untalented creator had been enamored of cobalt blue and the letter *R*. Shoving the hideous thing aside, I struggled to throw the latch, but the heavy metal door was nearly rusted shut. I grabbed a strong oak stretcher bar off the floor and used it to bang on the latch. With a mighty heave I managed to pry the door open about ten inches before it squealed and stuck again.

Dammit!

The night air poured in, cool and tangy with the salt of the Pacific Ocean, tempting and invigorating me. I shoved my right arm and leg into the narrow opening, and, bracing myself against the doorjamb, pushed with all my might. A lesser woman might have made it through, but my curvy hips had been fortified over the years by too many seafood enchiladas and pad thai noodles. Frustrated, I began grunting and swearing, using the stretcher bar as a fulcrum to force the door open just a few more inches.

"Leaving so soon, Annie?" A woman's deep voice rang out behind me.

Chapter 2

Experts agree that nearly one-third of museum holdings are forgeries, and that many of these fakes are superior to the originals. Am I less an artist than Paul Gauguin if I create a work of greater beauty than he? Should I be reviled for lending my talent to his fame?

—*Georges LeFleur, in "Barbara Walters Presents: The Fascinating World of Art Forgery"*

"Hello, Annette. I mean, Inspector."

I tried to sound nonchalant, which was no mean feat considering I had been caught, red-hipped, fleeing the scene of a suspicious hanging. On the plus side, I no longer hyperventilated every time I saw the inspector. In my world, that passed for "personal growth."

SFPD Homicide Inspector Annette Crawford and I had met last spring when she was investigating a series of art-related murders. A well-built woman in her late thirties, Crawford had flawless mocha skin, a piercing intelligence, and an innately imperial demeanor that encouraged criminals to confess their crimes and save themselves a world of hurt. I liked to refer to Annette as "my friend in the SFPD," but I was never sure if the feeling was mutual. A faux-finisher with a rap sheet didn't convey quite the same cachet as a cop, friendship-wise.

"Annette, I had *nothing* to do with *anything* . . ."

"Save it," she said shortly, though her sherry-colored eyes softened slightly. "Come along. Someone wants to speak to you."

I resumed banging on the door with the stretcher bar as I struggled to dislodge myself. Annette watched for a minute before sighing and giving me a hand.

"Thanks!" I said as I popped out.

"Anytime," she replied dryly.

I trotted behind the inspector as she led the way through Brazil's now nearly empty gallery. Outside on the street, half a dozen cop cars were parked next door in front of the massive Brock Museum. Their blue lights were flashing, and uniformed officers milled about beneath the large scarlet banners advertising the museum's extended Friday evening hours. The chaotic scene brought back unpleasant memories from last spring, when a custodian had been found murdered at the Museum.

I did not want to go to the Brock. Bad things always happened to me at the Brock.

"What's going on?" I asked, hurrying to keep up with Annette's long stride.

"Two things. Maybe related, maybe not," she replied curtly. "A body at the gallery and a theft at the Brock."

I hoped the thief was no one I knew. "I had *nothing* to do with *anything* . . ."

"So you said." Annette fixed me with a stern look as we mounted the museum's wide granite steps. "Annie, stop babbling before you implicate yourself in something I don't want to know about. Anthony Brazil confirmed that you were at his gallery all evening, so as far as I'm concerned you're off the hook. Not that you would have been a suspect in the first place. One day I'll have to give some thought as to why you have such a guilty conscience."

I hoped not.

"And," she continued, "no one is suggesting that you were anything more that the only person smart enough to tell the corpse from the tree."

"Hey! Annette, did you just make a joke?"

She flashed me a rare, beautiful smile. "It happens."

"Not bad," I conceded. "Sick, but not bad."

When we reached the museum's ornate bronze doors, Annette held up her gold badge, and a guard waved us through. The normally sedate institution was in an uproar, its grand hall filled with wary cops, bewildered museum personnel, and excited visitors. Agnes Brock's distinctive caw rose above the chatter of voices and static of police radios and bounced off the polished marble walls. Annette steered me toward a small office near the coat check station.

Bryan Boissevain sat huddled in a chair, a sky-blue blanket draped around his shoulders and tears coursing down his smooth brown face.

"Bryan!" I exclaimed, rushing to his side. "What in the world is going on?"

"Oh, baby doll, I cannot *tell* you the night I've had!" Bryan cried, his Louisiana bayou accent thickened by distress. "I *knew* Inspector Crawford was your friend in the SFPD. That's what I said. Isn't that what I said?" Bryan sniffed loudly and dabbed his eyes with a white silk handkerchief. "Oh, Annie, *what* am I going to d-o-o-o?"

I looped one arm around Bryan's shoulders. Years ago, after Agnes Brock fired me from the internship at the museum, Bryan had loaned me money, let me sleep on his couch for two weeks, and stayed up with me until four a.m. three nights in a row while I worked through my rage and humiliation. When I decided to open my faux-finishing business, he helped me find a studio space and threw a party to introduce me to his circle of well-heeled friends. And when I needed to infiltrate the Brock gala last spring, Bryan convinced a transvestite pal to lend me a gorgeous ball gown, devoted an entire day to getting me ready, and forgave me when, predictably enough, I completely ruined the dress. Bryan was a prince among friends.

He was also a major drama queen.

"Inspector Crawford, what's going on here?" I asked.

"A painting was stolen. No one knows much yet and no one is making any accusations," she said, eyeing Bryan suspiciously. "Inspectors Fielding and Woo need to talk to your friend here, that's all, but he became a little, um, over-wrought. I thought you might be able to calm him down enough to give a statement."

"Bryan, did you hear that?" I crouched before him and rubbed his cold hands. "The police just want your state-ment."

"That's not *all* they want, honey pie. Don't you believe that. Uh-uh." Following Bryan's gaze, I turned toward the door to see two men in dull gray suits enter the room. An-nette introduced them as Inspectors Fielding and Woo, and they nodded politely. Bryan was having none of it. "Mon-sieur *Thing* over there thinks we were in on it. He doesn't believe in *the Syndrome*."

"You mean this involves a kidnapping?" Annette asked.

"That's the Stockholm Syndrome," Inspector Woo, a neatly combed Asian man, replied. He looked at me. "Mr. Boissevain keeps referring to something called the Stend-hal Syndrome. Have you heard of it?"

Bryan squeezed my hands so tightly my knuckles popped.

I wrenched free of Bryan's death grip and stood to face

the inspectors. I didn't know much about biology, auto mechanics, financial planning, or gourmet cooking. But art? Art, I knew.

"The syndrome is named for Marie-Henri Beyle, who wrote under the pen name 'Stendhal,'" I lectured. "In the early 1800s Stendhal visited Santa Croce, the gothic Florentine basilica where Machiavelli, Michelangelo, and Galileo are buried. When he saw Giotto's ceiling frescoes Stendhal had what he described as an extreme physical reaction to their extraordinary beauty, and fainted. Similar incidents have been reported in travelogues ever since, and for years it was known in Italy as the 'tourist disease.' In the 1970s a Florentine psychiatrist wrote up several cases and renamed it the Stendhal Syndrome, after the writer."

There was a moment of silence.

"So you have heard of it," Annette said wryly.

"In fact," I continued, "a similar affliction has recently been identified as the *Jerusalem Syndrome.* . . ."

"Thank you, Doctor, that's quite enough," Annette interrupted.

"So, Mr. Boissevain, is it your statement that you were overcome by the Stendhal Syndrome and fainted at the sight of"—Inspector Woo paused and flipped a page of his black spiral notebook—"Gauguin's *Parau na te varua ino*?" He stumbled over the Tahitian words.

"I've never seen that shade of violet before," Bryan said, his puppy-dog eyes gazing up at the Inspector. "I never even knew it *existed*!"

Woo and Fielding exchanged a cynical glance.

"He's right, you know," I piped up. "Paul Gauguin's mastery of color is truly astounding, and can be appreciated only when viewing his paintings in person. Gauguin attained that shade of purple, you see, by painting its complementary color—green—underneath . . ." The inspectors were staring at me now, so I wrapped up the art lesson. "Anyway, I take it *Parau na te varua ino* was stolen?"

"Nope." Inspector Fielding, a middle-aged balding white guy with a sizable paunch, spoke for the first time. "A Chagall." He pronounced it "CHAY-gull."

"Shuh-GAHL," I said, absentmindedly correcting his pronunciation. "So why are you detaining Bryan?"

"They think we were a diversion," Bryan fretted.

"It wasn't just Mr. Boissevain who was involved," Inspector Woo explained. "A tour group from an adult-education class fainted in a pile on the floor and distracted the security guards. When everyone came to, the Chagall was gone."

"An *entire tour group* fainted?" I asked. The Stendhal Syndrome was described as an individual affliction, not a mass event. "Then why are you focusing on Bryan?"

"The others were more cooperative than your friend here."

"But Bryan isn't—"

"Thank you for your assistance, Ms. Kincaid," Inspector Woo cut me off. "Now that Mr. Boissevain is, um, calmer, we have a few more questions for him and then he'll be free to go. Thanks for your help, Inspector," he said to Annette deferentially.

"Good luck, guys," Annette said and led me to the door, one hand on my elbow.

"Bryan, do you need a ride home?" I called over my shoulder.

"Thanks, baby doll, but Ron's on his way," he replied with a loud sniff, a weepy smile, and a hearty hiccup.

Inspector Crawford and I made our way to the grand hall, past a knot of cops questioning the museum's staff, and headed for the front doors.

"Why are you involved in this, Annette?" I inquired. "You're a homicide inspector."

"I was called in to investigate the body at Brazil's gallery," she responded. "When the Brock's alarms went off I thought I'd see if there was a connection."

"Is there?"

"Don't know."

"If you find one will you tell me?"

"Don't count on it."

No surprise there.

"You!" a strident voice shrieked.

The grand hall fell silent, and the crowd slowly parted like the Red Sea. I was half expecting Moses to appear when Agnes Brock strode across the foyer like a vengeful Valkyrie and pinned me against one of the massive carved bronze front doors with a bony index finger. I winced as a sculpted eagle took a bite out of my scapula.

"Mrs. Brock, I—"

"That so-called *man* is a *friend* of yours? I might have known! Tell him to return my Chagall forthwith. Do you hear me, young lady? Tell him that if he doesn't return it, I will *personally* throw the switch on the electric chair!"

"Now, Mrs. Brock," Annette said calmly, "theft isn't a capital offense. If you'll just—"

"Shot by a firing squad!" Agnes railed on, her wrinkled, patrician face flushed with rage. "Drawn and quartered and fed to the seagulls! He should be *exterminated* for violating my lovely museum!"

"Wait just a minute," I protested hotly. "Bryan Boissevain is a wonderful person who happened to be in the wrong place at the wrong time. He may be a little emotional"—I heard Annette snort at this understatement—"but he's scrupulously honest. Bryan would never be involved in anything criminal, Mrs. Brock. I'd stake my life on it."

"You may very well have to," Agnes barked. "I *know* people, Annie Kincaid! I know people who *know* people!"

"Mrs. Brock, *please*," Annette interjected. "I assure you that Inspectors Woo and Fielding will thoroughly investigate this matter."

Undaunted, Agnes turned her beady black eyes on me and poked me in the chest. "You listen to me, young woman. That painting is of tremendous"—poke—"sentimental"—poke—"value"—poke, poke.

That last was one poke too many.

"No, *you* listen to *me*, old woman," I snarled, batting away her skeletal hand. "I don't work for you, I don't *like* you, and I don't think much of your tight-assed museum." The crowd gasped, and I heard Annette sigh. Never one to leave well enough alone, I continued, "And considering the quality of the museum's Chagall collection, it couldn't have been a very important painting anyway."

Agnes Brock paled. "Why, you *insufferable* child! That painting was given to my sainted mother by the great Marc Chagall himself! He told her to choose anything she wanted from his studio, anything at all!"

"With all due respect, Mrs. Brock, your mother did not choose very well."

"I know," she mumbled, suddenly deflated, and I imagined that she was as chagrined as I to find something we could agree on. Her mother should have selected one of the better-known works Chagall created to celebrate the contributions of Jewish culture to the world. His paintings of upside-down rabbis were both historically significant and worth a small fortune on the open market. "Mother didn't actually care for Chagall's modern style. She chose a simple urbanscape, with only a single floating woman."

"*That's* what was stolen?" I asked, recalling the painting. "What an odd choice. I would have taken—"

"Excuse us, please, Mrs. Brock," Annette interrupted, seizing me by the elbow. "I have police business to see to, and I need to speak with Ms. Kincaid. A pleasure, as always."

"*Annie Kincaid!*" Agnes Brock bellowed from the doorway as Annette and I started down the museum steps. "If that painting is returned within a fortnight, I shall ask no questions and will drop any charges against your friend. *Otherwise*, I shall see that he is prosecuted to the fullest extent of the law. And if the law fails, I have other resources at my disposal. *Do you hear me*?"

I heard her. The tourists at Fisherman's Wharf must have heard her. Agnes had an impressive set of pipes for a woman her age.

As Annette and I proceeded down the stairs, I thought about what Agnes' threats might mean for Bryan. He wasn't charged with anything, but as I knew only too well a lack of proof would not deter a Brock vendetta. Agnes had enough pull in this town to make his life miserable if she put her mind to it.

Arriving at the bustling parking lot, I sagged against a dusty Ford sedan and looked up to see Annette's partner joining us. Inspector Wilson was a taciturn man who reminded me of Ichabod Crane: Tall and skinny, he had a prominent Adam's apple and no discernible personality.

I nodded at him. He stared at me.

"Okay, Annie," Annette said, snapping open her notebook. "Let's take this from the top, shall we?"

I described recognizing that the corpse was not a sculpture and trying to convey that information to Anthony Brazil, who had not wanted to hear it. There wasn't much else to tell.

"Did you know the deceased?" Annette asked. "Tentatively identified as one Seamus McGraw, sculptor?"

"Never met him. What do you mean, 'tentatively identified'?" I asked. "Could it be someone else?"

"Until the coroner signs the death certificate it's always tentative. So. Have you heard anything that might suggest why someone would want to murder McGraw?"

"*Murder?* I thought it was a suicide."

"People who hang themselves don't chop their fingers off first," Ichabod said self-importantly. Annette shot him a glare and he fell silent.

"Chop off . . . ?" I felt bile rise in my throat.

"Any rumors about McGraw owing money, involved in drugs, anything like that?" Annette pressed.

"No, but I'm not exactly part of the City's gallery crowd, so I'd be unlikely to hear anything. Ask Anthony Brazil. Can I go home now?"

"Not yet," Annette said, all business. "How closely did you observe the condition of the body?"

"I could tell it wasn't a sculpture, but I tried not to get too close. Dead bodies aren't my strong suit."

"Did you notice that it was covered with powder?"

I nodded.

"Do you have any idea what that powder might be?"

"My guess would be stone dust, from cutting and shaping stone," I said. "Stone sculptors are usually surrounded by the stuff, like an artistic version of the Peanuts' Pigpen. We used to tease them about it at school."

"I thought McGraw sculpted in metal," Annette said with a frown.

"Most sculptors dabble in a number of media. I saw the manager of Marble World at the show, so I assume McGraw worked in stone as well."

"Mm-hmm. Anything else about the opening seem odd or different?"

Only that Janice Hewett had hired me to retrieve *Head and Torso* from its sculptor, but I decided not to share that information. If the police started poking around Pascal's studio I might lose my seat on the one-hundred-fifty-dollar-an-hour gravy train.

I shook my head and shrugged. "I don't know much about contemporary sculptors, and frankly I didn't much care for McGraw's work. Death, mutilation, torture . . ."

"I thought you artsy types lived for stuff like that," Ichabod sneered.

"Not me," I replied with a big, fake smile. "I only paint happy things. Like rainbows. And clowns. And big-eyed children . . ."

"You paint clowns?" Ichabod asked. "Could you paint a—"

"She's pulling your leg, Wilson," Annette interrupted, watching me with a ghost of a smile and shaking her head. "Annie doesn't paint clowns."

Twenty minutes later I trooped the four long city blocks to where I had parked my old green Toyota pickup truck, rooted around in my black leather backpack for my massive key ring, fired up the engine, and headed for China Basin, an old warehouse district just south of the Oakland Bay Bridge. My studio was on the second floor of a former chair factory that had been converted into artists' studios. The building had been bought last spring by J. Frank DeBenton, an entrepreneur whose brand-new Jaguar I had promptly rear-ended. This initial encounter set the tone for our occasionally contentious landlord-tenant relationship. Frank could be a real pain in the butt at times, but overall I had to admit he was a decent guy. He'd agreed to hold off on a proposed rent increase in exchange for some decorative painting in several of his commercial buildings, but with the work now completed I feared "double Annie's rent" had moved to the top of Frank's To Do list.

Being an artist was hands-down the greatest job in the world, except when it came to making money. After years of my working twelve-hour days, True/Faux Studios enjoyed a steady clientele, but there were still times when I scrambled to pay the rent.

This was one of those times.

For the past five weeks my assistant, Mary, and I had done little else but work on five sweeping, romantic panels in the Pre-Raphaelite style of Edward Burne-Jones for a chic new restaurant in the City's Hayes Valley neighborhood. The client's twenty-five-percent down payment went towards the cost of supplies, scaffolding rental, and Mary's wages. Three days before the grand opening, as Mary and I were working through the night to develop a crackled "aged canvas" effect on the panels, we caught the restaurant's owner sneaking a shiny new cappuccino machine out of the kitchen. He confessed—under duress, courtesy of Mary—that he had run out of money. A lawyer charged me two hundred dollars for the profound legal insight that I should try to get in line ahead of the restaurant's legion of outraged creditors and vendors, but admitted that my chances of getting paid were slim to none.

Worst of all, Frank DeBenton had warned me not to take the job because he'd heard the restaurant was undercapitalized. But I had been seduced by the romance of the panels and the ethereal beauty of the Pre-Raphaelite women I was painting.

Too proud to explain my situation to Frank, I grabbed the next paying job to come along, which was how I ended up painting the portrait of a Lhaso apso named Sir Frothingham

Snufflebums III for an elderly dog lover in Piedmont. I didn't mind Sir Snufflebums—hell, I wished all my portrait subjects were as good-natured—but I was reasonably certain this was not how the famous Venetian portraitist Rosalba Carriera had begun her career.

Still, I would be able to pay the rent as soon as Sir Snufflebum's check cleared. In the meantime I had been avoiding my landlord on the unproven and possibly dubious theory that if he could not find me he could not evict me. Since Frank's office was located at the foot of the staircase leading up to my second-floor studio, this strategy required good timing, a pinch of luck, and a willingness to work odd hours.

Like at nine o'clock on a Friday night. I pulled into a space in front of the stairs, set the brake, grabbed my bag, and slammed the locked driver's door before noticing that my keys were lying on the passenger's seat.

"Dammit! Dammit, dammit, *dammit!*"

Calm down, Annie, I scolded myself. *Remember what the yogi taught you.* I closed my eyes, took a deep breath, and tried to picture the ocean with my third eye.

Apparently it had a cataract.

I circled my little pickup, searching for an opening. The passenger's window was rolled down a quarter of an inch, allowing me to insert the tip of my pinkie finger between the glass and the rubber weather stripping. I wiggled it. It made for a cute shadow puppet but otherwise was not helpful.

I glanced around hoping to spot something I could use to jimmy the lock, but Frank DeBenton kept the parking lot as tidy as he did his office. My black evening bag yielded only a dead cell phone, my driver's license, a parking ticket, an overextended credit card, and a couple of crumpled dollar bills.

Rats. If only my assistant, Mary, were here. Mary could break into just about anything, a talent she had developed during her stint as a teenage runaway. I sighed. There was nothing for it but to spend the night on the couch in my studio and have Mary do a little breaking and entering in the morning. Too bad the key to my studio was also on the ring lying on the passenger seat, behind locked doors.

I knew Mary occasionally used the rear fire escape to enter the studio through the second-story windows. Skirting the outdoor staircase, I followed the picturesque brick walkway to the rear of the building. As I gazed at the rickety metal ladder high above my head, it occurred to me that my assistant was a full head taller, several years younger, and far more athletic than I. How in the world would I reach the release bar?

Aha! With a flash of inspiration I recalled the paintbrush extension rod in the bed of my truck. It had been there since the Hayes Valley restaurant fiasco, and had been annoying me for days, rolling around at every twist and turn. *This is why I never put it away*, I thought. It was destiny.

The rod was just barely long enough. After a good deal of swinging and grunting and a few choice swear words I brought the release bar within reach, yanked on it, and the ladder clacked toward me with a rusty screech. I clambered up to the second floor, cringing as my heels rang against the metal. Digging my fingers beneath the frame of one of the double-hung windows that ran along the back of my studio, I gave a mighty heave and the window inched up a crack. I braced my legs against the fire escape and went through a series of contortions that, considering the length of my skirt, would likely have gotten me arrested in half the states of the Union.

At last the window slid open; I threw my legs over the

sill and landed in my studio with a triumphant little hop. Brushing the grime from my hands, I felt absurdly pleased with myself.

Until I heard a beeping sound.

What was that? I glanced around at the packed bookshelves, the storage bins, the cluttered worktables, the large easels. I saw nothing out of the ordinary. It wasn't the telephone. It wasn't the computer. I would have noticed a dump truck backing up in the studio.

The noise was definitely mechanical in nature, and it was growing steadily louder.

What *was* that?

In the dusty recesses of my mind a memory stirred. Something about a memo from my landlord. Something about an alarm system. Something about a security code—

CLANG! CLANG! CLANG! CLANG! CLANG!

Aw, *geez*! Swearing at my stupidity, I thrashed through the litter on top of my desk until I unearthed the memo. "Dear tenant: On November 19th the building's alarm system will be activated . . ." *Get to the point, Frank. Get to the point.* Skimming frantically, I spotted the alarm company's emergency number and grabbed the telephone.

"Evergreen Alarm Systems, what is your code?" an exceedingly calm woman singsonged.

"I accidentally set off the alarm in my studio! How do I turn it off?"

"I'm sorry, ma'am, but I'll need the code before I can assist you in disabling the alarm."

"I don't have the code!" I yelled, the persistent clamor jangling my nerves. "It's a new alarm system and I don't have the code!"

"If you are a legal tenant you were provided with the code."

"I have no code!"

"Then I have no alternative but to notify the police," the woman declared coolly.

"Listen to me, please," I said, taking a deep breath. "I'm calling you from my studio. Would I do that if I were a burglar?"

"Ma'am, if you do not know the security code then you must remain in the building until the police arrive," Ms. Evergreen replied, sticking to her guns. "Remain in the build—"

I slammed down the receiver. Remain in the building my ass. If Frank DeBenton found out I'd set off the new alarm he would evict me for sure. I dove out the window and thundered down the fire escape, snatched up the paint rod extension, and raced around the building to the parking lot. I skidded to a halt and tried to hide the six-foot pole behind my back.

My landlord, Frank, was leaning against my truck.

Rats.

Chapter 3

Q: Where can I learn to become an art forger?
A: The best training for art forgery is an appren-
ticeship with a truly fine art restorer.

> —*Georges LeFleur, at an impromptu meeting of*
> *La Societée des Beaux Arts, Paris*

"Mindy at Evergreen Alarm Systems sends her regards," Frank DeBenton said as the blaring alarm came to a sudden and blessed end. Slipping a sleek silver cell phone into the pocket of his elegant suit vest, he crossed his arms over his chest and nodded his dark brown head. "Good evening, Annie. Is that a paintbrush rod extension or are you just glad to see me?"

I tossed the rod into the bed of the truck, where it landed with a resounding clang. "What are you doing at the office so late on a Friday, Frank?"

"I was having a drink with a client and came by to drop off some papers. I'd just pulled up when Mindy called to say some idiot had set off the alarm and phoned her. Said the woman didn't sound like a burglar, so she decided to call me instead of the police."

"More bungling than burgling, wouldn't you say?" I asked, swatting flakes of white windowsill paint from the skirt of my little black dress, which had earlier tonight been respectable, even fashionable. I was a mess magnet.

"That was my guess, too. How've you been lately, Annie? I haven't seen you around."

"I, uh . . . I've been keeping busy."

"Business is good?"

"Yeah, sure," I lied. The self-employed learned to always insist that business was good, especially when it wasn't. "Business is great."

A smile hovered on Frank's lips. It made me nervous.

"What?" I demanded.

The smile broadened.

"What?"

"Sounds like you've had quite an evening," he said enigmatically.

"You don't know the half of it," I muttered.

"As a matter of fact, I do. The client I was meeting tonight was Mayor Green. He told me about your discovery at Brazil's new gallery. You're the talk of the town."

I collapsed against the truck. "Just for the record, I had *nothing* to do with *anything*. I was a model citizen and answered all the cops' questions, and you know how I feel about that."

"I didn't imply that you were involved, Annie."

Silence filled the space between us. Suddenly tired, I gazed up at the night sky. The glow of millions of electric lights in the Bay Area obscured what should have been a spectacular display, but a few hardy stars managed to shine through. I tried to remember their names. I had learned the constellations years ago at Girl Scout summer camp, shortly before I'd been drummed out of the corps for conduct unbecoming.

Frank stirred and I wondered if he was thinking about

the stars, or, more likely, about the bottom line. *Might as well face the firing squad,* I decided with a sigh.

"I don't have the rent money yet, Frank. I screwed up. I should be good for it soon, if you can just wait a few more days."

"Is that why you've been avoiding me?"

"I wouldn't say I've been avoiding you exactly."

"So that wasn't you in the battered green pickup truck peeling out of the parking lot yesterday when I drove up?"

His voice, low and attractive, contained a note of suppressed humor. Was he making fun of me? Probably. Was I in any position to complain? Not really.

"It's not like I'm slacking off, Frank. It's just that I'm working sixty hours a week as it is and I still can't make ends meet. I should probably start looking for a new studio." I stared into the distance, fighting a wave of self-pity. I didn't ask for much out of life, just the chance to create my art without risking arrest and imprisonment. Why was that so hard?

"A new studio?" Frank asked, startled. "Isn't this a good location for your business?"

"Of course. Most of my clients are in the City. But the rents are too high."

"So there's no other reason you're considering moving?"

"No, I love it here. The studio space is perfect, my friends are here, and my landlord's a decent sort," I said, giving him a sideways glance. "Most of the time, anyway."

"And he's about to prove that this is one of those times," he replied. "Had you responded to any of my many phone messages, Annie, you would have known that I've been trying to propose a somewhat unorthodox business arrangement."

"What?"

"I said—"

"I heard you," I replied, thinking quickly. "Just how 'unorthodox' is this arrangement? Because I've had about as many surprises as I can handle in one night."

"It's not that kind of proposition, Annie," he said, his dark eyes holding mine. "As you know, DeBenton Secure Transport moves artwork for a number of top museums and dealers. From time to time accidents happen and I need the services of a top-notch art restorer. But the work must be done discreetly. *Very* discreetly."

"As in, I keep my yap shut and no one ever finds out?"

"Precisely."

"And in exchange for my services you are offering what?"

"I extend your lease for three years, and reduce the rent five hundred dollars a month in lieu of a retainer. You'll be my resident art expert."

"'Resident art expert,' eh?" I repeated, tempted but hesitant. "I like it. But let's be clear about one thing: I don't do restoration work that alters the value of a painting or its attribution."

The line between restoring art and forging art was a thin one that I preferred not to cross. To the best of my knowledge Frank was unaware of my past, and I hoped to keep it that way. I didn't think he would appreciate the irony of a former art forger working for an art security business.

"Not a problem. I'm referring to straightforward repair work, that's all. I would also like your opinion on questions of authenticity from time to time."

"Okay, then," I said, beaming. "It's a deal."

We shook hands solemnly. His grip was strong, yet gentle, his long fingers enveloping mine.

Not that I noticed.

"Just let me know when you need me," I said, thinking

that a bubble bath and a hot rum toddy would really hit the spot. With the wolf no longer baying at my studio's door, I could relax for the first time in months.

"How about now?" he asked, pushing away from the truck.

Or not.

"Now's good," I said cooperatively.

We crossed the parking lot to one of DeBenton Secure Transport's blue-and-silver armored cars emblazoned with the logo of a roaring lion, where Frank used a complicated series of keys and codes to open the rear doors. He climbed in and extended a hand to assist me, a chivalrous gesture I found both charming and annoying. I inched into the car, trying not to flash Frank in the process, which was not an easy task in heels and a short skirt. Switching on the overhead dome light, he locked the heavy doors behind us, hunkered down in front of a shallow wooden crate, lifted the lid, and took out a thick layer of foam packing material. Finally he removed a white silk cloth to reveal an eighteen-by-twenty-four-inch painting.

It was a Picasso, a colorful oil painting of a woman. At least I thought it was a woman.

"Amazing, isn't it?" he asked, his tone reverential.

"Yeah, sure. Amazing."

Frank looked surprised. "You don't like Picasso?"

"Of *course* I like Picasso!" I lied. "What's not to like? It's *Picasso*!"

"I can't believe you don't like Picasso," he said with a shake of his handsome head. "And to think you once called *me* a Philistine. Anyway, the question is: can you fix it?"

Fix what? There were no slash marks, no ink blots, no greasy pizza stains. Just a bunch of lines, pattern, and color.

I had to ask. "What's wrong with it?"

"The bright red mark? In the middle of the woman's breast?" He pointed to a red line in the center of an angular splotch that looked unlike any breast I had ever seen. "It wasn't there when I took possession of the painting. I'm investigating how it happened, but I can't surrender it to its owner in this condition."

"Oh," I said, squinting at the red squiggle. "How do you know it's not supposed to be there?"

"And here I thought you were the human art detector."

"Modern art's too cold and calculated," I explained. "I need to *feel* the art. Now if it were from Picasso's Blue Period . . ."

"Feel, schmeel," he scoffed. "The question is, can you fix it? I can't turn over a defaced multimillion-dollar painting."

"Okay, okay, don't get your knickers in a twist. Got a flashlight?"

Frank pulled one out from under a jump seat and turned its bright beam on the painting. I touched the surface of the red line gingerly, then tilted the canvas and examined it from the side.

By golly, it looked like a crayon mark.

Last summer, during a visit to my hometown of Asco, my two young nephews had reintroduced me to the wonders of Crayolas. I'd immediately bought a sixty-four pack, and Mary and I had experimented with them on all kinds of surfaces, including canvas. If I was right, it should be a relatively simple matter to lift the colored wax from the Picasso.

I glanced at Frank. Not only did I wish to bolster my reputation as "Annie Kincaid, Girl Wonder of the Art World," but in view of our new business arrangement, I needed my landlord to believe that he was getting his money's worth. So as he waited patiently, I cocked my head, frowned, and hmm'd. I squinted some more, sat back on my heels, and put my hands on my knees, bowing my head as if concentrating intently. Finally I shook my head and sucked air in through my teeth, making that reverse hissing sound that usually accompanies estimates for auto repairs.

"Well, Frank, here's the story," I said crisply. "I can help you. Yes, I can. But it's not going to be easy. I'll have to examine the mark under the magnifier to determine exactly what we're dealing with here, then do some tests to assess the pigment adherence index and the media distillates. I'll also need to analyze the canvas support integer, as well as the existing paint refraction, with a spectrum magnetometer. The last thing we want to do is to disturb the Master's original pigments and media."

Frank looked mystified, which wasn't surprising considering I had just spouted a whole bunch of hooey. If my original assessment was correct, then all that was necessary to remove the red mark was a careful application of low heat and wax-absorbent paper, a technique familiar to many a parent whose child had scribbled on the good linen tablecloth.

"I'll have to work on it in my studio, though," I said. "Will it be safe there?"

"Let me install some heavy-duty locks on the windows first. They're too easy to break into at the moment," he said as I avoided his eyes. "I'm also hiring a security guard, starting tomorrow. The painting should be safe enough so long as no one knows it's in your studio. I'll bring it upstairs in the morning. Will you be around?"

"I'll be here," I said.

Our eyes met and my pulse quickened at the fond expression on Frank's face.

"Thank you, Annie. I can't tell you what a relief this is.

I discovered the damage three days ago and have been trying to get ahold of you ever since," he said, carefully wrapping the Picasso in the packing material and securing the
crate.

"Sorry about that. I thought you wanted the rent
money."

"In the future, if you fall short with the rent, come talk
to me. I don't know why you make me out to be such an
ogre." Throwing open the rear doors of the armored car,
Frank climbed out and offered me a hand. I stumbled into
him during my descent but otherwise managed to remain
upright.

"I wouldn't say you're an ogre, exactly," I continued as
we crossed the parking lot. "But you have to admit that you
have occasional flashes of unexplained grouchiness."

"My alleged grouchiness is most often attributable to
certain unreasonable tenants," he said as he held up my key
ring and shook it so it jingled.

"How did you . . . ?"

Frank raised an eyebrow. "You think you're the only
one with skills?"

"Why, Frank," I purred, snatching the key ring and unlocking my truck. "I had no idea you were so talented."

"My dear Annie," he replied, closing the door as I
started the engine. "You *still* have no idea."

"The single most important thing about stealing art is
knowing where to find the art," Frank lectured the next
morning as I followed him up the stairs to my studio, sti-
fling a yawn. "Ergo, it follows that if a thief can't find it, a
thief can't steal it. Simple as that."

I knew from experience that foiling art theft was not
that simple, ergo or otherwise, but kept my mouth shut.
What Frank didn't know about my past couldn't hurt me.

"Where should we put it?" I asked, unlocking the door and ushering him inside. "Shouldn't you invest in a safe or something?"

"All a safe does is announce, 'The good stuff's in here!'" he replied jovially. "No, the safest place for this baby is right over there with the rest of the junk."

The man was positively glowing, I thought as I disarmed the security system with the code he had given me downstairs. Where was the grumpy-pants landlord I knew and loved to provoke?

"You feeling okay, Frank?"

"Just super," he replied, rummaging around under one of the worktables. "Thanks for asking."

My spacious art studio took up one corner of the DeBenton Building. The light, bright space included a fifteen-foot beamed ceiling punctuated by three skylights and two ceiling fans, as well as the original wide plank floor and redbrick walls. A bank of tall, double-hung windows along the northern wall let in a soft natural light that was perfect for painting. Near the door was a sitting area where I entertained clients and friends. In a fit of whimsy one rainy afternoon I had painted a faux fireplace on the wall, complete with a cozy roaring fire. In front of the fireplace I had arranged an old Persian rug, a faded velvet couch, two flea market chairs reupholstered with discarded fabric samples and my trusty staple gun, and a wicker trunk that doubled as a coffee table and storage for blankets for the nights I was too tired to drive home safely.

Most of the studio, though, was devoted to my work. Several large easels held paintings in varying stages of completion; a motley collection of garage-sale bookcases were jammed with art reference books, cans of paint, jars of applicators, cartons of brushes, and scary-looking bottles filled with scary-acting noxious chemicals; and along the rear wall were three large worktables, a light box, a steamer, and several heat lamps. Beneath the worktables were covered plastic bins packed with an assortment of faux-finishing tools masquerading as junk: goose feathers gathered from Oakland's Lake Merritt that were perfect for painting the squiggly veins of faux marble; old plastic sheeting for creating a wonderful texture when pressed into wet glaze; and Styrofoam blocks for stamping "bricks" into murals. Wherever I went I kept an eye peeled for odd bits of rubbish that I could use to create new effects.

Frank decided to stash his multimillion-dollar Picasso beneath a pile of Belgian linen canvas tucked behind a large carton full of plaster bunnies. I had acquired the bunnies at an auction two years ago for pennies on the dollar in what I could only describe as a triumph of creative optimism over practical sense. My assistant, Mary, had taken one look at the ugly rodents and informed me that I was no longer allowed to attend auctions.

"Safe and sound," Frank said as he patted the plaster bunny box. "Just don't spill anything on it."

"Like what?"

"I don't know. Coffee. Paint remover. Sticky buns."

"Sticky buns?"

"Just by way of example."

"Tell you what, Frank," I said. "If you'll install those window locks and let me get to work, I'll keep away from the Picasso when I eat my usual breakfast of coffee, sticky buns, and toxic solvents, okay?"

Frank laughed, picked up his toolbox, and got to work. I watched, impressed, as he efficiently unscrewed the old brass fittings, sanded down and puttied over the screw holes, drilled new holes, and screwed in tamper-proof steel locks. My landlord had never struck me as the type of man to know his way around power tools. Then again, last night he had extracted the keys from my locked truck neatly enough.

Finished with the window locks, Frank reminded me once more to set the alarm whenever I left the studio, and departed just as my friend Pete arrived. The two men nodded coolly, unconsciously puffing out their chests as they passed.

"How do you do, Annie?" asked Pete as he headed for the small kitchen enclosure. "Cuppa Joe to clench your thirst?"

Originally from Bosnia, Pete honed his English by watching soap operas and memorizing his word-a-day calendar, resulting in an impressive, albeit eclectic, grasp of American idioms, history, and culture. But whatever his linguistic quirks, Pete operated my fussy secondhand espresso maker with the skill of a master croupier at a roulette wheel. This was a very good thing because I had a serious caffeine addiction, and the rest of the gang put together could scarcely manage to boil water.

"Espresso, Americano, latte, cappuccino?" he asked.

"Double cappuccino, please."

Although he was six feet, six inches of rippling muscle, Pete was more teddy bear than grizzly bear, his animosity toward our landlord being a notable exception. Mary claimed it was due to a testosterone-driven territorial fixation and urged Pete to go ahead and pee around the perimeter of the studio. He had found Mary's suggestion bewildering but not altogether out of the question.

While Pete ground aromatic beans and noisily steamed water and milk, I checked my phone messages and my calendar. I needed to update sample books for the interior designers I worked with, finish the holiday displays for a local charity, and follow up on a bid for a "castle in the

clouds" mural for a little girl's room in the St. Francis
Wood neighborhood. I also needed to see how Bryan was
doing. Oh, and find a stolen Chagall.

First, though, I called Janice Hewett to make arrangements to be paid one hundred and fifty dollars an hour to
speak with a recalcitrant sculptor. She chattered for several
minutes about last night's excitement before giving me the
phone number and address of Robert Pascal's studio on
Tennessee Street, which was not far from the DeBenton
Building. I called the number twice, but there was no answer, not even voice mail. Looked like it was time for a
field trip.

"Mornin', Annie," my twenty-something assistant said
as she breezed in and threw herself onto the velvet couch.
Mary Grae was a tall, striking blonde who believed that,
when it came to clothes and eye makeup, any color other
than black was unnecessarily complicated. Today was her
day off, but I wasn't surprised to see her. She often took
refuge at the studio to escape the crowded apartment she
shared with the members of her pseudopunk band.

Close on Mary's heels was Sherri, her best friend since
kindergarten. A few years ago the pair had hitchhiked
cross-country from a small town in Indiana, where they
had outraged their elders by dying their hair, sporting tat-
toos, and forming truly wretched bands. Mary insisted the
only things of value she and Sherri had learned in three
years of high school were how to smoke, forge their mothers' signatures, and pee in a cup.

In San Francisco they seemed positively quaint.

"Mornin', Annie," echoed Sherri, a dark-haired pixie
whose high, tobacco-roughened voice sounded like Minnie
Mouse on a pack a day.

"Hello, young ladies," Pete called from the kitchenette.
"And how do you do today?"

Mary rolled her eyes at Pete's outmoded gallantry, but the better socialized Sherri returned his greeting and elbowed Mary in the ribs.

"What's up?" I asked, ripping open the mail in the vain hope that I'd won the Publisher's Clearing House sweepstakes.

"We were just—" Mary's reply was interrupted by the sound of heavy boots clomping down the hallway. Two young men—one tall and baby-faced, the other short and snickering—ducked through the open door. Their black leather jackets, black jeans, and spiky hair clued me in to their friendship with Mary. The bronze art-nouveau Tiffany lamp bases in Babyface's arms clued me in to the purpose of their visit.

"We made a bet that you couldn't tell which was the fake Tiffany and which was the real one," Mary said, bouncing up from the sofa and staring at me fixedly. "You have ten seconds."

"*Dude*, no way she can tell in ten seconds," Snickers said.

I sighed. I didn't pay Mary enough to refuse her the occasional moneymaking favor, and besides, I had spotted the fake the second the boys walked in.

I gestured with my pen. "The one on the right's the reproduction."

"*Dude!*" Snickers punched his friend in the arm. "She didn't even look! Lucky guess!"

"It's not a guess," I said, taking the heavy bronze lamp bases and turning them over. "See how the *Tiffany Studios New York* stamp is raised on this one? On real Tiffany bronzes of this period the maker's mark is die stamped, which means it's recessed into the metal. The real one also includes the model number. See there?"

Pete arrived with a tray of espresso drinks, doled out

napkins, and joined the impromptu lesson on spotting forged Tiffany bronzes.

"Also, note the patina—see how the fake has some chipping along the edges and at the tip of the nose? That's a dead giveaway," I explained. "Real patinas develop over time as the metal slowly oxidizes, but fake patinas are painted on. If you rubbed acetone—that's just fingernail polish remover—on the fake one, the patina would come right off."

"But you hardly even looked at them!" Babyface protested in a high, adolescent tenor, and I realized why he was the silent type.

"I didn't need to. Look at the features on the fake: the hands aren't fully modeled and the hair is crudely detailed. Tiffany would have melted down such sloppy work. Now look at the eyes. Most reproductions are made in Asia, so the eyes have an Asian cast."

I handed the bronzes to Snickers, who kept shaking his head and repeating "Dude" while Babyface dug a crumpled twenty-dollar bill out of his jeans pocket.

"Where did you get those, anyway?" I asked, gathering my things to head over to Pascal's studio. "The real one's worth a lot of money."

"It's my grandma's," Babyface squeaked. "She really loves it, so I wanted to get her another one. You know, like a matched set? So I bought one at the Ashby flea market, but Mary said it was probably a fake." He shook his head in disgust. "I paid fifteen bucks for it, too. Flea market dude said it was hot. He *lied* to me, man."

I watched silently as the boys clomped out of the studio.

"Mary?"

"Yes, Annie?"

"Let's make it a policy not to deal with those who traffic in stolen goods, shall we?"

"Does that policy include your grandfather?" she sassed, delicately sipping her espresso.

"It *especially* includes my grandfather," I replied, downing my coffee and setting off to make some easy money courtesy of Janice Hewett.

Chapter 4

Few art thieves are connoisseurs; most might just as well steal a big-screen television as a Titian. Not so the art forger. I am not only an accomplished artist, but a philosopher who challenges the popular definition of "art."

—Georges LeFleur, *in answer to the query, "Are you any different from a common thief?" on the BBC radio program* Ask the Experts

"Mr. Pascal! It's Annie Kincaid! Remember me? Dr. Harold Kincaid's daughter?"

I had been banging on the door of Robert Pascal's third-floor studio for ten minutes, with no discernable results. Maybe Pascal didn't care whose daughter I was. Maybe this was the butler's day off. Maybe the racket I was making had given Pascal a stroke and he was lying on the floor, cursing my name with his dying breath.

Someone was in there. The sleep-deprived denizens of the Internet start-up company on the first floor told me they had heard the whir of a pneumatic drill all morning. Those sounds ceased abruptly when I knocked.

Frustrated, I slid down the wall and sat cross-legged on the floor, drummed my fingers on the dull linoleum, and told myself I was being paid one fifty an hour to waste my time like this. Besides, I felt a tug of loyalty to a fellow artist. The Hewetts were prepared to sue Pascal, and their pockets were surely deeper than an elderly sculptor's.

Which reminded me: why wouldn't Pascal return *Head and Torso*? Artists were usually delighted to sell their old stuff so they could afford to create new stuff. And if they hated to part with something, well, there was nothing to stop them from making a copy, as long as they were up-front about it. After all, Edvard Munch had painted four versions of his famous *Scream*. So what was different about this sculpture? I wondered whether there might be a connection between Pascal's reclusive behavior and Seamus McGraw's peculiar death. Both had studied at Berkeley and were represented by Anthony Brazil . . .

But so what? The sculpting community was a small one, so it wasn't surprising their training had overlapped. And many artists aspired to be represented by Brazil, who owned one of the top galleries in northern California. Still, it did seem odd that Pascal had not come to the show last night if only—like me—to curry favor with potential clients. Had he somehow known not to go? Or was he just avoiding the Hewetts?

The answers, if there were any, lay behind his locked studio door.

Maybe if I were quiet for a while he would think I'd gone and come out to investigate. Of course, once he saw me he could just slam the door. I wasn't a cop or a bounty hunter. I had no idea how to extract the man from his studio, and no legal right to enter. With a decent supply of food and vodka he could hold out for days or even weeks, whereas I was likely to get bored and give up in an hour or two.

Actually, I was kind of bored already. I stood up and

wandered down the hall of the uninspired 1940s building. Nothing broke up the monotony of the dull beige walls except a profusion of cracks in the plaster. The only other door led to a janitor's closet, judging by the mop that nearly beaned me when I poked my head in. A single unadorned window at the end of the hall offered a view of dilapidated docks that had once bustled with longshoremen. The huge container ships from around the Pacific Rim now unloaded their cargo at the port of Oakland, abandoning this one to a handful of dry-docked ships and flocks of noisy seagulls.

I glanced at my watch. Fifteen minutes had passed.

Rats. Patience was not my strong suit.

Remember the money, I chided myself. That was good. Very motivating. Let's see, half of one fifty was seventy-five, which meant that in the past fifteen minutes I had already earned . . .

Math was not my strong suit, either.

I wandered back down the hall, sat on the floor again, and started sketching in the marble dust that fanned out in silky waves from beneath Pascal's door. I was putting the finishing touches on a nice rendering of Botticelli's *Birth of Venus* in the cartoonish style of Roy Lichtenstein when my cell phone trilled, startling me. I always forgot I had it with me.

"What's the deal with the Stand All thingee?" Mary demanded abruptly when I answered.

"Stand all?"

"Yeah, some kind of symptom?"

"You mean the Stendhal Syndrome?" I asked, surprised to be discussing the obscure psychological disorder for the second time in as many days. "It's a psychological condition where a person faints or loses control in the presence of great art. It was named after—"

"Oh, good." Mary, familiar with my tendency to digress, cut me off. "Sherri says everybody's getting it and I was hoping it wasn't some new sexually transmitted disease. Okay, bye!"

"Wait! I'm trying to get a sculptor to talk to me but he won't answer the door. I'm afraid if I go away he'll leave for good. Got any ideas?"

"Hold on, let me ask Sherri." Sherri and her husband, Tom, owned a process-serving business. Giving legal papers to people who did not want them had given Sherri unusual insight into human behavior. "She says to wait until he goes out for groceries or a doctor's appointment or something. She says they always leave eventually."

"I was afraid of that," I sighed.

"What's the matter?"

"I'm bored," I confessed. "And hungry." I had, as usual, skipped breakfast. A meal of coffee, sticky buns, and toxic solvents was starting to sound appealing.

"Tell you what! We'll join you! We'll bring lunch! It'll be fun!"

"Wait, Mar—"

She hung up. I started to hit redial, but paused. I was bored. And hungry. Pascal didn't seem to care what I did out here.

What the hell.

The phone rang again.

"Where the heck are you, anyway?"

I gave her directions, and while the phone was out I decided to follow up on Bryan's situation. With a little digging, I might be able to find out who had stolen the Chagall. Agnes Brock wasn't the only one who knew people.

I began with the one person at the Brock Museum who might still talk to me: Naomi Gregorian. Naomi and I had been semi-rivals in college and semi-colleagues when we were interns at the Brock, at least until I'd been outed as a former art forger. I hadn't spoken to her since the museum gala last spring, when she'd been in the wrong place at the wrong time and ended up locked in a closet with a killer. Odds were good she'd hang up on me, but what did I have to lose? I was earning $37.50 every fifteen minutes. I'd finally figured it out.

"Naomi Chadwick Gregorian," she answered in a newly acquired and ever-so-slightly British accent.

"Naomi!" I blustered. "It's Annie Kincaid! How the heck *are* you?"

My greeting was met with silence, but since this was par for the course for Naomi and me, I forged ahead. "I heard there was a ruckus at the Brock the other day. Something about a Stendhal Syndrome faint-in and a stolen Chagall?" The silence on the phone was replaced by sputtering. "Naomi? You still there?"

"Yes, Ann," she choked, calling me, as always, by the wrong name because she was just that petty. "I am here. What could you *possibly* have to say to *me*?"

"Well hey, old friends and all that. And after all, I did save *The Magi*, remember?"

The Brock Museum's Caravaggio masterpiece was actually an exquisite fake painted by my grandfather, Georges LeFleur. But if Agnes Brock was happy with it, who was I to enlighten her?

"You ruined the gala, is what you did!" Naomi screeched, and I winced. "The Diamond Circle gala! The most important, most exclusive event of the year!"

"Be fair, Naomi," I coaxed. "*I* didn't ruin the gala; the *bad guys* ruined the gala."

"You locked me in a closet!"

"Colin Brooks locked you in that closet because he was

trying to protect you. You know how crazy he was about you. He told me so."

I lied. Colin Brooks, also known as Michael X. Johnson, sexy art thief extraordinaire, had locked Naomi in the closet to keep her out of our hair.

"Colin said that?" Naomi asked, more subdued.

"Yes indeed. He also said that it was too hard to be with you when he knew he couldn't have you." *I should take up creative writing,* I thought.

"Why couldn't he have me?"

Oops. Cancel the career change. "Well, because . . . because he's already married."

"What?"

"Six kids, too."

"Six?"

"You did the right thing by letting him go," I continued. "You know what they say, if you love something you have to, um, get rid of it."

"That's true . . ."

"Trust me. Anyhoo, about that Stendhal situation . . ."

"I can't talk about the museum's internal affairs," she said primly.

"I appreciate that, Naomi, I truly do," I said. "But you *know* how much I rely on you to keep me abreast of what's going on in the art world." Naomi could never resist juicy gossip, especially if it meant reminding me that she was a professional art restorer and I was a lowly faux finisher.

"Well . . ." Her voice lowered and she forgot the British accent. "There was a group here. Adult Education types, so I guess we shouldn't be too surprised."

I bit my tongue to keep from reminding Naomi that her father, a gifted auto mechanic in Modesto, had gotten his GED at adult night school.

"They'd been touring the galleries when suddenly they

got all worked up and fainted in a heap on the floor. It was just *awful*, so *tacky*. Afterwards, Carlos in Security noticed a Chagall was missing. But you would know all this if you read the newspaper, Ann."

In college Naomi had fancied herself a policy wonk and hung out in cafés ostentatiously reading the *New York Times*. Just to annoy her I had started hanging out at the next table, reading *Le Monde*. Naomi had a tin ear for languages, and it drove her nuts that I could outsnob her. Too bad I always stopped reading as soon as she stomped out.

"Why do the police think the faintings and the theft were related?" I asked. "Maybe someone noticed that Security was preoccupied, grabbed the Chagall, and took off?"

"It wasn't that simple. The Brock installed an electronic sensor system last year, which should have triggered the alarm when the Chagall was removed from the gallery. But the system had been disabled. Whoever committed the theft knew what he was doing."

"What do the surveillance tapes show?"

Silence.

"Naomi?"

"The, uh, the cameras weren't exactly hooked up."

"Not hooked up?" For an art museum to disable its video monitoring system was an appalling breach of security that, unfortunately, was only too common. "What moron decided that?"

"Mrs. Brock thought, and the curators concurred, that the video system cost too much to maintain. It just didn't seem necessary. The cameras themselves should have been enough of a deterrence."

"So the museum has cameras but no videotape?"

"The gift shop and entry cameras are still monitored. And an eyewitness reported a man wearing a brown leather bomber jacket, a hat, and glasses coming out of the gallery about that time. But the painting was small enough not to be obvious in all the confusion."

"Surely the Brocks don't think the people who fainted were in on the theft? They're a bunch of folks taking an Adult Ed class, for heaven's sake."

"I'm just an art restorer, Ann. It's not up to me," she pointed out. "And speaking of which, if we're done with our little chat I need to get back to work."

"One more thing. Who was the Adult Ed tour guide?"

"That sort of thing is handled by Community Outreach. Art restorers are far too busy in the workrooms to attend to all that."

I gritted my teeth, thanked her, and hung up. I wouldn't trade places with Naomi for all the art in Florence, but the constant references to her flourishing career at the Brock rankled nonetheless. Naomi had a respected role in the fine-art world, as well as health insurance and a pension plan. I had squat. Every once in a while I was tempted to cave in to my grandfather's pleas to join him in creating brilliant forgeries and making fools of the establishment.

Too bad I hated prison so much.

According to Naomi, someone had disabled the Brock's security system and taken the Chagall in the confusion surrounding the Stendhal faintings. I had once been told by a highly impeachable but thoroughly knowledgeable source that many electronic sensor systems could be turned off remotely by someone with the technical know-how. But to stroll out of a museum in broad daylight with a painting tucked inside one's bomber jacket took a cool head and an abundance of self-confidence.

The very qualities possessed by a certain art thief I knew only too well. An art thief who once told me that a criminal's cardinal rule was to keep things simple. An art thief who habitually wore a brown leather bomber jacket.

Along with half the men in San Francisco, I chided myself. Besides, the missing Chagall was small potatoes. Michael X. Johnson hunted bigger game.

Not that he needed to worry about money after the Caravaggio heist last spring. Most likely Michael was lounging by the sea in Saint-Tropez, tanning himself in an indecent swimsuit. Or gambling his ill-gotten gains at the craps table in Monte Carlo. Or ensconced in a Prague penthouse, rolling around naked on satin sheets with a Czech chorus girl.

Not that I cared.

Still not a peep from Pascal's studio.

My stomach growled.

I gazed in vain at the elevator, hoping Mary and Sherri were on their way up. I banged on Pascal's door. Nothing.

Stretching my arms over my head, I tried some isometric exercises that a ridiculously fit friend had shown me. I closed my eyes, took a deep cleansing breath, found my center, started flexing, felt something pull, and quit.

One thing was clear: I would not be applying to the Police Academy anytime soon. I was not cut out for the stakeout kind of life.

Might as well delve into the Chagall theft a little more. I flipped open my cell phone and dialed Anton Woznikowicz, an aging art forger and my grandfather's protégé. Anton had a studio in the City and knew Michael X. Johnson. I would feel better if I could cross Michael off my list of suspects.

"Why, Annie! How nice to hear from you!" Anton answered. "How is your dear old grandpapa these days?"

"Last I heard, he's enjoying his book tour." My grandfather, Georges LeFleur, had recently published a book

detailing his long and illustrious career as an art forger—
and naming names. Interpol salivated and the art world was
furious, forcing the old reprobate farther underground than
usual. He was having a high old time being interviewed for
the BBC while in silhouette and using a voice-altering machine like a Mafia don, wearing elaborate disguises for impromptu book readings in Berlin, and granting interviews
to Reuters reporters, Deep Throat style, from behind the
Doric columns of the Parthenon. Part of me admired his
panache, while another part wondered if it was possible to
disown one's grandfather.

"Oh, such a time we had in Chicago!" Anton said. Last
spring, he and my grandfather had renewed their friendship
and swept first place at the "Fabulous Fakes" art show with
what turned out to be a genuine Caravaggio. Immediately
afterward Michael had absconded with the masterpiece.

"The reason I'm calling is sort of related to that. You
know that guy, Michael Johnson?"

"I don't know a Michael Johnson, Annie. Let me
think . . ."

"How about David? Or Patrick? Colin Brooks? Bruno,
maybe?" These were but a few of Michael's aliases.

"Colin Brooks! Well, of course! A fine fellow, fine fellow indeed. Oh! The meals we had, the tales we told," he
chuckled. "A randy young man, that one. Reminded me of
myself at his age. Excellent businessman, too. We shared
the proceeds from the sale of . . . Well, you know."

I knew. I did not want to officially know, though, because that might make me an accessory to fraud and grand
theft. This was a problem I encountered frequently in my
life, which was one reason I was trying to learn yoga.
"Would you happen to know where I might find Brooks?"

"You have something lined up, do you?" Anton's voice
dropped to a conspiratorial whisper. "If your uncle Anton

can be of service, you just give the word. Anything, anything at all— Oh, your grandfather will be so proud!"

"*No*, Anton, I don't have anything lined up." *Old folks
today—where are their morals?* "I need to talk with
Brooks, that's all. Just a quick little thing."

Why was I even bothering? Michael X. Johnson—the X
allegedly stood for Xerxes—was no doubt thousands of
miles away at the moment.

"—track him down. Not too hard since he lives here."

That caught my attention. "Where?"

"Here."

"Here?"

"Annie, are you all right, dear? Maybe you should have
your hearing checked. Do you need money?"

"No, I'm fine—there was just some static on my end." I
lied with ease, thanks to a genetic predisposition and a life-
time of practice. "So let me get this straight: Colin Brooks
is in San Francisco?"

"Why, yes, dear. I saw him recently at the Brock Museum."

"What do you mean *you saw him at the Brock Museum*?"

"Annie, is everything all right? You sound upset."

Wait until I got my hands on that no-good, lying, thieving, son of a—

"I was taking in the Brock's new exhibit of botanical
prints and early depictions of New World flora and fauna,"
Anton continued. "Have you seen it yet?"

"Unghh—" My mind reeled at the thought of Anton and
Michael, career criminals who had recently stolen the
jewel of the Brock's collection, casually taking in the museum's latest exhibit. For years I had been afraid to set foot
in the place and all I had done was get fired from a crappy
internship.

"It's marvelous. Simply marvelous," Anton went on. "You really must take time to see the exhibit, Annie. It's those sorts of pre-photographic, detailed depictions that remind us of a time before technology, when—"

"Anton!" Once Anton or my grandfather started philosophizing about art they were like runaway freight trains: impossible to stop without inflicting a lot of collateral damage. I feared I was becoming the same. "Tell me about Michael—Colin—whatever his name is. You say you saw him at the Brock?"

"He's grown a beard and was wearing eyeglasses. I scarcely recognized him." He paused, his tone thoughtful. "He was leading some kind of tour. Odd, that. A first-class art thief turned museum tour guide? One never knows where the money goes, does one?"

"Yeah, sure," I said glumly. "I let millions slip through my fingers every day. So, any idea how to get in touch with him?"

"Not really, darling, no. Your grandfather might know. Otherwise, I would try the usual haunts—fine restaurants, wine bars, that sort of thing. You know how the takers are."

In the lingo of the art underworld, the "takers" were the thieves while the "doers" were the forgers. The caste lines were clearly drawn, with the takers usually younger, brasher, and free with their money. The doers, with some legitimacy, thought of themselves as more artist than criminal and were often content to live fairly abstemious lives in exchange for the chance to create their art.

"I've got to run—take care of yourself, okay?" I said. "And if you speak to Georges, tell him to give me a call."

"Of course, Annie. You take care too, dear. Bye-bye!" Anton rang off cheerfully. He had been in high spirits since the successful forgery scam last spring, which had put to rest his concerns about living well in his golden years. Retirement was a worry for many of the self-employed. Even criminals.

I was beginning to nod off, my head resting uncomfortably on my knees, when the creaky iron elevator finally pinged its arrival. As I struggled up from my ungainly position on the floor the elevator door slid open to reveal not only Mary and Sherri but also our strapping Bosnian friend Pete and Sherri's husband, Tom, an ex-linebacker with a blond buzz cut and a skull and crossbones tattoo on the side of his neck.

"We're just along for the ride. You never know what could happen," Tom said as he deposited several large canvas tote bags on the scuffed linoleum. His eyes darted suspicious glances up and down the empty hallway, and his broad, freckled hands twitched at his sides. Pete stumbled out of the elevator, bumped into Tom, and nodded solemnly at me.

The air was suddenly full of free-floating testosterone. Mary and Sherri seemed to relish the display of machismo, but somewhere around my thirtieth birthday I had developed immunity. Now it just annoyed me.

"This isn't an armed invasion, guys," I protested. "He's a sculptor, for heaven's sake. Just a little old sculptor who—" I halted midsentence, distracted by the aromas wafting from the wicker picnic basket in Pete's arms. "What smells so good?"

"For you, my dear, I went all out," Tom replied, beaming.

Two years ago a motorcycle accident had landed Tom in a La-Z-Boy for six weeks with five broken ribs, a punctured lung, and nothing to do but pop pain pills and watch cable television. The combination had turned him into a devoted Martha Stewart fan. He and Sherri had recently bought a home in nearby Pleasant Hill, and Tom spent his spare time transforming the bland tract house into a shrine to gracious living. He had also become a wickedly good chef.

Tom spread a freshly laundered blue-checked tablecloth across the floor, knelt, and started unwrapping foil packets.

"Today's luncheon selection includes watercress salad with Italian mountain gorgonzola, organic walnuts, and balsamic vinaigrette—that's for you, my sweet," he said, winking at his wife. "There is also a warm casserole of boneless chicken breasts stuffed with sweet onion confit and topped with a wild mushroom glaze—I know that's your favorite, Annie," he said with a nod toward me.

Mary looked at him expectantly. "For the nuts-and-granola set, we have marinated baked tofu and curried brown rice. And for Pete, a loaf of rosemary sourdough bread, truffled mousse pâté, and three kinds of imported cheeses. Enjoy them, my friend."

"Thank you," Pete said gravely. "I am a man of the cheese."

"You had all of this food lying around the kitchen?" I asked, trying not to drool as I helped myself to generous portions of everything except the tofu. At my house, unexpected visitors were lucky to get canned tuna on stale saltines.

"He's been trying out new recipes," Sherri said, biting into a wedge of peppered brie. "We can't fit anything else in the fridge."

Tom was pouring the wine when my cell phone rang.

"Oh, *Annie*," Bryan sniffed loudly. "What am I gonna *do*?"

"Bryan, you've got to hang in there. What did the police say?"

"I'm a 'person of interest.' Can you *believe* that? They

told me not to leave town. Can you come over? Ron's at work and . . . I don't want to be alone."

"Oh, Bryan, I can't," I said. "I'm on a stakeout—"

"Ooo!" he squealed, his voice taking on its usual upbeat tone. "Can I join you, honey pie? I've never been on a stakeout!"

Having the flamboyant Bryan Boissevain on a stakeout was tantamount to inviting the proverbial bull into the china shop, but how could I say no? Besides, it seemed increasingly unlikely that Pascal would show his face, so I gave Bryan directions. I was about to sign off when Sherri grabbed the phone and asked him to bring a CD player and music, some pillows, and more wine. When I protested she tossed the phone to Mary, who pitched it to Tom, and by the time I wrestled it away from Pete, Bryan was no longer home.

"This isn't a social gathering, guys," I said sternly as Pete giggled. "This is business. *Serious* business."

"Yeah, we can tell," Sherri snorted. "You always conduct *serious* business like this?"

"Pascal probably escaped down the fire escape, anyway," I muttered. "And now I have to pee. How come that never happens to TV cops on stakeouts?"

"Because they're men, and men are superior to women," Tom announced with a belch. "We only need a jar."

"That is right," Pete added. "We are men of the jar."

"Yeah, peeing in a jar is the absolute pinnacle of human evolution," Mary interjected.

"Try the Internet company on the first floor," Sherri suggested sensibly. "I'll bet they won't mind."

When I returned ten minutes later Mary said Frank had called my cell phone, and over Pete's vociferous objections she had invited him to join us.

"You invited him *here?*" I squeaked.

"Give him a chance, Annie. I mean, when's the last time you even went on a date?" Mary said. "And hey, I've been meaning to ask: what's with all this powder? It's like a co-caine lab exploded in here. Which reminds me—Bryan's bringing more wine! We can party hearty!"

Great, I thought. This ought to impress Frank with my professionalism.

Chapter 5

Unlike writers or musicians, who keep copies of their art, the fine artist must forfeit her or his one-of-a-kind works in order to make a living. It is like giving up a child to the care of strangers.

—*Georges LeFleur, in* Parents *magazine*

Half an hour later Bryan burst out of the elevator accompanied by his friend Levine, another of the Stendhal fainters. After distributing pillows and wine, Bryan announced that he and Levine had PTS.

"But you're guys," Mary objected. "Y'all don't get PMS."

"He said P*T*S," I corrected her. "Post-Traumatic Stress Disorder."

"It's *dreadful*," Bryan said.

"*Hideous*," Levine whispered.

"Too bad you're not Norwegian," Mary asserted smugly, popping an organic cherry tomato into her mouth. "We don't get PTS or that Stand All thingee. Faint in a snowdrift and see how long your genetic line lasts."

Leaning back on a red satin pillow and pouring a glass of an Oregon Pinot Noir, Bryan launched into a colorful, comprehensive, and almost certainly exaggerated account of the faint-in at the Brock, from the first tingles at the sight of Gauguin's painting to the moment he was awakened by Brock security guard Carlos Jimenez. In answer to my questions he described their tour guide, Michael Collins, as "Fine, finer than fine, if you get my meaning," adding that Collins sported two of the greenest eyes Bryan had ever seen but was frustratingly committed to heterosexuality.

That clinched it. Michael Collins was the art thief I knew as Michael X. Johnson, aka Colin Brooks, aka the X-man. My mission was clear: find Michael, retrieve the stolen Chagall, and kill him for once again complicating my life.

By five thirty p.m. the rays of the setting sun were sifting through the grimy window at the end of the hall. The bad news was that I had given up all hope of seeing Pascal anytime soon. The good news was that it was Saturday evening and we had ourselves the beginnings of a first-rate party. Bryan cracked open a bottle of smooth Nicaraguan rum, Tom packed up the wicker picnic basket, Mary practiced palm reading on Levine, and Sherri taught Pete a Latin dance step. When the salsa music ended a skirmish broke out over control of the airwaves: Mary wanted to play a homemade CD of a friend's punk band while Pete made a heartfelt plea for Willie Nelson.

Neither alternative appealed to me in the slightest, so I suggested a sing-along to Gloria Gaynor's "I Will Survive." Bryan took lead vocals; Levine played the spoons; Mary, Sherri, and I sang backup and attempted a few coordinated dance moves; and Pete and Tom pounded out the bass line on any and all hard surfaces.

That Flor de Caña rum really packed a punch.

All things considered, it was just as well Frank seemed to have stood us up.

While the rest of us debated our next choral selection, Tom and Pete huddled in a corner, gesticulating wildly. "What's going on over there?" I demanded.

"We have A Plan," Tom said, his blue eyes shining. Pete giggled and Tom shot him a severe look.

"Uh-oh," Sherri said, perusing a box of chocolate truffles. "This has the earmarks of a Truly Bad Idea."

"Listen, you guys . . ." I began.

"Don't worry. We know what we're doing," Tom said, flexing his muscles and pounding his right fist into his left palm. "Bryan, Levine: You men keep an eye on the girls. I've got something in mind. Pete and I are going to check it out."

"Yeah," Pete echoed, mimicking Tom's flexing and pounding. "We're going to chicken out."

Tom sent Pete a withering look. "*Check* it out, Pete. *Check* it out."

"Yeah," Pete murmured. "*Check* it out."

"C'mon, dude. Time to *rock 'n' roll!*" Tom roared and thundered down the stairs, his arms and legs pumping furiously.

"Yeah, *rock 'n' roll*," Pete repeated less maniacally. At the top of the stairs he sketched a wave and proceeded down cautiously.

"Call me crazy," I said as Bryan topped off my glass of rum, "but I'm getting the distinct impression those two are a bit liquored up."

"Don't you worry none, baby doll," Bryan volunteered, a plate of hors d'oeuvres perched on one hip and a crystal goblet of wine in one hand. "Levine and I will protect you." He popped a shrimp canapé into his mouth and delicately brushed away an imaginary crumb.

Bryan was gym-toned and gorgeous, but the thought of his going toe-to-toe with anyone, even a little old sculptor, seemed ludicrous. Levine, meanwhile, was decidedly elfin and looked as if he could be blown away by a strong gust of wind. On the distaff side, Mary could likely inflict some real damage, and there was no telling what I could do given the proper motivation. After all, I had once knocked out a bad guy with a bronze garden elf. And Sherri, though petite, had a cooler head and more common sense than all the rest of us put together. If a brawl were to break out in the hallway, it seemed to me the women were likely to carry the day.

For several moments the hallway was quiet as we watched the sky outside the window change from a gaudy pink to a bright orange to a flaming red. Then Bryan started humming the overture from *My Fair Lady,* and before long we were performing "Wouldn't It Be Loverly," starring Bryan as Eliza Doolittle and featuring the rest of us as assorted street people, skipping up and down and singing off-key in atrocious cockney accents. We collapsed on the floor, laughing, and had just swung into a rollicking rendition of "I Could Have Danced All Night" when Pascal's studio door smashed open and a short, balding, unshaven man in a dirty white sleeveless undershirt and baggy cargo pants stepped into the hallway. So pale that his skin had a bluish cast, Robert Pascal was covered in stone dust and quivering with rage.

"*What* in the name of *God* in *heaven* is going *on* out here!" he screamed. "Will you people *please* shut the fuck *up*!"

"Mr. Pascal, I—" Scrambling over the detritus from our picnic, I knocked over a glass of wine and stumbled on a satin pillow. Bryan leaped up to steady me but stepped on a plate, sending shrimp canapés skittering across the linoleum, stomped heavily on Levine's sandal-clad toes, slipped on a rind of brie, and landed on the floor with a splat. Levine began hopping around screeching, holding his injured foot in the air, and when Sherri and Mary leaned over to help him they knocked their heads together with an audible thunk that made even Pascal wince.

"Oh my *gawd*! Are you all right?" Bryan cried and, rubbing his bruised flank, dragged himself over to the wine bucket and started distributing ice to the wounded.

Mesmerized by our antics, Pascal failed to notice as I sidled up and placed my foot on the threshold to prevent his slamming the door shut.

"Mr. Pascal," I said, ignoring the moans and groans behind me. "I'm Annie Kincaid, Harold Kincaid's daughter. We met years ago, do you remember?"

The sculptor's gaze was unfocused. Was he sick? Drunk? Appalled?

"Mr. Pascal?" I repeated more loudly. Seeing him now with the eyes of an adult I realized he was not nearly as old as I had imagined, probably only in his early sixties.

"Annie Kincaid?" he said vaguely. "Well, well. How long has it been?"

"I think I was about ten when we met." I smiled ingratiatingly, as if to say what's a mere twenty years between passing acquaintances?

"That's right," he replied, watching Bryan apply ice to Levine's foot while Mary and Sherri rubbed their heads. "What in holy hell are you doing in my hallway?"

"Um . . ." I glanced at my tipsy and injured friends, the spilled wine, the scattered food, the general air of debauchery, and ignored the question. "Why don't we talk in your studio?"

Pascal pulled a dirty rag from a rear pocket, wiped his hands, and nodded. I followed the sculptor inside and shut the door firmly behind us.

One corner of Pascal's sculpture studio was devoted to

a paper-strewn desk next to a clutch of boxy brown arm-
chairs surrounding a low coffee table. A partially opened
door to the right revealed a tiny room containing an un-
made army cot and a stack of cardboard boxes. The rest of
the space was given over to a huge workroom. Along one
wall were five magnificent windows that stretched from
floor to ceiling and cast light and air across the otherwise
uninspired venue. Mounted on a track like a sliding barn
door, the windows could be rolled open and, with the help
of the stout winch that projected from the building, Pascal's heavy sculptures could be hoisted in and out of the
third-floor studio.

Two worktables were piled with empty Cup o' Noodles
containers, maquettes of various shapes and sizes, and an
array of sharp tools that would have been at home in a medieval torture chamber. Several large objects—presumably
sculptures in progress—were hidden beneath canvas drop
cloths. Marble dust covered every surface like so much
powdered sugar sprinkled by a mad baker.

Pascal gestured to an armchair facing the windows and
took a seat opposite me. Clouds of dust poufed up from the
cushions as we sat down.

"Coffee?" he asked politely.

"No, thank you," I replied, relieved at his courteous
manner. Maybe this would be easier than I'd thought.
"You're probably wondering what I'm doing here."

"You've come to screw with my mind."

Maybe it wouldn't.

"Seriously, Mr. Pascal," I continued. "I'm an artist, too.
In fact, I have a studio not far from here. Isn't that a coincidence?"

Pascal's weary, red-rimmed eyes revealed nothing.

"So anyway, I was at Anthony Brazil's gallery the other
day and I met Janice Hewett—"

"No," he interrupted.

"Excuse me?"

"No. They can't have it back," he said dispassionately. "Not now."

"Not now?" I echoed. "Does that mean you'll give it back later?" I heard a muffled banging sound, but since it did not seem to emanate from the hallway I ignored it.

"I don't know." He shrugged. "Not at the moment, anyway."

"Why not?"

"Because I don't fucking want to."

"But you must know it's driving the Hewetts crazy."

"I don't care. It's my goddamned sculpture."

"Mr. Pascal, don't get me wrong—I'm a strong supporter of the integrity of an artist's vision. But *Head and Torso* belongs to the Hewetts. You sold it to them in 1968, and surely the check's cleared by now—"

"They're morons. They don't appreciate it."

My brief interaction with Janice Hewett inclined me to share Pascal's assessment, but that was not the point. If intelligence were a prerequisite for owning art, most of the world's finest palaces would have nothing on their walls except spiderwebs.

"They paid only twenty-five hundred dollars for it," Pascal continued. "It's worth nearly half a million now."

"I think I understand," I replied, choosing my words with care. "I know how hard it is to part with something that comes straight from your soul. But in the society we live in . . . well, the people who buy the stuff get to keep the stuff. Are you aware that the Hewetts are threatening a lawsuit if you don't return the sculpture?"

There was a scuffling sound high overhead, followed by a muted pounding, but Pascal either did not hear the noise

or chose to ignore it. He appeared to have admirable pow-
ers of concentration.

Pascal sighed heavily and shifted in his chair, his sad,
red-rimmed eyes watching me.

I changed tactics. "Did you hear about Seamus Mc-
Graw?"

"What about him?"

"He was found . . . uh . . . dead last night."

I thought Pascal paled a bit, but since he was already
deathly white I could not be sure.

"McGraw's an idiot," he said. "An untalented hack."

"Do you suppose his death had anything to do with
Head and Torso?"

"Don't be stupid," he snapped. "What could his death
have to do with me?"

"I don't know. The timing just seemed odd, that's all."

"Take some advice from an old friend of your father's,"
he said with an avuncular air. "Mind your own goddamned
business."

"But—"

"Do you have any idea, Annie, what it's like to be a
sculptor in a culture that doesn't appreciate art?"

"Actually, I'm an artist myself so—"

"I'll tell you what it's like," he said, and gazing at a
point on the wall beyond my left shoulder he launched into
a rambling discourse on the creative and monetary trials of
an artist's life.

As if this was news to me.

I was listening with half an ear, waiting for him to finish,
when I saw a thin vertical line in the center of one of the
windows. The line moved. What the hell was that? A rope?

"—cannot imagine the challenges—" Pascal droned on.

A pair of black motorcycle boots appeared at the top of
the window frame.

"—all over again, were I to have another chance at—"

Faded denim jeans lowered into view, followed by a black leather jacket, and the figure clutching the rope slowly started to spin.

Hoping to keep Pascal from turning around and witnessing the further antics of the stakeout flake outs, I nodded at him encouragingly.

"—career was a success, or so I thought, but in the art world there is no such—"

Tom's big blond head finally appeared as well as his broad hands, white-knuckled from their death grip on the rope. The spinning increased and was augmented by a pendulum motion. I watched, morbidly fascinated, as Tom began to swing from one side of the window to the other.

"—Sheila left me, which was probably as much a blessing as—"

Back and forth and round and round went my friend on the rope outside the window. The brief glimpses I caught of Tom's face revealed a mixture of nausea and terror.

"—financial success is, of course, important in the—"

Tom started yanking on the rope in what I hoped was a signal to Pete on the roof.

"It's my hands, you see," Pascal said. "They're useless."

He held up Exhibit A. I noticed a few liver spots and one really nasty blister, but they were not gnarled with arthritis as my great-grandmother's had been. According to the sculptor, though, his hands were too damaged to do the work that had been the great passion of his life.

I felt a surge of sympathy. When all you had was your work and your Cup o' Noodles, what did you do if you were forced to give up sculpting?

Pascal proceeded to tell me, droning on and on in excruciating detail.

"—clinic in Guadalajara—"

My gaze flew to the window as swirling bay breezes pushed Tom away from the building until Newton's Third Law of Thermodynamics pulled him back in. Blue eyes widened in a greenish face as Tom headed toward the glass before veering off a split second before impact.

My face must have registered my shock because Pascal turned to look at the window a split second after Tom swung out of sight.

"Beautiful view," I improvised. "Really amazing."

Pascal faced me again, frowning, and Tom drifted back into view. My eyes were weary from darting between the window and the sculptor. Pascal must be convinced that I either had some kind of eye trouble or severe attention deficit disorder.

I tried to refocus. "So have you thought about bringing in an assistant? You could do the design and detail work, and let the assistant do the heavier stuff."

"I had an assistant once," Pascal grumbled. "Years ago. Damned fool fell in love with me, so I fired him, and he went and killed himself. Pain in the ass, if you ask me. I'll never have another sculptor in here."

Tom's heavy boots were braced against the window frame as he attempted to scale the building. After a brief struggle he flipped over and hung upside down for several excruciating seconds before gradually righting himself. Suddenly the bay breezes caught Tom again and flung him toward the window.

"I'd love to see *Head and Torso*!" I exclaimed, jumping up. "Is it here?"

"Of course it's here," Pascal growled as he led me toward the rear of the studio. "Where else would it be?"

Tom hit the window with a thud, but thankfully the glass withstood the impact. Sneaking a peek over my shoulder, I saw one side of Tom's face pressed against the window, his breath fogging the glass. The rope started to jerk, and Tom inched skyward.

Pascal tugged on a fabric drop cloth to reveal a marble sculpture nearly seven feet tall and three feet wide. This was no head and torso as one saw them in nature, but a grouping of spheres meeting hard angles, softly polished surfaces meeting rough finishes, and naturalism meeting geometry. When it came to sculpture I was more a sixteenth-century, Donatello kind of gal, but there was no denying the power of this piece, which combined an unmistakably human form and a mechanical shell in a manner both alienating yet intriguing.

"I understand why you don't want to give it up," I said again, meaning it this time. I was a damned fine artist but had never created anything so compelling. And if I ever did, I could not imagine selling it to someone like Janice Hewett.

A movement at the window caught my eye again. This time it was Pete swinging past, staring into the studio and mouthing something at me, and I feared disaster could not be far behind. Time to rein in my macho minions.

"I appreciate your speaking with me, Mr. Pascal," I said. "And I do apologize for the noise; I didn't think you were here."

"So you decided to have a party?"

"Um, that's kind of hard to explain. . . ." I trailed off. My eyes fell on several steel chisels and soft iron hammers sitting by a marble block. They reminded me of McGraw. "Mr. Pascal, can you think of any reason someone would kill Seamus McGraw? Sculpture doesn't seem like a profession where one makes enemies."

Pascal looked incredulous. "What kind of art world do *you* live in, toots?"

"I meant *lethal* enemies. Most artistic types are content

with stabbing each other in the back figuratively, not literally."

"I wouldn't know. I have nothing to do with Seamus McGraw."

"But you knew him, didn't you?"

He grunted.

"You studied together," I pointed out. "And you were both represented by the Brazil gallery."

Another grunt.

"Did you two use the same stone supplier, Marble World?"

"Seamus worked in metal, not stone. They're very different media, technically and aesthetically, as you would know if you'd ever worked in three dimensions," he said, escorting me to the door. "Look, I appreciate your efforts on my behalf. But tell the Hewetts I said to go fuck themselves."

"Why don't I just tell them you'll think about it?" I hedged. "They're ready to start legal proceedings. Imagine a bunch of strangers in here with a warrant, pawing through your stuff, confiscating *Head and Torso* and who knows what else." Did I know how to hit an artist below the belt, or what?

Pascal's pale visage reddened under his heavy five-o'clock shadow. "And tell your goddamned friends to stay out of my hallway and away from my windows," he said angrily. "You guys can't sing for crap, either. Oh, and have a nice day."

The door slammed shut behind me.

Out in the hallway, I found Bryan and Levine sprawled on the red satin pillows sipping wine, Mary and Sherri slouched against the wall eating the last of the chocolates, and Pete and Tom in the stairwell breathing hard, ropes slung over their shoulders.

"Proud of yourselves?" I asked the two adventurers. "Just what did you hope to accomplish with that stunt? Did you even *notice* that I was trying to talk with our elusive sculptor?"

Tom refused to meet my eyes and Pete looked abashed. *What a couple of goofballs*, I thought fondly. "Let's pack it up and head home, guys. I'd say our first stakeout has been a qualified success."

Chapter 6

True egg tempera reads like a recipe for salad dressing, and indeed should be cooked up in your kitchen. Separate the egg yolks from the whites, and add eight to twelve drops of lavender oil for each yolk. Pour small quantities of the egg mixture into a glass bowl, whisking it, drop by drop, with sun-bleached linseed oil.

—*Georges LeFleur, in* What's Cookin', California?

After tidying up the hallway outside Pascal's studio, the party broke up. Mary had a gig at a new club downtown, and Sherri and Tom tagged along for moral support. Pete took off for his mother's house in Hayward in anticipation of tomorrow's big Sunday dinner, and Bryan and Levine opted to head to the Mission District for some tequila-lime fish tacos.

I was more tired than hungry, so I decided to head home. Hopping into my truck, I drove across the Bay Bridge to Oakland, exited at Grand Avenue, and veered right toward Lake Merritt. The meandering lake was highlighted by a necklace of romantic white lights, and even at this hour its two-mile path was crowded with energetic joggers, strolling lovers, and cranky Canada geese. It was one of those warm, clear, late-November evenings that explained why rents were so high in the San Francisco Bay Area.

Home sweet home was a once-grand Victorian built for a prosperous grocery merchant in 1869 and chopped up into apartments for working stiffs one hundred years later. I lived on the third floor in what used to be the maid's quarters, tucked up high under the eaves. What the building lacked in modern conveniences, such as decent electrical wiring, it made up for in graceful details, such as the intricate fantail window in the foyer and the elaborately carved newel posts on the stairs. The old Victorian's faded elegance was warm and welcoming, like the embrace of a beloved elderly aunt, and at the end of a long day I always looked forward to coming home.

I parked in the lot behind the house, let myself in through the solid mahogany front door, grabbed my mail from the hall table, and trudged up two flights to my apartment, my footsteps echoing in the silence. The building's other tenants were also single professional women who spent most of their waking hours on the job or out with friends, so I was not surprised to have the house to myself. But when I rounded the turn on the second-floor landing I came to a sudden halt. A light shone from under my door and the dead bolt lock had been thrown.

Someone was in my apartment.

I hesitated to call the cops. Among my varied acquaintances were one or two who were capable of breaking in and making themselves at home, and certainly none of my grandfather's felonious cronies would allow a mere dead bolt to stand in their way. I would never hear the end of it if I had one of Georges's friends thrown in the slammer. Surely a stranger bent on evil deeds would not be so blatant as to leave the door unlocked and the lights blazing.

I hoped.

Moving stealthily, I mounted the last few steps. On the landing next to the door was a brass spittoon where I stashed umbrellas and similar outdoor junk, including a sturdy oak stick I used while hiking last summer with Mary in Wildcat Canyon. I picked it up, slowly turned the doorknob, pushed the door open, and flattened myself against the wall. Nothing happened.

Okay, I thought, this is ridiculous. I was tired, crabby, and wanted a nice, long bath to wash away the residue of the gritty hallway, the dusty studio, and the miasma of Pascal's grim hopelessness. I was going in.

Holding the walking stick high in my right hand, I peered into the living room. The futon couch had been made up with my old blue-and-white striped flannel sheets and a yellow plaid wool blanket. My burglar was remarkably domestic.

"Honey!"

"Mom?" My voice was muffled by a Chanel-scented embrace. "What are you doing here?"

A stylish blond woman in her late fifties, Beverly LeFleur Kincaid held me at arm's length and looked me over from tip to toe. "What's the wizard's staff for, dear? And why are you covered with dust?"

"I, er . . ." I dropped the heavy stick in the brass spittoon and shut the door.

"You're looking awfully thin these days, honey. Are you sure you're eating enough?"

I loved my mother.

"Mom, what are you doing here?" I asked. "Why didn't you call?"

She shrugged and started straightening the mélange of books and magazines on the coffee table. "Oh, I just needed to get away for a couple of days, and you gave me a spare key to your apartment, remember? I hope you don't mind."

"No, of course I don't mind. But are you and Dad okay?"

She moved on to the messy bookshelf, efficiently alphabetizing my collection of cheap paperback mystery novels. "Why do you ask?"

I was the only one of my peers whose parents were still married, and with a shock I realized how much I counted on their normality to balance out my eccentric life.

"Just wondering," I said evasively. "You've never needed to get away before."

"Well, here I am. So what shall we do?" My mother's sweet, slightly husky voice betrayed her excitement. "Oh no! How thoughtless of me! Do you have a date tonight?"

I could not bring myself to admit to my mother that her wild artist daughter had planned to take a long soak and go to bed early, just as she had for the past few weekends. I glanced at the rhinestone-encrusted Krazy Kat clock on the kitchen wall: It was a quarter of eight on a Saturday night and I was ready to pack it in.

I was more middle-aged than my mother.

"Are you all right, dear?" she asked with concern. "We could stay in if you're tired."

"No, no, I'll be fine. I just need a quick shower to freshen up. What did you have in mind for tonight?"

"Something exciting. I know! Let's go to Berkeley!"

Only someone from a small Central Valley college town like Asco would stand within a stone's throw of San Francisco and opt to go to Berkeley in search of A Good Time. Then again, my mother had been a student at the University of California in the late sixties, so her experience with the town was no doubt more avant-garde than mine.

"Berkeley it is," I said, enjoying her enthusiasm. "Give me ten minutes."

"Take all the time you need, honey," she said gaily. "The night is young and you'll want to look your best for the Berkeley beaux!"

Berkeley beaux my patootie, I grumbled to myself as I scuffed down the short hall to the bathroom. Which was less likely to turn out well, I wondered, trolling for hot guys with my mother in tow, or finding an outfit she would think suitable for a big night on the town?

I took a brisk shower, toweled off, shook out my damp curls, and applied a fast coat of mascara to my eyelashes. Toilette accomplished, now came the hard part. My favorite clothes were comfy and artistic, which virtually guaranteed my chic mother would march me back down the hall to "change into something more appropriate." Thanks to last night's escapade my little black dress needed dry-cleaning. I sighed and wished, for Mom's sake, that I were more of a girly girl. Rooting through my messy closet I finally unearthed the black wool skirt I wore with a bland suit jacket for stodgy business meetings, some thigh-high black nylons, and a fuchsia camisole that I paired with a low-cut black cashmere sweater. I selected some dangling crystal earrings, slipped my feet into low-heeled black sandals, and looked in the mirror: monochromatic enough for Berkeley, fashionable enough for my mother, comfortable enough for me.

Mom was ready to go, wearing a beautiful red wool jacket, a red-and-white horizontal striped knit top, and snowy white linen pants. As I steered my mother's silver Honda sedan north towards Berkeley, I pondered how long I would be able to keep a pair of white pants clean. I gave it five minutes, tops.

A cruise up and down Telegraph Avenue turned up

hordes of homeless people, a handful of grungy carryout pizza places, and several crowded venues blasting hip-hop. None of these fit the bill, so I drove my disappointed and slightly disoriented mother to a bustling pub on Shattuck Avenue.

"Everything's changed so much," she murmured for the tenth time as we claimed a prime table near the French doors that opened onto a patio where a band played New Orleans–style jazz. "I guess I've been away longer than I thought. I wouldn't have recognized the town."

"It's been thirty years since you spent any real time here, Mom," I pointed out after we'd placed our drink orders. "I can't remember the last time the students at the university boycotted classes to protest anything."

"Is that so?" she said politely, though she seemed distracted. She took a surprisingly unladylike gulp of her Santa Barbara chardonnay and blurted out, "Tell me about Seamus and Robert."

I choked on my club soda with lime. "Seamus McGraw and Robert Pascal? How do you know . . . ? I mean, what do you . . . ?"

My mother looked over my head and smiled brightly as strong hands gripped my shoulders.

"Don't tell me this is your mother?" A deep voice, redolent of tobacco and whiskey, whispered in my ear. "I've missed you, sweetheart."

My stomach flip-flopped and my heart sped up, which pissed me off. I brushed the hands from my shoulders and twisted around. "Don't you 'sweetheart' me, you lying, stealing, double-dealing, abandoning, no good piece of—"

He laughed, my mother gasped, and a couple of frat boys at the bar turned to watch. I bit my tongue and scowled. The new beard emphasized Michael X. Johnson's piratical character, but there was no mistaking those piercing green eyes or that dazzling smile. The ensemble was topped with lush, wavy, dark brown hair, and the attached body was tall, broad shouldered, and slim hipped. In Bryan's immortal words, the man was finer than fine.

"I'm afraid Annie is angry with me, and rightly so," Michael explained to my mother, his eyes twinkling. I wanted to slap him. "I stood her up, but believe me it was not by choice. I had an unavoidable professional obligation."

True enough, I thought, if by "unavoidable professional obligation" one meant "absconding with a priceless Caravaggio."

"Won't you introduce me to your charming companion?" he asked, eyeing my mother.

I cleared my throat and reminded myself that for Bryan's sake I needed to be civil. There was plenty of time to kill Michael after he had given me the stolen Chagall. "Mom, this is . . . ?"

"Michael Collins," he supplied smoothly. "Delighted to make your acquaintance."

"Beverly Kincaid," Mom said, holding out her hand and nodding pleasantly.

Michael cupped her hand in his. "The resemblance was not immediately apparent, but I see it now. It's the eyes. And the smile. Your daughter has the most astonishing smile, Mrs. Kincaid."

And with that he drew up a chair, signaled the waitress for a Guinness stout, and joined our little party.

"I understand you're a talented watercolorist." Elbows on the table, Michael leaned toward my mother and cranked the charm up to high. Mom nearly slid to the floor.

I watched, nonplussed. Was Michael, the international art thief and occasional object of my unrequited lust, putting the moves on my mother? And was my mother, the thoroughly domesticated and loyal wife of my father, responding?

"Could I talk to you for a minute?" I asked Michael in a strained voice. "Outside?"

"You two stay right here and have a good chat," my mother said, standing up. "I'll just go find the little girls' room."

We watched as she made her way gracefully across the teeming room.

"Your mother's charming," Michael said.

"My mother's married," I snapped.

"Pity."

"I can't believe you're putting the moves on my mother!"

"I'm not 'putting the moves on your mother,' Annie," he said, looking at me with lust in his eyes. "There's only one Kincaid woman who interests me 'that' way."

"What way?"

"You know. *That* way."

"You mean in a love-'em-and-leave-'em-high-and-dry-in-Chicago-not-to-mention-everywhere-else kind of way? *That* way?"

Michael laughed and dropped the lover boy routine. "I simply think she's lovely. You're quite fortunate, you know. You'll look just like her in a few years. Except, of course, for the hair." He pulled one of my brown curls playfully, took a sip of my club soda, and made a face. "Why don't I buy you a real drink? It might improve your mood."

I snatched my soda away. "Listen, you felonious phony—"

"Oho! I like that. 'Felonious phony.' Too bad I'm not Phoenician."

"Michael, I swear to God . . ."

"Calm down, sweetheart. Anton said you were looking for me. I can't *tell* you how happy I was to hear it," he said quietly, green eyes searching mine.

"Is that right?" I cooed, and tossed my curls coquettishly, or as near to it as I could manage, which probably was not very close. "Any idea *why* I'm looking for you, big guy?"

"You've shaken that boring boyfriend of yours and you're after my body."

"What boring boyfriend?"

"The stuffed shirt you were hanging on to at the Brock gala last spring."

"Frank's not a stuffed shirt." That was sort of a lie. "And I wasn't hanging on to him." That was sort of the truth. "And I'm not after your body." That was pretty much a lie, too. I was not currently after his body because I was not entirely lacking in common sense. But there was no denying that Michael X. Johnson was a smoldering, broad shouldered, drive-your-grandmother-crazy kind of man who could inspire lust in an octogenarian nun. "How did you find us here, anyway?"

"I followed you from your apartment. And I wasn't the only one."

"What do you mean?"

"Another car was following you, a large black SUV. You didn't notice?"

"Who would be following *me*?"

"Maybe it was following your mother."

"Who would be following her? And anyway, how do you know? Maybe it was a coincidence."

"Because the three of us drove up and down Telegraph Avenue twice before coming here, that's how I know," Michael said grimly. "It was a damned parade."

Another shiver ran down my spine, and this time it was

not because of Michael. I could think of no reason anyone would be following me. On the other hand, we were driving my mother's car and she'd been acting strangely, starting with showing up at my apartment unannounced.

And she was taking a rather long time in the restroom.

Not for the first time Michael and I seemed to exchange thoughts telepathically. We rose as one and pushed through the crowd to the women's restroom at the rear of the bar. Michael got there first and burst in without knocking. I heard a shriek and a fresh-faced college girl rushed out.

"Beverly?" He searched the stalls and shook his head.

I scanned the restaurant for a red jacket but saw nothing except a crowd of boisterous students. I elbowed my way through a horde of athletic young men to the front door, which opened onto an alley off Shattuck. The passageway was packed with cigarette smokers.

"Did anyone see a blond woman in a red jacket pass by?" I asked, but the smokers shrugged and kept on puffing, so I hurried out to the street, where a disheveled man with strawberry-blond dreadlocks hit me up for spare change.

"Did you see a blond woman in a red jacket a few minutes ago?" I asked, groping in my shoulder bag for some coins.

He pointed to a black Toyota Highlander parked at the curb halfway down the block. Michael handed the man a five-dollar bill, trotted over to the SUV, and knocked on the tinted window.

Dreadlocks staggered up to us, his hands shoved deep in the pockets of a stained tweed overcoat. "Got yer back, homeboy," he said, slurring his words only a little. "That blond lady gave me a smile, man."

The SUV's window hummed as it slid down a few inches.

"Jess?" said a gravelly, accented voice.

"Jess who?" I demanded.

"He means 'yes,'" Dreadlocks interpreted. "That's how they say it, man."

"Where's Mrs. Kincaid?" Michael demanded, his voice quiet but fierce. "Blonde, red jacket, white pants."

"Patience," the voice hissed. "She be back."

The window slid back up.

"Open the door!" Michael demanded. "Open the car door right now!"

"Be cool, man," Dreadlocks said. "Blondie went into the deli."

Just then my mother strolled out of the convenience store clutching an envelope, a carton of orange juice, and two packs of Marlboro Lights.

"Mother, what are you *doing*?" I demanded. "You don't smoke."

"Here you are, dear," she said, handing the orange juice to Dreadlocks. "Don't be silly, Annie. The cigarettes are for . . . Well, why don't you and Michael just run along to the pub? I'll join you in a minute."

"Mrs. Kincaid, I'd feel better if we all stayed together," Michael said.

"We're not going to 'run along' anywhere, Mom," I said hotly, my fear having given way to anger. What the hell did my mother think she was doing? "You're coming with us."

"Oh, all right," she said with a little laugh. Those nervous titters of hers were starting to get on my nerves. "I just need to speak with Jose for a moment."

Quick as lightning, she opened the SUV's rear passenger door, climbed in, and slammed the door shut. Michael lunged for the handle, but it was already locked.

"That does it!" I started yelling and pounding on the

SUV. "Beverly Kincaid! Get out of there this instant! Do you hear me, Mother?"

"Easy, tiger," Michael said, placing a hand on my waist.

"Out! Out!" I shouted, kicking the SUV's fender.

The door opened and my mother emerged. "Really, dear. You're making a scene. Shall we?" She straightened her spotless white pants, shot the sleeves of her red jacket, and strode briskly down the alley towards the pub. I glared at the black SUV and trailed along behind her.

At the bar my genteel mother ordered a double shot of Stoli, straight up, and knocked it back in a single go. Michael raised an eyebrow, impressed.

"Mom, what in the world is going on?" I demanded. "You're acting very strangely."

"I'm sorry if I worried you, dear. Those fellows agreed to help me with something, that's all. Gosh it's been a long day, hasn't it? Shall we call it a night?"

"But . . ." I said, as my mother threw a ten on the bar and marched out. I looked at Michael, who shrugged and escorted us to the car.

Mom held out her hand. "So nice to meet you, Michael. I do hope to see you again soon. Perhaps you would be free to join us for Thanksgiving?"

"That sounds lovely," he murmured. "Let me check my calendar."

I couldn't take any more. "Mom—get into the car, please. Michael—go away, please." I fired up the engine, pulled away from the curb, and drove quickly through downtown Berkeley. "Mom—"

"That Michael is certainly charming, and so *handsome*!" she interrupted with a girlish giggle. "I do think you ought to consider forgiving him, just this once, for standing you up."

"It's not that simple, Mom."

"Sometimes love really *is* that simple, dear. He seems to care about you. You could do worse."

"I rather doubt it," I muttered. "Mom, *please*. My relationship with Michael isn't going anywhere, do you understand? It will never go anywhere. I'm not in love with him and I guarantee you he isn't in love with me."

"How can you be so sure?"

"Trust me."

"Now, Annie, I know you're still grieving the end of your engagement to Javier," she said gently, and I didn't know whether to laugh to cry. Javier was my old college boyfriend, and although he was a great guy—smart, hardworking, funny—we wanted different things out of life. After we broke up, Javier graduated with a veterinary degree from UC Davis and went on to make a fortune in the pharmaceuticals industry. Who knew there was so much money in giving Fluffy's hair its shiniest shine?

"It's time to move on with your life," Mom continued. "After all, you're not getting any younger. What line of work did you say Michael was in?"

"I didn't," I said, a bit stung by the suggestion that, at thirty-two, I was approaching my expiration date. Hadn't my mother heard that forty was the new thirty? "He's a friend of Grandfather's, if you catch my drift."

"Oh?"

"Mmm."

"Well, that's a shame."

"Tell me about it."

She was quiet for a few minutes, and I started to relax as we passed by Berkeley Bowl.

"Still," she started up again, "I suppose there's always a chance of reforming him. You know what they say: Behind every successful man is a good woman."

Who, me?

"Mom, don't take this the wrong way, but you have *got* to be kidding. I can scarcely keep myself on the straight and narrow, much less someone else."

"Now, Annie—"

"Mom, *please*. Give it a rest. There's no future for Michael and me. Trust me."

"All right. All right. You don't have to tell *me* twice. I just want you to be happy, my darling girl."

"I know, and I appreciate it. I really do." I looked at her, and she gave me a tender smile. My mother's smile was the first thing I'd seen in this life, and, like a duckling, I'd imprinted it. "Why are we even talking about Michael, anyway? Who were those men in the SUV, Mom? And why are you really here?"

"I don't know what you're talking about."

I harangued her for the twenty-minute ride back to my place, but she ignored me in favor of a running commentary on how much the Bay Area had changed over the years.

"By the way," she said as we climbed the stairs to my apartment, "I'm going to Seamus McGraw's funeral tomorrow, and I need you to promise me something."

"After the disappearing act you pulled tonight?" I asked, shepherding her inside and locking the door. "Not bloody likely."

"Anna Jane Kincaid!"

"Don't even *try* to 'Anna Jane Kincaid' me, Beverly LeFleur Kincaid, or I'll call Dad and drop a dime on you," I retorted, stomping into the kitchen to put the kettle on the stove.

"You'll do nothing of the sort, young lady. I am still your mother."

"Yes, but—"

"But nothing. Anna, I want you to leave Robert Pascal alone."

"I'm not—"

"Don't argue with me. Robert Pascal is a despicable human being, and there's no telling what he's capable of. Promise me you'll leave him alone."

"I can't do that, Mom," I said, thinking of Janice Hewett's ample bank balance, a portion of which could be mine.

"You most certainly can. And you will."

"But why? I don't understand. You and Seamus and Robert all knew each other at Berkeley, right? And Dad, too?"

She nodded.

"So what's going on? Do you know something about McGraw's death? Is that why you're going to the funeral of a man you haven't seen in thirty years? And speaking of which: Why isn't Dad going with you?"

"I'm not going to answer your questions, Anna. Just do as I ask."

"Tell me why you want me to leave Pascal alone, and I'll think about it."

"Time for bed, sweetheart. Just once in your life, do as I say, will you? And if you call your father I will never speak to you again."

I ranted for another fifteen minutes before admitting defeat. As I sat sulking at the kitchen table and sipping chamomile tea, I heard my mother moving around the living room, singing softly. She had a beautiful voice, and used to sing my sister and me to sleep when we were little. I had known Beverly LeFleur Kincaid for thirty-two years, and her behavior tonight was entirely out of character. How did she know the men in the black SUV? Why was she going to Seamus McGraw's funeral? Why was she warning me away from Robert Pascal?

I knew one thing: I was going to disobey my mommy and talk to Pascal again. He might be a despicable human being, but I was betting I could break him more easily than I could break my dear sweet mother. I wanted—*needed*—some answers.

As I put my teacup in the sink and headed to bed I spied the Evil Elf, an ugly bronze garden ornament I'd accidentally stolen last spring when Michael and I were set upon by a bad guy who resembled the Incredible Hulk. I had used it to save Michael's hide, not that he had appreciated it.

And speaking of whom . . . I had been so distracted by my mother's antics this evening that I'd forgotten to grill Michael about the stolen Chagall. Tomorrow I would ask Anton to relay another message to him.

But for now I needed to sleep. Early Sunday morning was the only time I could be sure to have the studio to myself in order to work on Frank's Picasso. I hated to leave my mother without a chaperone, but one could hardly ride herd on one's mother.

Not tomorrow, anyway.

In the half-light of dawn I slipped on a long-sleeved, black cotton T-shirt, wool socks, Birkenstocks, and my denim painting overalls. I caught a glimpse of myself in the bedroom mirror and sighed. Most days I tried to convince myself that I dressed like *an artist*, though in reality I dressed more like *a drudge*. Since I was usually cloistered in the studio covered in paint or faux-finishing goop, it hardly mattered. And anyway, it wasn't as if small children screamed when they saw me.

My mother, however, nearly did.

Beverly Kincaid looked beautiful in the early-morning light, her artfully tinted blond hair forming a soft halo that highlighted her delicate features and expressive blue eyes. She sat in a beam of sunshine, like a movie star in one of those soft-focused films from the forties, wrapped in a light blue silk kimono, sipping coffee. I made her promise to call me as soon as the funeral was over, and we agreed to meet for dinner at Le Cheval in downtown Oakland so we could have *A Talk*. Mom kissed me and told me not to worry so much.

I pulled up in front of the DeBenton Building just as Frank emerged from his office accompanied by a blond, Aryan-looking fellow and a graying man with a pronounced overbite. Both wore dark blue suits and aviator sunglasses, the reflecting kind favored by the California Highway Patrol for their intimidation value. They hurried past me and climbed into a beautiful maroon Jaguar without so much as a nod to me, which I attributed to the early hour. Or to my scruffy overalls. Frank, by contrast, was dressed in gray wool slacks, a starched white shirt with tiny black pinstripes, a burgundy tie, and glossy black Oxfords. His handsome face was freshly shaved and his dark brown hair was perfectly arranged. Seven fifteen on a Sunday morning and Frank looked as if he were ready for a summit meeting of the oil cartel.

"Heya, Frank," I said cheerily, trying to remember if I'd combed my hair yet. "Did the Secret Service call?"

"What do you mean?"

"I thought maybe you and the Giggle Twins were working on something dealing with national security."

"Nope, just an early business meeting. I'm glad you're here, though. I was hoping you'd found out something more about that project you're working on for me."

"Yes, well, there's a little problem with that."

"Oh?"

"I'm afraid the ultraviolet analysis showed some disturbing results." I wondered if, like Pinocchio, my nose would grow from all the lies I was telling, but feared that if Frank knew how simple the Picasso repair was he might renege on our deal. "I was hoping to find a cadmium base, because with cadmium there is a fairly standard mode of correction involving a series of metabolic solvents."

"I take it you didn't find cadmium."

"Afraid not. I found scarlet lake," I said, improvising.

"I thought that was a ballet."

"That's *Swan Lake*."

"Right. So what do we do about the scarlet lake?"

"It's a little complicated."

"Is that so?" he asked, sounding skeptical.

"Nothing I can't handle, though," I added as I headed for the stairs. "You can count on me. That's why I'm here so early. I wanted to work on it without being interrupted."

"Right. By the way, I hired a security guard," Frank said. "He's making his rounds, so you may meet him soon. I'll be around as well, in case there's any problem."

I peered over the railing. "What kind of problem?"

Frank let out an exasperated breath. "I don't know, Annie. But this is a very important project and you tend to attract trouble. Or haven't you noticed?"

"Is that why you didn't show up yesterday?" I asked, wondering why Frank was acting so oddly. Maybe Michael was right: maybe Frank *was* boring. "Or do you just hate parties?"

"I don't hate parties."

"You didn't come to the party."

"If you must know, I didn't feel up to dealing with your boyfriend."

"What boyfriend?"

This was the second time in twelve hours that I'd been accused of having a boyfriend. Did I have blackout periods when I dated up a storm but could not remember anything in the morning? Would I end up on television one day, begging a sleazy talk show host to run a DNA test to determine which of ten men was my baby's daddy?

"That guy you hang out with," he replied. "Peter."

Who the hell was Peter?

"The stained-glass guy."

"*Pete?*" I said with a bark of laughter. "Why would you think Pete was my boyfriend?"

Frank shifted uncomfortably. "He calls you *honey* and puts his arm around you, and looks as though he wants to take the head off any man who comes near you. I'm convinced the only reason I survived taking you to that Brock fiasco was because he was in a coma at the time."

"It did slow him down," I conceded. "But Pete is *not* my boyfriend."

Frank thought that over. "What does that mean?"

"What do you think 'not my boyfriend' means?" I replied impatiently, the entertainment value of this conversation having waned. "Let me put it another way: It means he's *not my boyfriend*."

"Does that mean he's really not your boyfriend? Or does it mean that you sleep with him but don't want to call him your boyfriend for some obscure female reason?"

I had to laugh. "You are too much, Frank. It *means* that the thought of my sleeping with Pete is ridiculous. It would be like sleeping with my own brother. And speaking of romance, Frankie, why aren't you at home doing the *Times* Sunday crossword with Elke?"

Frank's girlfriend was named Ingrid, though I referred to her by any name that sounded even vaguely Scandinavian. None of Frank's tenants had ever met Ingrid and a rumor was circulating—okay, I started it—that she did not actually exist. A few months ago the gang began a "Where's Ingrid?" pool, each of us pitching in ten dollars and choosing the day, time, and circumstances closest to the first verified Ingrid sighting. I was secretly rooting for Mary, who had chosen next Saturday, at three thirty a.m., being booked for drunk and disorderly at the Valencia Street police station.

"Ingrid's fine, thank you," he said with a slow smile. "She's very busy."

"I'll bet. Bring her by sometime. Everyone's dying to meet her. Anyway, I'd love to stand here and gab the day away, but I have *work* to do." I waggled my fingers at him and sashayed up the stairs to my sunny studio.

Once inside I bolted the door, punched in the alarm code I'd written on a piece of paper and taped to the wall next to the keypad—where any half-witted thief could find it—and dumped my jacket and backpack on my cluttered desk. Crossing over to a worktable, I unearthed the crate with the Picasso and carefully unwrapped it. I had to stifle a mental image of tripping and putting my foot through the canvas, or spilling dark French roast coffee on it, or in some other way destroying a multimillion-dollar master-piece.

I took a deep breath and lifted the painting onto a work-table. In addition to being a talented art forger, Anton Woznikowicz was a gifted art restorer, so when I called to ask him about Michael I would also verify the proper restoration technique. But first I wanted to confirm my ini-tial assessment. I switched on the lighted magnifier and peered at the Picasso, Sherlock Holmes–fashion. Yup, the red line still looked like a crayon mark.

Inspecting the painting further, I found a small, flat tab tucked between the canvas and the frame. A lot of valuable art these days was outfitted with locator devices such as this, which not only helped authorities track a piece if it was stolen but also set off alarms if the art was tampered with or taken beyond the boundaries of its acceptable zone, such as the perimeter of a museum or gallery. I assumed Frank was monitoring the Picasso and would not bring the FBI down upon my head if I unwittingly set off the alarm. Still, it made me nervous. If anyone could trigger an alarm, it would be me.

Rummaging around in a brightly colored storage bin full of miscellaneous art junk, I found a box of crayons, chose a deep red one, and pulled out a primed canvas. With a quick flick of my wrist, I drew a mark similar to the one on the Picasso and studied the two canvases side by side under the magnifier.

There was no doubt in my mind. The mark on the Picasso had been made by a crayon.

I tuned the radio to NPR, brewed a cup of coffee, and powered up the computer to check the Internet. My computer-savvy friend Pedro Schumacher had book-marked an art search engine when he upgraded my equipment last spring. Within seconds a color photograph of the painting popped up and with a click of the mouse I retrieved data on the paint and the varnish Pablo Picasso had used, as well as the composition of the linen canvas and the wooden supports.

Armed with this information, I returned to the work-table and placed the Picasso facedown on a clean, soft cotton cloth. I was checking for any bleed-through from the crayon to the canvas when a figure materialized on the other side of the table.

I yelped and jumped a foot in the air.

"It's nice to see some things don't change," Michael

said as he rounded the table, standing too close for my peace of mind.

"How did you get in here?" I demanded.

"The window."

So much for Frank's new steel locks and the crack security guard.

"I was, um, a little preoccupied," I said, blocking his view of the worktable and breathing a sigh of relief that the Picasso was facedown.

"What are you working on?" he asked.

"Oh, nothing much." I shrugged. "Just a restoration project."

"Is that right? Anton said you no longer did restoration, creative or otherwise."

Creative restoration was the disingenuous phrase art criminals such as Anton and my grandfather used in lieu of *forgery.*

"My work is none of your business," I snapped. "Why are you here?"

"I didn't get a chance to ask you something last night. How is your mother, by the way?"

"She's fine, thanks. Good ol' Mom."

"I'm so pleased to hear it. She's a lovely woman."

"So you keep saying."

"Of course, she can't hold a candle to her daughter," he whispered. I tried to ignore him, which wasn't easy when every nerve ending in my body was standing tall and screaming howdy. "There's a fire in you, lassie."

"And there's a liar in you, laddie."

"Ouch!" he cried, the big fake.

"Listen, sport, I want that Chagall."

"I don't have a Chagall."

"Yes, you do."

"No, I don't."

"*Yes*, you *do*."

"*No*, I *don't*."

"Why do we always go through this?" I groaned.

"It's one of the many things I enjoy about you, Annie," Michael said, reaching out a hand and touching my face lightly.

"Listen, Michael-Colin-David-Patrick-Bruno," I said, chanting a few of the aliases I knew him by. "I thought we were talking about a Chagall."

"We were."

"So where is it?"

"Annie, I don't have a Chagall. I do have a nice little Monet if you're interested—"

"You sold it already?"

"The Monet? No, that's why I'm offering it to you."

"No, the Chagall."

"What Chagall?"

"*Stop it!*" I yelled in frustration. "A dear friend of mine was on that damned museum tour you led, and he's taking the fall for your having stolen the Chagall. So stop denying that you have it!"

Michael looked puzzled. "But I *don't* have it. That's what I'm trying to tell you. I like Bryan. I wouldn't hang him out to dry. Annie, think: If I'd stolen the Chagall, why would I be here talking to you?"

"I don't know, but I'm sure you'd have some sneaky, ethically challenged reason. And how did you know I was referring to Bryan, eh?" The phone shrilled and I snatched it up. *"What?"*

"What's going on up there?" It was Frank. "We did agree on absolute secrecy while you worked on this project, did we not?"

"Yes, of course. It's the radio. Don't worry. Everything's under control." I hung up and turned back to Michael.

My good buddy, the professional art thief, held the Picasso in both hands.

"Beautiful, Annie. Just beautiful," he said, shaking his head. "But what's with the kid's crayon mark?"

Chapter 7

How is anyone to tell frauds from originals in modern art? Take, for instance, the discovery of a number of supposed Jackson Pollock paintings in a storage locker last year. The art experts and Pollock's heirs are arguing over the "behavior" of paint splatters!

> —Georges LeFleur, in Frontline: "The Mysterious World of Modern Art"

"Put that down," I commanded.

"Why, Annie." Michael cocked his head and a smile played upon his sensuous lips. "It's almost as if you don't trust me."

"Trust you? Why on earth would I trust *you*? You'd steal your grandmother's silver if you could get a good price for it. And may I remind you that you still owe me four hundred dollars from our little jaunt to Napa last spring?" I yanked the Picasso from his grasp and held it protectively against my chest. "Let's get one thing straight: I want that Chagall and I want it *now*."

Michael shoved his hands into the pockets of his perfectly faded Levi's 401 jeans and rocked back on the heels of his scuffed brown leather boots. His blue work shirt gaped open at the neck, revealing smooth, tanned skin and a few curly black chest hairs peeking over the collar of his white T-shirt. He looked good enough to eat, and I was pretty sure he knew it.

"Annie, darling, I don't have the Chagall," he began smoothly. "Had you read this morning's *Chronicle* you would know that the Brock Museum received a ransom note for it yesterday."

"What?"

"Yeah, can you believe it?" He chuckled and shook his head.

"The painting was *kidnapped*? Not stolen?"

"I'm not sure you can kidnap a painting. Don't you need a kid for that?"

Poor Agnes Brock, I thought, ignoring his banter. The Brock enjoyed a healthy endowment, but like most museums it didn't have a lot of spare cash. Having a painting stolen was bad enough, but paying a ransom for its return added insult to injury.

"How much is the ransom?" I asked, curious.

"Now, that's the complicated part," Michael said. "You might say its value is beyond mere money."

"Just tell me, please." I hated riddles. I even got stumped by knock-knock jokes, to the eternal delight of my young nephews. "What do the kidnappers want?"

"Peace in the Middle East."

"What?"

"I'm sure we can agree it's a laudable goal," Michael said, sounding pious. "Don't you want peace in the Middle East?"

"Of course, but the Brock Museum doesn't have any influence over the situation there," I protested. "That's crazy."

"So was stealing the Chagall. It's not especially valuable, after all. Doesn't it make you wonder, Annie, why a thief would go to the trouble of turning off the security system *and* engineering a diversion just to steal that particular painting?"

I stared at him. He was right. The Brock had any number of paintings with far greater market value than the Chagall, especially if ransom were the thief's objective. So why had that painting been taken?

Michael strolled over to the window, just your average world-class art thief passing a Sunday morning philosophizing with a friend. Sitting on the sill, he crossed his arms over his chest and continued. "The Gérôme—now, that's what I would have taken. Jean-Léon Gérôme's Orientalist realism has been greatly underrated. Mark my words: It's just a matter of time until he comes into his own, and when that happens, the value of his paintings will go through the roof."

"You're telling me the truth, aren't you?" I said slowly. "You really *didn't* take the Chagall."

A frown marred Michael's handsome face. "This isn't very complicated, Annie. I've been saying that from the beginning."

His gaze fell on the Picasso clutched in my arms.

"Whoa there, cowboy. Don't go getting any ideas about *this* painting. I could still finger you for the Caravaggio, you know."

"You could. But you won't."

"Are you so sure?"

"Reasonably sure, yes."

"And why is that?"

"Because you have a touch of larceny in your heart."

"You don't know that," I retorted. It was true, though. I was constantly fighting it.

He pushed away from the windowsill, sauntered over,

and gazed into my eyes. "But mostly because . . ." He paused for better effect. *What a ham,* I thought. My heart told me to shut up, and beat a little faster. "Because against your better judgment you have a soft spot in your heart for me."

"Not soft enough to cushion the blow of a stolen Picasso, you big fake."

Michael staggered backwards, a hand clutching his chest. "You wound me, Annie."

"You'll get over it," I replied. "I ain't jokin' here, big guy."

Michael straightened up. "In that case, let me remind you that should you finger me for the Caravaggio—which, for the record, I do not for a second believe you would actually do—I might, albeit only under torture or threat of indictment, be forced to spill the beans about your dear grandpapa's role in that little affair. It would break my heart, of course. And you? Could you do that to such a wonderful old man?"

"Just for your own damned record, *I* don't believe for a second that you would rat out Georges," I said with a glare. "Wouldn't that violate the code of honor among thieves?"

"You watch too many trashy movies, sweetheart."

This was true. "Was there a reason you came here today, Michael, or were you just bored?"

"You underestimate your charms."

"And you *overestimate* yours," I shot back.

He smiled. "I need a date."

I snorted. "Yeah, right."

"Seriously." He picked up a paintbrush from the worktable and caressed its sable bristles with his long, tanned fingers. I wondered if it was possible to envy a paintbrush. "I have been invited to an exceedingly formal and exceptionally dull cocktail party in Hillsborough next Tuesday, for which I need a date. A *respectable* date. You are the most respectable woman I know." He paused and grinned. "And I happen to enjoy your company."

Oh, please, I thought. San Francisco was full of lovely, well-educated, and eminently respectable women who would be delighted to accompany Michael to a barbeque in hell, much less to a cocktail party in Hillsborough, an exclusive enclave on the peninsula south of San Francisco. So why was he asking me?

"You're up to something," I said.

"Annie, my love, we really must work on your trust issues."

In the Bay Area we did not have disagreements, fights, hatreds, or to-the-death blood feuds; we had *issues.* I was beginning to have issues with people who had issues.

"Still ain't interested."

"Tell you what," he said, flipping the lucky brush into the air, where it rotated several times before landing, bristles up, with a clink in a glass jar. He strolled over and stood so close that I could feel the heat of his body. I wished he didn't smell so damned good. "If you come to the party with me on Tuesday, I'll make sure the Brock gets the Chagall back."

"I thought you said you didn't have it."

"I don't, but I might be able to locate it. *If* you will do me this one small favor."

Could he find the Chagall? Probably. Would he give it to me? Good question.

His green eyes wandered down my overalls and up to my face, gazing into my eyes with a soulfulness that communicated in a thousand ways that I was the most supremely desirable woman on the planet. Better than a supermodel lounging in the sun on a deserted tropical island. In a thong. Topless.

"Annie, my love," he said, his voice husky, and leaned in as if to kiss me.

I had no false modesty. I knew I was an attractive woman, especially when I made a little effort. I also knew it was highly unlikely that wars would be fought in my honor, that a king would give up his throne for me, or that my overalled and sleep-haired charms were sufficient to distract a professional art thief from thieving.

"Cut the crap, Michael," I barked. "I'm onto you."

The seduction routine came to an abrupt halt. "I'll pay you the money from last spring."

"You'll pay that anyway. You want my company? It'll cost you."

"All right. How much?"

"You get the Chagall back *and* Bryan off the hook, and quickly. And my going rate is a hundred fifty an hour."

Michael's eyebrows shot up in surprise. "Is that what faux finishers charge these days? That's almost as much as a first-class call girl."

I gasped.

"It's a deal," he said.

"Fine," I replied, surprised—and a little worried—that he had agreed so readily. Note to self: consider raising your price. "But I want the money you owe me *and* I want the cash in advance. And FYI: Your money buys my scintillating conversation. That's *all*."

Michael reached into his jeans pocket and extracted a thick roll of Benjamins. I gaped at it, though I supposed in his line of work Michael had to be prepared to hightail it out of town at a moment's notice without leaving a paper trail. The most I usually had on me was a twenty, and maybe sixty-eight cents on the floor of my truck.

Michael peeled off four of the hundred-dollar bills. "That's for last spring," he said and looked at me with an arched brow. "How long does a date take? Four or five hours? I pick you up, say sevenish, and have you tucked in by the stroke of midnight?" He counted off seven more bills.

"I need a new dress, too," I piped up. What the hell.

Michael sighed. "Make it sexy. But classy."

"And shoes," I said, going for broke. "Don't forget the shoes."

He handed me several more hundreds. "There. Shoes *and* a bag *and* silk stockings and whatever else you think you need. Just come through for me, Annie."

"Why, Michael, have I ever failed you?" I purred, batting my eyelashes and tucking the wad of cash into the bib of my paint-splattered overalls. Helen of Troy had nothing on me.

Michael smiled and headed for the window. "I'll pick you up on Tuesday. Seven o'clock sharp."

"Wait a minute," I called after him. "Where are we going?"

"To a private home. Our charming host made a fortune in the high-tech industry. There will be a number of businessmen from Hong Kong."

"I don't speak computer," I warned.

"Anton said you speak a little Mandarin."

"Emphasis on *little*, there, sport." When I was a child my grandfather had taught me how to say *Please*, *Thank you*, *Where is the bathroom?* and *How dare you accuse me of something so outrageous?* in seven different languages. Georges LeFleur was a practical man.

"*Hello* and *good-bye* will suffice. No one will expect you to do anything except look pretty anyway."

I scowled at him. He smiled at me.

"One more thing," I said. "Have you ever heard of Robert Pascal?"

"Sure. His stuff is too heavy to steal, too hard to fence, and too ugly to boot. Why?"

"Just curious."

"Don't be. There are some nasty rumors about him."

"Like what?"

"Stay away from him, Annie," he said soberly. "I mean it. Oh, and about that Picasso." I hugged the painting like a mother hugs a child threatened by a bully. "Didn't the Nazis steal that from the Steinbergen family during World War II?"

"No."

"How can you be sure?"

"Because Frank would never be involved in something like that."

"Frank DeBenton?" Michael queried, his eyebrows raised. "As in DeBenton Secure Transport? How much do you know about your landlord, Annie?"

"Enough to be sure he wouldn't traffic in stolen art. Unlike *some* people I could mention."

"No fair! You know I have rules."

"No group jobs?" I said, referring to his oft-repeated preference for solo thievery.

"No group jobs," he repeated. "And no looted art."

"Oh, that's right," I said sarcastically. "When it comes to stealing what's already been stolen, you're a veritable Eagle Scout."

"I should hope so," he said, not at all perturbed. " 'Til Tuesday, then." And with that he climbed out the window and silently slipped down the fire escape.

I gazed after him. What had he been implying about Frank? Why was he paying me a boatload of money to go to a cocktail party? And what were my chances the evening would end in a bail hearing?

The hundred-dollar bills in my pocket rustled as I locked

the window against further intrusions and hung a *Do Not
Disturb, Artist in Session, And Yes I'm Talking to You, Pal*
sign on the door. I placed the Picasso face-up on a worktable and began testing various absorbent cloths and heat
settings on the sample canvas I'd made. When I put wax-
absorbent paper over the crayon mark and applied a
medium-heat iron, the colored wax lifted out of the sample
canvas without leaving a residue. A quick call to Anton confirmed my approach was sound. I was sitting on the couch,
taking some cleansing breaths and screwing up my courage
to attempt the process on the Picasso, when the telephone
rang.

"*Chérie!* So you have some good news for your old
grandpapa, no?" It was my beloved grandfather, Georges
Francois LeFleur, world-class art forger and all-around
scoundrel.

"News? What news? Where are you calling from,
Grandfather?"

"Ah, my darling, you air zo modest. *Quelle charmante!*
Ze dashing Monsieur Brooks has set hees cap for you, eh?"

Georges LeFleur had been born in Brooklyn and spent
the first fifteen years of his life speaking Brooklynese. As
an adult he had reinvented himself—several times, in
fact—and now spoke English with a nearly impenetrable
French accent.

I adored my grandfather and understood him as few others could, but at times he drove me crazy. He would not
call me when I needed information, but burned up the international telephone wires when he thought I had hooked
up with a dashing, larcenous art thief.

A man much like himself, in other words.

"Grandfather," I said with as much patience as I could
muster. "'Colin Brooks' isn't even his real name. I know

him as Michael. And he doesn't want *me*. He wants something *from* me."

"Are you sure, my dahling?"

"Positive."

"Quel dommage." He sighed. "Zo, what does zis man want from you?"

"I don't know. He invited me to some cocktail party in Hillsborough, at the home of a computer billionaire."

" 'Illsborough, you say? Do you know ze 'ost's nehm?"

"No, I don't know the host's name," I replied, suddenly suspicious. "Why do you ask?"

"No reason, *ma petite. Ce n'est pas grave."* Grandfather's accent thickened in direct proportion to his guilt and his desire to conceal it. When he was flat-out lying he reverted almost exclusively to French, which was an excellent language to fib in.

"What's going on, *Grand-père*?"

"I must go, *chérie*! Bye-bye!"

"Wait! Grandfather, I have to ask you about Mom . . ."

"We air lozing ze connection! *Au revoir!*" Georges was a great believer in losing the phone connection whenever he found it inconvenient to keep talking.

Frustrated, I hung up. I knew Michael was up to something because Michael was always up to something. That he wanted me to play some role in whatever he was planning was annoying, and quite possibly unlawful, but not unexpected. What bothered me was that my grandfather, who apparently suspected what Michael was up to, would not tell me. Wasn't blood supposed to be thicker than thieves?

I sighed and shrugged off these thoughts. If I'd learned one thing about my grandfather it was that he was a stubborn old coot who would tell me in his own way and on his own time.

I turned up the radio and painstakingly removed the stray red mark from the Picasso. Anton had given me a few tips to avoid lifting the legitimate paint as well as the crayon wax, and on the whole it was a tedious job. But artists were accustomed to tedium. Not even the Old Masters stood in front of a blank canvas and dashed off a masterpiece. Come to think of it, Pablo Picasso might have been the exception, at least at the end of his long life. No wonder other artists admired him so.

By the time I'd finished it was nearly two o'clock. I examined the painting from all angles, held it up to a harsh light, looked at it under the magnifier, and double-checked it against the photograph on the Internet. It was perfect. I had done my job so well, in fact, that no one would ever know what I had accomplished. As a former art forger, I had long ago made my peace with anonymity.

Now that Michael knew I had the Picasso it seemed wise to return it to Frank as soon as possible. I packed it carefully in its crate, switched off the radio, and shut down the computer. Then I grabbed my backpack and keys, set the alarm, hoisted the crate in my arms, locked the door, and cautiously negotiated the outside wooden staircase. I found my landlord in his office, his dark head bent low over paperwork.

"Knock knock," I called out.

He jumped up to take the crate. "You should have called. I would have come to get it."

"I'm perfectly capable of carrying a painting, Frank. You've seen some of the things I've toted up and down those stairs—furniture and garden statuary and the like. Which reminds me—when are you going to put in an elevator?"

"If I put in an elevator I'll have to raise the rent. So, all done? Already?"

"Good as new," I said. "You're not going to try to back out of our deal now that you know how efficient I am, are you?"

"Of course not," he said, looking surprised. "I'm just impressed."

"I'm kidding, Frank. You're one of the most trustworthy guys I know."

The moment I said it, I realized it was true. Frank was as worthy of trust as Michael was of suspicion. Why was I entertaining even for a moment Michael's hint that Frank trafficked in stolen paintings? Still, I had to ask.

"So-o-o, funny thing, Frank," I said. "I couldn't help but notice that the Picasso looks a lot like the one the Steinbergen family says was stolen by the Nazis."

"Do you think I would transport stolen art?"

Talk about an awkward moment. I wished I'd kept my yap shut. "Maybe not knowingly . . ."

"There are online databases that track lost and stolen art from around the world, Annie. There's even a software program to send pictures from a camera phone to an image-processing server connected to the database. Whenever I take possession of a painting I access up-to-the-minute information on its origin and provenance. If it's flagged, I report it to the appropriate authorities."

"Really?" I said, impressed. *How does Michael manage to fence his purloined art?* I wondered. I filed that away as a conversation starter for our "date" on Tuesday.

"This Picasso is similar to the one the Nazis took from the Steinbergens, but rest assured they are two different paintings."

"That's a relief," I said. "I'd have hated to see you hauled off to San Quentin on my say-so alone. My next landlord might not be as reasonable as you."

"What a touching tribute," he said dryly. "I must say,

though, I'm pleased to learn that your ethics are as strong as my own."

Dear, naïve man, I thought. "Since you're so knowledgeable about art theft, could I ask you something? Why would someone steal an unimportant painting from a museum?"

"Is this a hypothetical question?"

"More or less," I dissembled.

"Well, that depends. Most art theft these days is connected to drug dealers and gun runners, but those folks want the big-ticket, high-profile pieces."

"What do drug dealers and gun runners want with fine art?"

"They use it as collateral for their deals, or else to launder money."

"I had no idea," I said, appalled. A spot of art forgery was one thing—it could be rationalized as a victimless crime if one's ethics were sufficiently flexible—but drug dealing and gun running left broken bodies in their wake.

"Art theft is the third most lucrative international crime, behind drugs and arms dealing," Frank said. "But that wasn't your question, was it? When a stolen piece of art is relatively unimportant or inexpensive the motive tends to be personal. I'd start with the museum's employees."

"An employee?"

"You worked at the Brock, Annie, so you know that most museum workers are underpaid and overworked. They're often art lovers themselves, and a few will yield to temptation. But since they're not motivated by profit their choice is usually a minor piece that's a personal favorite. Most of the time they take items from the storage areas and the theft isn't discovered for months or years, if at all. What's with this newfound interest in art theft?"

"Just idle curiosity."

"That right?"

"Don't you want to see the Picasso?" I said to distract him.

Frank opened the crate and examined the painting. When he looked at me, I saw relief in his eyes. "Amazing. You're a miracle worker, Annie, truly. I owe you one."

In the past six months Frank had rescued me from a goon holding a knife to my throat, escorted me to a gala I desperately wanted to attend, and reduced my rent so I wouldn't have to relocate my studio. All in all, I figured we were probably even. But I wasn't about to look a gift horse in the mouth.

"Oh, one more thing, Frank," I said as I started for the door.

"What's that?"

"Be careful. *Really* careful. Maybe return the Picasso to its owner right away."

"What's going on?"

"Nothing. Nosirree. But you might want to lock it in one of your trucks and drive away."

"Why?"

"I've got to run. Bye, Frank!" I waved gaily, raced out the door, and told myself I had done what I could.

After all, wasn't Frank the one who said I was a trouble magnet?

Chapter 8

Sculptures are tricky. If a bronze is poured in an artist's original mold, is it a genuine product of the artist, or of the foundry worker, or of the heir to the copyright? A Rodin sculpture cast by Rudier a century ago is now worth a fortune, while a cast made by the Rodin Museum in recent years is considered a mere copy.

—*George LeFleur, letter to the editor,*
Bulletin of the Society of Museum Curators

Flowers are amazing things. They inspire artists, lift flagging spirits, and seal romantic deals. They can even unlock doors.

I'd learned the secret of flower power from Sherri the process server, who once described how she used flower deliveries to gain access to her quarry and to soften the blow of being served distressing legal papers. The best source for flowers was the San Francisco Flower Mart at Sixth and Brannan, which opened at the crack of dawn and was jammed with Vietnamese flower vendors, Jewish florists, and mothers of every ethnicity looking to save a buck or twenty on wedding arrangements. I had once dragged my butt out of bed at four-thirty a.m. to witness the lily-scented free-for-all, but on the whole I preferred sleep to really fresh flowers.

After leaving the restored Picasso in Frank's tender care, I zipped over to the flower mart to pick up a nice mixed bouquet before heading over to Pascal's studio. Weaving through the Sunday traffic, I pondered how best to handle the wily old sculptor. My mother had confirmed a stronger connection to Seamus McGraw than Pascal had admitted to, and I wondered what he'd been hiding. If the two artists were old friends, why had he denied it? Worried, I sped up. Something was amiss in the world of Bay Area sculptors. Seamus McGraw had been murdered, Robert Pascal was lying his fool head off, and my mother's recent behavior suggested she was somehow in the thick of it. I was determined that Beverly LeFleur Kincaid would not be found dangling from an old oak tree.

I braked quickly to avoid plowing into a gaggle of bewildered tourists attempting to cross the street. Burdened by cameras and tote bags, sweating in heavy fall clothing, and clutching mangled street maps, they were out of place in this industrial area of the City. San Francisco's economy was heavily dependent on tourist dollars, so I muffled my impatience, plastered a welcoming Tourist Bureau smile on my face, and waved them across. Had I more time I might have directed them to the attractions they were undoubtedly seeking: the cable car station on California, Chinatown, Fisherman's Wharf, the Embarcadero, and the Depression-era murals at Coit Tower.

In contrast to those vibrant scenes, the old building housing Pascal's third-floor studio appeared grim and uninhabited. A light breeze blew trash across the cracked tarmac of the empty parking lot, and a seagull screamed overhead. I hesitated and wished someone were here to keep me company.

"Ecoutes-moi bien, chérie," my grandfather had said when, as a child, I'd hesitated to attempt a challenging design. "To be an artist is to embrace the courage of your soul. Without courage, an artist has no vision, and without vision an artist does not exist. *Tu comprends?"*

"Oui, Grandpapa," I'd dutifully replied.

"Alors, aux armes!" he'd cried, and burst into the Marseillaise. As an adult I came to realize my grandfather didn't actually know the lyrics to France's national anthem, but it hardly mattered. His words had given me courage then as they did now.

Armed with the bouquet and humming the Marseillaise, I pulled open the front door and literally bumped into a young Latina I had passed on the stairs yesterday.

"Hello," I said with a friendly smile. "I think I saw you here yesterday. Do you happen to know if the sculptor, Robert Pascal, is in?"

"Jess." She said, shaking her head. "No."

"Yes?"

"No."

"No?"

"Jess." She nodded.

"Okay, well, thanks." I really had to sign up for an Adult Ed Spanish class, and soon. "Do you know him?"

"I go . . ." she said, turning away and hastening down the street.

I shrugged and, on the pretext of needing exercise, opted for the gloomy stairwell over the creaky old elevator. In truth, I was afraid of getting trapped all night in that iron cage, with nothing to keep me company except my thoughts and a bouquet of flowers. Were flowers edible? I had a sudden visual of being discovered on Monday morning, caught between floors and stone-cold dead from acute flower poisoning.

A few minutes later, puffing a little from the exercise, I knocked on his metal door and waited, holding the bouquet in front of my face.

No response. I banged on the door again, yelled "Delivery!" and heard footsteps approaching. This was going to be easy, I thought smugly. I waited, poised to spring the trap.

And waited.

The flowers dripped on my foot.

Rats. Okay. Time to launch Plan B.

I set the flowers on the floor, clomped loudly down the hall, and hit the elevator call button, then tiptoed back and pressed myself flat against the wall to one side of Pascal's door. The elevator arrived with a ping; the doors slid open, paused, and closed. I held my breath. Sure enough, I heard a shuffling and a scratching, and the door slowly swung open. I leaped out and slammed one arm against the door, calculating that with the element of surprise on my side I would be able to out arm-wrestle Pascal.

This might or might not have been true. I never found out because it was not the old man, it was a large, very muscular young woman. Nearly six feet tall, with short, spiky, light brown hair and mild blue eyes, she looked a lot like one of the East German Olympic shot-putters we used to accuse of taking steroids during the days of the Cold War.

She barked in surprise and I squeaked in return. We gaped at each other for a long moment before I finally spoke. "I, uh—hi. I'm here to see Pascal. Is he in?"

"What, you was gonna jump him or sometin'?"

Not a hint of Bavaria in that accent. Bayonne, New Jersey, maybe.

"Whaddya want?" she demanded, eyeing me suspiciously.

"Um, yes, well, I was hoping to speak with Robert."

"Whaddya wanna see him for?"

"He and I spoke yesterday," I hedged. "He's an old friend of my parents."

"Yeah, right, I'll bet," she sneered, and from the expression on her face I half expected her to hawk a loogie and scratch her armpits. "Lissen, Miss Whoozits, Pascal don't have no friends far's I can see."

"And you are . . . ?" To my surprise she answered.

"Evangeline."

Of all the names in all the world, I wondered, how had she ended up with that one? "Evangeline" was a good name for a waif with flowing hair, rosy lips, and large doe eyes, the kind of romantic heroine who needed to be rescued as often as twice a day. This woman, in contrast, could face down a speeding Mack truck and probably come out ahead.

Evangeline held out a meaty paw and we shook hands vigorously.

"I'm Annie, Annie Kincaid." I handed her one of the business cards I carried in my overalls pocket:

True/Faux Studios
Annie Kincaid, Proprietor
Faux Finishes, Murals, Trompe L'Oeil
Not for the Feint of Art Alone

"What's foo—fox—fay-ucks?" she asked, puzzled.

"It's faux, rhymes with toe," I said. "It means fake. Or, in Vietnamese, noodle, like *pho*."

Evangeline stared blankly. "You make noodles?"

"No, I—" So much for my little joke. "I'm a painter."

"Yeah, hokay, Annie," she said in a friendly tone, and

slipped the business card into her dusty jeans pocket. "How *you* doin'? So what's wit' the flowers?"

"I was trying to get Pascal to open the door."

"Guess that worked hokay on me, huh?" she said with a snort. "Hey, hol' on—I thought you said you was friends wit' him."

"Actually, my parents are his friends. But I did speak with him yesterday. Is he here?"

"Nope. Hadda go to a funeral. Wanna come in and wait?"

"Thanks," I said, unsure what my next step should be. On the plus side, I was inside Pascal's studio and it had not taken six hours this time.

Evangeline set the flowers on the desk and my eyes flew to *Head and Torso*, which stood on a low pedestal in a pool of sunlight.

Correction. The sculpture looked a lot like *Head and Torso* but was not the one Pascal had shown me yesterday. And it wasn't just my freakish ability to recognize artwork that made me so sure. This piece was unfinished, the bottom left of the torso only roughly sculpted.

"Oops, I should pro'ly cover that," Evangeline honked. "Nobody's s'pose ta see it. Grab that side, will ya?"

I was getting the distinct impression that Pascal had hired Evangeline for her brawn, not her brain. Leaning over to grab a corner of a drop cloth, I picked up a small chunk of marble about the size of a matchbox and slipped it into my overalls pocket. For all I knew, there could be a way to analyze stone the way one could study paint pigments. It was a long shot, but I didn't trust Pascal. Together Evangeline and I draped the cloth and arranged the folds until the ersatz *Head and Torso* was shrouded.

"Is this what you've been working on?" I asked innocently. "It's very nice."

"I, uh," she stammered. "Nah, this is an old sculpture in for repairs. I help Pascal wid de repair stuff."

"Oh? Can I ask you something? Is there something wrong with Pascal's hands?"

"Ya mean like deformed?"

"No, like arthritis or something," I clarified. "Maybe he takes some medications?"

"He seems okay when he's workin'," she said. "Onliest thing I ever seen him take was a little blue pill once in a while."

Lord, I hoped that was not Viagra. *Now, Annie*, I scolded myself, *don't be closed-minded*. Maybe Evangeline was Pascal's mistress and I had stumbled into their love nest. Maybe Pascal was into big, beautiful, steroidal women, and Evangeline was into old, ugly, rude men. Maybe Pascal had not returned *Head and Torso* to the Hewetts because he wanted to offer the fruit of his youthful genius to his one true love, the fair Evangeline.

Said maiden was vigorously cleaning out one ear with a pinky finger, her eyes crossed.

"Do you sculpt, too?" I asked, averting my gaze.

"Um, yeah, sure. Mostly I do repairs with Pascal," she insisted, her face reddening. She fidgeted with a chisel and avoided my eyes.

I wondered why she felt compelled to lie. The best way for a new artist to learn to sculpt or to paint was to work with an established artist; this had been true in the days of the Old Masters, and it remained so today. So why had Pascal denied having an assistant?

Silence descended as I groped for a way to get her to spill Pascal's secrets.

"You want somethin' to drink?" Evangeline offered. "A Coke or somethin'?"

"Yeah, thanks. A Coke would really hit the spot."

"I like Pepsi better," she confessed. "But Pascal said he can't work without Coke, so that's what I bought. But then he started complainin' it wasn't sweet enough. Geez."

She disappeared behind a small partition separating a kitchen area from the rest of the studio, still grousing about the Coke versus Pepsi challenge. I took her absence as tacit permission to snoop and sidled over to an old-fashioned rolltop desk. Surrounded by cardboard boxes labeled by date in a bold handwriting, the desk was covered with a jumble of envelopes, folders, and bureaucratic whatnot in imminent danger of spilling to the floor. On top of the tallest pile were several pink invoices from the Mischievous Monkey Garden Supply. I recognized the name because last spring I had unleashed my arsenal of faux-finishing tricks to transform a truckload of their cheap cement statues into quaint "old" garden ornaments. But Pascal lived on the third floor of an industrial building surrounded by an asphalt parking lot. What would he need from the Mischievous Monkey Garden Supply?

Still, considering some of the artistic personalities I had encountered over the years, it could be just about anything. Maybe Pascal was experimenting with peat moss sculptures. Maybe he was indulging a lifelong passion for miniature bonsai trees. Maybe he liked to run his toesies through mounds of soft white sand.

Evangeline was vigorously chipping ice in the kitchenette, so I took a chance and picked up one of the pink sheets. It was not an invoice. It was a receipt for the delivery of ten plaster garden statues.

That was odd. Pascal's marble sculptures commanded top dollar from the best art galleries. Why would he be sculpting cheap plaster statuary for a garden supply store?

Evangeline appeared, carrying two large tumblers filled to the brim with chipped ice and cola. "Here's mud in your eye," she said handing me one, and we clinked glasses. I savored the cold tingle on my tongue as I wandered around the studio, studying the maquettes that lay scattered about the worktables amidst empty containers of Cup o' Noodles.

"So what's it like to work with the famous Robert Pascal?" I queried in an offhand, girl-to-girl kind of way.

Evangeline looked dismayed, slurped her soda, and uncorked a belch that would have awed my nephews.

"'Sokay." She shrugged. "I like California."

"So do I!" I said inanely. "Where are you from?"

"Upstate New Yawk."

"Did you move here to work with Pascal?"

"Yup."

"Didn't he have a bad experience with an assistant a long time ago?"

"Dunno," she said and belched again. "Pardon my French."

I laughed and she joined in.

Suddenly the studio door crashed open and Pascal appeared. Although it was a warm and sunny day he wore a threadbare green parka with the hood pulled up.

"Goddammit!" he swore. "What the hell's *she* doing here?"

"Hiya, Robert," I replied. "I dropped by to bring you some flowers. I felt just awful about disturbing you yesterday."

Pascal glowered as he shrugged off the parka and hung it on a wooden hook near the door. He had not shaved recently, nor, I was willing to bet, had he showered. He sniffed and wiped his nose with a blue bandana.

"Flowers my ass," he snarled.

"Crippled hands, my ass," I snapped back.

"What do you want from me, girlie?"

"What doesn't belong to you," I retorted. "The Hewetts'

sculpture. I also want to know why you lied about your hands."

"I lied about my hands to get you off my back, whaddaya think?"

"How is my mother involved with you and Seamus? You were at his funeral, weren't you?"

"Kiss my ass, little girl," he bit out. "And tell the Hewetts I'll give them their goddamned sculpture when I'm goddamned good and ready."

Evangeline looked shocked, and I wondered if her upbringing had been more genteel than it would appear. Mine had not been so refined, despite my mother's best efforts, and I stood my ground. "What kind of repairs are you doing, anyway?"

"Sculpting repairs," he said sarcastically, crossing his arms over his chest in an age-old gesture of mulish stubbornness. "I'm a sculptor, nitwit. Tell the Hewetts they have to wait their goddamned turn. I've got a bunch of other stuff waiting for repairs." He gestured at a covered pile of objects in the corner.

"See, now, that's something I don't understand. Why do so many of your sculptures need to be repaired? Do you have unusually clumsy clients?"

I worked in media that were not nearly as durable as stone, yet rarely was it necessary to repair my artwork. Barring a Visigoth invasion, how often did marble statues get broken?

"Get lost," he barked. He sniffed loudly again and turned on Evangeline. "Why'd you let her in?"

"She brought flowers."

"'She brought flowers,'" he mimicked, waggling his head. "Moron. Why I ever told your mother I'd take you on is beyond me." He looked at me. "Sister's kid. Dumb as a stump."

I waited for Evangeline to defend herself, but she just stood there, admittedly rather stumplike, so I spoke up on her behalf.

"Seems to me you're the moron here, Pascal. Don't your sculptures bring in good money? Why don't you go sit on a beach, enjoy your golden years, and spare the art world your charms? You might even find a use for that Viagra prescription. It's bound to improve your mood."

Pascal's otherworldly paleness purpled with rage as he took a step toward me. "Get out of my studio, you two-bit hack! And tell your mama she's not holding up her end of the bargain, you hear me?"

In his face I saw not just rage but something far more threatening: fear.

"What are you talking about?" I demanded, stepping back, stumbling into the desk, and dislodging a stack of black composition notebooks. They landed with a thump on the floor. "What bargain?"

"You okay, Annie?" Evangeline asked.

"I'm fine, thanks," I said, sparing her a smile before automatically leaning over to pick up the notebooks. Pascal stomped on them, barely missing my hand.

"Leave 'em," he growled.

Surprised by his reaction, I glanced at the composition books. *S. McGraw, 1971* was written on their covers in the same distinctive handwriting as the labels on the cardboard boxes.

I straightened, and Pascal and I stared at each other.

"What does my mother have to do with all of this?" I asked quietly.

Pascal deflated like a blow-up doll, collapsed in his ergonomic desk chair, and held his head in his hands. "Beverly . . . Ah, hell. Do yourself a favor, kid, and get out of here. Leave me alone."

"Listen, Pascal, if you return *Head and Torso* then I'll go away and you'll never see me again, I swear. But if my mother's involved in something dangerous, if she's threatened in any way, I will stick to you like a leech. I will be your worst nightmare. I happen to have a very close friend in the SFPD—"

Pascal shot from his chair like a demented jack-in-the-box. "I'll return the sculpture when I'm good and goddamned ready! Why don't you and your mommy go back to that dusty cow town you came from? I don't give a shit about the past, you hear me? Not one piece of shit!"

Rarely did I embrace the adage about discretion being the better part of valor, but under the circumstances I decided to give it a chance.

"You heard me," I warned as I headed for the door. "Leave my mother alone. Evangeline, can I give you a ride somewhere?"

"Nah, I'll be all right, thanks," she said softly. "He's got a temper on 'im is all."

For all my big mouth and bravado, I was shaking from a combination of anger and adrenaline as I hurried down the stairs, flew out of the building, and locked myself in my truck. What had just happened up there? Why was Pascal so vicious and embittered?

As I fired up the engine I noticed the young woman I'd seen earlier, returning to Pascal's building loaded down with plastic grocery bags from Safeway. Could she be working for Pascal? I doubted he needed human models for his angular creations; nor did the delicate-looking Latina appear strong enough to be a stone sculptor.

I headed towards the Bay Bridge, anxious to put some physical space between me and the lunatic sculptor. Traffic was light on this Sunday afternoon, and as I drove along I began to relax and think about my little tête-à-screaming-tête with Pascal. It now seemed highly unlikely that I would ever convince him to return *Head and Torso* to the Hewetts, which meant it would be unethical to continue charging them for my time. Cancel the meal ticket.

More important, though, it also seemed apparent that my mother was involved in something unpleasant, if not downright dangerous, related to Seamus McGraw's murder. But what? My mother was a small-town housewife who painted watercolors in her spare time and was married to an art history professor. What could she possibly know about—

I caught myself. Not only was Beverly Kincaid an intelligent woman, but she had been raised by her widowed father, the master forger Georges LeFleur, and spent her formative years in the great capital cities of Europe, in the bosom of the art world's shadowy underground. The odds were good my mother had learned at an early age how to handle the unsavory characters with whom my grandfather consorted. In fact, it was entirely possible that my mother took after Georges more than anyone in the Kincaid family appreciated—especially her younger daughter.

I wondered again what my grandfather might know about all this. Pulling over on Third Street, I scrolled down my cell phone's directory until I found his last known number in Paris. I left a message with a groggy French woman who claimed never to have heard of Georges LeFleur, a second with an equally sleepy man in Brussels who pretended he didn't understand English, and a third with an exceedingly polite desk clerk at the Hotel Royal in Prague who made me spell my name four times. The calls were going to be expensive and might not produce results, but it was the only way I knew to track down my elusive grandfather.

There was one other call I wanted to make.

"Inspector Crawford," Annette answered, her voice deep and authoritative.

"Annette! It's Annie! How are you?"

I heard rustling in the background and Annette's voice dropped. "This isn't a good time."

"I'm sorry, should I call back later?"

"That wouldn't be a good time, either. This number is for police business."

"This *is* police business," I insisted. "I'm calling about the stolen Chagall."

"Do you have information pertinent to the case?"

"Not exactly, but I—"

"Then it doesn't count."

Aren't we just the big-shot police inspector? I thought resentfully.

As if she'd read my mind, Annette's voice thawed slightly. "I'm sorry to be so abrupt, Annie, but I can't discuss this with you. It's not even my case. Perhaps I gave you the wrong impression when I asked for your help with Mr. Boissevain's interview."

"But Agnes Brock said that if I found the painting she would not make any trouble for Bryan."

"Annie, I suggest you steer clear of this case. Mrs. Brock has made some rather wild accusations. She seems to think you have connections to the criminal art world. I told her she was wrong, of course."

"I should hope so!" I blustered.

"Mm-hmm. Because if that were true it would be unfortunate for us both," she said. "I have noticed, though, that you do have a knack for showing up at the wrong place at the wrong time."

"You know what they say about the luck of the Irish. As for the Chagall . . ."

"Annie, I work homicide, remember? Everything I can tell you has already been in the news."

Note to self: subscribe to the stupid newspaper already.

"Indulge me?" I begged. "Please?"

"Hold on." Her muffled voice asked someone to get her a double skinny latte and a California roll. "Okay, I'm back."

"Coffee and sushi?" I teased. "Is that the dinner of champions these days?"

"I prefer to think of it as caffeine, calcium, and no fat," she replied lightly. "Where were we? Oh, yes, the stolen painting. As you would know—"

"If only I read the paper . . ."

"If only you read the paper, the investigation is focusing on a ransom note that mentioned the situation in the Middle East. A couple of days ago the Brock received an anonymous postcard claiming the Chagall was being held in the cellar of a house in Switzerland that used to be owned by some Nazi bigwig."

"Are you *serious*?"

"The FBI is checking it out with Interpol. That's all I know at this point. As long as your friend Bryan has no ties to the Middle East or to Nazis he should be fine. The inspectors may call him in for one last interview, so tell him to remain calm and bring his lawyer."

"The lawyer I can guarantee. Whether or not he'll remain calm is more doubtful," I said, thinking of Bryan's over-the-top response to something as mundane as toilet tissue hanging the wrong way on the roll. "Thanks, Annette. I appreciate it."

"You bet. And, Annie? Do me a favor?"

"Sure!"

"Forget you know this number unless you're calling about a murder."

I pulled into traffic, frustrated. If I could find the Chagall I could not only clear Bryan, but prove once and for all that Agnes Brock's suspicions of my character were unfounded. I could also cancel Tuesday's date with Michael, who, if he was running true to form, was almost certainly planning something criminal. Besides, I should be concentrating on whatever was going on with my mother, not traipsing around with an art thief, no matter how drop-dead gorgeous.

I was nearly at the entrance to the bridge when I was forced to slam on the brakes to avoid crawling up the rear of a metallic blue minivan that had cut into my lane. The van's *Free Palestine!* bumper sticker reminded me of what Annette had said. Ransom notes demanding peace in the Middle East and postcards hinting at a connection to Nazis in Switzerland had sent the FBI and the police hiving off after nonexistent culprits and diverted suspicion from likelier suspects. Frank had said museum personnel were often behind the theft of minor artworks. Agnes Brock's arrogance toward those in her employ was the stuff of legends, and likely to produce dozens of potential suspects within her own marbled halls.

But I didn't need dozens of suspects. I needed only one. Someone with a grudge against the Brock, access to the museum, and an intimate knowledge of its security system.

Well, duh. I could not believe I had not thought of it before. I would bet the family atelier that I knew who had taken the Chagall.

And I knew just where to find him.

Chapter 9

Museum workers are the unsung heroes of the art establishment, repairing artwork and safeguarding the halls of recognized art all over the world. Spending eight hours a day, every day, looking at and handling art is better training than any fine arts doctoral program in the land.

—*Georges LeFleur, in an interview with*
Smithsonian *magazine*

It took me twenty minutes to get across town to the Brock Museum and another ten to find a semilegal parking space. I forked over the five-dollar fee to the bored young man behind the glass at the entrance booth and handed my ticket to the docent at the turnstile. She looked like the universal grandmother: plump, bespectacled, and pink-cheeked. The name tag on her flowered nylon blouse read *Esther! Here to Help!*

I grinned. She beamed.

"Do you know where I might find a security guard named Carlos Jimenez?" I asked.

"Oh dear," she said with a shake of her head, the smile falling from her face. "I'm afraid I don't know them fellers. You might ask over there." She pointed to the security kiosk in a corner of the entrance hall and ripped my ticket in two. "Enjoy your visit!"

The kiosk was all of four feet square, with barely enough room for a cluttered desk, an old-fashioned intercom, and a black telephone. A security guard was hidden behind the sports section of this morning's *Chronicle*, his feet propped on the desk, only the bald spot on his head visible. Apparently the recent theft of a painting had not put the Brock's security force on a heightened state of alert.

I cleared my throat.

The poor man jumped straight out of his chair, knocking over a Styrofoam cup and splashing coffee all over the desktop. "Jesus Christ!"

"Samantha Jagger," I said, using my friend Sam's name in case Agnes Brock had issued a memo with *Annie Kincaid* circled in red and bisected with a slash mark. I handed him several brown paper napkins from a pile on the desk. "Sorry if I startled you. I'm looking for Carlos Jimenez."

"Chuck?" he barked as he mopped up the puddles. "Whaddaya wanna see him for?"

"I'm Chuck's . . . niece," I improvised. My paint-splattered overalls added ten pounds to my butt but took ten years off my age, and I emphasized the suggestion of youth by pitching my voice higher. "I'm here to see the botanicals exhibit? 'Cause I'm an art history major at SF State? And the last time I was here I didn't visit Tío Carlos? And when I got home my mama just about smacked me for not giving him a hug 'cause we're so proud of him, working at the Brock—"

"Yeah, whatever," the guard interrupted, consulting a clipboard hanging on a nail in the wall. "Chuck's downstairs, in Antiquities."

Hurrying down the central stairs and through the galleries, I spared a minute to appreciate two ancient Egyptian sarcophagi and some meticulous Roman mosaics but detoured through the Bauhaus furniture exhibit to avoid the Renaissance galleries. It would have taken me hours to savor the richly detailed portraits by Bronzino, Carlo Dolci, and Antonello de Messina; the lush, idyllic landscapes of Giorgione and Francesco Guardi; and the colorful still lifes of Bimbi and Luca Forte. And that wasn't even including the charming genre paintings by the likes of Caracci and Strozzi.

I might not appreciate Cubism, but I could recognize the work of Giovanni Domenico Tiepolo at fifty paces.

I reached the Antiquities gallery and roamed the rooms searching for a stout, barrel-chested man with merry brown eyes, jet-black hair, and a neatly clipped mustache. Carlos Jimenez and I had become buddies during my stint at the museum, brought together by a mutual dislike of aristocratic pretension in general and of Agnes Brock in particular. Carlos was the sort of man who bragged about his wife's cooking, horsed around in the yard with his kids, and mowed the lawn for the old lady next door. He dreamed of one day opening a restaurant in his hometown of Cerrito Lindo, near the Mexican border. After decades haunting the Brock's galleries, Carlos had become an art connoisseur who took his job very seriously. Accusing him of stealing the Chagall was going to take some finesse.

I finally spotted him near the Pre-Columbian ceramics, giving directions to a visitor in search of the African American quilts exhibit. His eyes widened when he saw me.

"Heya, Carlos," I said. "Long time no see. How are you?"

"Sure, okay. I'm okay." His eyes slewed away from me and he clasped his hands in front of his belly.

"I was hoping we could talk. Any chance you could take a break?"

"Gee, Annie, I'm afraid not. I'm on duty, you see."

Just then another uniformed security guard walked up. "Here to relieve you, Jimenez," the man said. "Lucky dog."

Carlos looked more hangdog than lucky. "Thanks, Roy," he mumbled, and strode away briskly as I trotted along behind.

Just past a display of jade and silver Mayan ceremonial masks, he halted and unlocked a door marked *Museum Staff Only*. Ever the gentleman, he waved me through before hurrying down the empty corridor. We reached an employee exit, where Carlos placed his right thumb on a small scanner to the left of the door, releasing the electronic lock.

"Wow," I said, impressed. "When was that installed? Thumbprint scanners, that's really something."

He ignored me, barreling down the sidewalk until stopping abruptly a block away from the museum. "What do you want?" he demanded fiercely, hands on his hips. We had shared so many easy laughs in the past that his belligerence took me by surprise.

"Well—"

"How much?"

"What?" I asked, puzzled. "I don't—"

"I should have known it wouldn't be this easy," he muttered, his eyes searching the quiet residential street. What was he looking for? A police dragnet? An armed accomplice? A Starbucks?

"Listen, Annie. Whatever you do just leave my son out of this."

"Your son?" Now I was really confused. "What does—"

"Leave him out of this!" Papa Bear loomed over me, prepared to defend his cub.

I took a step backwards. This was not the Carlos Jimenez I had known.

"Look, Carlos, I'm not here about your son," I said rapidly. "I'm here about the Chagall. The police think a friend of mine may be an accomplice in the theft, but we both know that's not true. I'm hoping the painting can be returned so my friend won't take the fall for a crime he didn't commit. That's *all*."

For the first time since we'd left the museum Carlos looked me in the eye. "Put it *back*? Are you nuts? I can't do that."

"Why not? Have you already sold it?"

"You think I sell stolen paintings?" He sounded deeply offended. "Is *that* what you think of me?"

"That is the usual procedure . . ." What was with these hypersensitive art thieves, anyway?

"It's not like that. But I can't return the paintings. Now, please. It's dangerous for me to even be seen with you."

He started to walk away, but I followed. "Carlos! What is going on? Why can't you be seen with me?"

"Everyone knows you're trouble, Annie," he replied more calmly. "Every time there's a problem you seem to be around."

This from a man who just confessed to grand theft.

Wait a minute. Did Carlos say *paintings*—as in more than one?

"Did you take more than the Chagall?"

"Stop it, Annie," he implored, his voice low. "The Brock is not hurt. No one is hurt, not really. It's none of your concern. For your own good, you must stop asking questions. Now leave me alone." He spun on his heel, walked quickly down the street, and disappeared around the corner.

I watched him go, baffled. Art thieves sold the art they stole; that was the whole point of the criminal exercise. So why had Carlos been so insulted by the suggestion? What had he meant by paintings, plural? And what did his son have to do with this? I presumed he meant his eldest boy, Juan, who had been a gawky teenager the last time we met, years ago. Had Juan grown into an art thief?

I needed some answers, fast. This was a job for a serious gossip. This was a job for Naomi Gregorian.

Back to the Brock I went, skipping up the monumental front steps, breezing past the ticket booth, and making a beeline straight to Esther.

I grinned. She beamed.

"I'm so glad you're still here!" I said. "I went out the wrong door, silly me, and need to get back in."

Esther gazed at me kindly. "Hello, dear. Do you have a ticket?"

"I gave it to you just a few minutes ago. Remember?"

She shook her head. "No, I don't think so."

"I was looking for a security guard."

"The security booth's right over there, dear." She gestured toward the kiosk. "But I can't let you in without a ticket."

"But—" I swore under my breath, returned to the ticket booth, and shelled out another five bucks. Normally I didn't mind giving money to museums, but I made an exception for the Brock. I glowered as I handed Esther the new ticket. She gave me a shaky, wounded look.

I felt like a worm. That look was going to haunt me all night.

"Sure do love the Brock!" I exclaimed. "Thanks so much for your help, Esther! It's always just great to see you!"

Esther's mild blue eyes lit up again, and she smiled sweetly.

I sauntered over to the archway that led to the museum's

offices and workrooms, unlatched the velvet cordon, slipped past, reattached it, and hurried down the paneled corridor. Sure enough, Naomi was in her office, hunched over her computer.

"Naomi!"

"Ann? What are you doing here?" she asked, closing the Web page she had been reading. Naomi's pale, nearly lashless eyes blinked behind oversized tortoiseshell frames, her frizzy red hair was captured in a lopsided French knot, and she was dressed in a boxy brown corduroy jumper that appeared to have been purchased from an outdoorsy catalogue. It had no style to speak of but was perfect for chopping kindling.

"Oh, you know, taking in the new botanicals exhibit," I lied. "Kudos to the curator."

"I'll tell her. What do you want?"

"I just bumped into Carlos Jimenez," I said, plopping into a hard wooden chair. "I haven't seen him for ages. He mentioned something about his son . . . ?"

"Juan? Yes, that was unfortunate. But if he can't be depended on to clean Mrs. Brock's office properly then he has no place here. Is that what you wanted to ask, Ann?"

"Nope. Here's what I wanted to ask: How many thefts has the museum suffered over the last year or so?" When it came to dealing with Naomi, I had learned, sometimes blunt was best.

"I can't imagine what you're referring to," she dodged. "And I'm very busy."

"I'll make it quick, then. Has the Brock been losing artwork?"

Naomi pressed her thin lips together. "And how is that any of your concern?"

"I may know someone who could get it back." Since everyone already assumed I was a player in the art underworld I figured I might as well take advantage of it. "But before I approach my, um, *friend*, I have to know the whole story. No way am I getting my guy involved without some assurances."

There was a long pause. Just when I was convinced she had decided to call Security—or, worse yet, Agnes Brock—she spoke. "There have been some losses, yes. Most of the items were not on display and no one realized they were gone until the annual inventory last month."

"What's missing?"

"A few paintings by minor artists, as well as several of the less important Pre-Columbian artifacts. Nothing especially important or valuable."

"Was a police report filed?" No museum liked to admit when its security had been breached, but a police report would be necessary if the Brock intended to submit an insurance claim.

"The Brock family does not wish to pursue it. The Chagall is a separate matter entirely."

"How do you figure that?"

"Because . . ." she blustered. "Because . . ."

"You're just repeating what you've been told, aren't you?"

"I am not!" Naomi said, snatching up the gauntlet I'd tossed at her feet. She glanced at the open office door and dropped her voice to a whisper. "Just between you, me, and the walls, I don't understand why Mrs. Brock's making such a big deal about the stolen Chagall. It's insured, and the rumor is that she was planning to sell it anyway."

"Sell it? Why?"

"Haven't you heard?" Naomi's voice became more animated. "Agnes Brock and her sister, Ida Cuthbert, had a falling out last year, and Ida's been threatening to sue for a share of the museum. Most of the collections belonged to

Agnes' late husband, Herbert Brock, but a few pieces, like the Chagall, came from the Cuthbert family. The workroom scuttlebutt is that Agnes decided to dump the Chagall, which she never really liked anyway, just to spite her sister. The thief took care of it for her."

"That's so petty."

"You mean that's so Brock."

Naomi and I shared a rare grin. "Anyway, I really should be getting back to work. If you have any information on the stolen Chagall I suggest you contact the police." She turned towards the computer, and logged back onto the Web site, a chat room for fans of J. R. R. Tolkien's *The Lord of the Rings*.

"I see you're really burning the midnight oil there," I teased.

"It's research for an upcoming exhibit," she sniffed. "I'll send you a ticket."

"Thanks," I said, though I wouldn't be holding my breath.

I plodded back to my truck, headed west on Geary, turned right onto Hyde, passed the gleaming dome of City Hall, crossed Market to Eighth, and took the Bryant Street on-ramp towards Oakland. Traffic congealed to a stop at the mouth of the Bay Bridge and, after flirting with indulging in a temper tantrum, I took a few deep yoga-inspired breaths and reflected upon what I had just learned: The Brock Museum was missing some artwork, and Carlos Jimenez was up to his keister in art theft.

Most puzzling was his reaction when I asked if he'd sold the purloined art. I would have understood had he flat-out lied about his role in the theft—given my upbringing that would have been the normal response—but to admit the crime yet deny the profits? That was just nuts.

Traffic inched forward and screeched to a halt again. I

flipped through the radio stations but nothing appealed to me, so I switched it off. Okay, let's say Carlos had been pilfering from the Brock Museum's storage rooms for years. Why would he risk taking a painting from one of the public galleries, where the odds of getting caught skyrocketed? Had it not been for the coincidence of the Stendhal faintings, Carlos would have been arrested and jailed. He had been lucky.

Unbelievably lucky.

Nobody was *that* lucky.

A long time ago my grandfather told me there were three kinds of luck in this world: bad luck, worse luck, and the luck that you made yourself. I was willing to bet Carlos' luck fell into the last category. What were the odds that Carlos *just happened* to change his modus operandi and steal a Chagall at the very moment Bryan and his friends *just happened* to faint in the Modern Masters gallery?

I rested my forehead against the steering wheel and groaned. Michael. Michael was behind this; he had to be. Why else would a world-class art thief be leading a museum tour?

A horn blared and I lifted my head to find that traffic was moving again, threw the truck in gear, popped the clutch, and peeled out. This was the advantage to driving a real working woman's vehicle, I thought as I nosed in front of a shiny red BMW convertible, whose outraged owner gave way as soon as he saw the truck's extensive collection of dings and dents.

The sunlight dimmed when I entered the tunnel at Yerba Buena Island, and it occurred to me that one thing Michael's involvement did not explain was why Carlos had targeted the Chagall. Did it, as Frank had suggested, have personal significance for him? Possibly. But what about the other missing items Naomi had told me about? Why would Carlos take them if he did not intend to sell them?

Of course, Carlos could be lying. Everybody else in my life had been lying to me lately.

Even my mother.

And speaking of whom, where the hell *was* that woman? It was a little after five now, and she had promised to call me after Seamus McGraw's funeral, which should have concluded hours ago. Maybe Mom ran into some old friends and spent the afternoon reminiscing in a Berkeley coffeehouse. I pulled off the freeway at Grand Avenue and tried her cell phone, but her voice mail picked up. We'd agreed to meet at Le Cheval in downtown Oakland at six o'clock, which gave me just enough time to get home, shower, and change.

Unless, of course, my mother needed to be rescued. But how would I know if she did?

I sped home and had just reached the second-floor landing when I heard the phone ringing in my apartment. I bounded up the remaining stairs two at a time, unlocked the door, and flung myself at the phone.

"Annie! Baby doll!"

"Bryan, is everything all right?" I imagined Bryan calling from the bowels of the city jail, clad in an ugly orange jumpsuit, a stern-faced Irish cop twirling a baton as he held the receiver of an old-fashioned, heavy black phone to Bryan's ear. What I lacked in actual knowledge of San Francisco's penal system I made up for with a fevered imagination.

"I'm just fine, honey. But you sound all out of breath. I didn't interrupt anything, um, *enjoyable*, did I?"

"Very funny," I said, collapsing onto the futon couch that my mother had expertly refolded. "I told you, I've embraced celibacy as a form of ritual purification."

"If you've embraced celibacy, honey, it's because you're *still* not gettin' any." He sighed. "What am I gonna do with you?"

"Throw me to the lions?"

"Lions like juicy meat, baby doll. Not vinegary old maids."

"Bryan! I am not a—" I heard him laughing. "Smart aleck."

"Anyway, the reason I'm calling, sweet cheeks, is because I have some *primo* info about that Pascal fellow." Bryan was plugged into San Francisco's gossip network in a way I could never hope to be. "That assistant he told you about? The one who *supposedly* killed himself? He wasn't gay *at all*. He had a *girlfriend*."

"Just because he had a girlfriend doesn't mean he wasn't gay. It was a long time ago, after all. Maybe he was afraid to come out of the closet."

"I don't think so, honey. There were a *lot* of rumors at the time that the 'suicide' had been helped along, if you know what I mean. What better way to throw the police off the scent than by playing the gay card? Make it seem more likely that he would kill himself?"

"I don't know . . ."

"Look, baby doll, all I'm saying is, ask around. I had a very informative talk with the girlfriend. She's a doll. Her married name's Francine Maggio and she lives out in the Avenues. She said to tell you to call and set up a date for tea."

I jotted down Francine's number and stuck it in my wallet, though I doubted I would call. I'd already decided not to bother Pascal anymore, and so far as I could tell, his former assistant had nothing to do with me or my mother.

Stepping out of my grungy overalls, I played my phone messages. My grandfather had called to assure me there was no need to worry, everything was "just superb!" and to express his best wishes for a lovely, interesting evening at the Hillsborough cocktail party with "ze dashing Monsieur Bruuuks." He said nothing about Mom and did not leave a call-back number. Thanks for nothing, Gramps.

There was a call from Evangeline, who said she needed to talk to me about something important, apologized for setting off my alarm, and asked me to call back as soon as possible. She did not leave a number, either. Did no one go to secretarial school anymore?

Next was a call from Frank, asking in clipped tones if there was a problem with my studio's burglar alarm. Apparently the gratitude felt this morning had dissipated like a San Francisco fog. Relieved that the Picasso was off my hands and out of my studio, I erased that message, too.

There was nothing from my mother. I dialed her cell phone again. Voice mail. I tried Pascal's studio on the off chance Evangeline would answer. Nothing.

I glanced at my watch and hurried down the hall to the bathroom. After a quick shower I dressed in a long purple velvet skirt, a stretchy celery-colored tank top, and a chartreuse jacket that fell in soft folds to my hips. I topped off the ensemble with a feathery, multicolored scarf that my sister, Bonnie, had knitted for me for my birthday, a pair of long beaded earrings, and a touch of mascara and lipstick. I pulled on a pair of black stockings and slipped into ankle-high boots. My mother would raise a delicate eyebrow when she caught sight of me, but if I had to confront mysterious men in black SUVs again I wanted to be comfortable. I snatched up my black leather shoulder bag and thundered down the stairs.

Le Cheval was on Clay between Tenth and Eleventh, a brisk fifteen-minute walk from my apartment. During the weekdays the streets and sidewalks of downtown Oakland were clogged with hordes of government employees and businesspeople, who crowded into the coffeehouses, sandwich shops, and supply stores. After five o'clock these folks disappeared into the suburbs and Oakland's formerly grand downtown felt more like a ghost town. The Merchants Association had been working hard to change that, so as I crossed Broadway's faded glory and hurried past Old Oakland's renovated Victorian town houses, I was not surprised to hear the strains of a rock band at the Washington Arms pub competing with a jazz trio at Jesso's Seafood Café. San Francisco was chic and Berkeley was funky, but Oakland was down-to-earth and friendly, and its fierce partisans, like me, were sure it was on the cusp of a rebirth.

Le Cheval was mobbed, the cavernous space sufficient to accommodate only a fraction of those in search of good Vietnamese food served in a lively ambience, and as a regular I had known to reserve a table as soon as the restaurant opened this morning. A tiny woman in black jeans and a sparkly red top led me to a table in the center of the room where my mother waited, dressed in a navy blue linen suit and matching Hermès scarf. Beverly LeFleur Kincaid was, as always, cool and elegant as she sipped a cup of steaming green tea and smiled graciously at all and sundry.

All, that is, except her youngest daughter.

"Anna Jane Kincaid," she scolded as I sat down. "I believe I told you to leave Robert Pascal alone."

"Hi, Mom. Good to see you, too," I said, relieved to find her unscathed, even if she was annoyed. "Something to drink?"

We placed our drink orders, decided to start with an appetizer, and settled in for what promised to be a very trying conversation.

"You don't understand, Annie," my mother said, her slim hand grasping mine. "This is very important."

"Then help me to understand. What is going *on*? Who were those men in the SUV last night? By the way, why haven't you been answering your cell phone, like *you* promised? I've been worried sick."

"Oh, you know how it is," she said, chagrined. "The battery went dead. These cell phones aren't as convenient as they're cracked up to be."

I laughed, and she joined in. It was a relief to be reminded that we had something in common. Lately I had begun to wonder if daughters were from Venus and mothers were from Alpha Centauri.

A waiter brought my *ca phé sua da*, an espressolike coffee that was mixed with sweetened condensed milk and poured over crushed ice. It tasted like a high-test milkshake, and I took a moment to revel in the sweet caffeine bliss.

"So. Mom. What are you doing here? And don't give me that 'Gee, I just needed to get away from Asco for a few days' baloney. It's almost Thanksgiving. Why aren't you busy decorating?"

"Oh, my. That reminds me. I haven't started marinating the rum cake yet. . . ."

"Okay, my fault. Let's stay on subject, shall we?" I said, interrupting her. "What the *hell* was going on between you and Seamus McGraw?"

"Language, young lady, *language*," she scolded, and I wondered, for the thousandth time, how it was that my mother had been raised by my rogue of a grandfather and yet seemed untouched by the coarser aspects of life. Then again, *she* had raised *me* and look how I'd turned out.

Mom took a deep breath. "If you must know, Seamus and I, were, you see . . . we . . ."

"You what?" I said, almost afraid to ask. I did not want to learn that my mother had not been the loyal wife I had

always believed her to be, not because I would love her any
less for being human, but for entirely selfish reasons: I
needed to believe that love could last because I hoped to
find it for myself one day. I was equally afraid that she was
in over her head but would not tell me about it out of a mis-
guided desire to protect me. I'd kept her in the dark about
my wilder exploits, partly because I didn't think she would
understand but mostly because there were some things a
red-blooded young woman did not want to share with her
mother. I mean, geez.

She took a shaky breath. "It was a different time, Annie.
It was Berkeley in the sixties."

"Uh-huh," I responded, dreading where this was going.

"Don't *uh-huh* me, young lady. You *asked*." She gazed
across the room at the huge mural of horses, the restaurant's namesake. "I put an end to it long ago."

A waiter brought a plate of *cha gio*, deep-fried rolls
served with lettuce, mint leaves, and *nuớc mam*, a salty fish
sauce. They went untouched.

"Put an end to what?"

"Seamus and I . . . well, all of us, your father and Seamus and Pascal and I . . . we were all friends back in the
day." She busied herself arranging lettuce leaves but did
not eat anything.

"Friends?"

"Good friends."

"What *kind* of good friends? The kind who posed nude
for one another in the heyday of bohemian Berkeley?"
Tears glinted in her eyes and I regretted my snide remark.
"Mom, I'm sorry, I . . ."

"I miss him," she murmured, dropping the lettuce and
dabbing at the tears that coursed down her smooth, powdered cheeks. "We haven't spoken in years, but I miss him.
I know his work had become violent lately, but he was such

a gentle man, deep down." Her cornflower blue eyes held mine. "What happened, Annie? How could Seamus have died like that? *Why?*"

"I don't know," I whispered, surprised that she was asking me, the daughter who never had the answers to anything. "Mom, I—"

"Good evening, Annie," a deep voice interrupted.

"Why, Frank," I said, surprised. "What are you . . . ?"

"Ingrid and I were having dinner with some friends," he said, looking relaxed in a charcoal-gray wool Italian suit.

I whipped my head around and scanned the room, hoping for a bona-fide Ingrid sighting.

"She just left."

"Of course she did. Oh, um, Mom, this is Frank DeBenton, my landlord. Frank, this is my mother, Beverly Kincaid."

"How do you do, Mrs. Kincaid?" Frank asked, as my mother shot questioning glances at me. I ignored them.

"Quite well, thank you, Mr. DeBenton," she replied. "Won't you join us?"

"Please, call me Frank," he said, taking a seat despite my glare.

I enjoyed serendipitous social encounters, but I was dying to learn what my mother was up to and she would say nothing in front of Frank. For the second night in a row our heart-to-heart chat had been preempted by a handsome but unsuitable man.

"Sorry about the burglar alarm, Frank," I said. "I think a friend may have set it off accidentally. I'll talk to her about it."

"I'd appreciate that," Frank said. "But enough shop talk. What are you lovely ladies drinking? May I propose some champagne?"

"No, you may not," I said.

"We'd love some!" my mother said.

Frank ordered a bottle of Veuve Clicquot, winked at me, and turned to my mother. "It seems I've been a little bit slow to put two and two together. Do you mean to tell me that you are related to the Asco Kincaids?"

"We aren't exactly royalty, Frank," I grumbled.

"I never doubted that, Annie," he replied, his cool brown eyes sweeping over me. I was pretty sure I'd just been insulted, but since my mother was at the table I held my tongue.

"Indeed we are," my mother interjected, breaking the tension. "From Asco, I mean."

"What a wonderful coincidence," Frank said, watching as the waiter poured champagne into three crystal flutes. *"A votre santé!"*

"Cheers!" my mother said gaily, clinking her glass against Frank's.

"Here's mud in your eye," I mocked, channeling Evangeline.

"As I was saying," Frank continued, "I've been negotiating with a Dr. Harold Kincaid to transport art to a conference to be hosted by the college in Asco next summer. I didn't realize you were related to the professor, Annie."

"He's my father," I acknowledged and, in view of the beautiful smile my mother kept flashing Frank, added, "And her *husband*."

"Isn't that something, your knowing my Harold," Mom said. "What a small world."

"We've only spoken on the phone," Frank replied, "but I hope to meet him soon."

Although my mother had at least fifteen years on Frank, I had to admit they looked good together. Both were elegant, graceful, and unfailingly refined. My father, in contrast, was more like me: clothes rumpled, hair askew, and mind usually somewhere else. I felt a sudden and unprecedented surge of empathy for good ol' Dad.

Frank and my mother looked at each other for a beat too long and I lost patience with the both of them. "What are you doing here, Frank, and why won't you go away?"

"Anna Jane!" Mom gasped.

Frank smiled. "I apologize if I'm interrupting something."

"You most certainly are not," my mother insisted. "My daughter seems to have misplaced her manners, that's all."

"Your daughter has many charms, Mrs. Kincaid—"

"Beverly."

"Beverly, thank you. Manners, alas, may not be foremost," he said, his warm brown eyes meeting mine. "But she makes up for it with talent and personality. You must be very proud."

My mother all but melted into a puddle. I wanted to rip his face off.

"Alas, I'm afraid I must run," Frank said, finishing off his champagne. "It was a pleasure meeting you, Beverly. Enjoy your dinner, ladies."

With one last smile and a nod to me, he left.

My mother glared as I bit defiantly into a spring roll. "What's gotten into you, young lady? I happened to notice there was no ring on his finger. It wouldn't kill you to make an effort once in a while. He looks like a successful man. You could do worse."

"Mom, I'm happy with my life the way it is. And need I point out that you said almost those very words last night, too?"

"That was before you told me what Michael did for a living," she chided me. "Are you saying this one's an art thief, *too*?"

"Keep it down, Mom," I said, glancing over my shoulder.

"I'm simply saying that for a girl without a date all weekend you seem to have a number of *very* handsome men expressing interest."

"Frank isn't interested in me, Mom. He was just being . . . Frank. He has a girlfriend; you heard him. Anyway, let's get back to our conversation. Do you know someone named Francine Maggio?"

She spat out some tea.

"I take it that's a yes?"

Two waiters flanked our table, set out clean dinner plates, and laid before us a fragrant, heaping dish of lemongrass chicken and a hot pot of rice, meat, and vegetables aptly named hot-pot stew.

The moment they left my mother reached across the table and gripped my hand. "Annie, how can I make this any plainer? Leave this alone. Do you understand me? For my sake as well as for yours." She took a deep breath and sat back in her chair. "Why don't we get this food to go? I think we're both exhausted."

"Mom, I—"

"I won't discuss this further, Anna. I'm going home tomorrow. I have a million things to prepare for Thanksgiving. The rum cake, of course, plus that yam-and-marshmallow dish your father loves so much. I do hope you will change your mind and join us. Just because I invited Javier and Tiffany. . . ."

"He's my *ex-fiancé*, Mom," I protested. "And I can't stand his new wife. Don't you think it might be a little awkward with me there?"

Javier was a good guy and all, but at some point during the visit he and my father would start crooning to old Julio Iglesias albums, crying in their holiday beers, and reminding me of the fortune Javier was making by selling grooming products to Sir Snufflebums and his pampered ilk.

I attributed our brief engagement to an excess of wine coolers, but in my parents' eyes Javier would forever be "the one that got away." I just wished he would go ahead and get away instead of hanging out with my parents on major holidays.

Mom kept yammering on about yams, and I stopped listening. While the waiters packed up our untouched food we argued over who would pay the bill only to discover that Frank had taken care of it. We drove home in silence. All in all, it was an uncomfortable ending to a very long day.

But it was made much worse by the death threat a few minutes later.

Chapter 10

Salvador Dalí is said to have signed tens of thousands of blank pieces of paper for lithographs he had never seen, much less created. For this brilliant attempt to evade poverty he has been dubbed a forger of his own work.

—*Georges LeFleur, quoted in* El País *newspaper*

"Stop asking questions," a sinister voice growled when I answered my cell phone. I let my mother into my apartment and lingered on the landing, prepared to deal harshly with a certain Bosnian friend of mine who adored sophomoric jokes.

"Pete, is that you?" I demanded. "Stop fooling around."

There was a pause.

"It's not Pete," the voice said, and I thought I detected a slight Spanish accent.

"Then who is it?" My heart started to pound as I realized this might be an actual threat. That sort of thing rarely happened to faux finishers.

"Stop asking questions or you will die."

"What is this about?" I was scared but also a little angry. "Have the guts to identify yourself."

"You know what this is about," the voice replied. *"And little girls shouldn't be so rude."*

A bully *and* a sexist. Could it be Pascal? "If I knew what you were talking about, I wouldn't ask."

"Fuck off," the voice whispered fiercely, and the line went dead.

Now, that sounded like Pascal, but I was sure it was not his voice. Besides, he was not the only jerk in the world who swore like a sailor. My cell phone indicated the telephone number was "not available" and when I hit "return call," nothing happened. Could it have been Carlos? Threatening phone calls seemed out of character for him, but then again so did stealing. How well did I know the man, after all?

I heard my mother bustling about the apartment as she packed for her trip and prepared for bed. I enjoyed her company, but this time I would be glad to see Mom head home.

Speaking of which—promises to one's mother be damned, Professor Harold Kincaid needed to know what was going on. What if Asco were not as safe as I'd been assuming? What if the mystery caller had intended to threaten her but called me because her cell phone's battery was dead?

I dialed my father but disconnected before it rang. Was I prepared to provoke a crisis in my parents' forty-year marriage? From what little Mom had told me, her affair with Seamus McGraw, or whatever it was, had been over years ago. So what was I going to say? "Hi, Dad—it's Annie. Listen, I think you should know that Mom was up to something with some sculptor guy who's now dead. No, I don't know anything more. No, I don't know why she hasn't told you. No, I guess I don't know anything really. Good talkin' to you!"

That would not be helpful.

I knew one thing, though: My mother had impeccable table manners. She would not have spat her tea across the table tonight unless the name Francine Maggio meant something to her. And I was going to find out what that was.

Taking a chance that it was not too late for a social call, I reached into my wallet and found the number Bryan had given me earlier. A cultured voice answered, and Francine Maggio suggested I come for tea tomorrow at four o'clock. I felt a bit skittish going alone—for all I knew the jilted lover of a suicidal sculptor was wanted in three states for feeding strychnine-laced scones to nosy strangers—and asked if I could bring Bryan along.

When I finally entered the apartment I found my mother tucked into her futon bed with a steaming mug of herb tea and a thick paperback book.

"Everything all right, dear?" she called out.

"Yeah, sure, Mom. I was just chatting with Bryan."

"That Bryan's such a nice man," she said. "So steady and reliable."

"He's a peach all right. Can I get you anything?"

"No, thank you. I'm just going to curl up with my tea and Maeve Binchy, and get some sleep. I've got a long trip ahead of me tomorrow."

Asco was a college town in the heart of California's great Central Valley, three hours away and straight up I-5, a freeway so flat it might have been engineered by a kindergartner. A native Californian would not think twice about making the drive. But Beverly LeFleur Kincaid had grown up in Paris, where an automobile was a luxury. She had gotten her driver's license in her midthirties and had never become comfortable behind the wheel.

"I'll say good night, then," I said, kissing her soft cheek.

"Good night, darling," she replied, hugging me tightly. "And, Annie—please trust that I know what I'm doing. Stay away from Robert Pascal."

I gave her a noncommittal smile, walked down the short hall to my bedroom, changed into an oversized football jersey, and flipped on my secondhand thirteen-inch TV. I had extended the reach of the rabbit ears antenna with bits of twisted aluminum foil but still received only two and a half channels, none of which was showing anything remotely interesting tonight. At last I popped in an old Hitchcock movie and drifted off to sleep.

Twelve hours later I staggered down the hall to find that my mother had departed. She left a note near my coffee mug thanking me for my hospitality and urging me yet again to reconsider joining the family for Thanksgiving. She had also cleaned out the refrigerator and scrubbed the kitchen until it sparkled.

I brewed coffee, heated up last night's Vietnamese food, sat at my kitchen table, and munched as I mulled over yesterday's phone messages. Was the fair Evangeline somehow connected to last night's threatening phone call? How was I supposed to call her when she hadn't left a number? Just for the heck of it I dialed Pascal's studio.

No answer.

I took another bite of fragrant rice. Evangeline's message had sounded urgent. As much as I disliked the idea, I would have to swing by Pascal's studio one last time and hope she answered the door.

Also on today's itinerary was a trip to Marble World, a marble and granite warehouse south of San Francisco in Burlingame. Reluctant as I was to make time for actual work-related activities, I was a week late ordering stone for a Beaux Arts home remodel that had evolved into the Monster that Ate Pacific Heights. The general contractor had left several increasingly frantic messages on my business phone and I hated to hear a grown man cry.

I rinsed my dish and trudged down the hall to dress. As I pulled on my trusty overalls, I felt something hard in one of the pockets. It was the chunk of marble I had swiped from Pascal's studio. Creamy white and beige, with a few streaks and splotches, it looked like a million other pieces of marble. Turning it over, I stroked its rough, cool surface. Why would Pascal make a copy of *Head and Torso*? And if he had, was it any business of mine?

The weather today matched my mood—dreary and overcast, with a decidedly autumnal chill. San Francisco was always colder than Oakland, flanked as it was by the Pacific on one side and the Bay on the other, so I grabbed my navy blue wool pea coat as I ran out the door, stopped for a tank of some of the priciest gas in the nation, fought my way across the crowded Bay Bridge, and headed south on the Bayshore Freeway. Ten minutes later San Francisco International Airport appeared on the left, and shortly thereafter I pulled off the freeway and headed toward a group of cinderblock buildings huddled on the edge of the Bay.

Marble World was a vast and undistinguished warehouse, a discreet sign on the front door the only indication that it imported stone rather than medical supplies or rubber flip-flops from Thailand.

I was climbing out of the truck when I spotted a contractor I knew emerging from the freight entrance. Josh Reynolds had been assigned to my volunteer crew last winter for Community Builders, a local do-good organization that fixed up the houses of elderly and disabled homeowners. Josh lived with a big brown dog named Mac in a house he had built himself in the woodsy Berkeley hills. With his longish sandy blond hair, tie-dyed T-shirt, and gold stud earring, he was an unrepentant hippie with the ripped physique of a construction worker, and even on a hot day, dripping with sweat, he always smelled delicious.

Distracted by this vision of masculine pulchritude, I tripped on the curb and nearly sprawled on the blacktop. Strong, tanned hands grabbed me by the upper arms to steady me.

"Hey there, boss lady," Josh said, concern written across his handsome face. "You okay?"

"Fine, thanks. Do I know how to make an entrance, or what?"

"I was thinking about you the other day," he said with a smile.

"Really?" Josh had been thinking about *me*?

"I was having lunch at the Chambers café. Did you do the mural there, the Tuscan vineyard scene with the dancing harlequins?"

"Sure did," I said, flattered that he recognized my work.

"Your style is distinctive," Josh said, and nodded toward the warehouse. "I was helping a client pick out some slate for a patio. How 'bout you?"

"I'm looking for stone for a Beaux Arts palace in the City," I replied, my senses acutely aware of how close we were standing. Josh's straightforward sweetness had always been alluring, especially when compared to such complicated men as Michael and Frank. And then, too, there was that gorgeous body.

"I like the Beaux Arts style," he said with a lazy smile. "Gloria's got some new blue granite from Brazil. Check it out; it's gorgeous."

"I sure will! I *love* the blues!" I realized I was babbling. "I mean, it sounds good."

Josh leaned against the nose of his dusty truck and

crossed tanned arms over a broad, muscular chest. In his well-worn jeans and leather work boots, Josh looked like an ad for the kind of cigarettes only the manliest of manly men smoked before coughing to death from lung cancer.

"So, how've you been?" he asked. "The last time we talked you'd had a bit of an adventure. Something involving the Brock Museum?"

"Yeah, well, usually my life's not that exciting," I said, dodging the question. My name had made the papers in connection with the Caravaggio fiasco, increasing my fame, or my infamy, more than I cared to think about.

"Guess you artists lead pretty interesting lives, huh?"

"Well, you know how it is." I shrugged. *You have no idea*, I thought.

"Get out much these days?"

"Out? You mean . . . Oh, um, no. Not really." Did he just ask what I think he just asked?

"Me neither."

"No? I thought you were with Misty? Cindy? Glinda?"

Last spring Josh had brought his girlfriend to the Community Builders project. A curvy, petulant blonde, she'd looked delectable in her teeny T-shirt and form-fitting overalls. Since she had no skills, other than the obvious, I sent her to work in the garden, where she lasted all of ten minutes before flopping down in the shade of a tree and nursing a wee blister.

We didn't exactly hit it off.

"'Glinda'?" Josh asked. "Wasn't she a witch in *The Wizard of Oz*?"

Oops. Now he was going to think I was a rhymes-with-witch. Which I probably was, though not on purpose. Which could be worse. Maybe it was just as well there was no romance in my foreseeable future, I sighed. I probably should not be allowed to reproduce.

"Yeah, but Glinda was the *good* witch."

"That's right. Anyway, we broke up last summer."

"Oh? I'm, uh, sorry." Not hardly.

"It was time. Past time, in fact." Josh watched the sailboats skimming across the whitecaps on the bay before turning his beautiful blue gaze on me. "Annie, I was wondering . . . Would you like to have dinner sometime? Maybe catch a movie?"

I was suddenly, deeply, and profoundly grateful that I had taken the time to comb my hair this morning. "That would be *great*."

"How about this week? I'm working in a soup kitchen Thanksgiving morning and going to my sister's house in Concord for dinner. But I'll be home after that. Or, if you don't have plans for Thanksgiving, you'd be welcome to join us."

Have Thanksgiving dinner with a hunky contractor instead of with my mysterious mother, my absentminded father, my clueless ex-fiancé and his plastic new wife? All my decisions should be this hard.

"We're pretty informal," Josh assured me. "They tease me about being a vegetarian and I tease them about watching football, and we all eat too much and play with the dogs and the kids. Not too exciting, I guess."

"Sounds like it's just my speed, actually," I said, delighted. "Can I bring anything?"

"Nope, we've got it covered. Why don't I swing by your place around three thirty? That should get us there in plenty of time. Let me just get your info."

He scribbled my home address and phone numbers on the back of one of my business cards. Josh had my "info." Had I been thirteen I would have giggled.

"Okeydoke," I said, and winced. Maybe I *was* thirteen.

"Stay out of trouble, now," Josh said with a wink and climbed into his truck.

I shot him a look. What did he mean by that? *Calm down, Annie*, I scolded myself as I waved good-bye. *It's just an expression.*

Sure, it was easy for Josh to say stay out of trouble, I groused as I entered the warehouse. *He* probably never had to protect multimillion-dollar Picassos from sexy art thieves, or hold out-of-control stakeouts in the hallways of recalcitrant sculptors, or help his grandfather the art forger evade Interpol.

The receptionist smiled and waved me towards Gloria Cabrera's office. Although Gloria looked scarcely thirty, with a plump physique and bountiful dark hair, she had celebrated turning what she called "the big four oh" last summer with a barbeque for her biggest clients and a few hangers-on like me. Gloria knew stone the way Ben & Jerry knew ice cream, and if the shiny new Mercedes convertible in her parking spot were any indication, the stone business was booming.

"Hey, girlfriend, what's up?" she asked in perfect, unaccented English, though she had just been speaking in rapid-fire Spanish to two of the warehouse workers.

"Countertops for a client in the City," I explained. "Something special."

"The stone's thataway," she said, handing some papers to the receptionist and pointing to a pair of double doors. "Let me know if you have any questions."

Customers were not usually allowed into the warehouse unescorted—one false move around the heavy stone slabs could prove lethal—but those whom Gloria trusted were permitted to roam freely through the aisles of marble, granite, limestone, onyx, and slate. The stone slabs were four feet tall and six or seven feet long, one to three inches thick, and weighed many hundreds of pounds each. The warehouse workers moved them with forklifts and a system of specially fabricated pulleys and winches suspended from the steel I beams high overhead. Steel A-frame racks held the slabs upright, and each time I came here I prayed an earthquake would not send the slabs crashing into each other in a deadly game of dominoes.

I lingered for a few minutes admiring a piece of golden Pakistani onyx that had been cut and splayed to resemble a glistening butterfly, before breezing past the granites and making a beeline for the fabulous marbles. My eye was immediately caught by a slab of leafy green stone rife with feathery veins of gold, gray, and black minerals. I was calculating the odds of convincing my conservative client, John Steubing, that it would be perfect for his master bathroom when Gloria walked up.

"Beautiful, isn't it?" she asked.

"Stunning," I agreed. "But I'm afraid it might be a little too much."

"Yeah, it's pricey."

"Cost isn't an issue on this job."

"Now, *that's* a client worth keeping. So what's the problem?"

"Let me put it this way: The client wanted to know what was wrong with a nice piece of linoleum." A successful entrepreneur, John Steubing was a complicated man with simple tastes. It had been a hard-won victory to wrench the Formica catalogue from his grasp.

"Yikes," she said with a grimace. "Hey, guess who was here this morning?"

"Who?"

"Gabe Jennings," she said excitedly. I must have looked blank, because she elaborated. "You know, the quarterback? For the Forty-Niners? The *San Francisco* Forty-Niners?"

"I live in Oakland. I guess that makes me a Raiders fan."

Gloria rolled her eyes. "Babe, *everybody's* heard of Gabe Jennings. Where've you been?"

"Oakland?"

"Look," she said, gesturing toward a large piece of stone. "His autograph."

There, in the marble dust that covered everything in the warehouse, was the signature of Gabe Jennings, Quarterback.

"Cool," I lied. "But how are you going to preserve it?"

"The guys and I were just talking about that," Gloria said. "What do you think? Maybe spray it with a fixative like polyurethane?"

"Maybe," I hedged. "You might want to get him to sign a piece of paper next time, though." My fingers curled around the piece of marble from Pascal's studio, and I decided to get Gloria's opinion. "What is this?"

"That's a chunk of marble, Annie," she said solemnly.

"I know *that*. What can you tell me about it?"

"Looks like travertine, nothing fancy. We've got some over here." She pointed to a slab of similar stone.

"Is there any way to tell the age of something like this?"

"Of stone? Maybe a scientist could run a test or something. Why would you want to, though?"

"Just curious. Okay, well, thanks anyway."

"I can tell you this much," she continued, holding up the piece I had given her. "It was quarried after 1985."

"How do you know?"

"Because the quarry this stone came from wasn't opened until 1985. Before then, this kind of travertine came from quarries in southern Italy and didn't have rust deposits. See the orangy-gold here?" She indicated a rust-colored vein in the marble.

So I was right. Pascal was sculpting a second *Head and*

Torso using marble from the newer quarry. What I could not understand was why. "Gloria, you import stone for Robert Pascal, right?"

"We used to. I haven't heard from Pascal for a while. Frankly, he's a pain in the butt, so who cares if he goes to another supplier? Know what I mean?"

"And you imported for Seamus McGraw, as well? I saw you at Anthony Brazil's reception the other night."

"Like I told the police, I didn't really know him," Gloria said, tight-lipped. "Listen, I'd better get back to my desk. Give a yell when you make up your mind." She scurried down the aisle and disappeared into the front offices.

I watched her go, then turned my attention back to the task at hand, finally settling on a creamy St. Michele fossil stone for the master bath and the blue Brazilian granite for the kitchen countertop. I still wasn't sure about the veined green marble, so I decided to show John Steubing a sample. I hailed a strapping young man driving a forklift and asked him to chip me off a piece. He nodded and his light brown eyes, partially hidden by a curtain of straight, mousy brown hair, focused on my humble chest.

I stood up a little straighter. "Do you know a sculptor named Robert Pascal?"

"Dude's always in here," he said, brushing his hair to one side with long white fingers. He had a sculptor's hands.

"Really? So you guys do all his importing?"

"Sure. We also ship a lot of stuff for him. This stone is so heavy you have to have the right equipment to crate it." He neatly whacked a corner of the green marble with his hammer and handed me a small piece. "We also import sculptures for him to repair."

"Thanks," I said, rubbing my thumb over the slick surface of the polished marble. "Wait a minute. Repair? You mean, not just his own stuff?"

"Yeah, from Mexico, all over. I've done a little work for him myself."

"You've done sculpting repairs for him? Do you know his other assistant, Evangeline?"

"Weird chick from New York? Yeah, I met her."

"You don't happen to know where she lives, do you?" He shook his head. "How often does Pascal get these shipments?"

"Every six weeks or so. There's one due sometime this week, I think. Why?"

"Could you call me when it comes in?"

He looked at me curiously and brushed the hair from his forehead again.

"I'd consider it a personal favor," I said, vamping a little. I rarely used feminine wiles to get what I wanted—partly out of principle but mostly because I wasn't very good at it—but once in a while they were the most obvious means to an end. "I've been working with Pascal on a project and want to take a look before he cleans everything up. You know how it is."

"Okay, sure." He shrugged. His pale fingers took the business card I handed him. "Annie, huh? My name's Derek. Maybe we could have a drink or something sometime, huh?"

Either the overalls were a good look for me, or I was registering off the charts on the pheromone-o-meter, because I'd received more masculine attention today than in the past six months. "Tell you what: You call me when Pascal's shipment arrives and I'll buy *you* a drink, 'kay?" I winked and headed for the front office. Gloria wasn't there, so I placed my stone order with the receptionist and left.

As I jockeyed for lane position on the Bayshore, I thought about what Derek had said. Why would a successful sculptor like Robert Pascal run a repair business? It was not unusual for artists to pick up jobs on the side—look at yours truly—but Pascal seemed to be operating on a large scale. How did he handle the volume of repair work he was taking on, plus create his own art, plus crank out cheap garden statues for the Mischievous Monkey Garden Supply? Even with an assistant or two, it would be a stretch.

Time to find out what Evangeline wanted to tell me.

Twenty minutes later I pulled up in front of Pascal's building. The door to the stairwell that had been open on Sunday was locked tight on Monday, so I went into the Internet company on the first floor and convinced the friendly receptionist to let me in. Kimmy explained as she did so that she had moved here from Tucson to "get in on the whole Internet thing." Kimmy looked to be about twenty-one, said she drove a Mini Cooper, and probably made twice the money I did. Why had I never thought to "get in on the whole Internet thing"? It had never occurred to me, not once, and I *lived* here.

The memory of our party a few days ago could not dispel the gloom of the third-floor hallway. I banged on Pascal's door, waited, and banged again. Then I ducked out of sight of the peephole in case the old ploy worked again. No luck. I pressed my ear against the door but heard nothing. Finally, I began to shout. Loudly.

"Open the door, Pascal! You hear me?" I bellowed. "I want to talk with Evangeline! Evangeline! *Evangeline!*"

At last I heard shuffling inside the studio, and Pascal's voice yelled from behind the door, "Go away! Crazy bitch!"

"Hiya, Bobby," I said, trying to peer in the peephole. "Let me talk to Evangeline and I'll go away."

"Evangeline? Who the hell's Evangeline?"

That was a new approach.

"What do you mean, who's Evangeline? She's your assistant."

"I told you, you stupid bitch, I don't work with assistants. Big pains in the ass, is what they are."

"Okay, fine, whatever you want to call her. Your sister's kid, remember? And what about Derek from Marble World? He said he works for you, too."

"You must be smokin' somethin', toots, 'cause I don't know what you're talking about," Pascal yelled. "And I don't have a sister."

"Whatever. Just let me talk to Evangeline and I'll go."

"There's no one in here but me, buttercup. I don't know anyone named Evangeline or Derek, and I never have. Now go the hell away or I'll call the cops."

My stomach clenched. I didn't know Evangeline's phone number, where she lived, or even her last name. If Pascal denied knowing her, where did that leave me? More to the point, where did that leave Evangeline?

"Listen, you miserable worm," I growled through the door. "You better find Evangeline and fast, because I'm not going to drop this, you hear me?"

"Fuck off."

I heard footsteps shuffle away and a pneumatic drill started to whine. Looked like our high-decibel chat was over. I stomped down the stairs and out to my truck, angry, frustrated, and worried. Try as I might, I could think of no reason why Pascal would deny knowing Evangeline.

Unless he had murdered her and disposed of her body.

I tried to push the thought away. Pascal was a gifted artist. True, he was a curmudgeon and a bit of a potty mouth. But that didn't make him a killer. He was pretty creepy, though. Maybe he'd started his sculpting career by digging up graves and carving human bones. . . .

Get a grip, Annie, I chastised. But my unruly imagination did have a point—how much did I really know about Pascal? What had Evangeline wanted to tell me? Why oh why had she not just said what she wanted to say?

I hated it when that happened in the movies. "I absolutely *must* see you tonight, Reginald, for I, and I alone, know the identity of the ruthless murderer. But I must tell you in person, not over the telephone. Meet me in an abandoned warehouse down at the waterfront at midnight, but be sure to wait until the fog rolls in. In the meantime I will do nothing whatsoever to protect myself." Lo and behold, they wound up dead every time. What was so wrong with saying the criminal's name on the phone? Would murder victims never learn?

I drove to the DeBenton Building, took the stairs two at a time—for the first half a flight, anyway—unlocked the door, tapped in the alarm code, and snatched up the telephone.

"Annie, is this in reference to a homicide?" Inspector Annette Crawford answered without preamble. I was guessing she had caller ID.

"Yes. No. Maybe," I replied. "Honest."

"Mm-hmm."

"Listen, Annette, I really think it might be. This sculptor guy I've been talking to, Robert Pascal? He has an assistant named Evangeline who tried to get in touch with me last night and now she's disappeared."

"What do you mean, 'disappeared?'"

"She's not at his studio."

"Have you checked her residence?"

"I don't know where she lives."

"So what makes you think she's not there?"

Okay. Good question. "Well, here's the weird thing. I just spoke to Pascal and he claims he doesn't know who I'm talking about."

"Pascal doesn't know his own assistant?"

"Exactly! Doesn't that seem suspicious to you?"

"It's strange, but it's not homicide. Maybe she quit. Maybe he fired her. Maybe she ran off with Cirque du Soleil. Lots of possibilities. I have to go."

"Annette, wait—I know I don't have much to go on, but I'm really worried. I can't help thinking that something might have happened to her. It just doesn't feel right."

I heard a long-suffering sigh. "Annie, I can't launch a homicide investigation just because a woman you barely know didn't show up for work—"

"And her boss claims not to know her."

"And her boss claims not to know her. Does anyone else know her? If someone files a missing person's report, we'll keep an eye out. Otherwise, it's not police business. Now, I *have* to go." She hung up.

I glared at the phone and thought some uncharitable thoughts about the evident uselessness of having a friend in the SFPD.

My pique subsided. It was unfair to expect Annette, who had actual dead bodies to investigate, to drop everything because someone whom I had met once had disappeared. Still . . .

As I gazed out the windows and watched the clouds roll across the bay, I heard my grandfather's voice whispering to me: "*Chérie*, a true artist must have a sixth sense, to see what others cannot, to see what is not there to be seen until *you* see it. Trust your sixth sense." True, my grandfather had been speaking of artistic vision, not of missing persons, but I figured it applied here, too. Either way, it gave me courage.

The door swung open, and I jumped three feet in the air, squealing.

So much for courage.

"You okay, love?" Samantha Jagger asked in her lilting Jamaican accent. Sam crafted gorgeous handmade jewelry in her studio down the hall. A decade my senior, she was hip yet sophisticated in an indigo and magenta batik-print oversized blouse, black silk pants, and a deep blue turban. The same outfit would have made me look like a clown.

"I'm fine," I replied as we hugged. Her elaborate breast-plate clanked softly and I caught a whiff of patchouli and sandalwood oils. "Just a little preoccupied. What's up?"

"I wanted to congratulate you on getting that sculpture returned."

"What sculpture?"

"*Head and Torso.*" She held out the *Chronicle*'s Arts and Leisure section and pointed to a black-and-white photograph. "Mary told me all about what she's calling *The Party Hearty in the Hallway.* There's something in there about the Stendhal Syndrome, too. It's been sweeping the City."

I took the paper and read:

Norman and Janice Hewett are thrilled to announce the return of their much-missed sculpture Head and Torso *just in time for their annual Thanksgiving Day reception for the San Francisco Symphony. As the lovely Mrs. Hewett, née Janice Bullock, explained, "We missed* Head and Torso *so much, you have no idea. This is truly an occasion for giving thanks." The marble masterpiece underwent a complete restoration at the hands of its reclusive sculptor, San Francisco artist Robert Pascal.*

I made a mental note to read the article about the Stendhal Syndrome later. I could only deal with one cause for fainting at a time.

"That's strange," I said. "I just spoke with Pascal and he didn't mention returning it."

"Perhaps he didn't want to admit it. Old folks can be funny that way. I seem to have missed out on quite the stakeout. Mary said something about singing the score of *My Fair Lady*? And to think all I ever do is sit in my quiet studio and make jewelry."

"Don't knock it," I sighed.

Quietly making art was sounding pretty good to me about now.

Chapter 11

Art dealers are like brushes: They can be divided into the soft and the stiff. And, like brushes, there are uses for both. While the stiff may be no good for washes, they are often handy for laying foundations.

—*Georges LeFleur, "Art Dealers and the Art Market,"*
Newsweek

Samantha and I chatted for a few minutes, and before leaving she agreed to accompany me on a shopping expedition in the morning to buy a dress for the cocktail party in Hillsborough. I puttered around the studio, straightening things up and thinking. I was beginning to dread tomorrow's date with Michael. Mingling with rich snobs quaffing martinis was sufficient to give me an attack of the willies under the best of circumstances, and my suspicion that Michael was up to something nefarious made my apprehension worse. But I feared that until the museum had its painting back, ransom notes and Nazis notwithstanding, Bryan would not be safe from the long reach of Agnes Brock's skeletal arm. Unless I could think of a way to get through to Carlos Jimenez, Michael was my ticket to the missing Chagall.

The dusty Elvis clock by the faux fireplace revealed I

had thirty minutes before I was supposed to pick up Bryan for our tea date with Francine Maggio. I flipped through my mental Rolodex searching for someone who might be able to help me figure out what was going on with Carlos. I knew a lot of artists, who were fun to hang out with. I knew a few art thieves and forgers, who were also fun to hang out with provided one didn't mind occasionally running from the cops. But for what I had in mind I needed a computer geek, preferably one who worked at home and was bored with his day job.

I dialed Pedro Schumacher.

"Annie! *Qué pasa?*"

"Not much," I said. "You?"

"Same old same old."

"Well, then, maybe I could talk you into doing me a favor. I need information on a guy named Carlos Jimenez."

"Sure, Annie. I'll just stick my head out the window and yell. There ought to be three or four on this block alone," Pedro quipped. Pedro and his girlfriend lived in Oakland's Fruitvale section, which was home to a large Spanish-speaking community, many of whom must have been named Carlos.

"I *know* who he is," I explained. "I was hoping you could use your unique talents to see if he's been up to anything unusual."

"Like what?"

"I don't know, maybe making large bank deposits or something? He's a security guard at the Brock Museum. He's worked there for almost twenty years."

"He an illegal?" Pedro asked, using the aggressively politically incorrect term. Although he was a second-generation American himself, Pedro didn't hold with illegal immigration and had never even visited Mexico, his mother's homeland. I imagined that his pugnacious attitude added spice to his relationship with his long-term girl-friend Elena Briones, a fiercely progressive Chicana lawyer who worked for the Oakland Public Defender's office.

"You got somethin' on this guy, Annie?" Pedro asked, his voice dropping to a conspiratorial whisper.

"I'm just trying to figure out how he fits into something I'm looking into. Sorry to be so vague, but I don't know much myself yet."

I heard the furious clicking of a computer keyboard in the background.

"Okay, *chica*, looks like Jimenez lives not far from here, off International Boulevard. You want me to go talk to him?" Five feet, six inches tall, Pedro weighed maybe 145 pounds, dripping wet. He looked more like a medieval scholar than a badass, but much preferred to think of himself as a hard-boiled private investigator than a soft-handed computer programmer.

"You found that out already? What are you, Pedro Super Sleuth?" I teased.

"Aw, you'd be surprised to find out how easy it is," he said modestly. "But then you'd never call me anymore. You want me to go over and shake him down?"

First Tom and Pete, now Pedro. I was starting to feel like a purveyor of macho adventures for my otherwise civilized friends. Maybe I should start a sideline business running men's retreats, I thought. I seemed to have a knack for encouraging mild-mannered suburban males to dream up crazy schemes of intimidation against alleged miscreants. It could be the new millennium's answer to the drumming circles of the 1980s.

"Thanks, but it's not really a shakedown situation. I just want some information on him. Anything out of the ordinary."

"If you insist." He sighed good-naturedly. "I'll call you with the results, okay?"

"Great. One more thing. Speaking of unusual names, I'm looking for a woman named Evangeline . . ."

"*Now* we're talking."

"But I don't know her last name."

"Oh boy."

"She's the niece of Robert Pascal, a sculptor with a studio on Tennessee Street. They're related through his sister, so she probably has a different last name." I filled him in on the little I knew about Evangeline. He promised to check it out, and I promised to treat him to dinner.

Teatime. I scrubbed the marble dust from my hands and face, and pulled on a pair of clean jeans and a long-sleeved black T-shirt from the old oak armoire. I tried to keep clean clothes on hand for the times when I was too messy—even by my loose standards—to meet with clients. Standing before the wardrobe mirror, I calmed my curly brown hair with a spritz of tap water and a wide-toothed comb, and applied a little lipstick. I'd read somewhere that lips pale as one ages, and for some reason the thought bothered me. God forbid I have pale lips.

I was now officially late, but hesitated. I should call Pascal's studio in case Evangeline answered.

"Yeah?" the old sculptor said brusquely after the second ring.

"Um . . ."

"Jose?"

I was tempted to pretend to be Jose but didn't think Pascal would fall for it. I've been told that on the telephone I sound like a fifteen-year-old girl.

"It's Annie."

He hung up. I hit redial.

Pascal picked up but didn't speak, so I dropped my voice as low as I could and said, "Jose here."

"Fuck off," he swore, and hung up.

This was kind of fun. I hit redial once more.

He picked up. Whoever Jose was, Pascal did not want to miss his call.

"May I speak with Evangeline, please?" I asked sweetly.

Slam.

I rushed across town and found Bryan tapping his foot on the sidewalk outside his Mission District apartment building. Dressed in buff-colored wool pants tucked into glossy knee-high black boots, and a stark white shirt topped by a brocade vest, he carried a tweed jacket folded casually over one arm.

"What, no jodhpurs?" I teased as he opened the passenger door.

"Very funny. Take the scones." Bryan handed me a basket of still warm baked goods that smelled scrumptious. His smile faded when he got a gander at my outfit. "Oh, baby doll, I wish we had time! You don't look *at all* the thing!"

I heard that a lot.

"Hey, these jeans are clean! Just because we're invited to tea doesn't mean we're being transported to Jane Austen's England."

He snorted in a most un–Mr. Darcy–like fashion.

I knew of no easy way to get from the Mission to the Avenues, so I skirted Laguna Honda Hospital, passed through the Forest Hill neighborhood, and went up Noriega to Thirty-first. This section of town was known as the Sunset, which was something of a misnomer considering how often the thick banks of fog hunkered down along its streets, obscuring the sunset along with everything else.

The Maggio house was typical of the neighborhood: a two-story, stucco-covered bungalow, with the garage and entrance at street level and the living quarters on the second story. Francine Maggio met us at the gate, a plump woman in her mid to late fifties with a round, attractive face, warm brown eyes, and blond hair liberally shot through with gray. She wore a floral dress topped by an immaculate lace apron, ecru stockings, and sturdy lace-up black shoes. Smiling graciously, she waved us through a flower-filled courtyard and up the stairs.

I paused in the foyer, taking in the scene. Every inch of wall space was papered in a riot of pink cottage roses and pale green stripes, the mahogany-trimmed furniture was upholstered in rose-colored brocade, and an oil painting of a big-eyed cocker spaniel hung with pride of place above the living room mantel. My eyes searched the shadows for a shrine to at least one member of the British royal family.

Francine urged us to have a seat on a hideously uncomfortable Victorian settee, bustled into the kitchen, and returned moments later with Bryan's scones arranged on a silver tray alongside what she referred to as "finger sandwiches." She sat in a Queen Anne armchair and commenced an elaborate tea-pouring ceremony. Bryan seemed at ease, but I felt like an anthropologist observing an alien culture.

"One lump or two?" she asked me, a pair of delicate silver tongs hovering over the painted china sugar bowl.

"Just plain, please," I replied.

"Surely some milk, then?"

Bryan caught my eye and inclined his head.

"Yes, please," I said. "Thank you."

Francine diluted the tea with milk and handed me the eggshell-thin china teacup, a teaspoon perched precariously on the matching saucer.

The brew was an unappetizing shade of beige. I took a sip. Tasted beige, too.

"Thank you for meeting with us, Mrs. Maggio," I said, relinquishing my tea to the coaster on the low table in front of us. "I know this must be difficult for you, but we were hoping you could shed some light on what happened between Robert Pascal and his assistant Eugene Forrester."

Francine took a fortifying sip of tea and dabbed her lips with an embroidered linen napkin. "Eugene and I had been seeing each other for about two years," she began. "We were both students at Berkeley. He was an art major with an emphasis in sculpture, and I was English lit. The fiction of Jane Austen was my specialty!"

Bryan and I nodded encouragement while Francine took a hearty bite of scone.

"Why, these are delicious!" she exclaimed. "Currants?" Bryan nodded, pleased. "Anyway, Eugene landed an apprenticeship with Robert Pascal, which was considered quite a coup at the time. Pascal was only a few years older than we, but already had a reputation as an up-and-comer. Eugene was very good, you know, immensely talented. Everyone said so. And we were so happy. . . ."

Her voice trailed off as she stared into space for a moment. She caught herself, picked up a silk-covered album from a side table, and handed us a photograph of a young man with light brown hair and long sideburns. Handsome and rather dashing despite the dated fashions, his eyes were bright and alert, brimming with life as if he were poised to race off someplace exotic and do something exciting.

Francine's eyes grew moist. "I'm sorry," she whispered, and I suddenly caught a glimpse of the young woman she had once been, head over heels in love with her long-haired artist. "I married a fine man and raised two wonderful daughters. I've had a blessed life. But I've never forgotten Eugene. Sometimes I think . . ."

"What? What do you think?" I asked a little too eagerly.

Francine started at the sound of my voice, as if she had forgotten we were there. Bryan leaned forward and rested a reassuring hand on her forearm. "You just tell us your own way, honey," he said, casting me a quelling look. It seemed I needed to repeat Interrogation 101.

"It was hard to put to rest because of the scandal. The police said it was suicide. Why, that's the most ridiculous thing I'd ever heard. Eugene was *not* the type to commit suicide."

I was not convinced. Francine would never admit that the love of her youth had been miserable enough to kill himself. Who would?

"Francine," I asked carefully, "do you have any kind of proof? Any tangible indication that something criminal happened?"

She shook her head. "I tried so many times to get the police involved. I did everything I could think of, but I was only twenty-one. What did I know? I even went to talk with someone in legal services, you know the free clinic they used to have in Berkeley? That's how I met Grady, my husband."

A man named Grady Maggio, I mused, seemed like an odd match for a woman with a passion for cottage roses and finger sandwiches.

"Grady pressured the police to investigate and tried to get the press interested. But Eugene had no immediate family and I was just the girlfriend, which didn't carry much weight with the authorities in those days." She shrugged. "And then Grady and I . . . Well, life went on."

"How can you be sure that Eugene didn't commit suicide?" I asked.

Anger shadowed her face. "He wasn't gay—I should know. The man wanted sex morning, noon, and night."

Bryan and I exchanged glances. It felt somehow unseemly for the demure Mrs. Maggio, nibbling at finger sandwiches in her starched lace apron, to speak so openly of sex. Then again, she and Eugene had been together in the late 1960s, an era that could teach current generations a thing or two about free love.

"And I suspect I wasn't the only woman he was seeing. Eugene always said I was a prisoner of bourgeois values and was free to see other men, but I never wanted to. He *loved* women. How could he have been gay?"

"Um, well, yes, but . . ." My turn to trail off. Now wasn't the time for a lecture on bisexuality.

"Plus, the police said Eugene shot himself," she continued. "Where did he get a gun? Eugene hated violence; we all did. He was prepared to declare himself a conscientious objector if he was drafted. He was not the type to shoot *anyone*, including himself."

Desperate people do desperate things, I thought.

"And besides, if Eugene was suicidal—without me or *any* of his friends or professors noticing—he would have overdosed on pills and alcohol, like every other Berkeley suicide. There were pills everywhere back then."

She had a point.

"Bryan, Annie," Francine beseeched us. "I know you're skeptical. I would be, too. But what you must understand is that Eugene hated Pascal, and vice versa. The apprenticeship went sour almost from the beginning."

"How so?" I asked, so absorbed in her story that I absentmindedly took a gulp of the nasty beige tea. I forced myself to swallow it and crammed a chunk of scone into my mouth. Bryan watched, amused. He was a seventh-generation Southerner from Louisiana whose mother had brought him up to be a gentleman.

Caught up in her story, Francine was oblivious to my gaucheness. "Eugene was working on a special piece, a large marble sculpture. Pascal hated it, and they had a huge row over it. And Eugene told me that Pascal hadn't been producing anything."

We waited for the denouement.

"Don't you see?" she asked.

We shook our heads.

"The *sculpture*. Eugene's sculpture! After Eugene's . . . body was found, Pascal sent me his things from the studio. But there were only a few small maquettes, nothing on the scale of what Eugene had been working on for months. I went by Pascal's studio to ask about it, but he wouldn't even open the door. Wouldn't answer the phone. Nothing."

"What did you do?" I asked, betting the answer would not be, "Sang the score to *My Fair Lady* until he cracked."

"I bided my time until Pascal's next show. And there it was," she said. "Eugene's sculpture was the centerpiece of Pascal's opening. Pascal called it *Head and Torso*, though Eugene had called it *Francie*—that was his pet name for me."

Francie seemed like a better name for a Barbie doll than a massive piece of carved marble, I thought, pawing through my backpack until I found the newspaper Samantha had shown me earlier. "Is this the sculpture?"

Francine stared at the grainy image of *Head and Torso* and started to cry. "Yes. That's *Francie*. I posed for it. See the hip, here? That's me." She pointed to a curve in the stone. "But when I told everyone at the opening that Pascal had stolen Eugene's sculpture, I was laughed out of the room. I had no way to prove it, and after all, Eugene was just an apprentice. Here, I kept a file of clippings."

She handed me a collection of yellowed newspaper articles from the *Oakland Tribune*. I skimmed them: "Young artist takes own life . . . single gunshot to the head . . . body discovered by the cleaning woman, Irma Rodriguez."

Could it be true? Had Robert Pascal murdered his young assistant thirty-something years ago because he was suffering from sculptor's block and wanted to claim *Head and Torso* as his own? If so, then the style Pascal had become famous for—that curious melding of machine and nature—had originated with Eugene Forrester, and Pascal's entire career was a sham.

That was a secret worth killing for. Had Seamus McGraw stumbled upon the truth and been murdered to ensure his silence? But if so, why—and how—would Pascal have hung McGraw's body from a tree in Anthony Brazil's sculpture garden?

This was news, *big* news. If it were true.

Bryan held Francine's hand and murmured comforting words. I was anxious to leave the cloying rose-covered room, but there was one other thing I had to ask.

"Francine, did you know any of Pascal's contemporaries, such as Beverly LeFleur or Seamus McGraw?"

"Yes, of course. They were art graduate students, and although Eugene and I were undergrads, it was a small department and we all socialized. Eugene even took a class with Seamus, and they shared studio space for a little while before Eugene started working with Pascal. In fact, Eugene went to Seamus when he thought Pascal was getting hooked."

"Hooked?"

"On drugs. Most of us experimented a little back then. I know how that sounds, but it truly was a different time," she added. "Eugene was afraid Pascal was getting in too deep. Seamus and Beverly tried to intervene, there was a huge row, and their friendship with Pascal was never the same." She gazed at the cocker spaniel portrait, a wistful expression on her face. "I heard Seamus died recently. Is that true?"

I nodded.

"Do you know if anyone is publishing his papers?"

"What papers?"

"Seamus always carried a notebook that he sketched and wrote in almost compulsively. He said it was an intimate record of the artistic process and talked about having his notebooks published as his legacy to the art world. I know he published excerpts here and there, but I wondered if he kept the project going all these years."

"I really don't know," I replied, thinking of the stack of black notebooks I'd knocked over in Pascal's studio.

"Oh well," she sighed. "Beverly LeFleur went on to marry a young man named Harold, which surprised all of us because we thought she would marry Seamus. She was lovely, and oh, *so* intelligent. I think even Pascal had a crush on her. Anyway, that art show was the last time I saw Pascal. People say he became a recluse. Perhaps he is living in his own private hell."

I remembered Pascal's hopeless, red-rimmed eyes, and thought she might be right.

"This is all we have of our lost loved ones, you know," Francine concluded with a loud sniff. "Memories. Remembrances of things past."

When your host starts quoting Proust, my grandfather once told me, it's time to leave.

At the door Bryan gave Francine a hug and promised to send her his recipe for currant scones. Francine grabbed my shoulders and enveloped me in a rose-scented embrace.

"You get him for me, Annie," she whispered fiercely. "You get that bastard Pascal."

As we crossed the courtyard, I glanced back at
Francine. Behind her was the image I had been searching
for earlier: a large photo of Princess Diana in a gold gilt
frame lit by a spotlight and surrounded by candles. I wondered what the defiant Eugene Forrester would have made
of it all had he lived to see his twenty-second birthday.

"So what do you think?" I asked Bryan as we pulled
away from the curb. "Do you believe her?"

"Oh, baby doll, *no one* could make up something like
that," he said, brushing away a tear. Bryan was a sucker for
lost love.

Maybe I had an overly active imagination, or maybe
Bryan needed to watch more soap operas, but Francine's
story didn't seem all that hard to fabricate. I didn't think
Francine was consciously lying, but I wasn't ready to trust
the interpretation of thirty-year-old events by someone
who kept a shrine to a dead princess.

"Thank you for arranging the meeting," I said as we
skirted the lush forest of Golden Gate Park.

"What's our next step?" Bryan asked. "File charges, or
what?"

"No, Bryan, we don't file charges," I said. The conde-
scension in my voice reminded me of the tone Annette had
used with me earlier that day, and I continued more gently.
"The police didn't take her suspicions seriously at the
time. I can't imagine why they would now."

"So you're saying we just let him get away with it?"
Bryan's handsome face was a study in moral outrage. "And
isn't Beverly LeFleur your mother?"

I jockeyed with a shiny silver Mercedes for position on
Oak Street, called the pinstriped driver a few choice
names, and turned back to the still misty-eyed Bryan.

"The problem is we don't know what really happened.
We're talking about a death that took place more than

thirty years ago." I shook my head and said, as much to myself as to him, "No, it's just none of our business. What we *should* be focusing on is your situation with the Brock. Has anything new happened?"

Bryan was peeved.

"Bryan?"

"No," he replied grudgingly. "The cops told me not to leave town, but I haven't heard anything else."

"Get a load of this, my friend," I said. "Inspector Crawford told me the police had received a tip that the painting was being kept in some former Nazi's house in Switzerland."

"Get out!" Bryan's dark brown eyes widened.

"First the Middle East, now the Nazis. Something weird is going on, don't you think?"

"You ain't kiddin', sugar pie."

"Bryan, tell me something. How did you hear about the Stendhal Syndrome?"

"Our guide—Michael Collins?—told us about it. He spent his childhood in Florence—he calls it *Firenze*—and knows how truly *sensitive* people respond to great art."

I'll just bet he does, I thought. But I still couldn't figure out why Michael would have bothered orchestrating the Stendhal faint-in. As he said himself, that particular Chagall was hardly worth stealing.

"Annie!"

"What?" I swerved.

"Pull in here! I need some *really* big pots for my espaliered pear trees."

"Don't *ever* yell at me like that unless I'm about to hit something, okay?" I snapped as we careened into the pitted parking lot of the Mischievous Monkey Garden Supply.

It was the store that had issued the receipt I saw on Pascal's desk.

It was kismet.

The Mischievous Monkey consisted of an office trailer surrounded by row upon row of brightly glazed ceramic pots from Asia and painted terra-cotta pots from Mexico. Stone Buddhas, plaster saints, and cement birdbaths and fountains abounded, ranging in degree of fussiness from the pure and simple to the baroque. The large yard was posted with *Beware of Dog!* signs, and I wondered if there really were thieves willing to hoist multi-hundred-pound clay pots over a ten-foot cyclone fence topped with vicious-looking razor wire.

Bryan hopped out to look around while I lingered in the truck and called Mary. "Any messages?"

"Some *incredibly* gorgeous hunk named Michael stopped by," she said with a breathy laugh. "Now *there's* a work of art."

"Oh yeah?" I swallowed hard and cleared my throat. "What did he want?"

"He said you two have a date tomorrow night and you'll probably try to weasel out of it 'cause you're so shy. I go, 'We talkin' about the same Annie Kincaid?'"

"That right?"

"So he's like, she has this 'winsome smile.' Then he goes on about your cute butt."

Cute butt? I yanked the rearview mirror toward me and smiled. Was that winsome?

"Who *is* he?" Mary demanded. "This guy is too hot for words."

"He's too old for you."

"Aside from the fact that he's got it bad for you, *I* don't have a winsome smile or a cute butt."

"You have a fabulous smile, as you should know from your legion of fans." Mary and her band had a devoted following even though she really did not sing very well. I was willing to bet her popularity was based on something besides her voice.

"So you're saying my butt's really huge and ugly."

I'd walked right into that one. "Your butt's adorable, and you know it. That's why you shake it so much when we go out dancing."

Mary laughed. "So? You're not going to stand him up, are you? I mean, you haven't had sex for what, months? Maybe years? And oh my God! What are you going to wear?"

Trust my practical assistant to get to the heart of the matter. No love life and no decent wardrobe. Could the two be connected?

"No, I'm not going to stand him up." *Unless Pedro comes through for me,* I thought. "As a matter of fact, he's *paying* me to go out with him."

"Are you serious?! You're working as an *escort*?"

"No, Mary, I . . ."

"I had a girlfriend who did that, and she said it was okay as long as you could say no to the creepy ones. Hey! I know! We could offer a *full-service* studio! We wouldn't even have to change the name—"

I cut her off before she could transform True/Faux Studios into a kinky art brothel, which wasn't such a terrible idea except for that pesky morals thing. "I am not, repeat, *not* working as an escort. Michael is a, um, colleague who needs someone to accompany him to a business meeting. That's all."

"Uh-huh. A colleague. Like you went to school with him?"

"Um, well, no . . ."

"Worked with him at the Brock?"

"No . . ."

"Painted for him?"

"Um . . ."

"So would this be one of your grandfather's kind of colleagues?"

Despite her unconventional past, or perhaps because of it, Mary was no slouch in the intelligence department.

"Michael's a colleague of sorts. Let's just leave it at that. But you're right that I don't have anything to wear. Sam and I are going shopping tomorrow morning. Want to come?"

"Totally. But I want to hear more about this guy. You should go to bed with him once, you know, just to see. Maybe he's one of those guys who *looks* great but doesn't have much to offer when it really counts. Maybe he's—"

"Got to go, Mary," I interjected before she could stir up any more inappropriate images in my already fevered brain. "My battery's beeping. See you tomorrow."

I set off in search of Bryan. I wanted to get on the Bay Bridge and home at a decent hour, and it was already almost six. Dusk was falling, but the bright outdoor lighting lent the garden statuary and pots a gay, almost festive air. I found myself admiring one pot after another and wondering if I should move to an apartment with a garden.

Great, something else to do with my spare time that required regular infusions of cash. Dream on, Annie.

I came to the end of a row of cobalt blue oil jars and stopped dead in my tracks. There, under a tin roof shelter, was a clutch of three-foot-tall plaster sculptures. Pascal's sculptures. Or, if Francine Maggio was to be believed, Eugene Forrester–inspired sculptures. They were much smaller than the ones I'd seen in Pascal's studio, but the style was distinctive.

"What did you find?" Bryan came up behind me. "I think they're ugly, Annie, to tell you the truth. I don't even get a tingle, and you *know* I'm sensitive to those Stendhal feelings."

"Help me turn one over," I said, grabbing a miniature of none other than *Head and Torso*. It was heavy, but with some grunting we managed to lay it flat on the ground. Kneeling, I examined it closely. I was betting the statue had an empty core because a solid one would have been heavier still, and started scratching at the statue's base with my car keys to see if I was right.

Just then a slight Asian man came up to us. He cocked his head to the side, trying to see what I was doing. "Help you?" he asked in accented English. "My name Van. You ask price on something?"

"Hi," I said, standing and tucking the keys into my jeans pocket as Bryan wandered off. The man could faint in a museum, but an awkward social situation mortified him. "I'm curious about these sculptures. Where do you get them?"

"Local artist. Old man. Kind of mean. You like them?"

"Can you tell me his name?"

"Aaaah . . ." Van shook his head. "I know what he look like, but no name."

"Is there anyone here who would know?"

Van led the way to the small office trailer where an elderly man, wrinkled and white haired, sat at a desk working on some papers. Van spoke to him in a staccato language I recognized as Vietnamese. I'd learned a few phrases during my frequent visits to Vietnamese restaurants and attempted a formal greeting. *"Chào Ông."*

The men smiled politely, but I could tell they were trying hard not to laugh. Tonal languages were problematic for the tone deaf.

I reverted to English. "What is the name of the artist who makes those sculptures?"

The old man spoke to Van, who translated. "He will look in the file."

After a moment of paper shuffling, the old man handed me an invoice. I was right. An internationally renowned sculptor was casting plaster knockoffs of his work and selling them for fifty bucks a pop to a garden supply store. According to the invoice, Pascal had delivered fifteen of the sculptures last month.

"Does he bring this many every month?"

"He say ten to twenty every month," Van translated. "He say they sell very well. You want one? Only two hundred dollars."

"I'm not really looking for a sculpture. But thank you for your help."

"You want some pot?" Van asked.

"Excuse me?" I wasn't current on the etiquette of drug dealing, but Van's approach struck me as rather forward.

"I see you like blue pot," he replied. "I give good price."

"Oh, right." *Pots*, not pot. "Yeah, okay, maybe one or two."

Bryan screamed.

Van and I bounded out of the trailer. In my absence Bryan had decided to explore the miniature *Head and Torso*. And found something.

"What is it?" Van asked, grimacing at the blackish mess that spilled from a hole in the base.

"Call the police," I said and swallowed hard. "Tell them you found something in a piece of garden sculpture. Tell them it looks like fingers."

Chapter 12

The contemporary artist can too easily become overwhelmed by color choices. The great Hals and Rembrandt used only four colors: Flake White, Yellow Ochre, Red Ochre, and Charcoal Black.

—*Georges LeFleur, "Modern Art or Modern Mess?"*
    Time

"Bryan, listen to me," I said, thinking rapidly as Van ran to the trailer. "We have to get you out of here. Go to the diner across the street and call a cab. I'll deal with the police."

"But, Annie—"

"Bryan, please. After what happened at the Brock last week, I don't think it's a good idea for the cops to find you here."

"Those are *fingers*, Annie. Somebody's *fingers*," he protested. "I won't leave you here to face this alone." Bryan might be a screamer, but he was no coward.

"Don't worry. You're not," I reassured him. "I'm going to call Inspector Crawford. Now *go*, please."

I did not have long to wait. A black-and-white cruiser screeched into the parking lot a few minutes later. One cop cordoned off the scene while the other began taking the names of witnesses. I was correcting his spelling of "Kin-caid" for the third time when I heard a familiar voice.

"Well, well. Look who's here," Inspector Crawford said with just a hint of sarcasm. "Imagine my surprise."

"Hi, Inspector."

She contemplated the gruesome sight. "Annie, tell me: how is it you *happened* to be shopping for yard decorations? Did I fail to notice a garden at your third-floor apartment or your second-story studio?"

"She buy some pot," Van said, and I sighed. Even in San Francisco pot dealing was a no-no.

"He means *flower pots*," I assured Annette. Van nodded and gestured to the hundreds of vessels surrounding us. "I thought it would really brighten up the fire escape."

"Mm-hmm," Annette replied. The cop who couldn't spell murmured something to her, and she turned back to me. "Who was the man that Mr. Van here says found the body parts in the sculpture?"

"Gee, that's hard to say," I lied.

She fixed me with the stink-eye. "African American male, thirties, about six feet tall, dressed in a vest and black boots? Ring a bell?"

"Doesn't sound familiar."

"You didn't know him."

"Uh-uh."

"Did you at least *notice* him? Maybe, say, when you ran out here to investigate why he was screaming?"

It seemed Van had been quite helpful to the police. "Mm, not really. I think I was distracted by the, um . . . Those *are* fingers, right?"

"Look like fingers to me," she muttered and, snapping on a pair of surgical gloves she'd pulled from her jacket pocket, she bent over to examine them up close. After a moment she straightened and spoke into her radio.

"Annette, what is it?" I asked. "What did you see?"

She ignored me.

"Annette?"

"Annie, did anyone ever tell you that you are a pain in the ass?"

"All the time, actually."

"Add me to the list," she said. "All right. Those *are* fingers and, judging by their size and hairiness, I would say they are a man's fingers. Furthermore, based on a description of the ring on the index finger, I would hazard a guess that these are the fingers of the recently deceased sculptor, Seamus McGraw."

Ick, I thought.

"Quite a coincidence, wouldn't you say?" she asked. "First you find a body without fingers, then you find fingers without a body. Care to comment?"

"I had *nothing*—"

"—to do with *anything*," she finished for me. "I know. You told me. Now tell me this: What can you tell me about the sculpture they were found in? I'm no expert, but this doesn't look like McGraw's work to me."

I saw no point in lying since she would find out anyway. "It's by Robert Pascal."

Her eyebrows shot up. "Would that be the sculptor you called me about earlier? The one with the missing assistant?"

"That would."

"And how is he connected to Seamus McGraw?"

What to say, what to say. I didn't want to implicate my mother, or Bryan, or myself. On the other hand, if the SFPD thought Pascal was capable of something like this maybe they would look for Evangeline.

"The two men have known each other for years. I was

hired on a completely unrelated errand to inquire about a sculpture that Pascal was repairing for a client."

"Mm-hmm. Client's name?"

"Isn't that, like, confidential?"

"The law doesn't recognize the artist-client privilege, Annie. Spill it."

"Janice Hewett. Anthony Brazil has her contact information."

"Okay, here's the deal," she said, removing the gloves and snapping her notebook shut. "You're going to wait for me while I attend to a few matters. Then you're going to buy me a cup of coffee at the diner across the street and tell me everything you know about Robert Pascal and Seamus McGraw. If you do, and if I believe you, then *maybe* I won't need to track down the well-dressed, screaming black man you claim you didn't notice. Do we understand each other?"

Hours later, awash in lousy coffee, I left the diner secure in the knowledge that Bryan was safe and that Annette was on her way to Pascal's studio to interrogate the cantankerous and perhaps homicidal old coot. I limped back to Oakland, lumbered up the stairs to my apartment, and nearly cried when my key stuck in the lock. Ignoring the dirty dishes in the sink, the light flashing on the answering machine, and the mail on the kitchen table, I downed two glasses of cheap Chilean merlot and fell into bed without brushing my teeth.

Tuesday morning came much too soon. I batted at the alarm, sending my new bedside clock skittering across the crowded nightstand and onto the floor. Maybe this was why my clocks always stopped working within days of their purchase. I craved sleep but had arranged to meet Samantha at ten o'clock to go clothes shopping for what was sure to be a fun-filled evening with an international art thief.

Unless Pedro Schumacher had come through for me. Maybe Carlos Jimenez had stashed the Chagall in a locker somewhere and posted a map to its location on some obscure chat room. Worth a shot. Without leaving the warmth of my bed, I dialed my tech-savvy friend.

"Yo, *chica*. I didn't find much," Pedro said. He sounded remarkably cheerful for so early in the morning, which ticked me off. "Your guy owns a ten-year-old Ford Taurus, has gotten two speeding tickets in the last five years, is a registered democrat, belongs to the public library—he's partial to science fiction, believe it or not—has a decent credit rating, lives within his means, and has a mortgage on a house in West Oakland that'll be paid off in five years. His financial transactions for the past six months indicate nothing out of the ordinary—paycheck goes in, bill payments come out."

"That's not very interesting, Pedro."

"Tell me about it. There is one weird thing, though: his gasoline card shows that he's been traveling to a town near the Mexican border every month or so for the past several years."

"So?"

"Doesn't that seem strange?"

"He's from that area, Pedro. He's probably just visiting relatives or something."

"Maybe—or maybe he's running drugs from Mexico!"

"Oh, very likely. He probably stuffs the trunk of his Taurus with kilos of high-grade cocaine and roars up I-5 because the CHP would never, *ever* suspect anything so clever," I said with a touch of sarcasm. "Probably deals it out of the Brock Museum. Hell of a cover, wouldn't you say?"

"It could happen."

"Pedro, the man's not a drug runner just because he goes to Mexico. It's a beautiful country. Lots of people spend their vacations there."

"There's one more thing. His son has been in rehab twice for methamphetamine addiction. Looks like Carlos took out a home-equity loan to pay for his treatment."

Poor Juan, I thought. And poor Carlos.

"At least tell me why you're interested in the guy, Annie."

I hesitated, not wanting to slander Carlos but worried that if I didn't tell Pedro the whole story he might come across something crucial without realizing it. "I think he may be connected to the recent theft of a painting at the Brock Museum."

"No shit? Maybe he's smuggling the paintings into Mexico to fence them, huh?"

"Yeah, I think there's a bar in Tijuana that specializes in that sort of thing." Pedro's image of Mexico seemed to be the Wild West with a dash of Casablanca. "Thanks for the research, my friend. I'm pretty sure the man's not running drugs, but it never hurts to keep an open mind. Oh and, Pedro?"

"Yeah?"

"You and I are going to take a little vacation to Mexico, you got that? You're going to love it and rediscover your heritage."

"I know my heritage just fine. Can you say the same?"

"Roger that, my friend. Mine keeps biting me on the butt, remember?"

We disconnected, and I wondered what my next step should be. Would I have to accuse Carlos of theft to save Bryan? Or had the stories of ransom notes and Nazis put an end to Bryan's problems with the Brock? What Carlos had done was wrong, but did I want to be the one to finger him?

Wait—that sounded wrong.

I decided to speak with Carlos one more time. I called his home number but got a machine, so I tried the Brock only to be told that he had taken some personal time. It was not clear when he would return to work.

I scuffed down the hall to the kitchen, put water on for coffee, and checked my phone messages. My mother had called to report that she was back in Asco, safe and sound. Pete had called twice to check on my welfare. Bryan phoned three times to see if I had gotten home. Michael left a message confirming he would pick me up at my apartment tonight at seven o'clock. Lastly, Josh had called "just to say hi." He was so sweet, with no discernible ulterior motives. Other than wanting to see me naked, but that was a motive I could get behind.

Humming to myself, I took the whistling kettle from the stove and poured boiling water over a coneful of freshly ground Peet's French roast coffee. It was fun to have gentlemen callers. True, one was gay, one was like a brother, and one was a no-good art thief. But still. I bet this was what Blanche Dubois felt like. Just call me the Femme Fatale of Faux Finishes. The Siren of San Francisco. The Chick of China Basin. The . . . Ogre of Oakland? Oaf of Oakland? How come nothing flattering started with an *O*?

The phone shrilled and I jumped, spilling coffee down my white T-shirt. I slammed the half-empty mug on the table, plucked the shirt away from my skin, grabbed a towel, and snatched up the phone. *"What?"*

"Good morning. Is there some problem with the alarm in your studio?" Frank DeBenton asked in his stuffiest landlord voice.

"Not that I know of."

"You do understand the concept of disarming and rearming the alarm in your studio, all in a coordinated fashion, upon entering or leaving?"

"Let me take a wild guess, Frank. Did the alarm go off again?"

"Yes. Yes it did."

"When?"

"About ten minutes ago."

"So why are you calling me? Maybe you should be looking for a burglar."

"We've already secured the premises and the guard is on alert. Since you are not the culprit, I am inclined to think that one of your many friends or acquaintances tripped the alarm," he said. "Perhaps you would be good enough to share with your many friends and acquaintances the fact that the studio *has* an alarm, and that said alarm will go off if the window is jimmied and/or the door rattled vigorously."

"'And/or'?" I teased, but my landlord was in tight-ass mode and did not reply. "Okay, Frank. I'll remind my 'many friends and acquaintances' that when they come to the studio they are not to break in the windows, jimmy the locks, pound on the door, or rappel from the roof."

"Why would anyone rappel from the roof?"

"You'd be surprised," I murmured, and hung up.

I took a moment to savor what remained of my coffee and gazed out the window. The kitchen's dormers were framed by large green leaves from the ancient mulberry trees lining the street. Each fall the trees dropped hard, round seedpods, and last year I had gathered a handful, dipped them in paint, and rolled them on a large canvas. It created an intriguing design that I'd dubbed *Autumn Solstice* and sold for a hefty sum during the Open Studios art show.

That was back when I did things like paint and earn a living. The past few days I had mostly spent chasing rumors and ghosts.

Take last night's gruesome discovery. First McGraw's body, then his missing fingers—how had I managed to find both? Assuming those were McGraw's fingers, that is. But if they were, how had they ended up in one of Pascal's sculptures? Was Francine Maggio correct in suggesting that Pascal was a homicidal sculptor who murdered his rivals? If so, he had taken his own sweet time about it. More than three decades separated the deaths of Eugene Forrester and Seamus McGraw.

But even if Pascal had murdered McGraw, why would he entomb his fingers in a sculpture? Maybe it was a matter of expediency—it beat stuffing them down the garbage disposal, I supposed—but then why hang McGraw's body in a high-profile art show? That sounded more like someone was making a statement. I wondered whether Annette Crawford had learned anything more at Pascal's last night.

One thing was clear: I was accomplishing nothing sitting in my kitchen in a damp T-shirt. I went to the bedroom and started to pull on my painting overalls when I remembered the morning's agenda. Even I wouldn't go clothes shopping in scruffy overalls. Rats. I opted for a dark blue linen wrap-around skirt and a light-blue sweater, and laced up my comfy boots. I hated shopping, but at least this time, with Michael's money burning a hole in my pocket, I could afford something nice.

I picked up a middle-aged man from the casual carpool, zipped past the bottleneck at the Bay Bridge toll plaza, and screeched to a halt at the mouth of the Yerba Buena Island tunnel. The commute was rarely this bad, so I switched on the radio for a traffic update. Sarah and No Name, of the Alice radio station, reported gleefully that a truckload of

Porta Potties had spilled their brimming contents on the western span of the bridge and proposed a "Name That Traffic Jam!" contest. I laughed out loud at the increasingly scatological suggestions. My favorite was "When the Shit Hits the Span," though my passenger hid behind his *Wall Street Journal* and ignored the Alice morning show and me. It took forty minutes to inch across the bridge, drop my boring carpooler at the corner of Howard and Fremont, and speed to the DeBenton Building, where I squeezed into a space next to Frank's gleaming Jaguar. I raced up the stairs, and when I opened the door to my studio the lovely aroma of dark roast coffee perfumed the air.

"Pete?" I called out, dropping my backpack on a crowded worktable.

His broad, friendly face peered around the partition separating the kitchenette from the chaos of my studio. "Annie! I called you twice yesterday! Your mother, she is here?"

"She had to get back home," I said, flinging open the windows to allow the fresh air from the bay to fill the studio. "I'm sorry I didn't call you back."

"The bondage between mother and child is most special," Pete said sagely and emerged with a tray bearing three cappuccinos, three spoons, and the sugar bowl. With surprising grace he lowered the tray onto the wicker coffee table near the sofa. "One day you must join my family for Sunday dinner. Mama's *cevapcici* were to decease for, as you say, and the *bosanski lonac*, well, what is Sunday dinner without it?"

"Sounds yummy. So, who's joining us?" I asked, glancing at the third cup and hoping to steer the conversation away from food. If Pete became inspired to make his signature cabbage rolls we would all be sorry.

"Morning, all." As if on cue, Samantha glided in, sat

next to Pete on the velvet couch, and availed herself of the third cappuccino. "So Annie, love, are you ready to worship at the shrine of the capitalist fashionistas?"

I had to laugh. Mary and I privately called Sam, a jewelry designer, and her husband Reggie, a social worker, Natural Born Capitalists. Twenty years ago they had bought a rundown building in a dicey downtown neighborhood and renovated it with an artistic eye and plenty of sweat equity. Their investments now brought in enough income to enable them to support progressive political causes, send their son and daughter to private colleges, and take care of their elderly parents in Jamaica.

"You bet!" I sang out with false cheer. "You know how much I like to go shopping!" Fancy pants department stores scared the bejabbers out of me. On our last expedition I'd started hyperventilating from a combination of the exorbitant prices, the size of my hips, and the climate-controlled air.

"Take a couple of deep breaths, now, you'll be fine," Sam crooned. "I must say, Annie, you give a whole new meaning to the phrase *shop till you drop*."

"Hey there!" Mary called out as she breezed in. "What's up?"

"Shhh," Sam said. "Annie's just breathing."

"Uh-oh. Where are we going?" Mary asked in a hushed voice.

"Neiman Marcus."

Mary gave a soft whistle. "C'mon, Annie. It'll be fun. Sam and I will protect you."

"Very funny, you two. I'm *fine*." I squared my shoulders and led the way down the exterior stairs, but when we reached the parking lot I realized we had a transportation problem. Mary biked everywhere and Sam refused to drive in the City. Public transportation in China Basin was sketchy, and a taxi would cost a fortune. That left my small truck. Mary won a round of "rock, paper, scissors" and slid triumphantly into the center of the bench seat, where shifting into reverse would provide her with an interesting diversion.

Neiman Marcus commanded one corner of Union Square, some of the City's priciest commercial real estate. A long bank of brass and glass doors beckoned the well heeled to enter the shrine, whose grand entry soared five stories and was topped with a magnificent stained-glass skylight. Sparkling glass counters filled the floor space and boasted tasteful jewelry, expensive perfumes, and custom-blended makeup from around the world. The counters were staffed by men and women in elegant dress eager to please the store's elegant clientele.

I glanced at my not-so-elegant outfit and had another crisis of confidence. I was happy in a Mexican bazaar, overjoyed in a Turkish marketplace, and at home at Paris' Marché des Puces. But drop me in an upscale American department store and I tended to use the restroom, spritz myself with perfume, and head straight for the exit.

Mary lagged behind at the makeup counters while Sam marched me to the elevator. We whooshed to the fourth floor, where the doors slid open with a muted ping to reveal the Designer Dresses department. She herded me toward an alcove to our left that offered a multitude of Little Black Dresses in silks, satins, and supple blends.

"How do you know about this place?" I whispered, poking halfheartedly through a rack of dresses.

"Oh, Mia loves this store." Mia was Sam's beautiful, accomplished daughter, now a freshman at Stanford. "I suppose it's sort of a rebellion against my natural fabrics and batik prints. Still, it's hard not to admire the quality, though it would drive me insane to pay the dry-cleaning bill."

A woman glided over, slender, chic, and impeccably well mannered in the way of all Neiman Marcus sales associates. She was attired in a tasteful charcoal pantsuit, her pale blond hair drawn into a sleek bun at the nape of her swanlike neck.

"Good morning, ladies. My name is Teri. May I be of assistance?" She sized me up, her tone polite but guarded.

"Good morning, Teri," Sam replied with an air of haughtiness, and Teri relaxed, reassured that Sam spoke the Code. She spared me not a glance, since it was clear I was not a Code Talker.

"We're looking for just the *right* thing for my friend here to wear to a cocktail party in Hillsborough," Sam said, flipping through a selection of high-priced ensembles.

"Ah?" Teri hitched her shoulders slightly and smiled. "What fun!"

Sam and Teri put their heads together in an intense discussion before falling silent and strafing me with their eyes. I smiled weakly. As if on cue, they broke the huddle and scattered. The Hunt had begun in earnest.

Twenty minutes later—just as I was considering slipping behind a bank of voluminous ball gowns for a catnap—Teri appeared and escorted me to a large changing room decorated in melting shades of bisque, cream, and peach. I sank onto an upholstered brocade bench and glared at the eight chic dresses that lined the wall with the precision and warmth of a firing squad. I fought a sudden urge for a cigarette, which was odd since I didn't smoke.

"In for a penny, in for a hundred thousand pounds," my grandfather used to say, so I left my comfortable clothes in a sad heap on the bench and stepped into the first dress, a black fitted number I could not get past my hips. I drop-kicked the offending garment into a corner and slipped on a sweet burgundy number with a swishy skirt. The good news was I could get the dress on. The bad news was I looked ready for a sock hop.

Go daddy-o.

Sam and Teri knocked on the louvered door.

"How's it going in there, ma'am?" Teri chirped.

"How do they look, love?"

"I haven't found the, uh, perfect thing yet," I said, chucking the sock hop dress and struggling into a frothy purple concoction with large white polka dots.

"Try this one," Teri said, thrusting a garment over the top of the door. "And this would be *great* with your coloring," she added, tossing in another. I scurried around, picking up piles of froufrou fabric and ducking when Teri lobbed in a pair of high heels to try on with the dresses.

"Let's see you, love."

I emerged, half zipped. Teri and Sam stared for a moment and returned to the Hunt without saying a word.

"Hey!" I called after them. "A little encouragement would be appreciated!"

Several demoralizing changes of clothes later I found an outfit that looked halfway decent on me. And, miracle of miracles, it seemed a little large. I could probably go a size smaller, if they had one. I slipped on the heels and tottered out of the dressing room, determined to prove to Teri and Sam that I could look hot. I finally found them huddled near the spring velvets. "What about this one?"

The women cocked their heads.

"Not bad. Not bad at all," Samantha said, her head tilted to the right.

"It's the right style," Teri confirmed, her head tilted to the left. "I'm not convinced it's perfect, though. And it is a little big. Oh! I know!"

She was leading us towards a clutch of disturbingly spangled gowns when I became aware of a strong odor. I looked to see if anyone else had noticed. Sam's nostrils were quivering, and Teri looked distressed.

"What *is* that?" I asked.

"I have no idea," Teri replied, her eyes squinting and a manicured hand held up to her nose.

"Gaack." I spied Mary rounding the corner.

"How's it going?" she called out, her face plastered in so many layers of makeup that she looked ready for Mardi Gras.

"What perfume *is* that?" I gagged as Sam coughed and took a step backwards.

"It's my *signature* scent. Whaddya think? I tried a few others first, you know, Chanel and Ralph Lauren and all the big names. I'm not sure how well they mixed with the botanicals, though."

"What's with the clown face?" I asked.

"New chick at the Marquesa Cosmetics counter." She grinned. "I kept telling her, 'More, more!' until the floor manager said I was scaring the other customers and asked me to leave. Cool, huh?"

By now our overloaded olfactory systems had shut down, and Sam and I started to laugh. Teri looked appalled. Mary lingered, making snide comments about the dresses, before growing bored and wandering off.

Sometime later Sam held up a black velvet dress and announced in triumph, "I found it!"

It was sleeveless and almost backless, with a modified halter top capped by a beaded band like a choker. Radiating from the neckband were long strings of beads that pointed toward where my cleavage would be. Spaghetti straps crisscrossed in back, which would allow my skin to play peekaboo above the invisible zipper. It was very pretty. Very stylish. It just wasn't *me*.

"There's not much to it, is there?" I said.

"Teri didn't like it either. Neither of you has any imagination. Just try it on, please?"

The aroma of inadvisably mixed chemicals preceded Mary's appearance by a good ten seconds.

"Guess what!" she crowed. "I'm getting my own personal shopper!"

We stared at her.

"They have this service where you tell them the sorts of things you like, they take your measurements, and when you need something, you call her up and she selects stuff for you. My personal shopper is LaTanya. Can you beat that? She's great. She's a Pisces, which is just perfect for me. . . ." She drifted off again.

Sam waved the dress at me. "Well?"

"Okay, I'll try it on." I returned to the dressing room and closed the door, but continued talking. "You'll have to find some kind of wrap to go with it, though, because I can't be hanging out all over the place. Not with this guy."

"Ooh, do tell," I heard Teri squeal. "Who *is* he?"

"He's one of *those* guys. You know the kind. Gorgeous, funny, interesting, smart. Gracious when he wants to be."

"And the problem is?" Sam asked.

"He's also a jerk. Totally unreliable. Probably has hundreds of girlfriends."

"But sexy," Teri said.

"Incredibly."

"So if he's such a jerk, why are you seeing him?" Trust Sam to get to the point.

"Well, I—"

"Because he's *paying* her, that's why," Mary's voice chirped. "Annie's his *escort*. We're gonna open up an escort service. Isn't that *awesome*?"

"We just lost Teri," Sam said with a muffled chuckle.

"I'm gonna go meet with LaTanya so she can take my measurements," Mary said.

"Girl, how in the world did you convince Neiman Marcus to give you a personal shopper?" Sam asked.

"I told them I was Francis Ford Coppola's niece. You know, Nicolas Cage's younger sister? They live around here. It's plausible."

I opened the door.

"Now, *that* is a *fabulous* dress," Mary said. Mary seldom offered compliments—she claimed it was a Norwegian thing, but I think it was more a Midwestern thing—which made it all the more meaningful when she did.

"Oh, honey," Sam added. "You look incredible."

I evaluated myself in a three-way mirror, twisting and turning to get the full effect. I did look good, though my back was mostly bare and my modest cleavage was on display. "You're sure I don't look like a stuffed sausage?"

"You look good enough to eat," Mary agreed. "What? Edible's good, right?"

"If you want to keep this guy's hands off you tonight, this might be the wrong dress." Sam commented. "Try this on."

She handed me a short, stretchy black jacket covered in tiny black jet beads. It appeared to be made from some NASA miracle fabric, probably one of those things that helped the Apollo 13 astronauts get home. The jacket hugged my shoulders and breasts, and fell away becomingly, hinting at my now-famous butt.

"I believe our work here is done," Sam announced.

I nodded. "Now for the moment of truth."

I looked at the price tags and winced. The dress and jacket together cost half a month's rent. *Oh well*, I thought as I waited for the shock wave to subside. It was Michael's money, after all. No doubt he was accustomed to spending exorbitant amounts on women's clothing.

The loudspeaker, which had been emitting only intermittent bings and boops, suddenly squawked. "Security, report to Personal Shopping. Security to Personal Shopping. Code four."

Sam and I exchanged a look. "Best get a move on, love."

We hailed Teri, who rang up my purchases as Mary stomped past accompanied by two highly pumped security guards. An unpleasant aroma followed in her wake.

"What will they do with her?" I asked Teri. Before I spent a fortune on evening clothes I wanted to be sure I wouldn't need the money for Mary's bail.

"They'll just escort her outside. Kids these days," she said, shaking her head. Teri must have been all of twenty-five years old herself.

I swallowed hard at the total—I'd forgotten to include the astronomical local sales tax in my mental calculations—and handed over a fistful of hundred-dollar bills. Teri looked surprised and a bit disapproving, and I imagined the cash transaction added to my reputation as a call girl.

As Teri hung the dress and jacket on hangers and swaddled them in plastic it occurred to me that unless I really was going into the escort business I wouldn't have much use for the outfit after tonight. I wondered if it would be ethical to return the clothes in the morning. If I were careful not to spill anything on them, no one would be the wiser.

After all, what could possibly happen at a Hillsborough cocktail party?

Chapter 13

For the working forger, the only good art is saleable art.

—Unnamed "deep background" source, "Fabulous Fakes: An Epidemic of Forgery Rocks the Art World," New York Times

"Was that totally random, or what?" Mary grinned as we joined her on the sidewalk. She glared at the gawking tourists, one of whom snapped her photograph to share with the folks back home. "You guys so *totally* freaked when I walked past with those Wide World of Wrestling rejects. I nearly lost it."

"So did we." Sam grimaced.

We trooped back to the truck and jammed ourselves in. Mary's signature fragrance filled the small cab despite the open windows, and by the time we reached the DeBenton Building even Mary was looking a bit green. Gravel spurted as I roared into a spot, yanked up the parking brake, and threw open the door. The three of us tumbled out.

"Whooo-eeee!" Mary yelled at the top of her lungs and stomped around the parking lot, shaking her head and flapping her arms. Sam and I stood hunched over like a couple of winos, hands on our knees, gasping for breath. Frank emerged from his office, sipping a bottle of sparkling water and eyeing us with a curious expression on his face. I straightened up and wondered if it was possible for me to look more foolish around the man.

"There was a little accident at the perfume counter," I explained. Mary snorted.

"How are you, Frank?" Sam asked, showing a great deal more poise. Frank smiled at her while Mary and I slunk up the stairs. I disarmed the alarm, hung my purchases in the oak armoire, and hit Play on the answering machine.

"Stop asking questions," a sinister voice hissed. *"Or suffer the consequences."*

"What the hell was *that*?" Mary demanded.

"Just some creep making crank phone calls," I said, erasing the nasty message. "It happens all the time."

"No, it doesn't. What's going on, Annie? Are you involved in something again?" For someone who had spent a summer picking up trash from the side of the highway as punishment for "borrowing" a car without the owner's permission, Mary was remarkably disapproving of my forays into the seamier side of life.

"It's *nothing*, Mary."

Sam stuck her head in the door. "Annie, love, when will you be going home? I have an idea for some earrings that will be perfect with your new outfit."

"Probably around four, four thirty."

"Are you going to tell her?" Mary demanded, her arms crossed.

"Tell me what?" Sam asked.

"Nothing," I said. "Mary's blowing something way out of proportion."

"'Nothing' my ass," Mary said. "Annie got a threatening phone call."

"What?" Sam turned to me, a cut-the-crap-this-instant look on her face.

"It's no big deal," I dissembled. Loving, caring, insightful friends could be such a pain sometimes. "Threatening phone calls are rarely followed with threatening behavior." I had heard that on a talk show once.

"'Calls'?" Sam said. "How many threats have you gotten?"

"Listen you two, I appreciate your concern. I do. But I've got everything under control."

My friends glared at me.

"Really."

"Annie, you're a grown woman, you've made your decision, and I have to respect that," Sam said. "But if anything happens to you, I want you to know that I will hunt you down and I will kill you."

"And I'll desecrate your body," Mary added, glowering at me.

Sam went to her studio, and Mary and I settled in to work. A well-funded local charity was sponsoring an interdenominational holiday festival at a children's center and had hired me to create the displays. We'd finished crafting the menorahs and were concentrating today on gilding the winged plaster cherubs I had carved and poured last week. I did make an occasional foray into the three-dimensional world of sculpture. I forayed into just about anything that meant getting paid for making art.

Classical water gilding technique calls for covering an object with a thin layer of earth-red clay called bole and floating tissue-thin sheets of real metal on top. Done properly, it yields a stunning—and expensive—finish. Real gold gilt was too pricey for today's project, so we cut corners by painting our cherubs with a red oxide acrylic base and applying composition gold and silver leaf with a water-based glue called sizing. When the sizing was dry we lightly sanded select portions to allow the red base color to show through, and aged the objects with a coat of burnt umber glaze. The glaze pooled in the pockets and recesses of the carvings, mimicking the grime that would accumulate over time. Next we spattered the cherubs with dark gray paint and sealed the finish with a coat of amber shellac.

The work went well, and by the time I looked at the clock it was after five. I felt a stab of panic. I had to get home, shower, and dress—with stockings, no less—by seven. Mary offered to clean up, insisted I take her illegal can of Mace "just in case," and shooed me out the door. I rushed down the hall to Samantha's studio, where she handed me a pair of gorgeous asymmetrical chandelier earrings of naturally misshapen dove gray pearls and jet-black beads. I thanked her effusively and thundered down the outdoor staircase just as a sleek maroon Jaguar drove out of the parking lot.

"Careful, Frank," I called out to my landlord, who was standing in the doorway of his office. "That looks like a newer Jag than yours. You wouldn't want anyone to show you up."

Frank tucked his hands in the pockets of his charcoal gray pinstriped suit. "Thanks for the warning. Oh, about the intruder this morning? Clive in 212 said he saw a man on your fire escape. Brown hair, nice build, good-looking. Ring any bells?"

"Let's see . . . Brown hair, nice build, good-looking. Gee, Frank, *you* weren't on my fire escape this morning by any chance, were you?"

"So you're saying I've got a nice build?"

"It'll pass muster. Not that I notice that kind of thing. I mean, you *are* my landlord."

"True," Frank said, his eyes flickering over me. "Samantha tells me you bought a sexy new frock. Have fun tonight. Don't do anything I wouldn't do."

"Why, Frank," I said, jumping into my truck. "You know me. I'm the soul of propriety."

The soul of propriety was running late. Traffic on the eastward span of the Bay Bridge had congealed as the result of a minor fender bender, and we all got to share in the joy while a couple of Type-As vying for lane position decided whether to exchange insurance information or lawsuits.

I finally squeezed past the holdup, crossed the bridge, zipped off the freeway at Grand Avenue, tooled up the street to my apartment, parked in the gravel lot out back, took the stairs two at a time, and flew in the door. I checked the clock on the mantle of my nonfunctioning fireplace: Michael was due at seven and it was now a little before six.

I hustled into the bedroom, hung my new "frock" in the closet, and headed for the shower, tugging off my clothes as I went. By the time I finished washing and drying my hair it was twenty minutes to seven and I still had to get dressed and do my makeup. I hurried down the hall to the kitchen and poured a glass of wine to calm my nerves. Ten minutes later I knocked the glass over reaching for a tissue and speared myself in the eye with the mascara wand, smearing black goop everywhere.

The front door buzzer rang. I ran into the kitchen in my underwear, mascara-smeared eye squeezed shut, and threw open the window. "Go away!"

"I'm your date," came a muffled reply.

"You're early!"

"No, I'm not."

"I'm not ready."

"I'll help you dress."

"In your dreams," I hollered into space, hoping my words fell in the direction of the front door. "You wait there like a good boy until I'm ready for you."

I slammed the window, darted into the bedroom, and wriggled into my dress. The short black velvet sheath with peekaboo back felt tighter now than it had in the store. The Chinese dumplings I'd eaten for lunch may have been a bad idea. I left it unzipped as I returned to the bathroom and cleaned up the wine-and-mascara mess, wishing I were crawling into bed with a pint of ice cream instead of rendezvousing with a suspicious character like Michael X. Johnson.

"Almost ready?" a deep voice queried.

"Michael!" I jumped, narrowly avoiding another mascara mishap, and glared at his handsome reflection in the mirror. I grabbed more tissues. "How did you get in here?"

"I do this sort of thing for a living, remember?"

"I could have shot you." Mascara in place, I reached for the tin of face powder.

"You don't have a gun."

"You don't know that I don't—"

Warm fingers caressed my bare skin and zipped up my dress. A shiver ran up my spine.

"That is one *fabulous* dress," he growled.

Our eyes met in the mirror. His lean body was dressed in formal black tie, his wavy brown hair was combed and styled, and his green eyes glowed beneath dark eyebrows.

"Get out of here, Michael," I ordered. "There's wine on the kitchen counter; help yourself. I need a few minutes. No joke."

"Your wish is my command."

"Since when? And by the way—did you set off the alarm in my studio this morning?"

His reply drifted down the hall. "I'm shocked, *shocked* that you would accuse me."

"Some thief you are," I muttered, finishing up my toilette with deep red lipstick, a color that was too dramatic for daytime but perfect for tonight. I hoped.

Now for the hair.

"How was I to know your studio had an alarm? It didn't the last time I went in the window." Michael leaned against the bathroom doorframe, wineglass in hand.

"You might have been tipped off by the fluorescent green *Premises Protected by Evergreen Alarms* stickers on the windows," I mumbled through a mouthful of bobby pins.

"Those stickers are everywhere. They don't mean anything." He took a sip of wine and grimaced. "Remind me in the future not to let you pick the wine."

"You're just spoiled. Now go away so I can finish. You're making me nervous."

"I don't know why," he said silkily. "You look stunning."

"Just *go*, Michael, or whatever your name is. And by the way—what *is* your name? Your *real* one, I mean."

"Sylvester. Or maybe Wolfgang. I never could keep it straight."

He had not moved an inch, so I set my comb on the porcelain sink, shoved him into the hall, slammed the bathroom door, and flipped the flimsy lock. Even I could pick that lock with a paperclip, but I thought the symbolism was important.

I piled my hair on top of my head, softened the effect with a few loose curls around my face and neck, and secured the mess with bobby pins. Testing it with a shake of my head, I decided it would hold unless Michael had a convertible.

"Hey!" I cracked the door and called down the hall as I mulled over my small collection of perfumes. Mary's escapade at the perfume counter had ruined me for anything dramatic. "Do you have a convertible?"

"Would you like me to have one?"

"Just answer the question, please." I spritzed myself with a light floral scent.

"I'll get you one if you'd like. Foreign or domestic?"

"It's a yes or no question, Michael. I'm not asking you to *steal* one."

I heard him rummaging around in the living room. The thought was annoying, but I didn't have anything to hide that he didn't already know about. I struggled into black stockings and slipped on my black high heels. They felt okay for the moment but would become uncomfortable after about an hour and a half. I had timed it once. I donned my sparkly jacket, grabbed my black evening bag, and stuffed it with my ID, a handful of cash, lipstick, comb, and my cell phone. I considered bringing Mary's can of Mace, but decided against it. At some point in the evening I might try to use it on Michael and get a snootful myself instead.

Ready at last, I found Michael lounging near a bookshelf and leafing through a photo album. And I thought *I* was nosy. "Find anything interesting?"

"You were a cute kid," he said, snapping the album shut. His eyes roamed up, down, and over my hips and legs, lingered at my exposed cleavage, and finally met my gaze. "And just look at you now."

He was close enough that I could smell his heady mixture of soap and shampoo with just a hint of maleness.

"Shall we?" I asked.

"But of course."

As we emerged into the cold night air, I looked for the

red Jeep he'd been driving last spring. Instead, Michael escorted me to a late-model champagne Lexus.

"New car?"

"Different persona, different car."

"Don't you ever get tired of it all?" I asked as he expertly maneuvered the luxurious vehicle out of the tight lot and onto the street. "I mean, who *is* Seymour, anyway?"

"I don't know. Who's Seymour?"

"You are. You said so earlier."

He merged onto the freeway and headed for the Bay Bridge. "I said Sylvester, not Seymour," he corrected. "Please, Annie. Allow me some dignity."

"I'm serious. Don't you ever get tired of that kind of life? The lies, the deception . . ."

"The travel, the excitement, the meeting new people and having new adventures? *That* kind of life? Most people's lives are fundamentally dishonest, Annie. The difference is that I only deceive those who deserve it. I love my life, just as it is."

I started to reply when Michael pushed a button on the dashboard and the lilting strains of *The Marriage of Figaro* filled the car's plush interior. If he had intended to shut me up he had miscalculated. My grandfather was a Mozart fanatic, and I'd learned every word to *The Marriage of Figaro*. I proceeded to prove it. Loudly.

I had to give Michael points for endurance. He lasted a good half hour, conceding defeat only when we reached the Hillsborough exit off I-280.

"Tell me, Annie," he said. "What's new in your life these days?"

"Work." Suddenly I didn't feel like chatting.

"Anything interesting?"

"Nope."

"How's that Picasso coming along?"

"Fine."

"Plan to finish it up soon?"

"Did. Don't have it anymore."

Wait a minute.

"Is *that* why you tried to break into my studio this morning, you thieving scumbag?"

"Whoa!" Michael said and turned toward me, his handsome face the picture of outraged honor. "I wanted to see you, that's all."

"You expect me to believe that?"

"Annie, had I wanted the Picasso, I would have taken it. But I would not have taken it from you. What kind of person do you think I am?"

"A liar and a cheat."

"I suppose you've got me there," he said with a slight incline of his head.

"And what's with engineering the Stendhal fainting at the Brock so that Carlos Jimenez could steal the Chagall?"

"Ah, so you figured that out."

"Answer the question."

"Which question was that?"

"How were you involved? And why?"

"I owed Carlos a favor from last spring's Caravaggio fiasco. When I realized the guys in Bryan's group were enthralled with the idea of the Stendhal Syndrome, it seemed like the perfect diversion. I planted the idea that the most sensitive among them might be overtaken with emotion in the presence of the Gauguin. I never imagined they would *all* hit the floor."

"I guess they're a sensitive bunch," I mused. "Why did Carlos want the Chagall?"

"I have no idea."

"And if you did, you wouldn't tell me?"

He shrugged.

"You are going to get the Chagall for me, though, right? That's our deal. I act nice tonight, and you get the painting back so Bryan's off the hook. *Right?*"

"A promise is a promise, Annie. It should be ready in the next day or two."

"What do you mean, 'ready'?"

"I mean I should have it for you in a day or two. Trust me."

I peered out the window, but darkness had fallen and the wooded landscape did not offer much in the way of night vistas.

"I'll bet being self-employed makes it hard to find a love life," Michael said as the Lexus snaked along the rural road.

"Not really. It just so happens I'm seeing someone."

"Oh, please," he scoffed.

"It's true!"

"Since when?"

"For a little while." Emphasis on *little*.

"I see. So who is this guy?"

"His name's Josh."

"Does Josh have a last name?"

"Reynolds." What the hell. Josh didn't have anything worth stealing that I knew of.

"Never heard of him."

"Why would you have heard of him? This isn't high school."

"Is he in the business?"

"What business would that be?"

Michael gave me A Look.

"It just so happens he's not currently wanted by the police, if that's what you mean," I retorted.

"Already done his time, has he?" Michael chuckled.

"What line of work is good ol' Josh Reynolds in these days?"

"He owns his own business."

"What kind of business?"

"Construction business."

"Oh brother . . . So that's it, is it?"

"What's it?" I bristled.

"You want some, bad."

"*What?* I do n—" Of course I did. But it wasn't any concern of his. "You are such a *jerk*!"

"Annie. You should have called me," he continued, unfazed. "I would've been happy to help you."

"Help me into jail, more like."

"Not on purpose," Michael mused. "Those construction guys have some muscles, huh?"

I rolled my eyes. "You're not my girlfriend, Michael. I'm not going to tell you about my lover's manly body."

Michael brought the car to a halt at a deserted intersection, set the parking brake, and turned toward me. "Girlfriend? Not hardly," he said, his voice low. "But I *do* know this: You'd rather be sleeping with me."

"You are the most arrogant, conceited, self-centered—"

Michael's mouth swooped down onto mine, my pulse shot into overdrive, my stomach plunged, and my toes began to curl. By the time his tongue started playing with mine my entire being had been reduced to the consistency of Play-Doh.

So much for playing hard to get.

I was on the verge of getting naked when he broke the kiss and reality came flooding back. "Hell, Annie," Michael whispered, his voice gruff, his green eyes piercing mine. "I'd be happy to help you with your lack of a love life anytime."

"Just drive the damned car," I said through clenched

teeth, and Michael put the car in gear. I didn't know what he was thinking, but I was preoccupied with corralling the raging hormones his kiss had released. They were putting up quite a fight.

"I didn't mean to put an end to our delightful conversation," Michael said, glancing at me from the corner of his eye. "But I've wanted to kiss you for quite some time."

"And my calling you names made me too hard to resist, is that it?"

"You don't believe me, do you?"

"What, precisely, are you referring to? I don't believe anything you say, as a rule."

"You don't believe that I've been wanting to kiss you?"

"I don't know what to believe, Michael," I sighed, dropping my head against the leather headrest and closing my eyes. "That's what comes from dealing with you folks in 'the business.' You know the saying 'once burnt, twice shy'? I learned the meaning of that the hard way."

I felt Michael's hand on the back of my neck, massaging very gently.

"You can believe the part about my wanting you. Annie, I—" He cut himself off. "We'll have to finish this later."

I opened my eyes to see a pair of massive black wrought-iron gates topped with a curlicued *H* highlighted in gold leaf. A circular driveway skirted an expansive green lawn, in the center of which was an ornate, ten-foot-tall fountain. Chubby cherubs frolicked with sea creatures as water splashed gaily about them. The façade of a magnificent red brick Georgian mansion was lit up like a theater production, highlighting the massive Corinthian columns that marched along the façade with military precision. Where were we—Tara?

Michael gave me an encouraging look and squeezed my hand. "Showtime."

"Cue the orchestra," I replied.

He rolled to a stop in front of the portico, handed his keys to a hovering valet, and came around the car to help me out. His grip on my arm was too tight.

"I'm not going to run away," I whispered. "Not in these shoes, that's for sure."

"Sorry."

Could the X-man be nervous? I wondered as granite chips crunched underfoot. I studied my escort out of the corner of my eye. I had assumed Michael was attending this shindig for reasons other than a love of cocktail wieners, but I never thought whatever scheme he was cooking up would unfold tonight. Was I about to become an unwitting—read: incredibly gullible and likely to be railroaded by the district attorney—accomplice? I doubted how long I'd hold out under even a half-assed interrogation. I'd probably crack if somebody so much as shone a forty-watt bulb in my face.

I was considering faking a case of sudden-onset food poisoning when a uniformed doorman materialized at the carved cherry double doors and ushered us in, demonstrating that being wealthy meant never having to turn a doorknob. I chanced another glance at Michael's tense expression. *Too late to back out now, Annie*, I thought. *Do it for the Chagall.*

The two-story foyer boasted marble trim with gold-leafed accents, a sparkling crystal chandelier, and a stunning hanging staircase along the curved rear wall. I stifled an urge to race up the stairs and sweep back down, à la Scarlett O'Hara, and declined the doorman's offer to take my jacket. Before I paraded around half naked in front of strangers, I needed a drink. Maybe several.

We were shepherded down a hallway toward the sound of muted conversation and tinkling glassware. A cavernous room was paneled in dark walnut with a vaulted, beamed ceiling and a massive stone fireplace where a fire roared. Heavy carved furniture and expensive Oriental rugs did little to disguise the room's outsized proportions or lend it an air of warmth, and I marveled at the number of trees that had been sacrificed so our hosts could live in such splendor.

A small man greeted us. He was in his late fifties and wore his salt-and-pepper hair swept back from a gleaming forehead. A pallid complexion and a pair of rosy lips, combined with prominent front teeth, gave him the unfortunate appearance of a rabbit. The man's pale gray eyes had a hard, calculating gleam as they looked me over from head to toe.

Make that a really *mean* rabbit.

"Ah! Raphael! So good of you to come!" The man spoke with an odd accent that sounded British with vaguely Germanic overtones. It was not from Australia or New Zealand, I was sure of that. It took a moment to realize the man was speaking to Michael.

Raphael?

"I am ver' heppy to be here," Michael replied in a straight-from-cable-TV Italian accent. "May I introduce Signorina Anna? Anna, this is Signore Nathan Haggerty."

"Charmed," Nathan assured me. "Delighted you could make it, Raphael, you und your charming companion. Do tell me what you've been up to since Johannesburg."

Aha! I thought. His accent was South African.

Nathan introduced his wife, Diane, a skeletal brunette in her late forties. I wondered if she'd been ill, or if she simply didn't eat anymore. Her slight figure suited her chic Jackie O–style dress, which she had accessorized with an ostentatious necklace of diamonds, rubies, and sapphires in filigreed platinum. I decided the stones had to be real because no woman in her right mind would wear something that hideous unless it had cost a fortune.

A waiter offered us drinks and we started to circulate. Most of the other guests were Hong Kong nationals who acted pleased when I attempted the few Mandarin phrases my grandfather had taught me. I omitted the one about demanding a lawyer.

I was engaged in a discussion with a physician about whether feng shui was a valid design philosophy or—as I had always suspected—just a bunch of hooey when a tall blond man named Kevin Something joined us. He seemed somehow familiar as his little piggy eyes squinted at me, and he hovered too close for comfort, gazing at my cleavage. For some reason Kevin decided we would like to know why South African apartheid hadn't been such a bad an idea after all.

As I listened to his tired racist twaddle I waited for our host or hostess to interrupt, but no one said a word. I figured I had two options. I could ignore him, in deference to my status as a guest in the Haggerty home. Or I could take him out, in deference to right-thinking people everywhere.

I took him out.

My words of denunciation rang out loud and strong. I was on my second glass of a smoky, twelve-year-old single-malt scotch and had not eaten anything in hours, a combination that made me unusually loquacious. The phrases "Hitler wannabes," "fascist scumbags," and "limp-dicked losers" may have made an appearance. When I finally wound down I realized the room had fallen silent and all eyes were trained on me. Michael smirked, the Haggertys looked surprised, and the Hong Kongers seemed embarrassed. Kevin the Nazi wore a ghost of a smile.

Once again I was a social pariah.

Warmed by the scotch and the argument, I excused myself and slipped into the hall, where a Latina maid hung my jacket in a closet. She glanced around furtively and winked. I winked back, and she disappeared into the kitchen. I longed to follow, since that was clearly where I belonged. Instead, I lingered in the hall, dreading a return to the hostile crowd and feeling more than a little exposed with nothing but air on my bare back.

And warm fingers running up my spine.

"That is one *hell* of a fine dress," came Michael's low, sexy growl in my ear.

"Do you like the earrings?" I asked over my shoulder. "My friend Samantha made them especially for tonight."

"I like them very much. But I *adore* this dress." He turned me around so that we faced each other, his hands resting lightly on my waist.

"Thanks for the support with Kevin the Nazi, pal."

Michael laughed, his eyes crinkling adorably. "Are you kidding? You didn't need my help. You could have taken him out with one hand tied behind your back." His voice grew more intimate. "He was outmatched and outgunned. You were magnificent, sweetheart. I love it when you pontificate."

"I do *not* pontificate!"

"*Au contraire*, my dear. You are the most pontificating female I have ever had the, ah, *pleasure* to know." He rested his forehead against mine. His skin was smooth and warm, and I felt his breath on my face. I had another *Gone with the Wind* moment, imagining Michael scooping me up in his strong arms and dashing up the curved stairs to have his wicked way with me. I swallowed, hard.

"Raphael, won't you two lovebirds join us, *per favore*? We're gathering in the library for a little show," our hostess called out with a gracious smile and a rotten Italian accent.

"Of-a course," Michael/Raphael replied, letting go of my waist.

"What's the story with this crowd?" I whispered as we followed Diane.

"Most are Nathan's business associates. He must have something in the works in Hong Kong. By the way, you womenfolk are supposed to keep your mouths shut and your opinions to yourself. Did I forget to mention that?"

He emitted a satisfying "oof" when I elbowed him in the stomach.

We arrived in the library, where the guests were oohing and aahing over a painting spotlighted above the stone fireplace. I halted midstride, transfixed, the babble of voices fading. When I finally tore my eyes away I saw Michael watching me.

So this was why he'd brought me here.

It was a magnificent oil portrait of an elderly man, his gnarled hands and wrinkled features exaggerated for effect as he gazed at the viewer with a stubborn yet serene air. The signature in the lower right corner of the canvas was that of Quentin Massys, the son of a blacksmith who had become one of fifteenth-century Antwerp's leading artists. In America the northern European Renaissance artists were not nearly as well known as the Italian masters, but in Europe Massys was famous for his dramatic triptych altarpieces and his expressive portraits, which emphasized the individuality of his subjects. The Massys above the Haggertys' fireplace looked to be one of his best.

Except Massys had not painted this portrait. Georges LeFleur, my grandfather and art forger extraordinaire, had.

"Anna?" I heard Nathan calling from what seemed like a great distance. "Is everything all right?"

I mentally shook myself and turned to smile at him. "What an extraordinary painting."

"Aah," Nathan said with a self-satisfied sigh. "An important Dutch artist. Do you know him?"

"Massys. But he wasn't Dutch. He was Flemish."

Michael chimed in. "You should-a take her word for it, Nathan. Anna knows a great-a deal about Renaissance art."

"Is that right?" Nathan replied, his tone an unpleasant combination of skepticism and lasciviousness. "Perhaps I shall test you, Anna. Would you say that this painting"—he nodded at the Massys—"is genuine? Or perhaps a clever imposter?"

"Since you asked the question," I replied, "I would say it's a fake."

Nathan roared with laughter. "But you *are* something of an expert, are you not? Raphael tells me that you studied with Anton Woznikowicz, the well-known art . . . restorer."

"Briefly, yes," I said. As far as the cops and the IRS were concerned, Anton was a legitimate art restorer. His real money, though, came from illegitimate art forgery. How much did Nathan know? And why was he playing these guessing games with me?

Kevin the Nazi came over to stand next to Nathan, and I realized why the two seemed familiar: I had seen them last Sunday morning leaving Frank DeBenton's office. The Giggles Twins. Did they recognize me, too? How were they connected to Frank?

"Perhaps, Anna, you would you care to see my private collection?" Nathan asked, voice as smooth as silk. "It is in my study. I do not share it with many."

Michael's eyes gleamed with avarice.

Reality check. Grand theft was a felony, and a blazing orange prison jumpsuit was not a good look for me. Michael was gorgeous and charming and one hell of a kisser, but he was also a thief and a liar, and he never hesitated to use me. Why did I keep forgetting that?

"Why, I would *adore* seeing your collection, Nathan," I whispered so only he could hear. As an art lover I *was* curious to see his collection; as a woman I was happy to spite Michael. "Could I get a *private* tour?"

Nathan's eyes widened. He nodded, said he would be right back, and rushed off.

Michael sidled up. "What was all that about?"

I shrugged. "Nothing much. Oh look, here's Diane."

Our hostess sank her claws into Michael's arm and dragged him away, chattering about her plans to attend Wimbledon next year.

Nathan escorted me up the plush carpeted stairs to the second floor and down a long gallery. Stopping in front of a stout mahogany door, he took a keycard from his vest pocket and swiped it in the card reader. The door unlocked with an audible click.

"I disarmed the sensors," he said, waving me into his study. "This is a *most* valuable collection. I don't allow *anyone* in here unescorted. I even dust the room myself!"

"Nathan, you are the *zaniest*!" I quipped, before the sheer beauty of the fifteenth- and sixteenth-century paintings lining the walls struck me dumb. The northern European masters were famous for their meticulous detail, use of dramatic light, and discerning portrayals of everyday life. I recognized two Marinus van Reymerswaele, another Massys, one Rembrandt van Rijn, two Jan Steen, and one each by Cornelius Bega and Adriaan van Ostade. There were three others in the same genre, but these were of lesser quality and I was not familiar with the artists.

I circled the room examining each. Both of the Jan Steen and the Rembrandt were forgeries, though I did not recognize the forger. The Rembrandt was not even particularly well done, I thought with a sniff, which surprised me because Rembrandt was not hard to forge. To my chagrin one of the Reymerswaeles and the van Ostade had been forged by my grandfather.

Not for the first time, I cursed the old man. I kept thinking Grandfather would become less prolific with age, but the opposite seemed to be true. But why did Nathan have so many of Georges' forgeries?

"This is quite a collection, Nathan," I said. "I see you have an affinity for the northern Europeans."

"Ah yes." He beamed with delight. "Yes, I have built the collection over many years, taking great care to acquire only the best."

Georges LeFleur is certainly the best, I thought.

"Would you like to see the brightest jewel in my crown?" Nathan crossed the room to an easel, where a painting was covered with a black cloth. He grabbed one end of the cloth, paused for effect, and whipped it off.

It was incredible. A beautiful, intricately detailed Vermeer. A young woman peered over one shoulder, as if the artist had caught her by surprise, her animated eyes and tentative smile so perfectly rendered it appeared she might at any moment spring to life. I approached the painting with reverence, losing myself in the shimmering colors and dramatic shadows and tingling to beat the band. It was genuine.

But what was Haggerty doing with it? Vermeer was a painstakingly slow painter in part because, unlike his contemporaries, he worked without the assistance of apprentices. One of the reasons Rembrandt was easy to forge was because his apprentices did so much of the actual work that many signed Rembrandts should more rightly have been attributed to them. But because Vermeer insisted on working solo he created far fewer paintings, and as far as I knew they were all accounted for in museums and well-known private collections.

Unless some of those Vermeers were fakes, and wealthy collectors such as Nathan Haggerty had been buying the real ones on the black market.

"It is amazing, is it not?" Nathan asked.

"Amazing."

"Would you say this one is fake or genuine?"

"Oh, genuine," I said without thinking. I met his eyes. "Why do you ask?"

He smiled his rodent smile. "I think, my dear, that you know rather a great deal about art. And the one in the library *is* a fake, but I imagine you know that already."

Did Haggerty know about my grandfather? Why hadn't Michael warned me? Okay, another item for the To Do list. First kill Grandfather, then kill Michael.

"And here is my newest acquisition," Nathan said, leading me to a canvas laid out on a walnut side table. "I haven't had her framed yet, and she doesn't quite go with the rest of the collection, but I absolutely fell in love with her."

"She" was a Picasso. And not just any Picasso, *the* Picasso—the one I had restored for Frank.

Nathan opened a mirrored liquor cabinet and poured two snifters of an amber wine from a crystal decanter. He handed me one, and I took a sip of a very fine Armagnac, my favorite brandy.

I forgot about my host for a moment while gazing in awe at the exquisite Vermeer.

"You are speechless," Nathan said with evident satisfaction. "I myself become this way around great art."

Great art might silence Nathan's organs of speech but it had no effect on his other organs. Rabbity Haggerty kept sneaking lascivious peeks at my cleavage.

"Thank you for showing me your collection. We should rejoin the party."

"Why, Anna, what's the hurry?" he asked, coming up behind me and brushing his hips against my rear. "Why don't we relax and enjoy ourselves?"

My temper flared. Bad move, pal. I had ridden public transit. In Rome.

I slumped a little and leaned back, then lifted my foot and stomped down hard, my pointy high heel drilling into the vulnerable bones at the top of his foot. Nathan let out a screech, and as he bent forward in pain I shot up to my full height, ramming the top of my head into his chin's soft underbelly. His teeth made a satisfying clacking sound. I spun around and tossed my Armagnac on his snowy white shirt.

"Ooo, Nathan! I'm so sorry! I didn't see you standing there! Are you all right?"

My not-so-genial host was hopping about on one foot, reeking of brandy, his eyes brimming with tears. *He must have taken one hell of a bite out of his tongue*, I thought, suppressing a grin. The crown of my head smarted, but the pain was well worth it. "I'll just go call someone," I said and hurried out of the room.

At the bottom of the stairs I paused to hitch up my halter top and take a deep breath. I was about to march into the library and demand Michael take me home when I had a better idea. Tiptoeing down the hall, I retrieved my jacket from the closet and slipped out the front door.

The valets were lounging against a maroon Jaguar, smoking and chatting. When they saw me they came to attention and tossed their cigarettes on the crushed granite driveway.

"The champagne Lexus, please," I said in a throaty voice. "The babysitter called. Poor little Timmy has a tooth coming in and is crying for his mommy. You know how it is."

A pimply faced valet, who looked to be all of seventeen, did not know how it was and did not really care. He ran off to get the car. I rummaged in my evening bag for a couple of crumpled bills, traded them for the car keys, and hopped into the driver's seat. The dashboard looked like a jet-liner's, but I managed to adjust the seat, shift the car into drive, and release the brake. As I reached the wrought-iron gates at the end of the driveway I glanced in the rearview mirror in time to see the front door fling open and Michael run out.

I floored it.

Chapter 14

Revenge is sweet, I chortled. I still didn't know what Michael's plan was, but I was sure it somehow involved me. True, abandoning Michael at the Haggertys nixed my chances of having sex tonight, but I was so pissed at him for using me I wouldn't have gone for it anyway.

Unless he did that neck rubbing thing again.

My problem now was finding the freeway. The area was densely wooded, with the twisty roads and lack of street signs common to snooty neighborhoods, and my initial surge of confidence waned. I *was* supposed to turn right out of the Haggertys' driveway, wasn't I? If not, I was headed further into the hills.

I pulled over at a wide spot on the road, fumbled around until I found the car's interior light, and rummaged through the glove box and door pockets for a map. Nothing. No map, not a scrap of paper, not even a tire pressure gauge or a stick of gum. Michael had probably rented the Lexus, the big fake.

Frustrated, I sat up and glared at the instrument panel. Aha! A little box glowed with the letters LOLA, a global positioning system that my friend, Miranda, swore by. Miranda was a realtor who could sell an igloo to the pope, but got lost in an empty room. Now all I had to do was figure out how LOLA worked. I pressed the button marked *power* and tried to read the small print on the screen.

I was hunched over, singing, "Whatever Lola wants, Lola gets," and poking buttons with abandon, when flashing blue lights filled the car's interior. I squinted out the rear window and saw a police car pull up behind me. For once I was glad to see a cop. The nice officer would know how to get to the freeway. Best of all, I was well dressed and nowhere near a crime scene.

The cop tapped on the window with his flashlight. I searched for the button to lower the window but succeeded only in locking and unlocking the doors. I hated power controls. Finally I just opened the door.

He jumped back, his hand going to his gun.

I held my hands up, an ingratiating smile on my face. "Good evening, Officer. I'm afraid I'm a little lost. Could you tell me how to get to the freeway?"

"Step out of the car, please, ma'am."

Officer Strong Jaw seemed less than friendly. Didn't he realize I was driving a Lexus?

"Is there a problem, Officer?" I asked as I climbed out.

"Not anymore," growled a deep voice I knew only too well. I'd heard it in my dreams, after all.

"How did you—?"

"LOLA ratted you out," Michael snapped. "GPS works two ways, sweetheart."

Michael thanked Officer Strong Jaw for his help and said he would make sure the doctor adjusted my meds. The cop nodded, got into his cruiser, and roared off.

So much for hearing my side of the story, I thought. Then again, I did kind of steal the car.

Michael stalked past me and climbed into the driver's seat. "Get in. Now. Or I'll leave you here," he said, his voice tight.

I hustled around to the passenger's side and jumped in. He peeled out, made a U-turn, and raced down the road without saying a word. I had a feeling I was witnessing Michael's anger for the first time, and it was not a pretty sight. I was silent as well, figuring it behooved me to be discreet for once. It was also the one surefire way to drive Michael nuts.

He held out until we reached the freeway. "What in the *hell* did you think you were doing back there?" he snarled.

"Let's see," I snarled back. "I believe it's called the *very same thing* you did to *me*. Twice, if I'm not mistaken."

"That was different."

"Really? How so? Oh, yes, that's right—it was different because it was *you* doing the leaving and *me* getting stranded. High and dry. All alone. No money, no friends, no—"

"All right, Annie. All right. You've made your point." He sounded a little abashed. Not much, but probably as much as an international art thief and general no-goodnik was capable of being. "Your little disappearing act put Haggerty on edge. He thinks you're working for someone."

"That's ridiculous. Who would I be working for?"

"Could be a lot of people. The FBI, maybe."

"The FBI?" I had been accused of many things in my

life, but never of being on the right side of the law. "Why would he think that?"

"He's a bit paranoid, though not without reason. He's been under scrutiny for a while." Michael shook his head. "I can't *believe* you took off like that."

We rode along in silence.

"So what did you see?" Michael asked, having recovered from his snit fit.

"See where?" I, on the other hand, had not.

Michael let out a breath, making a whistling sound. I saw a muscle in his jaw clench and smiled to myself.

"In his private collection, Annie. I couldn't believe how quickly Haggerty took you there. He took a real shine to you." Michael glanced at me. "Must have been the dress."

"Oh, of course. What else? Couldn't have been my obvious intelligence, my witty conversation, or my magnetic personality. No, sir. Must've been my—"

"Well?" he interrupted.

"Well what?"

More whistling.

"His collection. What does he have? Are the paintings genuine?"

I looked out the window.

"The guy's scum, Annie," Michael said. "Your grandfather did some work for him until he realized what Haggerty was up to."

"And what might that be?"

"He's been insuring the originals and replacing them with fakes. He then claims the paintings were stolen, collects the insurance money, and sells the originals on the black market. Turns quite a profit that way."

"Nothing new about that," I said, wondering why my grandfather had been so outraged at a spot of insurance fraud. Half of Georges' business came from people who wanted to sell the family heirlooms and replace them with fakes.

"Except Haggerty doesn't stop there. He uses the paper-work on the originals to convince buyers the forgeries are genuine, then uses the originals as collateral to finance arms deals. He does business with some very nasty charac-ters."

I recalled Frank's telling me about similar art-for-arms deals. No wonder Georges had been upset. "And you're helping him?"

"Of course not," he said, surprised. "I want a couple of his pieces, that's all. But I need to know which ones are real. No point in stealing worthless fakes. No offense to your grandfather."

"None taken."

"So that's where you come in."

"No, actually, that's where I step out."

"What do you mean?" he asked, casting nervous glances my way.

"I mean that I have no intention of getting involved in your little scheme. I can't *believe* you had me accompany you while you cased the joint—and now you expect me to tell you which paintings to steal? Didn't your mother ever tell you that stealing is *wrong*? Do you have any idea how long and hard I've worked to establish myself as a legiti-mate artist? How could you possibly think to involve me?"

"Annie, you're exaggerating. Now, listen. A lot of time, money, and planning have gone into this project. All I need to know is which paintings are real. You're not involved at all."

"The hell I'm not!" I was yelling now. "I could be pros-ecuted as an accessory and you damn well know it!"

"Oh, please. Could we have a little less hysteria here?"

It was my turn to clench my jaw and whistle.

"Here's a plan," I offered. "Steal them all and figure it out later."

"Annie . . ." Michael growled.

"No, really. Just cut them out of their frames and have done with it." This was a grave insult to a professional art thief. A thief who would cut a painting out of its frame—thereby destroying at least a part of the artwork—was not someone Michael would care to share his vocation with.

"What *is* it with you, Annie?" he demanded.

"What is it with *me*?"

"Yeah, *you*. What's the matter? Did you and Mr. Muscles take a vow to work at your boring, meaningless little jobs for the rest of your boring, meaningless little lives, scrimping and saving so that one day you could afford some crappy little tract house in Pinole and raise your 1.9 children? Is that it?"

"What are you saying? That I can't live a normal life and be happy? Is *that* what you're saying?"

By now we had both worked ourselves up and were hitting shrill, rather pathetic notes. Worst of all, I was no longer sure what we were arguing about.

"Why the hell would you want to be *normal*, Annie? I thought you wanted something more from life."

"What's wrong with being normal? Lots of people do it."

"You're *not* 'lots of people.' Face it."

"Maybe I could be if I didn't hang around lowlife scoundrels like you."

Michael snorted. "You couldn't be normal if you parachuted into the middle of Normalville, USA. Not even if you were elected the mayor of Normalville." His voice softened. "You're just not, Annie. You're special. It's a burden you'll simply have to bear."

I had no idea how to respond to that, so I punched the

buttons on the CD player and the strains of *The Marriage of Figaro* poured out once more. Sitting back with a huff, I considered what Michael was asking of me. I had no love for Nathan, that wascally wabbit, but stealing was wrong.

That sounded pretty good, I thought. Highly principled.

Too bad that wasn't why.

The real reason I didn't want to get involved in Michael's scheme was because I was afraid to put even one toe on that slippery slope. I didn't need an international art thief to tell me I had larceny in my heart. The straight and narrow was a confusing place for someone who had inherited her grandfather's talent and been indoctrinated by his flexible ethics. Some of the best moments of my life, the ones I would recall with fondness when I was a very old woman, had been spent on the wrong side of the law.

And on top of everything else, Nathan Haggerty knew Frank DeBenton. My relationship with my landlord was already strained by errant burglar alarms. I could only imagine how he would react to my involvement in the theft of his client's art collection.

We crossed the Bay Bridge and Michael switched off the Mozart. "Are you going to tell me which of Haggerty's paintings are genuine?"

"No."

"What about the Vermeer?"

I shrugged.

"Dammit!" He slammed the steering wheel with the palm of his hand.

"Michael, you should have told me what you wanted in the first place! I would have refused then and saved us both this aggravation."

There was a long pause.

"But then I wouldn't have seen you in that dress," he

grumbled, and I felt my face flush. "You were dazzling tonight. Magnificent with Kevin the Nazi. I was in awe."

I warmed under his compliments, even though I realized he was just trying a new approach. "I'm not going to tell you about the paintings, Michael."

"I know."

We exited the freeway and skirted Lake Merritt, beautiful in the clear night air.

"So . . . Are you going to invite me up to your apartment?" he asked.

"No."

"Yes, you are."

"*No*, I'm *not*."

"Don't be mad, Annie," Michael cajoled. He swung into the parking area behind my building and pulled up next to my truck. Shifting into park, he set the brake but left the engine running.

We sat there, in a warm, luxurious cocoon. Michael's strong hand cupped the back of my head and my heart started pounding.

He leaned in.

I leaned back.

"Gotta go," I said, reaching for the door handle. It was locked. I fumbled with the controls, this time sending the window up and down.

"Annie," Michael purred as he urged my head towards his, desire blazing in his green eyes.

For a split second I almost fell for it. But the seduction routine was too blatantly connected to my refusal to tell him what I'd learned about Haggerty's collection. Even I wasn't that desperate. Yet.

"Michael? If you don't open this door I'm going to start screaming. And you know how well I scream."

He sat back and sighed. "What am I going to do with you, Annie?"

"You're going to let me out of this damned car, that's what. And you're never going to call me again, or break into my studio again, or ask me for help stealing art again."

"You're breaking my heart."

"It's not your heart I want to break."

"Ouch!" Michael said, shifting his hips.

"Are you going to open the door?"

He hesitated. "Just tell me about the Vermeer, that's all. Is it worth stealing? None of the others are worth the risk. Just a simple yes or a no. Please, Annie."

I took a deep breath and exhaled. "I'll think about it."

"Annie, I—"

"No. I have to think about it, Michael."

"Fair enough. But thinking is easier with two heads. Why don't we go upstairs and I'll give you a relaxing massage? You seem a little tense."

"Your concern is touching," I said sarcastically. "I'll relax as soon as I'm in bed with Ben & Jerry."

"What about Mr. Muscles? Or isn't he into kinky four-somes?"

"Why? You interested?"

Michael looked shocked.

"Open the door, Michael. *Now*."

He pushed a button and the lock popped open. As I started to climb out, he leaned across the seat and grabbed my elbow. Our eyes met, his expression serious.

"This is important, Annie. Please. I need your help."

I wrenched my arm away. "What is it with you? Do you have a gambling problem or something? What happened to all the money from the Caravaggio you stole last spring? You really should think about saving some of your ill-gotten gain for a rainy day so you don't end up in the Old Felons'

Home. And I want that Chagall by this weekend. You promised."

I slammed the car door. Michael waited until I had the front door open before pulling out of the parking lot and roaring off into the night. He did not look back.

I muttered under my breath as I stomped upstairs, let myself into my apartment, and trudged down the hall to the bedroom to change. Tonight's sole triumph was that I had not ruined my fancy new dress. No wine or food stains, no tears; purse and jacket were accounted for; not even a run in my stockings. Even my high heels felt okay. I'd been so pissed off all evening I'd scarcely noticed how uncomfortable they were.

I kicked the shoes off with satisfying spite anyway, shrugged off the jacket, and reached over my shoulders to unzip the dress. I managed to lower the zipper about an inch before my arms were stretched as far as they would go. I tried curling one arm behind my back and snaking it between my shoulder blades, but the zipper's tongue was just out of my reach.

I hopped up and down. Nothing. Lying flat on my stomach on the bed, I reached behind me. That was even worse. I tried pulling the dress off, but my shoulders were too wide in one direction, and my hips were too wide in the other. No matter how I contorted myself, I could not reach the bloody zipper.

This makes no sense, I raged. I had been in and out of this dress before. How had I managed it? Then I remembered: I hadn't. Samantha had helped me at the store and Michael had zipped me up earlier this evening. Apparently it takes a village to unzip a dress.

I sank onto the side of the bed and cradled my head in my hands, tears of frustration stinging my eyes. What an incredibly maddening ending to an extraordinarily stupid evening. *This is all Michael's fault*, I thought. Had he not been a criminal and a schmuck he would be here with me now, and not only would I be naked but I would probably be having the first of ten orgasms. Shit.

The phone rang. I snatched it up. "Michael?" What the hell, if he was within the sound of my voice I was inviting him over.

"It's Derek. From Marble World?"

"Oh. Hi, Derek," I said, my heart sinking. "What's up?"

"We got a shipment in today, right after you left."

"It's kind of late. . . ."

"I know. But the truckers are supposed to pick it up first thing in the morning. We're working late seeing as how these containers all came in this afternoon. Gloria's here too."

I heard a shuffling of the phone, and Gloria came on the line.

"Hey, girl. Derek mentioned you wanted to check it out, and now's your chance."

"You made everybody work late, huh? You're a tyrant."

"Just Derek and my brother. I lured them with a couple of six packs."

"Which brother is this?"

"We call him Big Boy. He was at the last barbecue."

"I don't think we met." I glanced at the bedside clock. 10:07. At this hour I should be able to buzz over there and back, no problem. And Gloria could help me out of my dress! "I can be there in, say, twenty minutes?"

"Yeah? Okay. We'll stick around. Bye."

But wait. If I wore the dress to the stone warehouse it would get covered in marble dust and I wouldn't be able to return it to Neiman Marcus and get my money back. I spied my trusty overalls slumped dejectedly at the end of the bed. The dress was short enough and tight enough that if I hitched it up a little I could wear it under the baggy overalls. It would be wrinkled, but it would not be ruined.

I slid into the overalls and pulled on a loose white T-shirt to cover the top of the dress. The ensemble was pretty lumpy, but whom was I trying to impress? Pulling on a pair of old running shoes, which were in pretty good shape since I never actually ran in them, I slung my black evening bag over my shoulder and ran out the door. Construction on the Bay Bridge slowed me down, but I got through the City and down the Bayshore to Burlingame in just under half an hour.

Once I exited the freeway, my enthusiasm waned. It was desolate here at night. A cold breeze blew off the water, distant foghorns blared, and the lights of the East Bay winked through the wisps of fog. What had possessed me to come, alone, to a warehouse in the middle of the night, dressed in my evening finery and armed with nothing more dangerous than a plastic comb and a few bobby pins? What would I do if someone accosted me? Threaten him with a good grooming?

I had never understood movie heroines who repeatedly put themselves in harm's way until rescued by their heroes, who inexplicably fell in love, ensuring that their hare-brains would further contaminate the gene pool.

Apparently I was now one of those women.

I pulled up in front of Marble World, relieved to see a couple of vehicles in the parking lot and the lights blazing in the front office. I laughed off my fear. My good buddy Gloria was waiting for me with Derek and a brother reassuringly named Big Boy.

"Hello?" I called out. "Anybody here?"

No answer. I stuck my head in her office. "Gloria?"

No sign of Gloria, but I did catch a glimpse of myself in

a mirror. Yikes. My full makeup, dangling earrings, and the beaded neck of the dress playing peek-a-boo above the collar of the T-shirt made quite a statement. Paint-splattered overalls and sparkly evening bag completed The Look. Haute Grunge? More like Haute Homeless.

I pushed through the swinging doors into the warehouse.

The empty warehouse. No friendly Gloria awaiting me, no strapping Big Boy eager to watch our backs. Nothing but row upon row of cold, silent stone.

"Hello?" My voice echoed in the cavernous space as I crept down an aisle toward the loading docks. I had a case of the willies by now and jumped at imagined noises.

"Gloria!" I shouted, my fear making me angry. "Where *are* you guys?"

"May I help you?" an accented voice said.

I jumped about three feet in the air, yelped, and spun around. The man was four inches shorter than I and maybe 130 pounds. *Gloria's family must be into irony*, I thought.

"Hi, Big Boy," I said, smiling with relief.

The little man looked startled. "I beg your pardon?"

"Hello? Big Boy?"

"I do not approve of young ladies being so forward."

Who, me? "I'm Annie, Annie Kincaid. I'm supposed to meet Gloria?"

"What for?"

"She called and I, um . . ."

"And you came to ask more questions. I told you to stop asking these questions, but you insisted you did not know what I was talking about."

Uh-oh.

"How'd you get my cell phone number?" As the words left my mouth I realized that I could hardly have focused on a less important detail. I should have been focusing on the fact that this man had threatened to kill me. My heart sped up and I started to stammer. "I . . . uh . . . was just leaving?"

"I think not," the dapper little man said with a shake of his head. He had a dark goatee and was balding on top. A couple more years and a few gray hairs and he would look like a short, malevolent Don Quixote. "I do not approve of nosy young ladies who do not know how to keep themselves healthy."

He inclined his head and two enormous men emerged from between the stone slabs. One was so pumped up with muscles that his arms stuck out from his barrel chest at a forty-five-degree angle, while the other was so hairy it looked like his mother had run off with a gorilla. Neither was likely to be surprised by any of the moves I'd learned in the YWCA's six-week Respect Your Self-Defense class.

Barrel Chest grabbed my arm and started to frisk me.

"Tiene algo," Barrel Chest said, looking confused.

"He says you've got something," Don Quixote said, frowning. "What are you wearing under those, er, pants?"

"I've got a nice dress on, that's all. I don't have any weapons." *Oh, nice move, Annie*, I thought. *Just go ahead and tell him he's free to kill you, why don't you?*

"Why are you wearing a dress under there?" The Don seemed genuinely curious.

"I didn't want to ruin it."

He raised his eyebrows.

"Look, it's a long story. And I'd really like to go home. I'm sorry if I offended you with that Big Boy remark. And please don't take this the wrong way, but some friends of mine will be meeting me here at any minute."

Don Quixote took a slim gold cigarette case from his coat pocket, flipped it open, and selected a cigarette. He tapped one end on the case, stuck the other end in his mouth, flicked a gold lighter, and lit up in blatant violation of the state law banning smoking in public buildings.

He blew a stream of smoke out his nostrils like a bull in children's cartoons and came to stand with his face close to mine. His breath reeked of cigarettes. I turned my head away but was held fast by Ape Man and Barrel Chest. "You are a very nosy girl. A most *inappropriate* girl. Why do you keep asking questions when I tell you to mind your own business?"

"I, um . . . You're right. But I've learned my lesson, boy have I. I'm going straight home and minding my own business from now on, you bet. You can count on me."

"Yes, your mother told us you were nosy."

"My mother?" I said, anger slicing through my fear. "What does my mother have to do with this? If you touch one hair on her head . . ."

"Calm down, *chica*," Don Quixote said with a peculiar smile. "Your mother is a lovely woman. I like her very much. But to my great disappointment, she is married. I do not believe in breaking the sacred vows of matrimony."

Wasn't that just typical? I meet a guy who believes in commitment and he turns out to be a psycho.

"Your mother is much more appropriate than you. She went away like we told her to. She promised us you would do the same."

"And I will. Right this very second, as a matter of fact."

"Sadly, it is a too late for that. Tell me what you know. Who has been talking?" His voice was calm but fierce.

"I don't know. I really don't," I babbled. "No one's been talking to me, that's for sure. Nobody ever talks to me."

He held the cigarette out to me.

"Thanks, I don't smoke," I said.

He raised the glowing tip to my face, so close that I could feel its heat.

"Tell. Me. Now. Was it Pascal?"

"I—" My heart was pounding and bile rose in my throat. Torture was something one saw in movies about political prisoners, not in warehouses in Burlingame. "Please, I don't know—"

"Haggerty?" he hissed. I squeezed my eyes shut and tried not to move. I felt the excruciating pain of a burn on my upper cheek, even though the cigarette had not yet touched my skin.

"The FBI? *Tell me!*" Don Quixote sounded as if he was losing control, but he had nothing on me. I think I peed my pants a little.

A cell phone rang. Don Quixote swore and answered gruffly, taking a deep drag on the cigarette. He turned to me and rolled his eyes, and I wondered if I was supposed to commiserate over the frustration of being interrupted at work. Speaking in rapid Spanish, he tossed the cigarette absentmindedly to the floor and crushed it under the sole of a tooled leather boot. I was never so glad to see someone litter in my life.

"Okay, okay," he groused, and snapped the phone shut. He looked at me speculatively. "What do you know about Robert Pascal?"

"Pascal? Well, he's an artist, a sculptor. He's awfully rude. He's best known for developing a style called . . ."

Don Quixote gestured impatiently and the goons shoved me to my knees. I fell hard, wincing as bits of gravel dug into my skin through the worn overalls. The Don stood over me and punched me in the face. Pain shot through me, and I saw stars and sagged to the ground. Rough hands pulled me back to my knees.

Ape Man giggled. The Don rebuked him. The cell phone rang again.

More Spanish flew, but I did not even try to understand.

My eye was throbbing, my cheek burned, and I felt dazed. I realized I was covered in stone dust like a corpse I'd seen not so long ago. I was starting to put the pieces of the puzzle together, and not liking what I saw, when I was yanked to my feet and dragged. I struggled and was kicked in the thigh, hard.

"Stop it!" I cried impotently.

Ape Man giggled again.

A motor started up, and the heavy steel hook that was used to move the stone slabs lowered. Barrel Chest slipped the hook under the rear strap of my overalls, the hydraulic lift engaged, and suddenly I was three feet off the ground. Don Quixote grabbed the front of my overalls and pulled me toward him until I was almost horizontal. We were nose to nose, my butt sticking up in the air.

"If you live through this night, do yourself a favor," the Man of La Mancha hissed. He hung my once-posh evening bag around my neck like a sign and smiled cruelly. "Mind your own business. And stay away from Haggerty and Pascal."

He gave me a shove and I started spinning as the cable hoisted me higher. I was dizzy and nauseated and petrified that my overalls strap would tear, sending me plummeting to the concrete floor. When the cable at last ground to a halt, I was five feet from the ceiling.

"Don't leave me here!" I yelled at the retreating figures. "*Por favor?* Let me down!"

Ape Man pulled out a gun and fired in my general direction. I ducked, which made me swing even more. My assailants laughed as the bullet ricocheted off the metal roof and several stone slabs before burying itself in a bag of mortar. I heard the muffled sound of a distant door slamming. Silence descended.

I reached behind my head and grabbed the cable, forc-

ing myself to take slow, deep breaths to control the nausea
and to relax. It was nearing midnight and I was alone in a
stone warehouse, dangling several stories above a concrete
floor, held up by the grace of denim and a couple of brass
buckles. A boring life in a crappy tract house in Pinole was
sounding pretty good right about now.

Clear the mind, Annie, that's the girl. Now, *think.* It was
late Tuesday night. What time would the Marble World
people arrive for work in the morning? Seven? Maybe
eight? I could hold on until then, no problem. I just wasn't
sure if my overalls felt the same level of commitment.

The spinning gradually subsided, and I wished I had not
procrastinated about losing those extra fifteen pounds. Tilt-
ing my head back cautiously, I looked up. Near the ceiling,
where the cable met the joist, was a wide steel I beam and
what looked like a ladder that was probably used to work
on the pulley mechanism. All I had to do was shimmy up
the cable, swing over to the I beam, hook one arm around
the ladder, and climb on down.

It was a good plan. Unfortunately my upper body
strength was, to be kind, laughable. Even when I had been
in peak physical condition—which was to say when I was
in the eighth grade—I had not been able to do a single pull-
up. Since then my shoulders hadn't gotten much bigger,
but my hips and butt sure had. A shimmy up the cable was
not in my future anytime soon.

I needed a Plan B. Think, Annie, *think.*

Nothing, absolutely nothing.

I felt a bubble of panic start to grow. Time to look on the
bright side.

Bright side? I was *dangling* from a *hook*!

Okay, try logic. If I survived, I was going to have one
hell of a story to tell at cocktail parties. If I fell, there was
an outside chance it would not be fatal. And if it was fatal,

well, we all had to go sometime. At least it would be quick. And I would not have to pay off my swollen credit card bill.

But still. My sister, Bonnie, would take it hard. And Mary. And Sam. And Pete. Maybe even Frank. I sniffled a little, thinking about my memorial service. My mother and father looking pale and stunned. My grandfather, supported by his old friend Anton, would have aged twenty years since he'd heard the news. The chapel would be filled with flowers and sobbing friends. Maybe Naomi Gregorian, even. Agnes Brock would send a gaudy floral wreath with a sash inscribed, *So Young, So Lovely, So Long.*

And in the corner, a handsome, green-eyed stranger would struggle for composure as he realized his one love, his true love, was lost to him forever. Why oh why had he been so cold, so cruel, so abandoning? The organ, which had been playing a melancholy hymn, would fall silent as the minister stepped up to the pulpit. "Dearly beloved, we are gathered . . ."

No, wait. That was the wedding ceremony. Talk about your Freudian slips.

I heard a muffled trill. Wha—? My cell phone! Geez! I had been so focused on not plummeting to my death I had forgotten I had it with me. Now I felt like an idiot on top of everything else. *Don't hang up*, I prayed to the unknown caller. *Please don't hang up.* My right hand carefully released its death grip on the cable and reached for my handbag. I unzipped it, fished around for the phone, and hit the on button.

DON'T DROP IT!

"Hello?"

"Annie? Listen, I know you think I'm a jerk, but—"

My eyes started to tear up, and my voice shook. "Michael! Oh, thank God! I need you!"

"And I need you, too, my darling," he replied, sounding surprised but pleased. "I'm so glad you've reconsidered—"

"Not *that*, you moron! I need help!"

"Annie, what is it? What's wrong?"

"I'm at Marble World! In Burlingame! I'm hung up, high up, and I don't know how long my overalls will hold out!"

"Take it easy," Michael said calmly. "I'm on my way. You say you're at Marble World, hanging somewhere?"

"Yes, on a cable, suspended from a hook near the ceiling."

"Are you in imminent danger?"

"Only if I fall."

"Annie, honey, that's kind of what I meant . . . Stay on the line with me, now. What are you doing in Burlingame? You're supposed to be eating ice cream in bed."

"I know, I know. I wish I were, too. Hurry, Michael." I hiccuped.

"I am, sweetheart. I am. Are the police on their way?"

"Um, no, I sort of forgot I had the cell phone. Should I call 911?"

He paused. "Do you think you can hold on for ten more minutes? Be honest."

"Um . . ." I thought about the straps that were holding me up. They weren't ripping or anything. Yet. "Yeah, I'm okay. Ten minutes, no problem."

"Because if you're sure you can hang in there, it would probably be best not to call the cops. They're going to ask a lot of awkward questions, like what you're doing at a stone warehouse in the middle of the night."

"Yeah."

"Annie?"

"Yeah?"

"What the hell are you doing at a stone warehouse in the middle of the night?"

"It's kind of a long story. Just get here soon, okay?"

"I'm going ninety-five, sweetheart. What exit do I take?"

I gave him the directions, which were luckily pretty simple since I was in no shape to convey anything complicated. Michael stayed on the line, talking soothingly. "Hang in there, sweetheart. I'm almost there."

"Michael?"

"Yes, darling?"

"The Vermeer's real."

There was a pause. "I was coming to help you anyway, Annie. You know that, don't you?"

I sniffed.

"Don't you?"

"Unghh." I was usually pretty good in a crisis—not especially effective, but reasonably levelheaded—but with rescue in sight I was fast becoming a wreck.

"Okay, I'm pulling into the parking lot. I see your truck. Where are you?"

"In the warehouse. The front door was open before; I don't know about now."

"I'll find a way in," he said confidently, and I did not doubt it for a second.

A few minutes later I heard some banging and slid the cell phone into my overalls pocket. The double doors to the warehouse flew open and there he was, my very own knight in shining armor. I gazed down at Michael soulfully. He gazed up at me and burst out laughing.

Asshole.

"I've got to hand it to you, Annie Kincaid. You are hands down the most unpredictable woman I've ever known."

"Michael, will you *please* shut up and get me down!" I had the mother of all wedgies.

He saluted, sprang into the control booth, and fiddled around until the winch engaged and the hook started to lower. I held on tightly and watched the floor rise up to meet me, experiencing an overwhelming rush of relief tinged with nausea. I was a good eight feet from the ground when the cable stopped and Michael climbed out of the control booth. He stood below me, his arms crossed.

"Is the cable stuck?" I asked anxiously.

"No."

"Then what—"

"Tell me what's going on."

"*What?* Get me *down*, Michael!" I judged the distance to the floor—not far enough to be lethal, but I could break an ankle. And that would make it harder to catch Michael in order to kill him.

"What's wrong with your face? Did somebody *hit* you?"

"The guys who hung me on this hook weren't exactly gentlemen," I said. "Dammit, Michael, let me down!"

"No can do."

"Why the hell not?"

"Because I have a few questions for you, and as soon as you're on terra firma you'll start lying and tap dancing your way around them."

"I don't tap dance!"

"Oh, please. You are the Queen of the Tap."

"No, I'm not."

"Yes, you are."

"No, I'm—"

"Annie? Tell me what happened here. Then tell me why you went ballistic at the Haggertys'. Then tell me which of Nathan's paintings are genuine."

"I did not go *ballistic*!" I said this with as much dignity as I could muster, which under the circumstances was not a lot. "I had every right to be angry that you would use me like that, and I didn't want to be involved in a felony. Is that so hard to believe?"

Michael shrugged. "Fine. So what happened here? Why do you have what promises to be a very impressive black eye, and why are you hanging from a hook?"

"I was trying to get some information about a sculptor and things got, um, out of hand."

"Would that be Robert Pascal by any chance? Didn't I tell you to stay away from him?"

"Maybe." One thing about hanging from a hook—it was hard to squirm.

"Why don't you ever do what you're told like a good girl?"

"Maybe because I'm not seven years old?" I said, losing what remained of my patience. "If you don't let me down immediately, Michael, I will go straight to Interpol. Don't think I won't!"

"Calm down, sweetheart. Just tell me which of Nathan's paintings are genuine."

"If I tell you, will you let me down?"

"Scout's honor," he pledged, holding up three fingers.

Looked like Michael had been an even worse Scout than I. He was saluting with the wrong hand.

I thought about what he was asking of me. As long as I did not help him steal the paintings how could the district attorney prove I had played a role? Sure, I had a few opinions about some paintings. Who didn't? And just think of the character witnesses I could call. Agnes Brock and her lapdog "art expert," Dr. Sebastian Pitts, would be delighted to testify that I was a no-talent hack.

Reassured by the art world's low opinion of me, I decided Nathan could take care of himself and told Michael which of Haggerty's paintings were real and which were fakes.

"Really?" he said, surprised. "Both of the Jan Steens? And the Rembrandt?" He shook his head and grinned. "That grandfather of yours is a busy boy. Who did the other forgeries?"

"Don't know and don't care. By the way, my esteemed grandfather wouldn't like how you've kept me dangling up here."

"And the Vermeer?"

"I told you, that's real. Why don't you steal it from Nathan and return it to its rightful owners? It might help redeem your soul. *Now* will you let me down?"

"Any idea if there's a reward?"

"Probably. Vermeers are few and far between. Here's some career advice: Steal art *for* museums and collect the reward money. Now *let me down!*"

"Are you going to stay out of trouble? No more sneaking around abandoned warehouses like an idiot?"

"No more."

"I'm serious, Annie. That would have been quite a fall. And your face looks like hell." He powered up the winch and lowered me to the ground. When my feet touched mother earth, my spirit failed and I crumpled into a heap on the floor.

"You sure you're okay?" Michael crouched beside me. "Shall I carry you?"

"No, you *shan't* carry me," I spat and sat up.

Michael wrapped his arms around me. "Give yourself a minute there, tiger. It's not a crime to lean on someone once in a while, you know."

I closed my eyes, took a deep breath, and relaxed. I heard Michael's heart beating and felt his strength and warmth. It was nice. Too nice. I pushed him away and got to my feet, teetering a bit but upright. "How did you know how to operate the stone winch?"

"A misspent youth. Maybe I'll tell you about it some-time."

"You're a very strange man, Michael."

"Need I point out that *I* was not the one dangling from a hook?"

"I just had a terrible thought. I was supposed to meet Gloria and her brother here. Where do you suppose they are?"

"Probably took off already."

"What if they're hurt, or hanging somewhere? We have to look for them."

Michael gave me a long-suffering look. "This isn't my sort of thing, Annie. I'm not in the rescue business."

"C'mon, Michael. Be a mensch."

We scoured the building but found no one. Then I re-membered the shipping container supposedly filled with Pascal's sculptures. We located what seemed to be the right one, but it was sealed shut. We banged on it and yelled for Gloria, but got no response.

I nodded to Michael. "Okay, go ahead."

"Go ahead and do what?"

"Break in."

"How would you suggest I do that?"

"Use your magic thieving stuff."

"My *what*?"

"The stuff you use to thieve with. I mean, to steal with."

"I don't carry around my *magic thieving stuff*, Annie. Especially when I'm going to a cocktail party where my car will be searched."

I gaped at him. "Haggerty searches his guests' cars?"

"He does when he's afraid they'll try to steal his paintings."

"Still seems rude, though."

"True."

"So what about this container? Is there any way in?"

"None that I can see, except by brute force. It looks like there are some pry marks on it, but look here, Annie: It still has the customs seal. I don't think it's been opened."

I hesitated. My cheek throbbed, my head hurt, my knees ached, and I was dying to get home and crawl into bed. But how could I leave if Gloria and her brother needed help?

"Why don't you try calling your friend?" Michael suggested.

"I don't know her number," I said, defeated. Being beaten and suspended in the air had taxed my internal resources. And that had been only *part* of my day.

"I'll bet it's in the office."

We went to Gloria's office, where Michael quickly located the personnel files. I sat at Gloria's desk and called the number listed on her employment form. She answered on the third ring, sounding wide-awake, and I heard the *Late Show* playing in the background.

"Gloria?"

"Annie?"

"I thought you were going to meet me at the warehouse."

I heard a muffled sound, as if she had covered the receiver for a moment. "Um, yeah. We couldn't wait. I didn't think you were coming."

"But I told you . . ." I trailed off. "Anyway, I wanted to make sure you were all right."

"Yeah, okay, thanks. You're all right, too?"

"Uh-huh. Okay, talk to you later."

Hanging up, my eyes fell on Gloria's employment form.

Gloria Cabrera, 5701 Elwood Street, South San Francisco. Not far from here. Next of kin: Irma Rodriguez Cabrera. That name sounded familiar. . . .

"Let me guess," Michael said, interrupting my thoughts. "Gloria wasn't here when you arrived, and instead you were met by some bad guys. Does that sound about right?"

I nodded.

"Let's get out of here."

"I thought she was my friend."

"Betrayal's a hard one to stomach, Annie," he said as he put the file away. "I know. But remember, you don't have the full story. She may have been threatened, or promised you wouldn't be hurt. People do what they have to do to survive."

We turned off the lights, crossed the lobby, and walked into the cold night.

And tripped over a body. At least I did. Michael maintained his balance.

It was the young warehouse worker Derek, and his throat had been cut. Michael checked for a pulse, and shook his head. I watched as if through a fog. The alabaster skin on Derek's hands was torn and bloodied, as though he had tried to defend himself. Those long fingers would never again brush his long hair from his forehead or lay chisel to stone.

Michael grabbed my arm and hustled me toward the Lexus. "Let's get the hell out of here." He unlocked the passenger door. "Get in."

"But we can't just leave him here," I cried.

"You can't help him, Annie," Michael said as he shoved me into his car. "No one can."

"My truck—"

"You're in no shape to drive, Annie," he said. "It's the adrenaline crash."

"But . . ."

Michael started the engine, and drove quickly out of the parking lot. "I know a guy. I'll have him take the truck—where? Your studio or your apartment?"

Ensconced in the luxurious Lexus, my mind was unable to grapple with his questions. My eyelids felt heavy, and my last conscious thought before succumbing to sleep was that my dates with Michael so often ended in death.

Chapter 15

It is a burden, ma chérie, *to be an A+ student in a C– world.*

—*Georges LeFleur, in a letter to his granddaughter Annie Kincaid*

I awoke facedown in a pillow so soft it felt like a cloud. Too bad the throbbing of my eye and the pounding of my head made it difficult to enjoy. My shoulders and neck were killing me, my knees stung, and my thigh ached. I nearly cried out in pain when I moved.

Along with the hurt came the memories: of vicious, laughing men; of my own panic and sense of impotence; of the shock and horror of finding a dead body. Would the young man with the pale hands be alive if not for my questions? What role had Gloria played? Would Neiman Marcus still take back the dress?

I rolled gingerly onto my back and looked around. I remembered nothing after leaving the warehouse, and it finally registered that I was in a hotel room. An expensive hotel room, where the furniture was what a person might have at home if that person were stinking rich.

"Michael?" I croaked. "Hello?"

It was the second time I had spent the night with

Michael, the sexy international art thief, but I had no memory of either occasion. Did that say something about me? About Michael? About the quality of our relationship? At least I'd awakened in more luxurious surroundings this time. In a weird kind of way, things were looking up between Michael and me. On the other hand, it didn't say much for our budding romance that he had taken off rather than linger in this soft bed, waiting breathlessly for me to wake up.

An unwelcome thought pushed its way to the forefront of my bruised mind. Now that I'd told Michael about the Haggerty collection he had no further use for me. He had wined me, flattered me, kissed me, rescued me, and abandoned me. Again.

Well, shit.

"Remember the LeFleur motto, *chérie*," I heard my grandfather whisper. "Anger is the food of fools. Revenge is the food of gods." He'd said it in French, but I remembered it in English. I had a sneaking suspicion Georges had made it up, armed with a vivid imagination and a good French-English dictionary. But it was a hell of a motto, and it rather suited me at the moment. First I would heal; then I would gorge on revenge.

On the bedside table was a clock that read 10:47 a.m., along with a black leather folder with the hotel's name embossed in gold: *The Fairmont*. I'd been here before, as a child, to visit my grandfather on one of his rare visits. The Fairmont was one of Georges' favorites. All things considered, I could handle being abandoned at one of the City's finest hotels.

Unless Michael had stuck with me the bill again.

I sank into my cozy nest of down pillows. Tomorrow was Thanksgiving, and I was reconsidering the wisdom of going with Josh to his sister's house. Since I could scarcely open my left eye, the odds were good I was not looking my best. Plus, after the violence last night I felt more like wrapping myself in one of the hotel's fluffy white terry-cloth robes, ordering room service, and vegetating in the Jacuzzi. The Fairmont seemed like a good place to lie low for a few days.

Still, there were a number of things I needed to do, beginning with figuring out who had nearly killed me—and murdered Derek—last night. And finding out what my mother knew. And locating Evangeline. And making sure the Chagall was returned to the Brock. Oh, and running a faux-finishing business. Mary and I had made a lot of progress on the holiday display but we still had to paint fifty glass ornaments and assemble Kwanzaa decorations, including a giant red, green, and black candleholder known as a kinara.

Just thinking about it exhausted me. How much work would anyone do on the day before Thanksgiving, anyway? State offices were closed, and regular folks were either gassing up the SUV for the trip to Sacramento to visit Grandma, or were deep in the poultry section of the local grocery store squaring off against a determined Fremont homemaker for the last fresh turkey.

Realizing I wasn't going to be capable of any rational decisions until I took a long hot shower, I inched back the covers and discovered that except for a skimpy pair of underwear I was nude under my T-shirt.

Michael had seen me naked. He owed me. That clinched it.

I picked up the phone and dialed the front desk. "I'm calling from Room"—I glanced at the center of the phone dial—"1208. I wanted to verify the credit card we put the room on?"

"Certainly, ma'am. One moment, please." I heard some

clicking sounds as the clerk checked her computer. "The room is registered to Dr. and Mrs. Patrick Collins, and is charged to Dr. Collins' American Express card. I have you down for one night's stay, checking out at noon today."

"Actually, the doctor and I have been *so* looking forward to touring Alcatraz—*such* a touristy thing to do, I know, but what can I say? We get to the City so rarely, and we're hoping to extend our stay another night."

"Certainly, ma'am. Shall I charge it to the same account, Mrs. Collins?"

"Please do. Oh, one more thing—I want to be sure we're charging this to our *personal* AmEx account, not the doctor's corporate card. It wouldn't do to be unethical, now would it?" I laughed gaily, hoping I wasn't overdoing it. She read me the account number, which I jotted on the memo pad next to the phone. "Thank you *so* much; that is correct. Now, would you be a dear and transfer me to room service?"

I ordered a Caesar salad, garlic bread, and linguine with clams in a butter, garlic, and white wine sauce. In deference to the hour, I added a side of bacon and a carafe of coffee. Reckless with Michael's credit card, I dialed the concierge and ordered a manicure and an in-room massage. My shoulders were killing me.

Stumbling into the marble-lined bathroom, I made the mistake of looking in the mirror. My eye was swollen, the skin beneath it dark purple and sickly yellow, there was a small round burn on my cheekbone, and dried blood from a scratch along my hairline. I was encrusted in stone dust. Adding to the horror show were the smeared remnants of last night's makeup. My hair looked—well, it looked the way it always did in the morning. No two ways about it, Mrs. Patrick Collins was a fright.

And I wondered why Michael had abandoned me.

I showered with care, cleansed my wounds as best I could, wrapped myself in a white Fairmont bathrobe, held a cold washcloth to my eye, and settled in at the desk near the window. Gazing out at a picture postcard view of the Bay, Alcatraz, Angel Island, and the Golden Gate Bridge, I dialed my answering machine. Pedro and Annette had each left a message to call them back. Mom had phoned to urge me once more to join the family for Thanksgiving. Grandfather had called to ask how things had gone in Hillsborough and to tell me that my present was in the dead letter section of the main St. Louis post office. I had no idea what he was talking about, but this was the kind of cryptic message I had come to expect from him. Lastly, Josh had called "just to say hi." Hearing his warm, deep voice reminded me why I wanted to see him. Josh was a nice, normal, steady-as-a-rock kind of man who would never, under any circumstances, ask for someone's help in casing a client's house and leave her half naked at the Fairmont.

Good ol' Josh.

On the other hand, I did seem to have a talent for attracting trouble, as Frank had remarked on more than one occasion. Maybe Josh was also an international art thief. Maybe he was an undercover agent from Interpol, sent to check on my connections to wanted art forgers and thieves. Maybe his beefy nice-guy-construction-worker persona was a façade—had I ever actually seen him build anything besides that wheelchair ramp for Community Builders?

As I dialed Pedro's number, I debated asking him to run a background check on Josh, but decided I was being pathetic.

"*Hola*, Annie. Where you been?"

"I spent the night at the Fairmont—"

"Yo, *chica*, good for you. I knew you had a wild side.

Elena and I were just talking about you. So who sprang for the room? Some rich dude, huh?"

"You wouldn't believe it if I told you. Were you able to track down Evangeline?"

"Have I ever failed you? Full name's Evangeline Simpson, she lettered in high school wrestling in Utica, New York, and dropped out of art school at NYU two months ago. Moved to 1849 Tennessee Street last May."

"That's Pascal's studio."

"It's listed as her residence. Is it a live/work space?"

"Yeah, but I thought Pascal lived there. There's only a tiny bedroom with an army cot."

"Maybe they're a real close family."

"Very funny. Any idea where she might be right now?"

" 'Fraid not, but I left a voice mail on her cell phone, and with the clerks at the video store where she's a regular. She's partial to Clint Eastwood spaghetti Westerns."

"I don't suppose you found anything more on Carlos? Anything on the drug angle?"

"Last time we spoke you dismissed the idea!"

"Just curious."

"Nope, nothing like that. Hey, here's something: did you know Carlos is Jewish?"

"He is?"

"According to the Internet, there was a small but significant Jewish immigration to Mexico in the mid-twentieth century. You know, I've been thinkin' about what you said. Maybe I should visit. Seems like an interesting place. Anyway, Carlos Jimenez gets nothing but stellar references from his neighbors. And if he's a drug dealer he sure ain't livin' like one. He may be a big shot in his hometown, but around here he and his wife lead a pretty humble life."

"What do you mean he's a *big shot*?"

"According to the *Cerrito Lindo Courier*, the mayor

gave Carlos the key to the town at the harvest festival last weekend in recognition for—hold on, let me call it up—oh, yeah: *In heartfelt appreciation and gratitude for the many munificent donations to the Cerrito Lindo Museum by one of the town's most golden native sons.* Who *writes* that kind of crap? Anyway, according to the paper, Carlos helped to design the town's museum."

"Were these financial contributions?"

"Nah, from what I can tell it was mostly time and energy, like some pro-bono consulting, though he did hook the museum up with some pre-Columbian artifacts on the cheap. But no paintings of note, at least not that I could find."

Not surprising, I thought. The missing Chagall would be kept under wraps until things died down. The more I thought about it, the more it seemed entirely out of character for Carlos to have stolen the painting for personal profit, but entirely in character to have taken it for his hometown. The choice of the Chagall made sense now that I knew he was Jewish and that Agnes had been planning on dumping the painting.

"Did you find out anything else about his son Juan?" I asked.

"Looks like he's doing okay. He moved to Cerrito Lindo last spring and—get this—is in charge of the new museum. This article says Juan Jimenez *brings a wealth of hands-on museum experience to our fair town.*"

Can't get more hands-on than scrubbing the museum floor, which was the only experience Juan had gained at the Brock. I thanked Pedro, left him my room extension in case he found anything else, and hung up.

Next on my list was Annette.

"Inspector Crawford," she said in her rich alto.

"Annette. It's Annie. What's up?"

"Where've you been? I need you to come down to the station to answer a few questions about this Pascal character. By the time we got to his studio he'd cleared out. The place was a wreck, smashed sculptures everywhere. No body parts, but one hell of a lot of dust, and evidence that someone had burned a fire in a portable barbecue pit."

"Did you find any notebooks?"

"There were fragments of scorched paper in the barbecue, but three or four cardboard boxes were full of them. All had Seamus McGraw's name on them."

"Did you read any?"

"Not yet. There's quite a lot there. Why?"

"I was wondering why McGraw's notebooks were at Pascal's studio."

"I wondered that myself. Anyway, I also wanted to tell you we found Evangeline. Live and kicking, with one heck of a New York honk. She came in to file a missing persons report on Pascal. You know, the guy you tried to convince me had killed her?"

Cancel my subscription to *True Detective*.

"When can you come in? I want to get a formal statement from you."

"Gee, I'm out of town for Thanksgiving," I lied. "How about Monday?"

"Make it Friday," she said. "And, Annie? If you don't come to me, I'll come to you."

"Sounds like a threat, Inspector."

"Just so we're on the same page. So where are you headed for Thanksgiving?"

"To a friend's family's house."

"Friend as in boyfriend?"

"Sort of."

"What about that landlord of yours? I saw him this

morning when I dropped by your studio. You two made a cute couple at the Brock gala last spring."

"No, we didn't. Besides, Frank hates me."

"I rather doubt that," she said. "And don't even *try* to tell me you've never thought about him. It's a felony to lie to a police inspector."

"Really?"

"No. But it should be."

We signed off and I braced myself to tell Josh I was bailing on our date tomorrow. Fate cut me a break for once, and his voice mail picked up. I left a vaguely plausible excuse about feeling guilty for not being with my family on Thanksgiving, and as a sop to my conscience gave him my cell number. Not that it would do him any good, since its battery had long since run out of juice.

I looked out at the glorious blue sky and started to relax. Mom was out of harm's way. Evangeline was alive and honking. I'd figured out where the Chagall was, and I was willing to bet Michael had known from the start. Poor Derek's death was best left in the hands of the police, though when I saw Annette Friday I should probably mention the little I knew about *that*.

But for now I was in a bathrobe at the Fairmont, a long holiday weekend stretching out ahead of me, and I had Michael's American Express card number.

A discreet knock announced room service had arrived. A nice young man set the meal on a little café table, laying out silverware and china on a linen tablecloth. I signed for the meal, added a huge tip, switched on the TV, poured myself some coffee, and dove into the clams.

The phone shrilled. I ignored it. After five insistent rings I caved.

"Your cell phone's turned off," came Michael's sexy growl.

"Thanks for the tip, scumbag. I just ordered a massage, on your tab. Plus a manicure. I'm thinking of an in-room movie later. And I—"

"I need your help, Annie," he interrupted.

"What is it?" I asked, mentally reviewing how much money I would be willing or able to post as bail. If Michael had done more than run a stop sign he was on his own.

"There's a, um, kind of situation."

"What kind of situation?"

"A sort of stuck kind of situation."

I slurped up some linguine and thought that over. "Like in a drain pipe?"

"What would I be doing in a drain pipe?"

"That was my next question."

"No, not like in a drain pipe. Like at the Haggertys'."

"The Haggertys'?"

"Yes."

"You're stuck at the Haggertys'?"

"Is this a difficult concept?"

"What do you mean?"

"Annie, will you please be quiet for a moment and listen? I need help. I'm trapped in their panic room."

"What are you doing in their panic room?"

"Panicking."

"Makes sense." I had been introduced to panic rooms while overseeing a remodeling project for a neurotic client from Blackhawk, an upscale East Bay community. Panic rooms were reinforced structures with their own ventilation system and phone lines, stocked with food, water, medicine, contact lens solution, and whatever else one needed to survive for a few hours or days. The house could burn down or be ransacked by evildoers, and those inside the room would be safe. The project's architect had proudly shown his plans to the entire construction and design crews until I pointed out that panic rooms were supposed to be a secret.

"Annie, I'll be happy to tell you the whole story later. Right now I need you to get your pampered ass over here and help me."

There was a loud knock.

"Hold on. That's my massage." I opened the door for Clint the masseur, who started setting up his table.

"Send him away," Michael ordered when I returned to the phone.

"I will not. My shoulders are killing me after last night. I need a massage."

"And I need your help. I'm serious, Annie. You have to get everyone out of the house long enough for me to escape."

"I don't get it, Michael. You got in there, why can't you get out?"

"I *can* get out," he said, sounding as if his teeth were grinding. "I need you to make sure that I'm not spotted on my way out."

"Uh-huh," I said, eyeing Clint, who was remarkably well built. "What about that guy?"

"What guy?"

"Last night, when I asked who was going to pick up my truck, you said you had a guy. Where is my truck, by the way?"

There was a pause. "I'm sorry, we don't seem to be communicating very well. Wasn't I the one who rescued you from a fall to certain death last night? Wasn't I the one who set you up at a fancy hotel for the night?"

"Weren't you the one who abandoned me here?"

"Is *that* it? You're pissed off because I wasn't there when you woke up? Or is Mr. Muscles-for-Brains there entertaining you?"

"No, *Mr. Muscles-for-Brains* is not here," I protested, and rolled my eyes at the masseur. He smiled.

"Your truck's in the hotel garage. The valet stub is on the dresser. Annie, I swear to God, I need you. Please."

It was the *please* that did it. My body ached and I was loath to give up an indulgent afternoon watching movies in bed, but Michael *had* gotten me off the hook last night, literally. And apart from laughing at me and extorting information from me, he had done so with surprising good grace.

"Hold on," I said again. I apologized to Clint, signed the tab, tipped him well, and sent him on his way. "Okay, so why don't you trigger a fire alarm or something?"

"Too risky. This whole place is monitored by remote cameras. I disabled the ones along the route I was taking, but can't get to the others from here. I'd be spotted along any other route, and Nathan is in his study, right outside the panic room. Diane's somewhere in the house, as well. They arrived unexpectedly."

"Can't Nathan hear you talking on the phone?"

"The room's soundproof. I can watch him on remote, though. He and Kevin are working at his desk. They've been there an hour. I have no idea how long this could go on, but I have to get out of here."

"Why don't you just wait until they leave?"

"I can't."

"Why not?"

"I'm claustrophobic."

"You're *claustrophobic*?"

"Yes, goddammit, I'm claustrophobic."

"Doesn't that get in the way of being an art thief?"

"You mean like now? Yes, yes it does."

Well, what did you know? A chink in the mighty Michael's armor.

"What can I do?" I sighed.

"Come here and make up something, anything you can think of to get everyone out of the house. All I need is ten minutes."

"All right. I'll be there as soon as I can. How do I get there?"

Sounding relieved, he gave me the directions. My fancy dress and dingy overalls hung limply in the closet, offering me a choice of extremely formal and wrinkled or extremely informal and wrinkled. Then I realized my only footwear was my old running shoes. Maybe if I showed up at the Haggertys' wearing last night's sexy dress and smelly running shoes they would be so stunned Michael could slip out unnoticed.

I needed a plan. At this hour on the day before Thanksgiving the freeways and bridges heading out of town were going to be clogged, so zipping home to Oakland to change was out. I didn't have the time or inclination to buy a new pair of uncomfortable high heels. Who might be able to help? Sam and Reggie were at her sister's home in San Diego, and Bryan and Ron were visiting Ron's parents in Petaluma. I knew a few women in the City well enough to ask a footwear favor, but everyone I could think of had already left town for the holidays.

That left Mary. I threw on my overalls, grabbed my dress and evening bag, and ran out the door. I retrieved my truck from the garage, made it across town in record time, and flew past Frank's office with a quick wave. I found Mary in the studio working on the Kwanzaa candelabra. "Hey, Mare—"

"What the hell happened to *you*?" she gasped, getting up from the floor and gently touching my face.

"It's a long story, and I'm in a rush. I have to make a trip to Hillsborough to see a client, but can't go like this. Do you have any of that liquid makeup goop that covers things up?"

"You mean foundation? No way is it gonna cover up that shiner. Were you in a *fight*?"

"I'm fine. Don't worry. Do you have any clothes I could borrow?"

"Sure. But don't give me any of that *walked into a door* or *you should see the other guy* crap, all right?" Mary handed me a well-worn black leather makeup bag and started pulling clothes from the oak armoire, flinging them across the sofa and chairs. Black web netting and ripped black silk abounded.

I applied Mary's makeup with a generous hand to hide my rapidly developing black eye. Foundation, powder, mascara, and lipstick helped me look slightly more re-spectable, and I combed my hair out and gathered it on top of my head again. After considering the limited clothing options I settled on a short black skirt, a black teddy, a silky black scoop-neck T-shirt, a pair of black tights that bagged a bit at the knees and ankles, and a black velvet cropped jacket.

I inspected myself in the armoire's mirror. Funky. In a slutty kind of way.

"Shoes?"

Mary handed me two pairs: mid-calf black leather boots with silver buckles and clunky black Doc Martens.

"Nothing a little more establishment?"

Mary looked hurt. "These are my most normal shoes. I thought you liked them."

"I do," I assured her. "It's just that this is a pretty straight client."

The Doc Martens made me look like a kid playing dress-up in mommy's hooker clothes and daddy's prison brogans, so I went with the boots. The overall effect was a tad on the dominatrix side, but judging from my interaction with Nathan last night I thought that might work in my favor.

"Wow, Annie," Mary said, appreciatively. "That's a great look for you. A couple of well-placed rips and you could sing with the band."

"Um, thanks."

I grabbed the evening bag, wished Mary a happy holiday, and ran out the door. As I clomped down the stairs I appraised my truck with a critical eye. What would the Haggertys think if I drove up in a dusty pickup truck? The shiny Jaguar parked next to it, on the other hand, would be right at home in Hillsborough. *Don't even consider it*, I told myself. *There's no way in hell.*

"Heya, Frank," I said, opening his office door.

"Annie," Frank replied with a nod. His cool glance flickered over my ensemble, paused a moment on the boots, and returned to my face. "Interesting outfit. What happened to your eye?"

"Well, you know how it is—you should see the other guy. Hey: remember when you said you would return the Picasso favor sometime?"

"You mean the rent reduction wasn't enough?"

"No. I mean, yes. I mean, it's great. Anyway, I was wondering—"

"Annie, could we speed this up? I'm working on a report that's going to take me several hours, and I'd like to finish before the holiday."

"Sure, sure. I just need to borrow your Jaguar."

"Excuse me?"

"For heaven's sake, Frank, it's a car, not a holy relic. May I borrow it, please?"

"No."

"Why not?"

"Because."

"That's not an answer."

"Okay: no, Annie, you cannot borrow the Jaguar."

"You mean to tell me you would ruin our budding friendship by denying me the use of your car for a very short period of time when you're not even using it?"

"If we are indeed friends, Annie," he intoned, "then I hardly think my not lending you my car would ruin our friendship."

"If we are indeed friends, Frank," I replied, "then I hardly think you'd balk at lending me your car. I'm not going to hurt it. What can I do to get you to trust me?"

"Be a different person."

Well, dang. That kind of hurt my feelings.

"Forget it," I said with uncharacteristic dignity and headed for the door. "I'm sorry I put you on the spot. And you're right—we aren't good enough friends to trust each other with something of value."

I left *like an irreplaceable Picasso* unsaid, hanging in the air between us.

I heard a loud exhalation of breath. "Annie—wait. Come back here. Why do you need the Jaguar? Is something wrong with the truck?"

"The truck is old and battered and while I love it for precisely those reasons, I have an important meeting with a wealthy client who is very status conscious, and I have to pick him up at the airport. I tried to rent a nice car, but they gave away my reservation and offered me a pink Geo Metro, and I can hardly pick him up in a pink Geo Metro, now, can I? And now his plane's due in twenty minutes and I'm late, and I thought maybe you would be willing to lend me your car for a couple of hours. I mean, what could possibly happen?"

I winced slightly as I said the last sentence.

"Take it," he said tossing me a set of keys. "But you had better be back here, with the vehicle intact, by four o'clock. Do you hear me?"

"Loud and clear." I fumbled the catch, retrieved the keys from the floor, and added, "Four o'clock, yessiree, no problem."

"That's four o'clock *today*. And bring it back clean, if at all possible."

"As a whistle. And Frank?" I tossed him my keys. "No joy rides in the truck, wild man. You hear me?"

Chapter 16

What in the world is an autograph masterpiece, *I ask you? As if an autograph cannot be replicated! As early as the sixteenth century, printmakers learned the power of adding a signature to forged Albrecht Dürer prints, thus tripling their value.*

— *Georges LeFleur, in an interview in* Die Zietung

Traffic out of the City on the eve of a four-day holiday was a nightmare. It took me nearly forty-five minutes to get to the Hillsborough exit, a distance of roughly fifteen miles. As I wound my way through the hills I wondered how to get the Haggertys out of the house. Had Nathan been alone, I would have lured him out with the promise of a frolic in the sunshine, but with Kevin and Diane and possibly others, as well? I supposed I could try for an orgy, but my loyalty to Michael only went so far.

In the light of day the Haggerty estate's massive gates and the fountain's frolicking cherubim looked even more glaringly Pots o' New Money with Lots o' Bad Taste. I drove the Jaguar up the semicircular driveway, parked in front of the door, and tried to think of something clever to tell them.

Nothing, absolutely nothing.

Annie, I lectured myself sternly as I clomped up the front steps, *do not hyperventilate*. As hard as it is now, it will be even harder if Nathan comes to the door and you have a paper bag over your head. You will just have to lie like a shag rug. And what do we do when we are fresh out of lies? We call on our grandfather, that's what we do.

Ah, but zat is easy, chérie, Georges replied. *Tell your dear new friends Monsieur et Madame Haggerty zat zere was somezing zey simply had to see at ze end of ze drive, and would zey be so kind as to indulge you? And zey will say, but of course, my leetle friend.*

But how do I get the others out of the house, Georges?

Ah, chérie. Zat, I am not so sure.

C'mon, Grandfather, I prayed. *Don't fail me now.*

Alors, chérie, here is a better one. Tell zem zat you had just been informed zat a bomb had been placed in ze home by a radical antiapartheid group operating in ze Bay Area and zat zey must leave ze premises tout de suite.

But, Grandfather, that's ridic—

The door opened and a harried-looking woman with mousy brown hair glared at me.

"Hello," I said with an ingratiating smile. "I'm here to see Nathan Haggerty, please."

The mouse looked me over and frowned. "Is Mr. Haggerty expecting you?"

"Not really, but this is important. Vitally important. In fact, I wouldn't stay in the house if I were you. I regret to inform you that we've received a tip that a radical antiapartheid group has placed a bomb in the house and that it is set to go off at"—oh, lord, what time was it? I never wore a watch—"soon. *Very* soon."

"An antiapartheid group?"

"That's right, ma'am. Please, we must hurry."

"But apartheid ended years ago."

"Not everyone agrees."

"Like who?"

I had to hand it to Ms. Mouse. She was standing her ground.

"Please, ma'am, I was a guest at a party here last night and I feel responsible for the well-being of the household. Perhaps you could tell the Haggertys that I'm here, and that I need to speak with them?"

She looked at me. I looked at her. Our optical duel lasted for several seconds, until she stepped aside and waved me in.

"Thank you, ma'am, but I'd rather not. I've called the bomb squad, so I'll just wait here, thanks, where I probably won't be killed by the initial blast and might even stand a chance of surviving my disfiguring wounds. Best tell the Haggertys to hurry."

"Yes, all right." Ms. Mouse was beginning to look a little nervous.

I hummed while I waited. It occurred to me that Michael might be able to see me on camera in the panic room, so I slapped on a winsome smile. Was he still panicking? Who would've figured him for a claustrophobe? And since my cell phone was dead, how would I know if he'd gotten out? I'd just have to trust he was on the ball enough to escape when he had the chance.

"Annie! What a delightful surprise!" Nathan said, as he scurried down the sweeping staircase. "Good lord, what happened to your face?"

"Nathan! Thank heavens! Listen to me! A bomb has been planted in the house. I've called the bomb squad, and—"

"But, Annie, what nonsense is this?"

"Everyone must leave immediately, Nathan. We must

all gather at the end of the drive until the bomb squad has declared the property safe."

"But I don't understand. Why . . . ? How . . . ? Who . . . ?"

"Nathan, I lied to you last night. Yes, I did. I am not a struggling artist, that's just my cover. That's why I'm dressed like this. No, I am in reality, um, part of a crack SFPD undercover squad tracking radical antiapartheid cells working in the Bay Area and targeting, um, wealthy South Africans such as yourself."

Nathan looked dumbfounded. "But apartheid ended years ago."

"Try telling that to these guys. They're fanatical. Take Ken, for example."

"Who?"

"Kevin, right. Sorry. Ken's his code name. How well do you really know Kevin, Nathan?"

"Why, he's worked for me over a year."

"Has he? Has he *really*? Didn't you find his racist comments last night a little, shall we say, overstated? Didn't you ever wonder what he might be hiding by being so extreme? Kevin's not what he appears to be, Nathan. That's all I can say right now." I dropped my voice to a whisper and Nathan leaned in close. "It would cost me my badge if anyone found out I told you this. We're not supposed to get personally involved in our cases. But after our very special time together last night I couldn't stand by and let this happen, and I knew I was closer than the bomb squad, who, frankly, seem to be taking their own sweet time getting here. But I can't stay any longer. Nathan, I beg of you, for the love of God, get everyone out of the house, *now*!"

I was afraid that last bit might have stretched credulity to the breaking point, but Nathan started shouting, "Every-

one out of the house! Diane! Sweetheart! Janice! Everyone!"

He did not go inside to rescue his beloved Diane, but
joined me on the front porch. He did keep shouting,
though, I had to give him that. Ms. Mouse emerged with a
longhaired cat clamped under one arm and a purse under
the other; Diane appeared wearing a white tennis outfit
with a short flouncy skirt; and a thin man in his seventies
limped toward the door with the help of a cane. Last to arrive was Kevin the Nazi, who swept past me with a glare.
I noticed Nathan looked at his employee askance.

"What about the household staff?" I asked.

"Servants' day off," he replied. "Let's go."

I herded them down the driveway, wondering how much
time Michael needed to get out of the house. Nathan
whipped out his cell phone and I froze, afraid he was calling the cops, but relaxed when I heard him trying to explain the situation to his insurance agent. He gave the agent
his cell number, and I made a mental note of it so I could
call him after I left. It seemed mean to leave them standing
in the chill November air on the day before Thanksgiving,
worried there was a bomb in their house and awaiting the
mythical bomb squad.

As soon as they were all chatting by the side of the road,
I figured it was time to make my escape. I held up one hand
like a school crossing guard, and they fell silent.

"On behalf of the SFPD undercover squad, I'd like to
thank you for your cooperation in these trying circumstances. So. Here's what we're going to do. I'm going back
in. No—don't try to stop me."

No one did.

"No matter what happens, even if I get called away, it is
imperative that you remain here, away from the house,
until you're given the official all clear. Got that?"

Five heads bobbed up and down in mute assent, though Kevin frowned. The cat hissed.

I continued in my take-charge voice. "Let's hope it's a false alarm, but one never knows with these crazy leftists. Thank you and Godspeed."

As I hurried back up the drive I heard Diane say, "I thought she was rather a leftist herself, didn't you, darling?"

"It was all a façade, my dear. I saw right through it," Nathan replied. "She's a crack undercover agent. Damn good, too."

"Nice car for an undercover agent," Kevin muttered.

I crunched up the driveway, jumped in the Jaguar, and gunned it. Granite chips spurted as I zoomed past the astonished Haggertys and their entourage. Deciding to call Nathan from the nearest pay phone, I scribbled his cell number on a scratch pad my uptight landlord used to keep track of his gas mileage. I approached a stop sign and debated which way to go.

"Take a right," came a voice from the backseat.

I swerved and sent the Jaguar careening across the road, regaining control only after a close shave with a gold BMW.

"Michael! Dammit! You're going to get us killed, you backseat-driving thief! How did you get in here?" I yelled, my heart racing.

"Why, the door, of course. It's the easiest way. Nice shiner. How are you feeling?"

"It's not enough that I perjure myself in front of the Haggertys, now I'm to be scared to death in my own car?"

"It's not your car," he retorted, caressing the buttery leather upholstery. "It is very nice, though. Whose is it? You didn't tell anyone our little secret, did you, Annie?"

"Of course I did. I called my investigative reporter

buddy at the *Chronicle* and told him I was on my way to rescue an art thief who'd gotten stuck in some wealthy sucker's panic room after exchanging his valuable paintings for my grandfather's worthless fakes. You mean I wasn't supposed to?"

"Annie," he tsk-tsk'd. "Why are you so dismissive of your grandfather's work? The forgeries are quite wonderful. As Georges so often says, if a fake is as beautiful as the original, why is it less valuable?"

"Because it is."

"But why? Are you really so devoid of feeling—"

"Cut the philosophical crappola, Michael," I snorted as the Jaguar hummed around the twists and turns. As furious as I was, I had half a mind to follow Skyline Boulevard along the crest of the Santa Cruz mountain range. When would I get another chance to drive such an amazing car? "Tell me something, you big art-stealing fake: if the forgery's as good as the original, then why do you bother to steal the real ones? Why not just enjoy the fakes and be done with it? Answer me that."

He shrugged. "Everybody's got to make a living."

"Give me a break. And your cell phone," I said, holding my hand out.

"Why?"

"I want to call Nathan."

"Why?"

"To give him the all clear."

"Why? Or are you enjoying being Secret Agent Annie Kincaid, part of a crack SFPD undercover squad investigating radical antiapartheid groups in the Bay Area?"

"You heard that, huh?" I squirmed.

"I heard it all, sweetheart. The entire astonishing performance, from soup to nuts."

"It was nuts, all right," I muttered. I glanced in the

rearview mirror to see if he was laughing at me. His handsome features were arranged in such an innocent expression I was immediately suspicious.

"I don't know what I admire most: that you could come
up with such a preposterous story, or that you could make
it sound so plausible. You are a gifted liar, Annie."

Great. Being admired by a sexy art thief for my ability
to tell a first-class whopper wasn't exactly one of my life's
goals.

"It's in the blood," I said, gritting my teeth. "Now, give
me your phone. I can't leave them there, standing in the
cold the day before Thanksgiving."

"I don't see why not."

"Because it would be mean," I snapped. "Give me your
damned phone."

"No."

"I don't believe this! I interrupt my spa day, come all
the way out here, lie through my teeth so you can make a
clean getaway, and you won't lend me your stupid phone!"
I was shouting now. "Why not?"

"Because Nathan will capture my cell phone number on
his caller ID, and then we'll both have some explaining to
do. Nathan knows some important people, Annie. I'd just
as soon we didn't all get acquainted."

"Oh." I deflated a little. "So. Shame about Nathan's
paintings, huh?" I asked as we zipped along.

"In what sense?"

"Well, you set up this elaborate scheme and got me to
go to that stupid cocktail party, and paid me lots of money,
and forced me to tell you which paintings were worth
stealing, and then got trapped in the panic room and, well,
here you are."

"Yes, here I am."

I gritted my teeth. "Best-laid plans, I mean."

"I don't know about that—I think all in all it was a pretty good plan."

In the rearview mirror I saw Michael nonchalantly watching the scenery. Here was my chance to lord it over him for failing to steal the paintings, and he was being obtuse. "So too bad your plan didn't work, huh?"

"How do you figure that?"

"Duh, Mr. Big Time Art Thief—maybe because you don't *have* any paintings?"

Michael's eyes met mine in the mirror. "Oh, I got the paintings all right."

"No, you didn't."

"Annie. Of course I did."

"So where are they?"

"In the trunk."

I slammed on the brakes and we screeched to a halt by the side of the road. Michael wasn't wearing a seat belt, and the momentum propelled him forward until his forehead thumped against the back of my seat.

"Jesus Christ, Annie! Are you trying to kill me? That's the second time you've given me a head wound."

Last spring Michael and I had had a bit of an adventure during which I'd inadvertently bashed him in the head. He'd forgotten that I'd saved his butt that time, too.

"You'll live," I said. "Are you telling me there are stolen paintings in the trunk of this very expensive, very *borrowed* car, thereby implicating in your crime not only me but the car's owner, as well?"

"Must you be so dramatic? The paintings are in the trunk. No one knows they're there—*you* didn't know they were there—and no one ever will know they're there unless, of course, you insist upon attracting attention with your wretched driving."

Swearing under my breath, I put the car in gear and

pulled onto the road. A click from the backseat indicated Michael had decided to buckle up.

"So, tell me, *Dr. Collins*, just how were you planning to make your getaway if the Jaguar hadn't been parked in front of the house?"

"The secret to great thievery, my dear *Mrs. Collins*, is to keep your options open," he replied. "That way if Plan A doesn't work out, you move on to Plan B."

"I see. So I guess that explains how you got trapped in the panic room, huh?"

"No plan is foolproof."

Michael reached forward and started to give me a neck rub. It felt so good it was hard to keep my attention on the road.

"Oh! Look! A gas station," I said with relief. The station was closed on this Thanksgiving Eve, but there was a phone booth near the office. I pulled up next to it, grabbed the sheet of scratch paper with Nathan's cell number, realized I had no change, and began searching Frank's Jaguar. There was only paperwork in the orderly glove compartment, so I started rooting around between the front seats.

"What in the world are you doing?" Michael asked after a moment.

"Looking for change." I perched on the passenger's seat and stuck my head into the driver's footwell to search under the seat.

"Is that where your friend keeps his change?"

"What friend?" I pulled up the floor mats.

"Mr. Boring Fat Cat. Your date for the Brock Gala."

"Frank is not boring, he's not a fat cat, and he wasn't my date. He's— How did you know this was his car?" I switched sides and started searching the passenger's seat.

"Let me get this straight. You're seeing Mr. Muscles *and*

Mr. Boring Fat Cat, both at the same time? Plus hanging out with me? My my, you *are* a busy girl, aren't you?"

I sat upright in the seat, frustrated, and realized that with my short skirt I had been giving Michael quite a show. Yet another reason why I seldom left the house without my overalls. I yanked the skirt down and glanced at Michael. The international art thief was relaxing in leather-lined luxury, arms crossed over his muscled chest, watching me with amusement.

I crossed my arms over my scantily clad chest and raised an eyebrow. "Tell me something. How can you be claustrophobic if you're a thief? Don't you get into a lot of tight situations?"

"I overcome my fear through force of will."

"I guess that would explain your tone of voice when you called for help, huh?" I replied. "And Mr. Boring Fat Cat is my landlord, nothing more."

"You know, Annie, you might not want to get too close to that landlord of yours."

"Is that right? Too bad I see him every day."

"I'm serious. He's not our kind of people."

I thought that was a little harsh. Frank couldn't help it if he was from Topeka.

"And what kind of people would that be, Michael?"

"He's in the security business, Annie. The *art* security business."

"I know, but he's a transportation guy."

Michael snorted. "When do you think a lot of art gets taken?"

"Leave Frank alone, Michael."

"I intend to. And I'd prefer that he left me alone as well. The fact is, Annie, the guy's good. His testimony helped put Curt Dodson away for ten to twenty last year, and Curt was a pretty cautious guy."

"Don't be absurd. Frank's my landlord; he's not a threat."

"All I'm saying," Michael continued, "is that someday somebody will let something slip, and your landlord is going to put two and two together. When he realizes you're Georges LeFleur's granddaughter, it might get uncomfortable. He has a reputation to protect, after all."

"Yes, but I'm not a crook, Michael. I don't have to be afraid of Frank."

Michael shook his head. "I can't believe you're falling for this guy. If your grandfather were dead he'd be rolling over in his grave."

"Let's get something straight, my thieving friend. I'm not falling for anybody. Least of all you, in case you were wondering."

He ignored that. "Tell me, Annie. What do you suppose ol' Frank would think if he knew you were using his Jag to aid and abet the theft of valuable artwork?"

"I have no idea"—actually, I had a damn good idea, which is why I didn't want to think about it—"but it doesn't matter since he'll never find out, will he?"

"He won't hear it from me. But I'm serious, Annie. You can't mix the two worlds and expect to remain unscathed."

I looked at those green eyes framed by sooty lashes, at the sensual lips and thick dark hair. It seemed wrong that he should look like an angel but be such a devil.

"*I'm* not mixing the two worlds, Michael. *I* live in Frank's world, in Josh's world, in Samantha's world." Better leave Mary off the list. "*You* are the one intruding on *my* world. I helped you today because I owed you for last night. But no more. And if you bring up the tract home in the burbs again, I'll hit you. That's not the only option for a normal, legal life, you know. And having 1.9 kids offers its own rewards, I'm sure. At least I won't grow old as a lonely criminal who can't even remember his real name."

Michael gazed out the window, his mouth tight, and if I didn't know better I would have sworn I'd hurt his feelings. He reached into a pocket and handed me some coins. "Make your phone call," he said, his voice flat.

I had a sudden visual of him tearing down the road in the Jaguar while I punched buttons in the phone booth. "I'll, um, wait. I can call him from the City."

"Annie, I'm hardly going to steal your boyfriend's car and have you put an APB out while I'm hauling stolen paintings. I may be sad and lonely, but I'm not stupid."

I took the keys with me for good measure, even though I was pretty sure Michael knew how to hotwire a car. He seemed the type.

Nathan answered on the first ring, and I told him we'd apprehended one of the leaders of the cell who had admitted the bomb threat was a hoax. He was beginning to sound skeptical, and I prayed our paths would never cross in front of Frank's office. I marched back to the Jaguar and slid behind the wheel. Michael had switched to the passenger's seat, making me feel a little less like I was driving a getaway car.

"So, Mr. Big Time Art Thief," I said as I maneuvered onto the freeway on-ramp. "Enlighten me. I identified the genuine paintings just last night, right?"

"Right."

"How did you happen to have first-class forgeries on hand for the switch? Wait a minute. It was my grandfather, wasn't it?" I demanded, exasperated. "He's an old man. Surely he'll slow down one day?"

"Your grandfather's a genius, Annie. Never doubt that. But he knew the collection. He stayed with the Haggertys while he painted the Massys, as well as a few others.

Georges and Nathan had a bit of a falling out, and Nathan brought in someone else to paint the other forgeries."

"Who?"

"No idea. Anyway, there was no love lost there, and when I told your grandfather Nathan had gotten his hands on a Vermeer, Georges suggested we liberate the genuine paintings. He had already forged most of Nathan's collection from memory. We just needed you to tell us which were the new forgeries. I'm sure your grandfather will find a use for the fakes we didn't use."

Yeah, like selling them on the black market, I thought.

"What am I supposed to do with you, Michael?" I asked. Traffic moved along at a good clip as we headed into the City, though it was at a standstill in the southbound lanes.

"I can think of several possibilities, each more delightful than the next," he purred, his fingers caressing the back of my neck and giving me goose bumps.

"I meant, where should I drop you off?"

"I left my car at the Fairmont."

"Don't you have a hideout?"

"You mean like the Hole-in-the-Wall Gang?"

"You know—some warehouse where you stash your stuff. Where we pull in and the switch is made."

"It's clear you were trained on the forgery end of this business, sweetheart, not the taking end."

"I'm not *in* the business at all, Michael, as I keep telling you. So where do you live?"

"Nowhere."

"You have to live *somewhere*."

"No, I don't. I'm just a lonely man with no home and no name," he said with a forlorn smile. "Just an old, rambling, bag o' bones . . ."

"Shut up."

"Anything for you, my love."

I exited at Ninth, crossed Market to Larkin, took a right on California and a left on Mason.

"So you think I'd be better off with you than with Frank, huh?" I could not leave this topic well enough alone.

"I never said you'd be better off with me. I said you should stay away from Frank. Those are two different things."

We pulled up in front of the Fairmont and a valet rushed over. Michael got out and spoke to him for a moment, the young man nodded, slipped the bill Michael handed him into his pocket, and waved us into the garage. Michael told me to drive to the second level, where the Lexus was parked near the elevators. I pulled the Jaguar up behind it and popped the trunk. While Michael moved his ill-gotten cargo from Frank's car to the Lexus, I rested my forehead on the steering wheel and squeezed my eyes shut in the vain hope that if I didn't see it happening, I wasn't aiding and abetting. The switch completed, Michael squatted on his haunches next to the open driver's-side window, his face level with mine. We gazed at each other for a moment.

"It occurs to me that we have some, shall we say, unfinished business," he said, his voice low and sexy. "Maybe I should escort you back to the room."

I couldn't bring myself to agree. I had to return the Jaguar to Frank, which was going to be uncomfortable since I was pretty sure it was past four o'clock. Plus, my entire body still ached. But the real problem was that I needed a gesture of faith from Michael before I was prepared to finish up our unfinished business in bed.

"No to the Fairmont, Michael. Take me to your place."

"What?" he said, surprised but pleased.

"Take me to your place. Then have your way with me."

"That's quite an offer."

"The offer's contingent."

"I realize that. All right. Follow me."

Wait a minute. That had been too easy.

"You have to prove it's your place, though."

"Annie . . ."

"You're planning on taking me somewhere else, aren't you?"

"Like where?"

"How should I know? A girlfriend's, who works nights. A client's, who's out of town. A colleague's, who—"

"Okay, okay. I get the point. You don't trust me, is that it?"

"I've never trusted you; you know that. That's not the issue here."

"It isn't?"

"No, it isn't. The issue is whether *you* trust *me* enough to show me where you live."

"Let me get this straight," Michael said slowly. "Taking you to my place is a prerequisite for getting you in my bed. Is that right?"

"Getting me in *your* bed is a prerequisite to getting me in your bed, yes."

Michael pushed away from the car, let out an exasperated sigh, and ran his hand through his hair. He leaned back through the car window and caressed my face. "You're a real pain in the ass, you know that? Happy Thanksgiving, Annie. Oh, and by the way, the Chagall has been found at the St. Louis Post Office. The Brock will have it back soon enough."

"*The* Chagall, or *a* Chagall? Did my grandfather paint it?"

"Does it matter?"

"Yes, it matters."

"Who deserves the painting more, Annie: a rich old lady

who was planning on selling it cheap to spite her sister, or a humble working man trying to honor his cultural heritage and his hometown museum?"

Words failed me.

"Agnes Brock will never know the difference," he said. "Trust me."

And with that he climbed into the Lexus, fired up the engine, and drove off, his tires squealing in the silence and the gloom of the underground parking garage.

Well, shit.

Chapter 17

There is no shame in settling out of court.

—*Georges LeFleur, on his personal mantra,*
Yoga *magazine*

"Something wrong with your watch?" Frank demanded, his gaze glued to his computer screen.

"Funny you should ask," I replied in what I hoped was a jovial tone. "I have one of those weird body chemistries, you know, the kind with an electromagnetic field or something, that breaks watches? Seriously. Every watch I've ever worn stopped running. I had a watch repair guy explain it to me once, and at first it sounded like a load of baloney, and then I thought maybe he was just coming onto me, you know, saying I had a magnetic personality and all that, but I don't think that was the case because he seemed very married, and he swore he was telling the truth. Of course, he also gave palm readings."

I waited, but Frank said nothing. So after a brief pause, I continued.

"I do have a clock, you know, on my cell phone? But I just can't seem to remember to charge the damned battery, so it's not working, either. Good thing you are, though, huh? Working, I mean, so you probably hardly even missed the Jag, which I would have washed for you, of course, except that it's the night before Thanksgiving, so no one's open. I know, 'cause I drove by several places, but they were all closed up. Shut and shuttered. Tight as a drum. I did fill it with gas, though. The good stuff, too. High test. High octane. Practically rocket fuel, they sure charged enough—"

"The issue is not your alleged magnetic field or the fact that you never remember to charge your cell phone," Frank barked as he leaned back in his chair and clasped his hands over his flat stomach. "The issue is whether you can be bothered to keep a promise. Did it ever occur to you that I had to be somewhere shortly after four o'clock? That I am only still here, working, because you failed to return as promised?"

As a matter of fact, it had not. I felt like a jerk. "Oh, Frank, how late is it? I'm so sorry, really. I didn't dawdle or anything, but traffic was insane and, well . . . You're right. It was thoughtless of me. I'm so sorry."

What kind of loser was I, anyway? Frank had been very generous and I couldn't even manage to return his car on time. I was alienating all the men in my life. First Michael, now Frank. I hadn't spoken with Josh, so maybe he was okay with being stood up. Otherwise, at the rate I was going I might never have sex again in my life. Fifty or so long years of celibacy stretched out before me. . . .

"—Annie?" Frank's voice broke into my unhappy reverie. He was standing in front of his desk now, hands in his pockets.

"Hmm?"

"I said, are—you—all—right," he repeated slowly.

"Yeah, sure, Frank. I just feel terrible for letting you down like that."

"You didn't," he said, and for a second I perked up. "I rather expected you to be late."

Stung, I stared at him. That was kind of mean, even if it was true.

Frank's tone softened. "What happened to your eye, Annie? Are you in trouble?"

"Me? Trouble?" I was aiming for bewilderment but hit squeaky guilt instead.

"Tell me what's going on. Does it have anything to do with the Picasso?"

I flashed on the abstract painting I'd seen in Haggerty's collection and wondered if Frank knew about it. Or had Michael nabbed it along with the others? "I gave the Picasso to you, Frank. I'm not responsible for it anymore, remember?"

"I didn't suggest that you were," he replied, his dark eyes searching mine. "If you're in trouble, Annie, I might be able to help. Come on," he cajoled. "You can tell your Uncle Frank."

Uncle? I'd thought of Frank in many ways, but never in the avuncular. My unruly mind flashed on an image of Frank in the buff. Either I didn't think of him as an uncle, or I'd suddenly developed a tolerance for incest. Did I need therapy?

No, what I needed was to relax. Sitting in more traffic and going home to an empty apartment did not fit the bill. The room at the Fairmont was still mine, and along the way were stores aplenty dispensing junk food all night long, holidays included. As I knew from my time in Europe, one of America's great contributions to human comfort was the twenty-four-hour convenience store. So that's what I'd do. I would eat ice cream and watch movies in my luxury hotel room. My spirits lifted and I was infused with energy.

"Frank, listen. I'm fine, really. Got to go. Have a great Thanksgiving, okay?" I snatched my keys from the top of Frank's desk, leaving the Jaguar's keys in their place.

Frank grabbed my wrist. "Hold it. Are you *sure* everything's all right?"

I looked at him, surprised at the expression on his face, which spoke of greater-than-average interest. Maybe Annette was onto something and Frank really was interested in me romantically. I couldn't be sure, though, because his eyes were focused on my chest, where Mary's blouse gaped open. Maybe he was just a red-blooded hetero guy sneaking a cheap peek.

"How's Hedvig these days?" I asked, to distract him.

"Hedvig? Who's Hedvig?"

"Heidi. Sonja. Gerta?"

Frank laughed and released my wrist, crossed his arms over his chest, and leaned on his desk. "Ingrid. And she's doing very well, thanks. Why do you ask?"

"Just being polite." I tried to sound innocent, which was a stretch because we both knew I wasn't.

"What's the deal with you and Ingrid?"

"What are you talking about, Frank? I've never even met the woman."

"Do you and the gang upstairs have some kind of contest afoot concerning Ingrid?" he asked with a slight smile.

"A 'contest afoot'?" I huffed. "Don't be absurd. What kind of people would have a pool on the first verified Ingrid sighting? That would be pretty sad, huh?"

"Annie, you never cease to amaze me," he said, and started laughing, a genuine laugh this time, not one of his patented mirthless chuckles, and I joined in. Our eyes met, and there it was. A definite tingle. It made me nervous, especially coming on the heels of my desire to sleep with

Michael. And that reminded me of how I'd deceived Frank into loaning me his car to aid and abet a felony.

I needed that ice cream. And maybe a fifth of scotch.

"Anyhoo, I've got to run. Thanks again for the use of the car. It was a lifesaver, truly."

"No problem," he replied, returning to his computer. "Happy Thanksgiving."

I felt a vague disappointment as I started up the stairs. *What did you expect?* I chided myself. That Frank would sweep you up in his strong, masculine arms, forever shattering the invisible barrier of pride that had kept apart our two lonely, aching hearts, so we could be united in an eternity of lusty fulfillment and blissful oneness?

Whoa—where had *that* come from? I halted on the landing and ran a quick self-diagnosis. I was in greater need of comfort than I'd thought.

I charged up to the studio as fast as I could in Mary's too-big boots. My assistant was on the computer, surfing the Internet. "Hey, Mare."

"Hey, Annie. How'd it go? I've been worried about you, what with that eye and all. Who've you been hanging with in these mysterious *client meetings*?"

"Never mind that. I've got an all-expenses-paid room at the Fairmont tonight. Whaddya say? Me and thou, a couple of pints of Ben & Jerry's, and some in-room movies?"

"I am *totally* there." Mary's eyes lit up and she shut down the computer. "We've got it all night?"

"Yup."

"What are we waiting for?"

Mary's vagabond lifestyle meant she always carried a toothbrush and clean underwear in a tote bag, so she was ready to go. I, on the other hand, was acutely aware of my lack of personal effects. Along with ice cream, potato chips, chocolate, and booze, I would buy a toothbrush, some hair goop, and a *People* magazine. After putting a few things away and keying the alarm system, we thundered down the stairs and hopped into my trusty truck. It wasn't a Jag, but it would get us where we wanted to go, so who was I to complain?

Forty-five minutes later we were happily ensconced in luxury, eating ice cream from the carton and flipping between *The Maltese Falcon* and *When Harry Met Sally* on cable. Mary kept me amused doing Humphrey Bogart voice-overs for Harry and Billy Crystal lines for Bogie.

A ringing telephone intruded into our hedonistic cocoon. Mary muted the television. "Might as well answer it," she said. "If you don't, you'll be wondering all night who it was."

There was a terrible wailing on the other end of the line. And a honking sound.

"Evangeline?" I asked. "Is that you? What's that noise?"

"Yeah, sorry. I was jest knockin' on your door and your alarm went off again. Hol' on a sec."

I heard garbled voices shouting above the alarm. Uh-oh.

Evangeline came back on the line. "That was the little guy from downstairs. He seems kinda pissed."

"Little guy?"

"Yeah, the hoity-toity one in the fancy duds."

Only Evangeline would refer to Frank as a *little guy*. "How did you know where to find me?"

"That friend of yours? Pedro? I called him back, and he said I should maybe call you at the hotel. What're you doin' at the Fairmont? That's a pretty ritzy place, huh?"

"You could say that," I said, distracted by the alarm blaring in the background. "Listen, Evangeline, did you call the alarm company? Tell them it's a false alarm?"

"Oh. You want I should do that? Won't that guy do it?" The alarm choked off. "See there, it stopped."

"Great," I said, rubbing my temples. "Where have you been? What's going on with Pascal?"

"That's what I was callin' about. Can I come over?"

This was what happened when I answered the phone, I thought. You'd think I'd learn.

Twenty minutes later, hotel security called, reluctant to allow Evangeline upstairs. When I opened the door I understood why. Evangeline wore a stiff black leather outfit, studded with dangerous-looking silver spikes and decorated with zippers and chains with no discernible purpose other than intimidation.

"Great outfit," Mary piped up as I stood in the doorway, dumbfounded.

"T'anks loads," Evangeline said, clanking and creaking her way into the room. "See, I knew this would be a fancy-schmancy place. Hey, looka here, a minibar."

I looked to Mary for help, but she just grinned. "Evangeline? What's going on? Where's Pascal?"

"I think maybe he's dead. It's kinda hard to say. There was some wise guys lookin' for him." Evangeline cracked open a bottle of Perrier. "But this afternoon, I get this call, all crying and emotional, from this chick who lives with him at the house." She took a swig of the mineral water and wiped her mouth with the back of her hand.

"Pascal has a *house*?"

"That's what I said! I figgered he had an apartment somewhere, not a fancy-pants house. But it's on Telegraph Hill, and that's a pretty nice area, right?" Evangeline guzzled more water, and started to open and close drawers, finding only a Gideon's Bible.

I nodded. A house on Telegraph Hill was a nice asset indeed.

"Anyway, she was pretty hard to understand 'cause she don't speak English good. Only Mexican. And then I thoughta you, 'cause I figgered you could understand her." She belched loudly.

"Good one," Mary said, and Evangeline grinned.

"Why would you think I speak Spanish?" I asked.

"Dunno. You seem the type."

"Um, Evangeline, it's a holiday and my friend and I—"

"Oh! Youse two, you're like, together, huh?" Evangeline poked her head into the bathroom, and I wondered what she was looking for. "I never woulda believed the way peoples live out here, if I hadn'ta seen it fer myself. Like getting married 'n' havin' kids and stuff. I mean, don't get me wrong, it's not like it bugs me, or nothin'. Live 'n' let live, huh? But girls with girls, and guys with guys, no way you'da seen that sort of thing back home."

I looked at Evangeline's muscled bulk, packed into the studded black leather pants and jacket, and wondered how many people assumed she was a lesbian from the get-go.

"Mary and I are friends," I said. "We happen to have the hotel room for the night and thought we'd just relax and—"

"Cool. Whatcha watchin'?" She moved toward the bed, and Mary scooted over to make room. Evangeline's face clouded. "Oh yeah, I forgot about Pascal's chick. She seemed pretty upset."

I was getting a bad feeling. "Upset how, Evangeline? Why do you think Pascal's dead?"

She shrugged, her attention focused on the commercials playing silently on the television. "These guys came lookin' for him. They wasn't happy. Somethin' about him owin' them money, or somethin'. They said he shouldn'ta been sellin' the statues to the garden store. Anyways, after that he burned a buncha stuff and took off."

"What did the woman say when she called?"

"Well, like I says, she was talkin' partly in Mexican. She kept saying somethin' about a *dedo*. What's a *dedo*?"

"You mean dildo," Mary suggested, and I fervently hoped she was wrong.

"Did you call the police?" I asked Evangeline.

"Nah. She was pretty clear on not doin' that. I think she's illegal."

I was rapidly losing Evangeline's attention, so I grabbed the remote and turned the television off.

"Hey!" said Mary.

"Hey!" seconded Evangeline.

"Sorry, Mare. Stay with me here, just for a minute, Evangeline. You think Pascal's dead or at least in trouble, and that a woman called from his house on Telegraph Hill to talk about a *dedo*. Is that about right?"

"Yeah, pretty much. She was cryin' and shit."

"And then you came to find me. Why?"

Her mild blue eyes were soft and vulnerable. "I figgered you'd know what to do."

I sighed and picked up the phone. In much of California the hospitality business could not function without immigrant labor, so it was a safe bet the housekeeping department included at least a few native Spanish speakers.

"I have a rather odd question," I began.

"Not at all, ma'am," a sweet-voiced woman replied. "What can I help you with?"

I could only imagine what thoughts were skimming through her brain. Hotel staff saw a whole lot of the seamier side of human nature, or at least its residue.

"Can anyone there tell me what *dedo* means in Spanish?"

"*Dedo*? *Dedo* means *finger*. Or *toe*, if it's *dedo de pie*."

"*Gracias*."

"*De nada*."

Finger? Toe? I turned to Evangeline. "Let's go find Pascal's mystery woman."

"I want to come," Mary said.

"You do know where his house is, Evangeline?"

"Yeah, she gave me th' address. Whaddya think's up with her?"

"Hard to say," I said. "Probably she's just upset because Pascal's disappeared. Damn, I wish one of us spoke Spanish."

I glared at my companions. It was ridiculous that every schoolchild in California did not start learning Spanish in kindergarten. I could handle French pretty well, but French was usually useless except when dealing with my grandfather and the nice folks at Interpol.

Mary and I shed the Fairmont's comfortable bathrobes and Mary dressed in her black jeans and torn black pullover. I had left my overalls at the studio, so I put on the hooker clothes I'd worn to the Haggertys'.

"Youse two look real good together," Evangeline said.

"Thanks, but we're not *together*, together," I began.

Mary slung an arm around my shoulders. "Come on, sweet cheeks."

In the elevator I realized we had a transportation problem. "What are you driving, Evangeline?" I asked, hoping against hope for a sedan.

"Beemer."

"Really?" Being an assistant sculptor must pay a whole lot better than being a faux finisher. "Is it in the garage?"

"Nope. It don't take much space, so they said to leave it out front."

"Can we take it to Pascal's?"

Evangeline looked doubtful. "Dunno about all of us."

"Why? Is it a convertible?" I persisted.

"Kinda. You get lots of fresh air."

"Are the windows missing or something?"

"Nope. Don't have no windows."

"Oh! I know!" Mary said, pleased with the game. "It's not a car, is it?"

"It's a motorcycle." Evangeline and Mary did some sort of complicated high five and down low.

Ten minutes later we were on our way to Pascal's house in my truck, Mary perched on Evangeline's lap. The human booster seat made Mary too tall for the cab, so she hung her head out the window, doglike.

After several twisty laps around the hilly neighborhood I found a barely legal parking space and we tumbled out of the truck. Hundreds of steps led to Coit Tower at the summit of Telegraph Hill, and Pascal's house was about halfway up. Evangeline trucked straight ahead, Mary hot on her heels, while I lagged behind. I arrived at Pascal's house, out of breath and short of temper. The house was ultramodern white stucco, with large plate-glass windows shrouded by heavy drapes. From the street the structure looked small, but as we drew closer I saw a lower level carved out of the hillside that opened onto a steep, curving driveway.

As we approached the front door we heard voices inside. Female voices, I realized with relief. In my experience, female people were not nearly as likely as male people to hang other people forty feet in the air, or to hit them in the face. I rang the bell and the door swung open.

Marble World Employee of the Month Gloria Cabrera gaped at me for a moment before shutting the door and throwing the dead bolt. First she set me up with the goons at the warehouse, and now she slammed a door in my face? *Like hell*, I thought. I wanted some answers, and I wanted them now. I pounded on the door.

"Gloria! Open the door this instant!" I yelled, as if expecting her to apologize and invite us in for cocktails. "I'm warning you, Gloria! Sisterhood is powerful!"

Evangeline and Mary looked puzzled. I shrugged.

The three of us backed up and looked around. On the right was a stand of fragrant eucalyptus trees. On the left was a narrow catwalk hosting a trash can and two recycling bins. We crept along the catwalk to a small balcony at the back door. It was locked, but the window next to it was wide open without so much as a screen. Being by far the smallest, I was the likeliest candidate to go through the window. Fabulous. I didn't have a good track record when it came to breaking and entering.

"Okay, guys," I said. "Somebody give me a boost."

Evangeline grabbed me by the waist and hoisted me onto the sill, where I paused for a moment before a firm hand on my butt propelled me forward. As I tumbled into the kitchen two women ran in. Gloria and the young Latina I had seen near Pascal's studio. She was sniffling and speaking rapidly in Spanish.

"Annie, for God's sake, don't you ever give up?" Gloria demanded. "I thought you were smart enough to stay out of this."

"Think again." I sneered as I extricated myself from the sink. The younger Latina offered a hand to steady me, which I thought was rather brave of her since I probably outweighed her by a good forty pounds. "I want to talk with you about your friends at the warehouse last night. And what's all this about a *dedo*?"

A wail and a fresh barrage of tears burst forth from the young woman. Gloria rolled her eyes and sighed.

Mary shouted to unlock the back door, and I let them in.

"What's up?" Evangeline said, gesturing with her chin towards Gloria.

"*Dios*, not her again," Gloria swore.

"You two know each other?" I asked.

"Hey! You look familiar," Evangeline said suspiciously. "Oh yeah, the stone chick, right?"

Mary turned to the younger Latina. "And you're Pascal's chick, right?"

Pascal's chick spoke in soft, accented English. "I am Consuelo. B-but I d-don't know where P-Pascal go." She hiccupped. "His, his *dedo*—" She began to cry again.

I reflected that it was a good thing I knew what *dedo* meant. I shuddered to think what my imagination would have come up with.

"What's going on, Gloria?" I demanded. "What's all this about Pascal's finger?"

"Why don't we all take a seat in the other room and talk?" Mary suggested, her Midwestern breeding showing.

"You're not staying that long," Gloria sniped.

"We're staying long enough for an explanation," I replied. "Otherwise I'm calling the cops and you can explain to *them* what's going on, and who those goons were in the warehouse."

"They got a little carried away," Gloria said. "It happens. You're not good at taking a hint."

"Hints are one thing," I said. "Murder's another matter."

Consuelo began whimpering again. It is a flaw of mine, for which I will no doubt spend a considerable amount of time in purgatory, that people who whimper bring out the worst in me. "What the hell's wrong with her, Gloria?"

Gloria sighed and shuffled into the living room, where she sank onto a white leather sofa and held her head in her hands. The rest of us perched on the modern, clean-lined, and dreadfully uncomfortable chairs.

"This whole thing has gotten out of hand," Gloria muttered.

"What whole thing?" I demanded.

"You can't call the police."

"Nobody's calling anybody just yet. Tell me what's going on."

She remained mute.

"Listen, Gloria," I said. "The last thing I want is to get involved in anything illegal."

Mary raised an eyebrow and I scowled at her. Then I scowled at Gloria. For good measure, I scowled at Consuelo and Evangeline.

Consuelo stopped crying, Mary and Evangeline remained silent, and Gloria started talking. Maybe I should scowl more often.

"A long time ago, Pascal killed his assistant Eugene Forrester."

"Go on."

She obviously expected more of a reaction, but continued. "Eugene Forrester was my mother's boyfriend."

"Who's your mother?" Could Gloria be Francine Maggio's secret love child? No, the ages weren't right.

"Irma Rodriguez. She married Guillermo Cabrera when I was eleven, and he adopted me. But I adored Eugene. And that bastard Pascal killed him."

"Nah, I don't believe it," Evangeline interjected. "Pascal's a jerk, but he ain't the type to whack nobody."

"I *saw* it happen. I was only ten, but I know what I saw. Eugene took me with him to the studio sometimes. He told me stories about how the stone trapped ancient spirits, and it was his job to release them. I think that's why I went into the stone business . . . Anyway, I was there the night he was killed."

"Tell us about it," I said.

"Pascal and Eugene were arguing over Eugene's sculpture, *Head and Torso*. My mother modeled for it."

Eugene had been a busy boy, I thought. He'd kept two

women on the string, each of whom believed she was his true love and muse.

"That's the one we was workin' on," Evangeline added. "Pascal said he hadda do it over again cuz the first one wasn't quite right."

"You mean the first one wasn't quite his," Gloria sneered. "Pascal's been using cocaine pretty heavily and got it into his head that some guy from the Brock—a real prick named Dr. Sebastian somebody—was trying to 'out' him. I told him he was being paranoid, that nobody could tell who had sculpted something just by *looking* at it—I mean, c'mon—but Pascal insisted it was possible and that to protect his reputation he had to sculpt a *Head and Torso* himself. Made me ship in one fuckin' heavy piece of marble for it, too, let me tell you."

Pascal was worried about Dr. Sebastian Pitts, from the Brock Museum? That was a laugh. Sebastian would be lucky to spot a child's scribblings in a stack of Picassos, much less out a stone sculptor on the basis of technique alone. "What happened between Pascal and Eugene Forrester?" I asked.

"They started arguing, and I hid under a worktable. There was a terrible scream. I'll never forget it. And a gunshot." Gloria's voice shook and there were tears in her eyes. "I peeked out and saw Pascal standing over Eugene's body with a gun in his hand. I hid there for hours, until my mother came for me and called the police."

So much for the newspaper report of the body being found by "a cleaning woman."

"But if you knew Pascal murdered Eugene, why didn't you say something? And why do you do business with him?"

"My mother was afraid nobody would believe me, and besides, she was an illegal immigrant. She could have been deported. When I went into the stone-importing business I knew I would run into Pascal, and I figured I could use what I knew to my advantage."

"You mean blackmail?" I asked.

"Whatever."

"What does this have to do with the goons in the warehouse? Or with Consuelo?"

"They sent Consuelo Pascal's finger."

"Eeeeewwww!" Mary said.

"Cool," added Evangeline.

"Was this, um, recent?" I was afraid of the answer.

"It's right over here." She got up, crossed over to a sleek white-oak credenza, and held out a small cardboard box.

I leaned away, my nose wrinkling. "That's okay. I believe you. Maybe later."

Gloria, clearly made of sterner stuff, opened the box and shook her head, a bewildered expression on her face. "I don't know what those guys are thinking."

Consuelo started crying again, muttering in a mixture of Spanish and English.

"What *guys* are we talking about, Gloria? The same guys who hung me several stories above the concrete warehouse floor? Those guys?"

"Who *hung* you—?" Mary began, but I silenced her with a look.

"The wise guys lookin' for the money, right?" Evangeline said.

Gloria nodded. "Pascal was holding out on the last shipment."

"What kind of shipment?" I asked.

"I don't know the details," Gloria protested. "I *don't*. I didn't want to know."

"How did you get involved with them?"

"Jose approached me a couple times over the years

about importing some containers from abroad. I had always kept my nose clean and didn't want any trouble from customs, so I said no. But then my mom got sick and had to go into a nursing home. All she had was Medicare and Social Security. You know what kind of a hellhole that pays for? I got to thinking about Pascal. He shipped in stone all the time anyway. Plus, if he got caught he'd go to prison like he deserved. And I could say I knew nothing about it, which is true."

"So you hooked up Jose and Pascal?" I asked.

She shrugged. "What of it? Pascal had to cooperate because of what I knew about Eugene and *Head and Torso*. He was a junkie by then anyway."

"Where were the drugs hidden?" I asked.

"In the shipping containers, I guess. How the fuck should I know? I made a point of not asking stupid questions, okay? I got paid to do the customs paperwork and keep my mouth shut. I wasn't involved."

"No, all you did was turn a blind eye to murder and drug smuggling," I said, my sympathy for the little girl Gloria had been replaced by disgust for the woman she had become.

"I bet he hid the drugs in them garden thingies," said Evangeline. "Pascal tol' me he had 'em cast in Mexico, cheap, for some o' his clients. They was always breakin' 'n' shit, and he hadda glue 'em back together then sold 'em to that garden place, Monkey Madness or whatever it's called. He was rippin' them off, too, cuz plaster falls apart in the rain."

"What happened to Seamus McGraw?" I asked.

"Pascal hid something in McGraw's studio," Gloria said. "The boys went to get it back but I guess Pascal had already moved it. They would up killing McGraw, then strung him up at the art show as a warning to Pascal."

"What about McGraw's fingers?" I asked, appalled at the savage story Gloria recounted so calmly. And I thought I needed therapy.

"Jose's boys put them there as a joke; none of us knew Pascal was selling the statues to the garden supply store," Gloria said with a shake of her head. "He was supposed to break up the plaster and melt it down. Cheap bastard wanted to make a few extra bucks by selling them, which meant he didn't destroy the evidence. I've seen CSI. They can pick up all sorts of traces off stuff like that. What an idiot." ·

"And Derek, your employee?"

"Derek started snooping around and demanded a piece of the action. He even tried to pry the container open. I feel kind of bad about what happened to him, but you have to understand Jose and the boys are scared too. They work for someone else, somebody even worse." She met my eyes, and I saw sadness there. "It's not what you think, Annie. I didn't mean for any of this to happen. All I wanted was to be able to afford some nice things for my mother. Pascal owed us. Nobody was supposed to get hurt."

"Except Pascal."

"Like I care," she said with a snort.

"And Seamus McGraw. And Derek."

She shrugged.

"Why did they send Pascal's finger to Consuelo?"

"I guess they think she knows something about the missing stash. She doesn't, though, so I came over to help her deal with them. This has got to stop. These guys are out of control if they're slicing off fingers and killing people."

"Gee, Gloria, you think?" I asked sarcastically. "Wait a minute—are you saying they're on the way over? *Now?*" I squeaked. None of us was packing any firepower as far as I could tell, and in light of two dead bodies, numerous severed fingers, and my adventure in the warehouse, I had an aversion to meeting up with Jose and the boys again. I stood. "Let's get the hell out of here."

"You know, I never bargained on any of this," Gloria said, dropping the box with the bloody finger on the credenza and heading out the front door. "I'll leave Consuelo in your capable hands. I'm outta here."

I wondered whether to give chase, but decided against it. Gloria had already told us what she knew, and I didn't relish trying to hold her captive while waiting for the police.

"Yep. That's his fat little finger, all right," Evangeline said with a shake of her head as she peered into the box. "When Pascal said he liked coke, I thought he meant soda pop. Who woulda took him for a junkie?"

I turned to Consuelo. "Where are the statues?"

"Down there." Off the small foyer was a flight of stairs to a room on the lower level composed almost entirely of windows, the view obscured by the floor-to-ceiling curtains. The space was crammed with packing material and sculptures of various shapes and sizes in the Eugene Forrester style. Most lay on their sides or were broken in two.

"Those are the new ones," Consuelo said.

I tried to pick up one of the intact sculptures, but it was too heavy. Evangeline came over and hoisted it onto her shoulder. "Where'd'ja want it?"

I was getting a major case of the willies in this cold white house with the bloody finger and the mysterious statues, and longed to be cradled in the bosom of the SFPD. This last was such an unusual impulse that I thought I should honor it.

"Okay, here's the plan," I said, improvising. I tossed Mary the truck keys, glad I'd taught her how to drive a stick shift last summer. "Mary, go get the truck and pull it into the driveway. We'll take this statue with us before Jose and his boys can get rid of everything. We'll take it to the police and let them deal with it."

Mary nodded and ran up the stairs.

"Policía?" Consuelo asked.

"Don't worry," I assured her. "I have a very good friend in the SFPD."

"No! No, I cannot. I cannot!" Consuelo cried, and began speaking rapidly in Spanish.

"Tol' you she was an illegal," Evangeline said.

"We don't have a choice. Those guys are killers. Consuelo, is there an exit at this level? We'll never get this statue up those stairs."

She pulled aside the curtains, revealing a sliding glass door that opened onto the driveway.

"Evangeline, put the statue in the back of the truck when Mary gets here," I ordered. As she carried the statue outside, I turned to Consuelo. "Are you undocumented?" I asked in a voice as gentle as I could muster.

Consuelo nodded. "Come with us," I said, holding her by the upper arms and speaking slowly. "We won't take you to the police, okay? You will be safe."

She looked blank. I racked my brain for the Spanish equivalent, and recalled the bilingual emergency instructions that were stenciled in BART cars in the event of an earthquake. *"Seguro!* You will be *seguro."*

Now she looked confused, so I tried again. *"Vámanos por seguridad—"*

"Youse guys better get your heinies out here," Evangeline interrupted. "Somebody's comin', and they look an awful lot like those wise guys who were lookin' for the money."

Chapter 18

Q: Do you have a personal hero?

A: Absolument! *Han Van Megeeren, without a doubt. Facing a possible death sentence for selling a Vermeer to Nazi official Hermann Göring, Van Megeeren admitted he had forged the painting, and demonstrated his talent by producing a brilliant new forgery,* The Young Christ Teaching in the Temple, *while in police custody. The charges against him were commuted to forgery, and a poll showed he was one of the most popular men in the Netherlands, right behind the prime minister.*

—*Georges LeFleur, in an interview with* Paris Match

I hustled Consuelo outside as Mary pulled the truck into the narrow driveway. Evangeline dumped the statue in the bed of the truck and climbed into the cab. I thrust my weeping undocumented alien onto Evangeline's lap, where she was encircled by a pair of muscular arms, and hurried around to the driver's side. A glance through the trees bordering the drive revealed a man behind the wheel of a shiny black SUV pointed uphill. Don Quixote, whom I presumed was really Jose, and his evil assistant Ape Man were pounding on the front door. Because of the way Pascal's house was situated on the hillside, we were below them and around a slight bend. But it wouldn't be long before they spotted us.

Panic spurring me on, I tried to squeeze behind the wheel as Mary scooted over, but there wasn't enough room on the truck's narrow bench seat for all those womanly hips. Mary twisted sideways, facing me, and I managed to shove my way in and lock the door. I stomped on the gas and we took off with a lurch.

I checked the rearview mirror. The driver of the black SUV was executing a many-pointed turn on the narrow, car-lined alley while Don Quixote and Ape Man ran down the street towards us, guns waving.

"Yikes!" Mary yelled and I turned my attention to driving just in time to avoid a UPS truck laboring up the hill. I heard some popping sounds I feared were gunshots and stepped on the gas. Consuelo began reciting what sounded like the Lord's Prayer in Spanish while Mary watched out the rear window and provided a running commentary on the progress of Jose and the goons. Only Evangeline remained silent. A quick glance revealed her broad face to be unusually pale.

"They're jumping into the SUV," Mary warned. "Look out, they're coming."

We careened down Telegraph Hill and I took a right on Grant, then a left on Chestnut. The normally packed streets were quiet this holiday eve, but I wasn't sure if that was a good thing.

"Should I go somewhere crowded?" I asked of no one in particular.

"Crowded's good," Mary replied.

I turned left on Mason and left again on Columbus, which put us right back in the center of North Beach. If anywhere in the City would be crowded the Wednesday before Thanksgiving, it would be North Beach.

"Okay, they're caught in traffic," Mary reported with relief.

"Yeah, but so are we."

"Uh-oh," Mary said.

"What? *What*?"

"They're driving on the wrong side of the road and are no longer blocked by traffic."

I glanced over my shoulder. Jose and his boys were two blocks behind us, which was not far enough to lose them, but not close enough for them to shoot at us. They were gaining ground, fast.

Mary's arms didn't fit in the meager space allotted her, so she had one arm around the back of my shoulders, and the other hugging my waist. I wasn't wearing a seat belt, and I hoped she could hang on tight enough to prevent me from sailing through the windshield if we crashed. Then again, since she wasn't wearing a seat belt either, I supposed we would fly through together.

"What do I do? Where should I go?" I pleaded as I swerved around a double-parked delivery truck, and sped down an alley, tires squealing. The statue rolled around and hit the side of the truck with a thud.

"Go to Lombard!" Mary cried.

I jerked the truck around a startled pedestrian in a pilgrim's hat. "What?"

"Lombard!"

I hung a sharp right and we raced through Chinatown, at one point veering onto the sidewalk to avoid several little old ladies wearing hand-knit caps and carrying bright pink plastic grocery bags, then swinging around a truck unloading squawking chickens. Curses and shaken fists followed in our wake, and I wondered if anyone could possibly think we were joyriding.

"Why Lombard?" I yelled, as we skidded onto Chestnut. "Is a police station there?"

"That's where everybody goes for a car chase in San Francisco!" Mary replied. "There must be a reason!"

Lombard was a normal street except for a one-block stretch dubbed *the crookedest street in the world* because it zigzagged to compensate for the forty-degree slope of the hill. Vermont Street at Twentieth was actually more crooked, but who was I to quibble with the tourist brochures?

"Yeah, well, they also always have a Chinese New Year parade in San Francisco chase scenes, even though that happens only once a year. We need a police station! Where's a police station?" I demanded, my fear making me jumpy. "C'mon, you guys. You mean to tell me that none of you has ever been arrested? Why do I find that hard to believe?"

"There's a substation near my apartment," Mary offered. "That's off Valencia. You think we can make it that far?"

Consuelo sniffed and offered the address of the passport office, but unless we were going to demand an emergency deportation this was not helpful. She seemed to be working her way through the Catholic prayer book, while Evangeline maintained a stoic silence.

We were now racing past the Cannery, heading toward the Marina and the Presidio. There was much less traffic around here, and I heard the popping of gunshots again. Shit! I was fresh out of ideas. I hazarded another glance in the rearview mirror and saw the black SUV only half a block behind us.

"Look out!" Mary yelled, and I swerved to avoid a

brightly colored Kreamy Do-Nut delivery van, complete
with a giant smiling Kreamy Do-Nut on its roof, pulling
out at a stop sign. The SUV was not as quick and smashed
into the van with a squealing of brakes, the smashing of
glass, and the groaning of steel.

"Yes!" Mary said. "They crashed!"

We cheered and hooted. I should have been driving, not
celebrating, because the truck ran over a curb, taking out a
big blue mailbox. The statue slammed into the truck's cab
as we screeched to a halt.

Luckily I had slowed before the impact and after a moment of shock, I backed onto the road and looked behind
us. Our pursuers leaped from their disabled vehicle and
yanked the stunned driver out of his delivery van. Ape Man
jumped behind the wheel, with Jose and Barrel Chest rid-
ing shotgun.

"They're coming after us!" Mary cried. "They've hi-
jacked the doughnut mobile and they're coming after us!"

I stomped on the gas, taken aback at being pursued by a
giant doughnut. Sure, I thought, the bad guys got a van full
of Kreamy Do-Nuts while I was stuck with a penitent
Catholic, a speechless giant, and a petty criminal who
didn't even know where the nearest police station was.

The van sped along faster than I would have thought a
doughnut mobile could go. I raced through the flat residential streets of the Marina, leaning on the horn in the hope
that some public-spirited citizen would call the cops. I decided Mary was onto something with the Lombard suggestion and was willing to bet my trusty old truck could climb
hills better than the doughnut mobile.

I headed straight up Divisadero, a very steep hill. At the
summit was an intersection controlled by a stop sign, but I
didn't hesitate. The hilltop flattened out and we sailed up
in the air, across the intersection, and slammed to earth on

the other side, jolting the truck and its contents. The statue rocketed around the bed of the truck, banging into the tailgate as we headed uphill, jumping toward the cab when we went airborne. I heard a horrible groaning noise and scanned the dashboard for a red *Check Engine Because You're About to Die* light until I realized the noise was coming from Mary.

"What's wrong?" I demanded. "Mary, what's wrong?"

"Eye it eye ung," she mumbled.

"What?"

"She say she bit her tongue," Consuelo replied, momentarily interrupting a volley of *Ave Maria*s.

"Are you okay?" I asked anxiously.

"Uh-huh," she nodded, craning her neck to see out the back window. "Ere opping o-uhts."

"What?"

"She say, they are dropping doughnuts." Consuelo appeared to have found her calling as a translator for the lingually impaired.

I was too busy gripping the wheel to look for myself. Consuelo pulled a tissue from her pocket, which Mary pressed tightly against her tongue. After a moment, speech restored, Mary resumed her blow-by-blow description of the drama unfolding behind us.

"The back doors of the van are swinging open! They're dropping Kreamy Do-Nuts everywhere! It's a fried-dough massacre!"

I concentrated on avoiding driving into the knots of people gathering on the sidewalk to watch the chase. *Surely someone would have the presence of mind to call the cops,* I thought. At the moment, though, they seemed mesmerized by the carnage created as the Kreamy Do-Nut van sped along, spewing its cargo.

"Glazed doughnuts are rolling down the street! A whole

bunch of jelly-filled hit the pavement! An Alfa Romeo is skidding in the jelly! Ew! It looks like blood!"

For every steep upside to a hill there is an equally steep downside, and since we had just crested the hill there was only one way for us to go. To buy time until the cops arrived, I took a left off Divisadero, doubled back onto Scott, and swung right on Green. The street nosedived towards the Bay, and I was hoping the doughnut mobile would lose control on the steep downgrade.

"They're gaining on us!" Mary cried.

I heard another round of popping, and the doughnut van banged into us from behind. My heavy steel bumper absorbed much of the blow, but I feared we were about to join the jelly-filled Kreamy Do-Nuts in the Roadkill Hall of Fame. I laid on my horn to warn anyone entering the intersection at the bottom of the hill that we were barreling towards them. At last I heard sirens approaching, but before I could feel relieved the doughnut mobile rammed us again, this time with more force, and we careened onto the curb, bounced off a light pole, and landed back on the road. I was fighting to control the truck when the larger, heavier doughnut mobile, unable to slow its momentum, streaked past us and skidded into the intersection, where it T-boned a police cruiser. There were terrible sounds of metal crunching, glass shattering, and tires exploding before both the doughnut mobile and the cruiser came to a rest in the middle of the intersection.

We cheered again, savoring our rescue, until I realized I couldn't stop the truck in time, and we slammed into the back of the doughnut mobile, the nose of my truck coming to rest just inside the open rear doors of the van. Doughnuts rained down upon the windshield and a chocolate cake doughnut with rainbow sprinkles lassoed the radio antennae. The statue in the bed of the truck launched into the air and smashed onto the asphalt. In one last act of defiance, the giant Kreamy Do-Nut emblem creaked, trembled, and rolled off the roof of the van, impaling itself in the police cruiser's windshield.

There were several long seconds of eerie, unnatural calm.

Then Consuelo started wailing, police sirens shrieked, and car alarms screamed. A crowd gathered on the sidewalk, speculating noisily. There were assorted shouts, more popping sounds, and general bedlam as the watching crowd shifted and surged around us.

I tried to climb out the driver's door, but it was jammed against the delivery van and wouldn't budge.

"Is everyone okay? Evangeline, try to get out your side," I said. She wrenched her door open and practically flung Consuelo to the sidewalk, then tumbled out. Mary bounced across the bench seat and climbed out, and I followed more slowly. As I emerged, the Kreamy Do-Nuts that had fallen onto the truck's roof shifted, and I felt the cool goopiness of vanilla custard land with a splat on my head.

My companions looked at me and started laughing, even Consuelo. I joined in, and then none of us could stop.

Failing to see the humor in the situation, the cops surrounded us, weapons drawn. Mary and Evangeline tried to explain, adding to the confusion. I sat on the truck's bumper, giggling in my custard-encrusted hooker clothes.

An officer was inspecting the statue, which lay in pieces on the pavement. He nudged it with his foot and plastic baggies of white powder spilled out.

Oh boy.

While the police were distracted by this new development, I looked up to see Consuelo disappearing into the crowd. For a stranger in a strange land, her timing was impeccable.

Chapter 19

"No comment."

—*Artist Annie Kincaid, asked about her grandfather*
Georges LeFleur's bestselling new book,
San Francisco Chronicle

The headline screamed DARING DAMSELS, DESIGNER DRUGS,
AND DAFFY DOUGHNUTS ON TURKEY EVE DISASTER!!! On
what must have been a slow news day, the story was fea-
tured above the fold on the front page of the *Chronicle* and
was illustrated by a color photograph of Mary, Evangeline,
and me squatting amid the doughnut carrion cackling like
a trio of madwomen. On my long list of public humilia-
tions, this one ranked right at the top.

The press coverage alerted my mother to my predica-
ment, and within hours of spying the article over her
Thanksgiving-morning coffee Beverly LeFleur Kincaid
had driven down from Asco, enlisted the aid of a former
boyfriend who was now an influential attorney, and fina-
gled a bail hearing from a judge with a soft spot for well-
spoken, prettily tearful mothers of felons.

Mom's reluctant and generally pissed-off ally in this
legal wrangling was Inspector Crawford. Irritable from a
sleepless night spent helping to interrogate first me, then

the Ape Man—Jose and Barrel Chest had escaped in the confusion—she assured the assistant district attorney that I was too clueless to be a drug trafficker, and that my wild story about Robert Pascal and Gloria Cabrera might even be true. The harassed ADA was anxious to get home to a turkey dinner with his fiancée and future in-laws and reduced the charges against me from drug trafficking, assault with a deadly weapon, and littering, to misdemeanor reckless driving. He dropped the charges against Mary and Evangeline altogether.

We were released from the City jail at four thirty in the afternoon, "just in time for pumpkin pie," the cheerful desk clerk pointed out. Annette caught up with us in the vestibule and informed me in a clipped voice and no uncertain terms that henceforth I was to call her Inspector Crawford—or better yet, not to call her at all.

"Geez, she sure seems pissed," said Evangeline.

"What's *her* problem?" demanded Mary.

I shrugged, depressed at the end of my friendship with Annette. My mother herded us toward her Honda sedan, which was parked directly across the street from the gray stone Bryant Street police station. Mom had serious parking karma.

"Where to first, girls?" she chirped.

"I live on Valencia, and Evangeline's gonna stay with me for a few days," Mary said, no worse for the wear after a night in the slammer. She and Evangeline had been cellmates and caught some sleep, whereas I had been isolated and interrogated by narcotics inspectors throughout the night.

"Yeah," Evangeline chimed. "On account of I don't have no job no more, and I can't stay at Pascal's, not for a while leastways. S'gonna be great. Whaddaya think, Annie?"

"Sounds like a plan." I nodded, so tired I couldn't keep my eyes open.

I awoke twenty minutes later as Mary and Evangeline disembarked at a Valencia street taco stand and bid us farewell. Mom pointed the car north, away from the approach to the Bay Bridge.

"Where are we going?" I asked.

"I have an errand to run."

"On Thanksgiving?" I whined. "Mom, thanks for everything, really, but all I want to do is take a shower and crawl into bed for a week."

"First things first," she sang, though I thought I saw a nervous twitch over her left eye and her voice rang false.

"What kind of errand are we talking about, Mom?"

"I need to retrieve something from Anthony Brazil's gallery. Something personal. Don't worry about it."

"What could you have left at Anthony's new gallery? You've never even been there, have you?" She didn't reply. "Anyway, the gallery's not open on Thanksgiving."

She turned up the Vivaldi and sped across the City, the streets deserted on this national holiday. I dozed again, awakening when we pulled into the small parking lot attached to Anthony Brazil's swanky gallery. The place looked deserted as did the Brock Museum next door.

"You see, there's no one—" I began.

"Beverly, I wish you would take my advice and reconsider," a thin-lipped Michael said as he materialized at the driver's window. "Surely whatever it is can wait a day or two until the gallery owner . . ."

My mother ignored him, opening the car door so fast he had to jump out of the way.

"Thank you for unlocking the gallery, Michael," Mom said with a gracious smile. "You needn't have waited. Run along now and enjoy your Thanksgiving dinner." She started marching toward the door of the gallery as if she owned the place.

I got out and glared at Michael across the roof of the car.

"It's not my fault," he said, holding up his hands in surrender. "I'm here against my better judgment."

"Then why did you come?"

"Your grandfather called in a marker." Michael did a double take as I walked around the car and he caught the full effect of my crusty clothes, snarled hair, and sleep-deprived face. "*Jesus*, Annie. You look worse every time I see you."

"Thanks. You sure know how to make a girl feel special."

"Are the alarms off?" Mom called from the entrance.

"I took care of it hours ago," Michael replied, and she disappeared into the gallery. "I'll just be running along now."

"Fat chance, buster," I said, grabbing his arm. "You're coming with us. You have to turn the alarms back on and lock up as if we were never here. Mom?"

She screamed.

Michael and I sprinted toward the door. He ran through first, was bashed on the head, and collapsed on the hard slate of the entryway. I tripped over him and rolled to a stop at the feet of none other than Jose, who was holding a gun to my mother's elegant head.

"You see what happens when you do not listen to your mother?" Jose scowled. "You have involved her in this unpleasantness, when she should be protected from such things."

My eyes darted around the gallery, noting four men in addition to Jose and Barrel Chest.

"Listen, she doesn't know anything," I beseeched Jose.

"It's me you want, because I'm the one who can testify about the drugs. Let her go and—"

"It's too late for that," he snapped. "Get up, *now*."

A man with a jagged scar on one cheek yanked me to my feet. "What are you doing at Brazil's gallery?" I asked Jose, hoping to buy time for Michael to wake up and rescue us, or for a clown to stroll in with the French prime minister and a frog on a leash, proving that this was all just a very bad dream.

"We caught up with that *cabrón* Pascal at the airport this morning. The *hijo de puta* thought he could escape to the Bahamas. With a little encouragement he told us he had hidden the missing product in one of McGraw's sculptures before they were picked up for the show." Jose nodded at McGraw's statue of a prim librarian armed with a bronze cattle prod. "I do not understand modern art. It is so . . . so *vulgar*."

"True," I said, thinking to distract him with a discussion of art. It worked with my friends. "But don't you think Mc-Graw's portrayal of social isolation—"

"Enough!" Jose released my mother, who put an arm around my shoulders. He barked an order in Spanish, and Gloria Cabrera emerged from Anthony's office. Her face was swollen and bruised, and as she knelt to tie up Michael, she glanced at me and mouthed, "I'm sorry."

"I—what is *that*?" I asked, my attention drawn to the window overlooking the walled sculpture garden. There, amidst the torn crime scene tape, a man hung from the old oak tree. Still alive, he was perched precariously on the back of a chair, his toes struggling for purchase.

"Pascal," Jose said. He shrugged at my mother's horrified expression. "The boys thought it was funny. It's the tequila, you see. Terrible drink." He gazed adoringly at Mom. "*I* don't drink."

"That would mean a lot more to me if you would also refrain from using guns," my mother murmured. "Please put the weapon down, Jose, and we can talk. I give you my word that we will not try to escape."

He looked at me. I sure as hell wasn't giving *my* word.

"Jose—" my mother began.

"Take that *unfortunate* man down from the tree *this instant*!" an imperious voice commanded. Agnes Brock, all five feet of her, quivered in outrage in the doorway. She did not seem to notice the guns pointed at her.

"Will *someone* please lock the damned door?" Jose snapped at his minions. "Pardon my language, my dear Beverly. But, really, this place is busier than Union Square. Who unlocked it in the first place? We came in the back."

"Don't be absurd, young man," Agnes said in the contemptuous tone I had heard her employ with a hapless art restoration intern who had used phthalo paint—a twentieth-century invention—on a landscape from 1898. Stepping regally over Michael's unconscious body, she flung out an arm and pointed her scrawny finger at Jose. "*You*, sir, ought to be ashamed of yourself. This is an *outrage*."

"Madam, I have no idea who you are, but—"

"I am Mrs. Agnes Brock, director of the world-renowned Brock Museum. I have an excellent view of the sculpture garden from my office next door, and I know the proprietor of this establishment very well indeed. I witnessed those thugs of yours hanging that poor man and have summoned the police."

"You lie, old woman," Jose said. "Only a fool would act so rashly."

"Why, you little *pipsqueak*," Agnes continued. "Have you any idea with whom you are dealing? I have had to fight for my rightful place in the art world for *fifty years*! Do not think I will be cowed by the likes of you!"

And with that she strode through the gallery to the sculpture garden, slapped Barrel Chest's hands away from a thick rope anchored to a low branch of the oak tree, and set about un-hanging Pascal. At a loss for how to respond to such a force of nature as Agnes Brock, Barrel Chest looked helplessly at Jose. Jose moved over to the garden doors, dragging my mother and me with him.

"Shoot him," he ordered as Pascal tumbled down to the ground, moaning.

"What about her?" Barrel Chest asked.

"Shoot her, too."

"No!" my mother and I cried.

"She's a little old lady," Barrel Chest protested. "I can't shoot a little old lady."

Jose let out an exasperated sigh. "You'll sing a different tune when she's testifying at your trial. Bring her in here and tie her up, then. Let's get what we came for before the cops . . ."

Two men walked out of Anthony's office.

"Nathan?" I said, surprised. "Kevin?"

"Anna?" Nathan said, shocked. Kevin the Nazi shook his head and looked disgusted.

"How do you know this annoying girl?" Jose asked. "She works for the FBI."

"No, I'm—" A gun was shoved in my face.

"She's with the SFPD, but we have a mutual acquaintance." Nathan toed Michael's inert form. "What is he doing here? Is he dead, I hope? The man was after my collection. Happily my security system was too sophisticated for him."

Jose gestured toward me. "This girl works with Frank DeBenton, who is working with the FBI. She did something to the Picasso, the one you offered as collateral." He eyed Nathan suspiciously. "You wouldn't be double-crossing me, would you, my old friend? Perhaps working with the FBI yourself?"

"FBI?" Gloria gaped at me. "You work with the *FBI*?"

"I don't work with the FBI, and neither does Frank." I turned to Jose. "How do you know Frank?"

"Everyone shut up about the FBI!" Nathan yelled. "You"—he gestured to Barrel Chest—"get rid of those women and let's get what we came for already!"

"I'll shoot that one," Barrel Chest said, pointing at me. "But I can't shoot this one. She reminds me of my *abuela*."

Agnes smiled at Barrel Chest and rested a bony hand on his arm.

"Ay, *que la chingada*," Jose muttered, closing his eyes.

"Jose, we don't have time for this," Nathan said. "Let's find the rest of the product and get out of here."

"Do you really think you can—" I began.

"Stop asking questions!" Jose yelled and slapped me. My mother flew to my defense, whacking Jose under his chin with her fist. He staggered backwards, banged his head on the sculpture of the homicidal *Postman*, and lost hold of his gun.

It skittered towards us, I lunged for it, and all hell broke loose. Kevin the Nazi pulled out a gun and as I swung toward him, he fired at Jose. Someone else shot Kevin, who went down, but not before wounding several others. Nathan aimed his pistol at my mother and me, and just as suddenly collapsed.

Agnes was behind him, a stun gun in one hand. She looked pleased, and we shared a fleeting grin.

"Get down!" someone shouted.

I shoved Mom behind a sculpture of a flayed corpse, draping myself over her, while Agnes ducked behind the bronze rendering of a maniacal nursery school teacher. Gunfire erupted and bullets zinged around the room, ricocheting off McGraw's metal sculptures and pulverizing a marble bust of Caesar. A bile yellow abstract painting entitled *Lips* took a bullet right in the kisser, and what sounded like automatic-weapons fire laid waste to a ceramic toilet seat decorated with American flags.

Gloria started screaming and bolted for the front door, flinging it open as a stream of cops in helmets and bulletproof vests rushed in, each leaping over Michael's unconscious body. More cops swarmed into the sculpture garden and poured in through the French doors.

"Put your weapons down! Hands over your heads! Over your heads! *Nobody move a fucking inch!*"

There was a moment of silence as we remained hidden behind our sculptures. Then Jose threw out his weapon and emerged, his hands in the air. Barrel Chest followed his example, along with the scarred-face man and several others. At least three men had been shot in the exchange, including Kevin.

The police started cuffing and frisking people in the gallery while out in the garden two officers watched as a paramedic checked out Pascal and loaded him, handcuffed, onto a stretcher. The still-unconscious Nathan was carried from the gallery.

Kevin sat slumped on the floor, his back against a wall. Holding one hand over the wound on his thigh, he reached slowly into his breast pocket and pulled out an FBI badge. Either the FBI was recruiting neo-Nazis or I had been doing my level best to interfere with a federal investigation.

"Annie?" a voice called out. "Are you okay?"

"Frank?" I croaked. I pried myself off of my mother and crawled out from behind the flayed corpse. "What are you doing here?"

"Funny, I was going to ask you the same thing," he said,

his dark eyes worried. He scooped me into his arms and held me tight for several seconds. Then he shook me. "Are you all right? Answer me."

"I'd be fine if you'd stop shaking me. I'm a little bruised, that's all."

"You look like hell," he said, holding me by the shoulders. "Mrs. Kincaid, is that you? Are you hurt, Beverly?"

He released me and helped her to her feet.

"I'm fine, just a little"—she took a deep breath—"just a little shaky."

From somewhere outside I heard Agnes Brock barking orders to the police and wondered how they were taking it. *The smart money's on her,* I thought, regretting the many, many nasty things I'd said about Agnes over the years. Her quick thinking when Nathan was about to shoot my mother and me meant I owed her, big time. Maybe I could square things a bit by returning the Chagall.

Frank escorted us out to the street, where I saw Michael perched on the bumper of an ambulance, talking to a middle-aged man in a brown rumpled suit, the kind favored by police inspectors. Michael held my gaze for a moment before turning his attention back to the cop.

If anyone could talk his way out of a complicated situation, it was Michael. I hoped.

"Frank, wait—that man was trying to protect us," I said, pointing at Michael. "He didn't have anything to do with Jose or Nathan."

"I'm sure the police will sort it all out."

"But—"

"I have no authority here, Annie," Frank said. "I was helping the FBI set up a sting operation, that's all."

An inspector drew my mother away for questioning, and I sat down on a low wall to wait my turn at interroga-

tion. I looked again for Michael, but didn't see him anywhere.

Frank sank down next to me and we observed the scene.
Uniformed officers were cordoning off the area, interviewing participants, holding back a growing crowd of onlook-
ers, and taking measurements. Poor Anthony Brazil would
go ballistic when he returned, stuffed with turkey and
dressing and pumpkin pie, to find his gallery shot up. I
doubted I'd be invited to another of his art shows anytime
soon.

"Frank," I said, "was the Picasso part of the FBI sting?"

He nodded. "You can imagine how pleased I was that
Georges LeFleur's granddaughter had neither absconded
with it nor forged it."

"You know about Georges?" I asked, my voice scaling
upward.

"Annie, I'm a security guy, remember?"

"How long have you known?"

"Long enough."

"Yeah, well, Mr. Security Guy, just so you know: I
found the sensor on the Picasso right away."

"You found a decoy. I've been working with a Swiss
company to develop an undetectable microchip that's virtually impossible to remove. That's why the FBI contacted
me in the first place. Someday, Annie, technology is going
to put your grandfather out of business."

Wanna bet? I thought. "Still, it seems like an awfully
big risk to take with such a valuable piece of art."

"You're right. Except the Picasso's a fake."

"What?"

"You didn't know? I was sure you did."

Well, wasn't *that* embarrassing? So much for my reputation for spotting forgeries. "I guess I'm not very good

with abstracts. Maybe if it had been from Picasso's Blue Period . . ."

"Maybe so."

I thought he might be humoring me, but was too exhausted to call him on it. "Frank, did you really think I would steal the Picasso?"

"No, not really. I thought I had a pretty good read on your character, and I've noticed that although you may be prone to an occasional lapse in ethics, you're fiercely loyal to your friends, and I flattered myself that I was in that category. But your mother had been spotted with Jose, so suspicion arose. We—I—had to be sure."

As if on cue, Beverly Kincaid walked up. "How are you feeling, honey?" she said, checking me over. "Were you hurt? Are you all right?"

"I'm fine. Not a scratch on me. Mom, how did you know Jose?"

"Who, dear?"

I thought I heard Frank stifle a chuckle. "Mom, don't even start."

She sighed, and sat on the wall next to me. "When Seamus . . . passed away, I was surprised at how hard it hit me. I was reading some old letters and was reminded of the notebooks he used to keep. It occurred to me that one thing I could do to memorialize my old friend was to have his notebooks published. He had shown me portions of them over the years, and they offer amazing insight into the artistic process. But then, Seamus was an amazing, insightful man."

She paused, and Frank and I waited for her to continue. "The thing is, the notebooks were also his personal diary, and contained passages that I didn't want anyone else to read. I'm not proud of everything I've done, but I've always loved my husband and I value our marriage, and if the notebooks were published unedited, your father might get the wrong idea. So I decided to retrieve them."

"Were these the notebooks at Pascal's studio?" I asked, recalling the stack of composition notebooks I had dislodged on one of my visits to Pascal's studio.

She nodded. "When I heard Seamus had died, I drove to his studio in the City as fast as I could, but Pascal had already been there. You see, Seamus told me once that he suspected Forrester had sculpted *Head and Torso*, though he couldn't prove it. I imagine the notebooks discuss those suspicions in some detail. So I went to Pascal's studio to confront him, but he wasn't in. That's where I met Jose. He agreed to help me recover the notebooks if I kept you away from Pascal."

"Why didn't you just tell me?"

"Because you would have tried to get the notebooks yourself. Don't you think I know my own daughter?"

"So that's why you nearly got killed? For a bunch of old *love* notes?"

"Not love notes exactly, but references to an emotional attachment that would have been very hurtful to your father. Obviously I didn't realize Jose was involved in drug smuggling, nor that Pascal was a murderer," she said, her expression prim. "I also wanted to publish an edited version of the notebooks, Annie. I may not be an artist in the same league as my father and my daughter, but I do understand the inherent beauty of the artistic process. I hoped to make it possible for others to understand it, too."

I felt tears in my eyes and hugged my mother, hard. *Art's a funny thing,* I thought. It can inspire great joy, but also great pain.

Mom, Frank, and I sat on the little stone wall, watching the commotion and lost in our thoughts.

I noticed Kevin being loaded into an ambulance. "Is he going to be all right?"

"It was a flesh wound," Frank answered. "He should be fine."

"I think I owe him an apology."

"He was surprised to see you at Nathan Haggerty's the other evening. He says you have quite a way with words."

"Um . . ."

"Kevin's a very progressive guy in real life," Frank said with a smile. "He's also an old friend of mine."

But of course, I thought. My best friends were thieves and forgers; Frank's best friends were FBI agents. Could this relationship be saved?

"How did you spot my mother with Jose?" I asked. "Were you following him?"

"Not me, personally. The FBI's had a surveillance team on Nathan Haggerty and his associates for over a year. He's been orchestrating a drug and arms smuggling operation, using stolen paintings as collateral. It looks like Jose and his men were bringing in the product with the help of the stone importer. Apparently Pascal skimmed off part of a cocaine shipment. From what I've gathered, he panicked and hid several kilos in McGraw's sculptures before they were picked up for the art show. But what I don't understand is why you two came to the gallery today."

He looked at me, and I looked at my mother.

She pulled a thick bundle of letters from her handbag and smiled sadly at them.

"Love letters?" asked Frank in a sympathetic voice.

"Of a sort," replied my mother. "A deep friendship, really, not what most people would have considered an affair. But they might have been misconstrued had they been found. Jose told me they were in the leather mailbag of Seamus' *Postman* sculpture."

"The letters are probably evidence, Beverly," Frank said. "I suggest you keep them under wraps."

"Speaking of letters," Agnes Brock said as she joined us. "I received a very interesting call yesterday from a man at the St. Louis Post Office. He claims he found my Chagall."

"Really?" I said. "How did he know to call you?"

Her lips pressed into a thin line. "There was a note on the back of the painting, saying, *If found, please return to the Brock Museum, San Francisco, for a reward.* It included my private telephone number."

"That's wonderful, Mrs. Brock. Are we square, then? Bryan's off the hook?"

"Dr. Sebastian Pitts must authenticate it, of course," she said, sizing me up. "But it seems as though you and I are, as you say, square. My dear."

My mouth fell open as Agnes Brock swept majestically towards the Brock. "Did she just say what I think she just said?"

"Looks like the start of a beautiful friendship, Annie," Frank said.

Mom whispered, "That *If found* note is a trademark, if you know what I mean."

I did. Georges LeFleur had struck again. The real Chagall was no doubt squirreled away in Carlos Jimenez's hometown until the fuss died down and it could be hung in Cerrito Lindo's new museum. I silently wished Carlos well. "Listen, Mom, I have to stick around to answer a lot of questions, especially since what happened here ties into last night's fiasco. Why don't you go to my apartment and get some rest?"

"Thank you, dear, but I think not. I'm going to wait for you right here and then I'm taking you home to Asco for a delayed Thanksgiving dinner. And, Frank, I insist that you join us. I have a house full of food, and I believe none of us has done justice to a turkey yet."

"Mom, I don't think Frank wants to—"

"Me? I'm starved," Frank said. "You look like you could use a little sustenance yourself, Annie. Beverly, you have a deal."

My mother went to stash her purloined letters in the car.

"You don't know what you're getting yourself into, Frank," I muttered. "You really don't. This isn't some walk in the park with gun-toting drug dealers and homicidal sculptors, you know. There are an ex-fiancé and Julio Iglesias albums involved."

"Annie, I'm a security guy," Frank said, his dark eyes dancing. "I don't scare easy."

I snorted. "You told me once that *I* scared you."

"You? You're scary as hell. But somehow I'm feeling up to the challenge."

Annie's Guide to Gilding the Lily

Gold gilding requires patience, concentration, and practice. Once mastered, however, it is a simple and wonderfully dramatic way to enhance trim, decorative objects, frames, furniture . . . just about anything.

Loose-leaf Gold Leaf*
Red oxide acrylic paint
Slow-drying Gold size (specialty varnish) or water-based quick-dry size
Very soft, dry brushes
Very soft, clean rags—velvet or silk are best

Before you gild:

Work in a draft-free area. The gold leaf is thinner than tissue and will float away, bend back on itself, and wrinkle with the slightest breeze—including human breath. Make sure you are in an area of maximum stillness.

Prepare the surface. Sand the object with fine-grit paper or steel wool so that the surface is as smooth as possible. Every bump and blemish will be magnified by the shiny gold leaf.

Paint the base coat. Red oxide approximates the earth-red clay that was the traditional base for gold gilding. Other colors may be used for different effects, such as lemon yellow for a mellow gold or sap green for an aged, tarnished look. Your imagination is the only limit, but remember that the base color will show through in some areas.

Apply the gold size. Brush the size onto the object with a clean varnishing brush. I like the slow-drying oil-based varnish, though the impatient artist may use a water-based quick-dry gold-leaf size. Just make sure before you start to note the "open" or workable time so that you have sufficient time to complete your project.

Check for the right "tack." Check size for tackiness by touching it with the back of your knuckle. You should not "sink" into the varnish at all; rather, when you pull your knuckle away, it should make an audible *tsk*ing sound, as though you were pulling away from Scotch tape. If there is no audible noise, the size is too dry. In this case, you can reapply the size and start again.

Applying the leaf:

Lift the leaf. Refrain from touching the leaf with your fingers, which have oils that can mar the finish. Instead, try rubbing a large, flat brush on your clothing or against your cheek. As you pass the brush over the leaf, it should lift onto the brush through static electricity. Alternatively, you can gently hold the "book" of leaves over the object and let the leaf fall, blowing it gently into place.

Tears and wrinkles happen. No need to worry. These slight imperfections add to the distressed look of the finish. During the burnishing process they will be smoothed out.

Tamp down gently. Using a very soft bristled brush, tamp down gently if needed to fill crevices and dips in ornate trim.

Repair. Reapply the leaf onto large "skips" or tears. The size should still be tacky enough to take the leaf; if not, dab on spots of size and wait until it is ready to receive the leaf, as described above.

Allow to dry thoroughly. This could be several hours or overnight, depending on the size used.

Final Steps:

Burnish. Using your silk or velvet rags, rub the gold into the surface, bringing out its luster and ridding the surface of extra leaf.

Distress. If desired, the gilded surface may be distressed by using steel wool or a rough rag to wear off some of the metal leaf, allowing the color underneath to show through.

Protective Finish. The whole object should be sealed with a clear or tinted varnish. To age the object, try using an amber varnish or tinting the varnish with artists' oil paint. For example, use burnt umber for an antiquing wash, whitish gray for a French "pickle" effect, or a green oxide for a tarnished look.

Hint: Don't feel constricted to gold leaf. There are as many colors and types of metal leaf as there are metals, and then some: several different shades of gold, as well as silver, copper, aluminum, and composites in shades of pink, blue, and green. Check with your local art store or on the Internet for specialty suppliers.

*The price of genuine gold leaf fluctuates with the gold market, and is usually prohibitive for any but the smallest projects. "Composition" gold is an imitation metal that is slightly brassier than the real stuff, but by the time the leafing is burnished and distressed, no one will be able to tell the difference.

About the Author

Hailey Lind is the pseudonym of two sisters, one a historian in Virginia, the other an artist in California. Their identities are a closely guarded secret . . . unless someone really wants to know. They love to hear from readers: www.haileylind.com.

Look for Annie Kincaid's next adventure in the Art Lover's mystery series

Brush with Death

Coming from Signet in July 2007

Working nights to restore murals in a building full of cremated remains is strange enough, but chasing a crypt-robbing ghoul through a graveyard is downright creepy. In *Brush With Death*, San Francisco artist Annie Kincaid finds herself drawn into a decades-old mystery involving some illustrious graveyard residents and Raphael's most intimate portrait, dubbed *La Fornarina*, or "the little baker girl." Could the Raphael "copy" hanging amid funerary urns actually be the priceless original? Is the masked crypt-robber somehow connected to the Raphael? Or is the painting part of a larger puzzle involving Annie's unrepentant grandfather, master art forger Georges LeFleur, and an Italian "fakebuster" out to ruin him? Annie's under pressure to figure things out ... before she finds her permanent home among the ashes.

THE FIRST IN THE MYSTERY SERIES
STARRING ART-FORGER-GONE-GOOD
ANNIE KINCAID

FEINT OF ART

An Annie Kincaid Mystery
by
Hailey Lind

Annie breaks the news to her curator ex-boyfriend
Ernst: his museum's new Caravaggio is a
fifteen-million-dollar fake. Then the janitor is killed,
Ernst disappears, and a dealer makes off with several
Old Master drawings. If she breaks the case using her
old connections, Annie can finally pay the rent.
But doing so could also draw her back into the
underworld of forgers she swore she'd left behind.

0-451-21699-7

Available wherever books are sold or
at penguin.com